ATTACKED BY NATURE ITSELF

"A whirlwind!" shouted the soldier. "That's a—killer storm! It spins so fast it can throw a house in the air! Don't you see those trees catching hell?"

Gull peered. The tornado was closer now, though he was still unsure how far off. Distances were impossible to judge against an ocean of green. But now he recognized the bits being flung in the air: evergreen trees seven or eight feet high. As the storm spun, it lofted dozens in all directions, as a saw throws sawdust.

When the impact hit him, all he could say was, "Oh, my."

That tornado was hundreds of feet tall, tearing a swath through the forest fifty feet wide, no more than a mile away.

Coming straight at them.

Look for
MAGIC: The Gathering

Arena
Whispering Woods
Shattered Chains
Final Sacrifice*

From HarperPrism

*Coming Soon

MAGIC ™
The Gathering

SHATTERED CHAINS

Clayton Emery

HarperPrism
An Imprint of HarperPaperbacks

HarperPaperbacks   *A Division of* HarperCollins*Publishers*
             10 East 53rd Street, New York, N.Y. 10022

Cover illustration by Kevin Murphy

First printing: March 1995

Printed in the United States of America

HarperPrism is an imprint of HarperPaperbacks.
HarperPaperbacks, HarperPrism, and colophon are
trademarks of HarperCollins*Publishers*

❖ 10 9 8 7 6 5 4 3 2 1

*Dedicated to
my brother Frank, the wanderer.*

CHAPTER
1

IT WAS THE BOY, STIGGUR, ATOP HIS CLOCKWORK beast, who first saw the danger.

"Gull! To the north! It's a—a—I don't know what it is!"

Everyone in camp looked up. There were dozens of people of every shape and size and color, bundled in colorful clothing against the early winter snow that covered the ground. From there one could see nothing but evergreen trees just taller than head-high, trees that seemingly went on forever.

Gull the Woodcutter dropped his dinner, dashed across camp, and vaulted to the rope ladder that dangled down the side of the clockwork beast. The general of this erstwhile army had started as a woodcutter, and looked it. He was tall and bronzed from a lifetime outdoors, with long brown hair barely contained by a rawhide tie at the nape of his neck. He wore a leather tunic, much scarred, over a wool shirt, and a leather kilt with red leggings and sturdy knee boots. His breath frosted as he mounted the ladder.

The clockwork beast was a contraption like a giant horse of wood and sheet iron with guts like a millworks, all whirring wooden gears and leather belts and pulleys and levers. They had yet to discover if the construct creature was alive or not: they only knew it ran all the time, humming like a beehive, and could be steered by levers atop its oaken skull.

The owner, or master, or friend of the beast was an orphan boy named Stiggur, whose name meant "gate," which is where he'd been found. He was a thin lad of perhaps thirteen, bundled like a sausage in leather and wool after the manner of his hero, Gull.

Gull mounted the ramshackle saddle-nest Stiggur had built aloft. In the months since he'd gained the beast, Stiggur had added to it, piling on gadgets and armor and weapons, then loading sacks and satchels and baskets to carry for the rolling camp. Gull felt as if he were standing on a mobile warehouse as he gazed out over the tops of the evergreens. Standing, he was almost thirty feet off the ground.

The taiga, a subarctic evergreen forest, did seem to wend forever in this flat-bottomed valley. In the east was a high plain, almost a mesa, flat as a tabletop, that reached north out of sight. Far to the west was a sierra, a range of saw-toothed mountains so high an eagle couldn't pass. So the makeshift patchwork army could only forge ahead through the taiga and hope it ended somewhere.

Except something now blocked their way.

A cone, thought the woodcutter. An inverted cone that—wiggled?

In the clear frosty air, he felt he could reach and touch the thing. It was tall, hundreds of feet high, and flat on top, like smoke from a forest fire flattening against a thunderhead. The cone tapered to almost nothing at the ground. Where it touched—the forest?—it spit bits and chunks into the air. As if a dog were digging and flinging dirt between its legs.

"What is it, Gull?" Stiggur reckoned Gull knew everything.

But the woodcutter disappointed him. "I don't know, lad. It's a dark—column of—spinning smoke? Is it dangerous? And how far away is it? I've nothing to judge the distance. . . . " Yet those bits being tossed through the air seemed familiar. And was that a howling he heard far off . . . ?

A thrumming of hooves muffled by snow interrupted his thoughts. Parting dark evergreens, Bardo the Paladin came prancing into camp on his white warhorse. A professional soldier dedicated to his god, the man wore chain mail under a leaf-brown woolen cloak that allowed his gypon to show his holy symbol: a winged staff in red. Gull had never bothered to ask which god it represented: there were so many. Disciplined and meticulous, Bardo headed a small pack of hunter-scouts. Two of the men were with him now, which left four elsewhere. All carried longbows jutting from saddle cases, and long swords either slung across their backs or from saddle scabbards.

Bardo was long-jawed, with blue eyes the color of the glaciers in his far northern homeland. Under his mail coif, his hair was as yellow as straw. He pushed his horse to the base of the clockwork beast. His accent was thick in his excitement. "Gull! Riders in the nort'! They're skirting the mesa, heading this vay! Ve think t'irty of them! My scouts investigate vhether there's a matching party vest! My guess is t'ere are!"

"What kind of riders? Cavalrymen? Any merchants with them?"

A shake of the head. "No. T'ey're girded for var."

"Well . . . " Gull felt foolish and helpless, as usual. Somehow, he'd been appointed leader of this motley army, and folks expected him to make decisions. Not that he was qualified, he thought. He was a woodcutter. Ask him to fell a hawthorne without bruising its neighbors, and he could drop it on a needle. But ask him how to scotch encroaching cavalry . . .

"They must be after us, because there's nothing else out here. Stiggur, sound a general alarm." The boy raised a gold-chased ram's horn and blew a honking blast that rattled Gull's skull. "Bardo, signal your scouts to watch but not engage, however you do that.

Dispatch Helki and Holleb to the, uh, west, so you won't be ambushed. And send someone to our rear so we're not surprised."

Bardo frowned. "I don't have enough for t'at."

"Oh, right. Well, I'll get it. Move out! No, wait! Climb up here and see if you recognize this thing." Below him, soldiers stuffed dinner in their mouths and shirts and snatched up weapons. Soldiers' wives and husbands helped them strap on war gear. Cooks and other retainers scurried to secure the camp. People ran everywhere. Two soldiers cannoned into one another following their sergeants' barked orders.

Bardo never walked when he could ride, so he nudged his horse sideways and caught the scaling ladder from the saddle. Squeezing alongside Gull—the back of the clockwork beast was narrow—he frowned at the twisting cone in the north. "Never seen it before."

"And you're from the northlands. . . . " Gull mused. "Varrius, where are you? Varrius! Climb up here, will you?"

Varrius was a thin man with knotty arms, a thick black beard, and skin bronzed by southern suns. He left a corporal in charge of assembling his soldiers and dashed to the clockwork beast to mount.

When he reached the top, his crisped skin turned pale. "Arms of Hyperion! That's a tornado!"

"Tor-na-do?" asked Gull. Again, he reflected that an ignorant woodcutter who'd lived his first twenty years in one village made for a poor adventurer. "What's—"

"A whirlwind!" shouted the soldier. He wore more clothes than usual, for his blood was better suited to hot lands. Over all was a breastplate of mail like fish scales. He wore a padded helmet with a tall red plume. His war harness was hung with a short sword and long dagger almost as big. "That's a—killer storm! It spins so fast it can throw a house in the air! Don't you see those trees catching hell?"

Gull peered. The tornado was closer now, though he was still unsure how far off. Distances were impossible to judge against an ocean of green. But now he recognized the bits being flung in the air: evergreen trees seven or eight feet high. As the storm spun, it lofted dozens in all directions, as a saw throws sawdust.

When the impact hit him, all he could say was, "Oh, my."

That tornado was hundreds of feet tall, tearing a swath through the forest fifty feet wide, no more than a mile away.

Coming straight at them.

Panic swept the camp, a windstorm by itself.

The camp lay asprawl a hacked-out clearing of short stumps and trampled twigs and needles. There were no breaks in this endless forest, so each campsite had to be created anew: trees chopped down, the resinous evergreens burned. Amidst the slush and churned mud and scattered branches was a hodgepodge of tents and bedrolls with no order at all. The cooks' kitchen area was neat enough, and that of the cartographers and librarians, but the rest . . . There weren't even any proper latrines: it was probably only the cold that had kept them free of disease so far.

Once things quieted down, Gull thought, they *had* to get organized.

People ran every which way, tripping as they went. Bardo and his scouts vanished into the greenery without a trace. Helki and Holleb, a wife-husband team of centaurs, clapped on their fluted painted helmets and hoisted their feathered lances high. They wore sweaters under their ornamented breastplates, and horse blankets under their war harness around their glossy roan-colored flanks. The ancient giant, Liko, with two slow bald heads and one arm, clambered upright only to get in the way. He alone could see over the trees, but it would take a while for the danger of the windcone to penetrate his thick skulls. The scale-mailed sergeants in red—Tomas, Neith, and Varrius— barked at their motley squads, slapping food from hands, demanding to see weapons for inspection. Three Muronian holy dervishes spun in circles, shrilling that the moment of doom was at hand. One's flailing foot knocked a cook sprawling and dumped a caldron of steaming soup into the snow. Others ran, jumped, asked each other questions.

Into this teeming midst leapt Gull, bellowing orders that no one heard. "Stiggur, get your beast moving, away from camp! You lot, get under cover! Here, grab those horses! Peg 'em to trees, but spread—hey! I'm talking to you! C'mere! Move this—"

Someone upended a basket and dumped out a scrawny gray-green form no bigger than a child. It was a goblin, that most useless of species, named Egg Sucker. Feeling the cold snow under its bare feet—it was wrapped in rags and looked like a pile of leaves— the goblin jumped for something warm and landed on both of Gull's boots. Angrily, the woodcutter grabbed the goblin and chucked him squawling into the evergreens. Egg Sucker was a mascot of sorts, useless but indespensible. Before Gull could turn around, a young woman crashed full into him with an armload of scrolls. Gull didn't know her name, only that she was a student of magic his sister Greensleeves had met somewhere on the road. The girl apologized and scrambled to pick up scrolls from the slush.

Gull felt a log bang his wool-and-leather padded shoulder, and flinched. But it was only the giant, Liko, asking what he should do. Despite the weather, the giant wore only a long sleeveless smock made of patched canvas, old ship's sails, and raw bullock hides bartered from a slaughterhouse. The mountainous dullard had lost his left arm in an earlier battle, chewed off to the elbow. To compensate, Gull and other craftsmen had fashioned a long club studded with iron that weighed as much as the brute's good arm, and lashed it to the stump, so he might walk without listing. Gull craned his head back and scratched his head. "What to do? Um, just . . . go *that* way, see if you see any riders on horses. Let them see you, then come back and tell me, all right?" The giant nodded and stomped off, dirty bare feet sinking deep into the slushy loam. He didn't even feel the sharp stumps that abounded in the campsite.

People were disappearing, though Gull couldn't say exactly where except into the trees. Let them go, he thought. He dashed for one of three big tents at the edge of the clearing. Trying to duck inside, he almost banged heads with his sister.

Greensleeves lived up to her name, dressed all in green, some of the clothes fine, some ragged. She'd even donned shoes for the snow. Her ragged old shawl, knitted by their mother, lay around her shoulders atop a green plaid cape. Her head, as always, was bare, her brown hair tousled like Gull's. They were much alike, except the sister only came up to her brother's breastbone. At her feet chittered a badger with a notched ear, a pet of sorts. Perched on her shawl was a chickadee named Cherrystone.

"Greenie! Take Lily and get under cover! There's a tornado, a big wind coming!"

"Wh-which w-way?" Until a few months ago, Greensleeves had been a half-wit all her life. It was only after leaving behind their homeland, the Whispering Woods, and its befuddling enchantment that her mind had cleared and she had learned to talk. She was still slow at it.

Yet the enchantment had also suffused every fiber of her being, making her a powerful, natural—and unschooled—wizard.

When Gull pointed north, she only disappeared inside, the badger scuttling after. "I m-might have so-something . . . "

"Greenie! Come—Oh!"

Lily was backing out. Another natural and untrained wizard, and Gull's source of love and bewilderment. Dressed in winter white, like an ermine, Lily wore a belted gown and short jacket brocaded with flowers, sturdy laced shoes, and a white cloak embroidered around the edges with more flowers in blue, red, and yellow. Her face was olive dark, with black hair twisted behind her head and entwined with white ribbons. She flashed him a bright smile, instinctively craned on tiptoe to give him a fast kiss, then remembered herself and halted—and tore the wound in Gull's heart once again.

She moved stiffly, for in recent months she'd suffered a broken leg and arm. It wasn't that old pain, but a burden on her heart that kept her distant from Gull. She muttered only, "I'll tend Greensleeves. You see to the camp."

"But—" She was gone.

By now, Gull could hear the moaning of the spinning wind, hear wood breaking. He gave up worrying about the women. Both could probably ride a tornado like he could ride a milk cow. He'd get back to his job, being a general of this rabble.

Not that he knew much about generaling.

Finally, the camp saw some order, if only that most of the nonfighters had run to hide in the low forest. The "red sergeants," so-called for their tatty plumes—Tomas, Neith, and Varrius—had assembled their troops into rough ranks. Some snapped to attention when Gull trotted up. Others fiddled with their tackle or snuck more bites of their interrupted dinner. Tomas, big and bald and black bearded and bronzed, barked, "What are your orders, sir?"

Gull waved his huge double-headed axe feebly. Times like this, he preferred woodcutting. "Tom, take your men out about, uh, two hundred paces and fan them out in a line to the northeast. Var, do the same northwest. We're to protect the camp. Neith, take yours behind us and fan out to cover our rear. If you're engaged by superior forces, fall back toward camp. Otherwise, keep 'em away from the center. And get your heads down if that storm cloud sweeps through. Got it?"

Clearly, they got it, but had a dozen more questions that discipline forbade them to ask. In best military fashion, they'd "muddle through." Gull watched them trot off through the stubby trees.

He took stock of himself. He had his axe and,

looped through his belt, a new blacksnake whip such as he'd once used to pop flies from his mules' ears. But where were his longbow and quiver? He'd unhooked them from the side of the clockwork beast, hung them on his tent pole, but they were gone. Who could have—

Someone ran to the fire, grabbed a burning brand—Gull couldn't see why—and dithered as to which way to go. Gull shouted, "Get under cover, you idiot!" Shaking his head, his longbow forgotten, he pressed through the evergreens for the front lines. Wherever they were. And that giant windstorm.

He'd just closed on the lines and answered a sentry's challenge when a bloodcurdling chorus of screams split the frosty air.

There was no way to tell what the attack looked like, or whence it came, except from ahead. Or perhaps to the side, or behind.

As the screams welled up again, Gull cursed and pushed on. The forest didn't change an inch. The valley floor was flat, sand under layers of dead brown needles, and stretched for miles east and west. With plenty of sunlight and no competition except from neighboring evergreens, the trees filled out until their stiff sweet-smelling branches interlocked. In every direction, it was like a sea of breast-high water.

A bad place to fight, Gull berated himself. A real general would have picked another site. And where were the rest of the troops?

The only landmark was the tornado, which he could see now, despite being surrounded. It towered in the sky, dead north, whirling, spitting out shredded trees like watermelon seeds. Yet it looked no closer. Could such a thing just hover in place? Could a wizard conjure one and then direct it? That would be like steering a mountain.

He saw soldiers ahead and around him, a head here, a hat there, spaced in their curving irregular line. But for the enemy . . .

Then he saw one.

Dark—darker than Tomas, even—almost black skinned. Black beard. Wrapped in a woolen robe of a brilliant blue like an evening sky. Even the man's head was wrapped with cloth. A turban, Gull had heard it called in a seaport. The man's horse was dark brown, with an ornate gold-stamped leather harness. Over his head he waved a sword curved like a crescent moon, yet he didn't hack at the trees, for the horse could dance nimbly amidst them. He saved his hacking for enemies.

Gull saw one of his soldiers—he didn't know the man's name—back up swiftly, fetch up in tangled branches, then set his feet and raise his long sword. A short bow was cased on his back, but he hadn't had time—or the wherewithal—to nock and draw. Now he waited for the cavalryman's attack.

Spears, damn it! thought Gull. We should carry spears! Or, better, lances that could be planted in the ground to tear mounted troops from the saddle.

But to stand against cavalry with swords was futile.

The rider, much higher than the infantryman, coming so much faster, easily batted aside the sword, then swung backhanded with his curved saber. Shocked by the sudden attack, the infantryman lost the top of his head to the razor-sharp blade.

Gull winced as he watched in horror and damned himself for their lack of preparation. He crushed branches with his elbows, grabbed for the longbow slung over his shoulder.

Except it wasn't there. He remembered then. It was lost back in camp somewhere.

Gull gaped as the rider spun the horse in his direction. The sickle blade swung high over the man's shoulder. Shrieking like a demon let out of hell, he charged the woodcutter.

For lack of any other defense, Gull ducked. And kept going.

The trees grew thicker closer to the ground. Though the branches were long dead and needleless, they were still as tough as wires. Gull wouldn't have liked to crawl amidst them, except now he had the strength of the desperate and hunted.

Slithering, crawling, low as a snake, he rammed his head and shoulders through branches, which snapped with a deafening noise. Jamming, pushing, gathering bushels of needles in his hair and down his neck, he battered a path for a dozen feet. He was hampered by his heavy axe clutched in his left hand, which lacked the last three fingers, pinched off in a tree-felling accident. Similarly, he was hampered by a lame right knee, from yet another oak twisting the wrong way on its stump. No soldiers had ever wounded Gull as badly as fetched-up trees.

Gasping for breath, as if he had plunged underwater, Gull decided he'd gone far enough, squinched his eyes shut, and crashed upward through interlocked branches like some giant demented rabbit.

In the wrong place.

The blue-robed horseman was a dozen feet away, still charging. But he currently searched along the other side of his mount. He'd seen Gull disappear there and hadn't followed his almost-underground passage.

His mistake.

Spitting out needles and twigs, the woodcutter hoisted his axe and crooked it over his shoulder as if for splitting wood. He'd never make a proper soldier, he thought, for he couldn't strike from cover. *"Here, you scut!"*

Surprised, the rider turned just in time to not shy fast enough. The horse seemed to dance under his expert guidance, but waves of greenery trapped it neatly. The rider raised his scimitar, half-attacking, half-flinching . . .

And Gull's eight-pound axe head fell.

The heavy wedge, sharp enough to shave hair, clove through the horseman's right thigh, his saddle, and his mount's rib cage. The horse snorted, ready to whinny, but had no wind to spare, for his lung had been nicked and quickly filled with blood. The rider only blinked as his thigh separated, and the lower half of his leg fell free to dangle from the stirrup. Gull noted incongruously the man wore leather shoes that turned up at the tip and held a tiny silver bell. Then blood was spurting everywhere: onto cedar branches, into the air. Off balance, his heart already failing, the rider pitched the opposite way. Yet, disciplined, he held onto his scimitar and the reins. His weight slewed his mount's head around, but the animal was gasping, frothing red at the mouth, and it veered, struck a tree, and stopped, then slowly sank. Gull felt sorry for the animal, for it would be a long time dying.

And its rider, Gull guessed, was no doubt another commoner like himself, plucked from some remote stretch of the Domains at a wizard's whim, compelled by geas to battle so the wizard might—what? Grab more power from another wizard?

Balls! thought Gull. If he ever forgot his purpose in life, the world kept reminding him. He and his sister and army were out to stop wizards any way they could, stop them from ravaging whole countrysides and disrupting commoners' lives.

Even though his sister, and his lover—or former-lover or almost-lover—Lily were wizards themselves.

Brushing thinking and paradoxes aside, Gull rammed through the trees, searching for his soldiers. Where had they gone? Had he gotten turned around? He turned in a slow circle, seeking the landmark windstorm. But it was gone. The sky was ice-blue, clear as only winter air in the mountains could be. How . . . ?

He heard shouting, turned and pressed in that direction. Calling "Friend, friend!" he came up to a ragged woman with a crossbow and pike. She nodded Gull on toward Tomas.

Soon, standing breast to breast in the mad maze of green, Gull asked, "Did you capture any riders?" Getting captives was their first desire, for captives brought knowledge—something hard to recall in the heat of battle, as Gull had just demonstrated.

"Maybe, sir. Istu knocked a man from the saddle.

He might survive," reported the soldier, sheathing his short sword and using both bloody hands to emphasize each word. "They came at our right, so we know there are two parties out here trying to flank us. We got three, we think, lost one of ours, before they pulled back. They hallooed in some godsforsaken tongue, probably calling us jellyfish, then they slipped away, back north."

Standing so close, Gull could smell Tomas's sweat, the garlic on his breath. He and his southerners put garlic in everything. "Could they be circling around to gain the camp from the rear?"

"Can't say, sir." He waved a hand around. "They could'a gone anywhere."

Gull raised his voice. "Did anyone see where that windstorm went?" He realized he could only see four other soldiers. He wondered where the fallen horsemen had landed. Their blood and bones would feed trees for years, he supposed.

No one answered, so Tomas spoke. "We was busy pushing off the attack, sir."

Gull frowned at the sea of green. From now on, he'd stay atop the clockwork beast, use it for a mobile tower, or ride between Liko's thick heads so he could *see* what the hell the enemy did. "Well, let's pull back to within, uh, a hundred paces of camp. We need to get within shouting distance of each—"

He paused, mouth agape. Tomas turned and swore.

Zipping through the sky, directly overhead, by the dozens, went swordsmen and women on flying carpets.

"The camp!" bleated the woodcutter. The tornado must have been a distraction to drive them from camp.

Whirling, he raised his axe to bat aside the cedars, then halted.

Facing him was a black hairy man-shape. Even hunched like a bear, it was wider, taller, and stronger than Gull.

It opened a red mouth lined with fangs and roared.

CHAPTER
2

NORREEN EASED HER SLEEPY CHILD ONTO HER lap and relaced her bodice. The boy Hammen, dark like his parents, murmured sleepily. He fell asleep nursing every night. Now if she could only lift him into his cradle without waking—

"Papa?" gurgled the child. His eyes opened wide, deep turquoise blue, like his father's. "Where Papa?"

Norreen felt a twinge. "He's—outside, dear. Checking that the animals are safe."

"Oh. But me want Papa to . . . " Gravity won, and the child's eyelids drooped. By then, his mother had levered him into his cradle. He grew so fast he barely fit, his large feet planted against the footboard. He'd be a big child, a towering man, like her side of the family, which she hadn't seen in so long. Another twinge. She tried to concentrate on her child. He was talking now, real speech; the boy needed a bed, not a cradle. But his father wouldn't make him one. He was too busy.

This final twinge brought tears to her eyes. Misty, she tightened the laces of her bodice. At least she could take some pleasure in the way her chest and stomach were flattening again. Gods, but childbirth took a toll on a woman's body! She'd suffered fewer scars and disfigurements on the battlefield. Now that little Hammen could run and manage alone outside, Norreen could get more exercise. She should get back to training. Get the feel of the sword and shield and dagger and bow back in her arms and shoulders. Dressed in a peasant woman's plain wool gown and laced bodice, her black hair grown long and a slightly wavy, there was little that marked her as a former warrior. Except for the seven-pointed star tattooed on her left forearm.

And her memories.

Shaking her head, she searched for her husband.

Outside the cottage, the air was cool and damp. The night sky was half-clouded, but the Mist Moon was a gray fog in the western sky. Here the Southlands were rolling hills and small forests, mostly cultivated to feed the voracious appetite of the city of Estark in the north, gently rolling southward till they met the Endless Sea, and the Green Lands of backwoods Gish. Their cottage nestled against a hill covered with catulpa trees and quaking aspens, bordered by a clear-running stream and overlooking a small valley.

Lining the face of the valley were grape arbors, lattice works head-high that marched in rows across the slope, and, below, pastureland. With her husband, Norreen owned all the land within sight, for they'd once been rich and were now rich in land. It was good land; the slope faced the south and got plenty of sun and rain, and the nights were never cold. The vineyard had been fruitful, the finest in the community, when they bought it.

Now it might as well be an ashheap.

Her husband stood brooding above the slope, staring without looking, not thinking of the farm. Or her.

She approached him warily, scuffing her feet.

From years of training and hardscrabble surviving, it wasn't safe to surprise either of them. A person could get dead very quickly.

"Garth?"

"Eh?" He jumped, whirled upon her. Bringing his thoughts to earth, he answered, "Oh, Norreen. It's you."

"Who else would it be?" she asked petulantly. Besides herself and the child, there were only three servants on the farm. "What are you doing? Hammen asked for you to put him to bed."

"Eh?" He'd turned away. Piqued, Norreen prodded his back with a sharp finger. Again he jumped like a tiger, then relaxed.

Norreen could have cried all over again. Five years since they'd battled for their lives, yet both of them were still as skittish as starved wolves. Would they never know peace?

"Listen to me! I'm your wife, damn it! Stop mooning at the sky and *tell* me! What's going *on*?"

"Oh, nothing . . . " Garth was a thin man, not tall, with scruffy dark hair ill-cut—Norreen was no barber. Although he wore a farmer's shabby wool breeches and plain shoes, he yet retained a heavily embroidered shirt, black with blue thread. Around his shoulders hung a tattered leather cape with an embroidered hem. He carried a dagger, a queer tool for a farmer, and a small satchel of tooled leather. Norreen especially hated to see that.

Garth's only arresting features were his eyes: deep turquoise blue, like their son's. Around the left eye were vivid white scars with jets radiating in all directions, so his blue eye resembled some child's drawing of a sun.

Altogether, he looked like a scarecrow. But at one time, he'd been the most dangerous man in the Western Realms.

Garth, once Garth One-Eye, bore two eyes now because he'd grown one back. The eye had been gouged out when he was a child, purely for spite, before he was consigned to flames where the rest of his household died. Yet Garth had survived, and learned magic and more magic, and returned years later to the city of Estark and its annual wizards' festival, and its arena. Single-handedly, he had joined first one house and then another, fought innumerable duels, sustained torture both physical and psychic, pitted one master against another, one house against another, and finally established himself the premier wizard of the Western Realms. From there, he'd met a planeswalker, once a man, now almost a god. He'd ascended to walk between the planes, and had battled that god and defeated him, and had returned, the first wizard to ever come back to the arena. From there, he'd exacted his revenge upon all the houses of Estark—Fentesk, Kestha, Bolk, and Ingkara—for the conspiracy that had razed the House of Oor-Tael long years ago. The resulting chaos had been labeled the Time of Troubles, a neat phrase that encompassed the death of thousands, the destruction of a city, and the ruin of the ruling class of Estark.

All worked by this one "scarecrow."

And along the way, he'd stolen the heart of Norreen of Benalia. Confident, daring and dashing, mysterious and yet vulnerable, he'd won her love even before she'd saved his life—and he saved hers—in the arena.

Together, they'd left behind the plaguey smoldering city and come south, bought a farm and tended grapes, for Garth was fond of wine and wished to become a vintner. He'd wanted only to live in peace and start a new family after being alone and lonely for so long.

For a while.

Yet lately the vines languished, tended half-heartedly by the servants, for their master had lost interest. More and more, Garth prowled the night, gazing at the stars and moons, whispering to himself.

Once he'd used magic, Norreen thought bleakly, wielded it like a god. Now magic used him.

"I've been thinking, Norreen . . . " Suddenly she

hated that name, for it wasn't her real one. "I've been thinking I might—"

"Go away," she interrupted. "Again."

A frown crossed his bony face. By the slim light from the cottage door, the white scar-star around his left eye glowed. "It's purely for business. I want some new grafts for the vines. If we irrigate too much, the grapes will split because they're a northern variety. I thought if I searched south, where the sun's hotter, there'd be some variety—"

"Spare me!" She held up a hand, and he flinched. "You said that the last two times and returned with nothing! The grapes don't need grafting, or magic twiddling, either! They need a gentle hand to trim and shape them, and weed and water and prune! Weeks of backbreaking labor, not a week's jaunt through the ether! If you don't stay here and grub in the soil, we won't *have* any crop, just a murder of grape-fattened crows!"

Before he could say anything, she pointed angrily at the satchel slung by his side. "If you're going after cuttings, why do you carry *that*? All I ever saw you pull from that was more accursed magic! Magic won't help this farm! And it won't help me!" Then she was crying, damning herself for a show of weakness.

Her husband wasn't listening. He wasn't even there. A man who'd walked among the stars would never plant his feet on the earth again, not fully. He'd tasted the infinite and found the finite wanting, as a man who'd tasted fine wine could never settle again for water.

"I'm going," he announced. "I'll return—"

"Don't bother!" she shouted through tears. "I won't be here when you come back! And neither will Hammen!"

The frown returned, starker. "You will. I order—"

"You don't command me!" she snapped. Instinctively she snatched at her side for a dagger, her favorite fighting weapon, but she wore none. "No man does! I am a Hero of Benalia, of the Clan Tarmula!"

"The magic calls me. We'll talk when I return."

Reaching into his satchel, he pulled forth something blacker than the night. Frail as a spiderweb, the black threads spun like film from his hand to enwrap him. The blackness coalesced until he was invisible inside the black cocoon.

Then it fell away, like gossamer on the wind, and he was gone.

Norreen swore, cried, stamped her foot, clenched her fists. She damned Garth and magic and her own helplessness. Of course she'd be here. She had no place to go, could not go home, though these days she thought of home more and more and wished her child could know his heritage. And she loved this farm and the simple people of the valley and village nearby. She wanted to live here, be happy here, but Garth was lured away by the siren's call of magic—

A squawl froze her. Spinning, she turned.

Tall shapes flickered in the candlelight of the cottage that moments ago had held only her child.

She grabbed her skirts and she tucked them in her belt, wishing for her old fighting togs of neat leather. Dashing, she plucked up an iron hoe from the kitchen garden before the cottage, tore off the blade to leave an iron-tipped pole—deadly enough. Warrior's caution took control, and she tiptoed to approach the door obliquely. If these were bandits, they'd regret their raid on this house. For endangering her child and home, she'd open their veins and let their blood flow downhill to feed the vines.

Back against the door, she listened, but the thieves had gone silent. Had they heard her? Had she lost her touch, fallen this far from training?

Another squawl from her baby set her moving.

Better a direct attack. Shrieking "*Tar-mu-la!*" she whipped around the corner with the improvised quarterstaff leveled.

And froze.

All three wore black: leather jerkins, skintight trousers, floptop boots. And war harnessess holding short swords and daggers, all sheathed, so far. Two men and one woman, lethal as tigers. The biggest man, in back, held her bawling son cradled in his arms.

Tattooed on their left forearms were seashells, the mark of Clan Deniz.

"You are Rakel of Clan Tarmula?" demanded the black-clad woman. Blond hair was bound in a long braid down her back, tied with black leather.

"Yes, that's her," the tall man answered. "Though you wouldn't know it for those clothes. Have you been shoveling cowshit or slopping the hogs, Rakel?"

Inadvertently, Norreen gasped. She knew the man. She'd trained with him. Natal. They were heroes of Benalia. What could they want here?

Ah. Her.

"Put down my son, Natal, or I'll kill you first. The rest of you, get—"

Eyes flickered, and the blonde exploded into action. With one leap she crossed the room, kicked Norreen's pathetic hoe high, then spun and kicked again. Struck in the breastbone, Norreen slammed against the wall. Winded, her vision spinning, she clutched at a table leg. Anything was a weapon in the hands of a hero, her people said. She could—

A casual boot kicked away her hand, numbing it. Another hand seized her hair, twisted her neck, slammed her to the dirt floor of the cottage. Her cottage, her home. And Garth's and Hammen's.

Wrists twisted behind, locking her arms straight, she breathed dust and tried to think. There was a way out of this armlock—what was it? She was so slow, so helpless. Tears squeezed from her eyes and spotted the dirt.

"Are you *sure*," sounded the blonde's snide voice, "she's a hero? She's helpless as a milkmaid and slow as a cow!"

"That's her," came Natal's voice. "Guyapi!"

From the corner of her eye, Norreen saw a man

step forward from the darkness of the corner. He wore a dark jerkin similar to the warriors', but embroidered with a star-and-moon motif across the breast and down his ribs. A Benalish wizard. The man who'd conjured this assassination squad here and would conjure them out. Once Norreen was dead. And her child? Fresh tears stained her cheeks. And she'd told Garth she wouldn't be here when he returned. Now he'd find their skeletons picked clean by coyotes and rats.

"Guyapi, take us home."

The wizard didn't reply, only spread his hands wide. The heroes, Natal still holding the sobbing Hammen, clustered together. Sparks flew from the wizard's fingertips—a foolish vanity, Norreen knew, from Garth's explanations. Only minor wizards wasted magic in pyrotechnics.

Yet they'd said "home." Would she . . . ?

The sparks increased, flaring, filling the cottage. Norreen found it too bright to watch. Would the sparks set fire to their home? Would Garth find a smoking ruin and never know what happened to them?

Would he even return?

Then she felt a tingling all over, as if the sparks had got under her skin.

Then she was falling. Crying.

When the sparks faded, Norreen found herself in a small room without windows. The tiny room sported rich though muted tapestries on the four walls, and an iron chandelier for light.

She was still pinned facedown, held by two heroes now, who fitted an iron collar around her neck, then affixed it to manacles on her wrists, trussed behind her back. By straining her arms upward, she didn't choke. The blond woman laughed. "This is like fitting an elephant's ankle chain on a mouse."

"You know the rules. Are they ready for us yet?" asked Natal. He silenced Hammen's cries by pinching his nose and mouth shut, so the child couldn't breathe. Hammen gasped for air when released. Norreen writhed in her iron bonds helplessly. She could only hope they'd kill her and her son quickly, not send them to the dungeons to be practiced upon by apprentice torturers.

At the door, Natal said, "They're signaling. Let's go. Look smart now, heads up, shoulders back."

Pride before anything else, thought Norreen. Had she really been born of these hard-hearted folk? Then her bonds were jerked savagely, and she was hauled from the tiny waiting room—

—into a luxurious chamber like a throne room, had Benalia had royalty. But the city-state did not have a king; it had rotating castes instead. And with a sinking sensation, Norreen realized which of the seven castes was on top this season. And who ruled that caste.

Dozens of retainers, hangers-on, and layabouts lined the room, all in expensive but plain clothing, all eager to be entertained. Down the center lay a long blue runner decorated with pink seashells, the color and emblem of the current ruling caste, Clan Deniz. At the end of the room was a dais with a long glossy table, very plain but costly, as was everything in Benalia. At the table sat seven elders, leaders of their caste. Centermost was the Speaker for the Caste. Norreen knew him all too well.

At one end of the table stood the exchequer with a scroll edged in red. The color of blood, a matter of life and death. Hers. As the seven elders and the court listened, and the heroes behind kept a tight grip on Norreen's manacles and her child, the exchequer read, "Rakel of Dasha of Argemone of Kynthia," citing the names of Norreen's mothers, "you stand accused . . . "

It was very flowery, and went on some time. To Norreen it was old news. She had been shield-bearer to the warlord, a woman named Alaqua, killed in battle. By rights and custom, Norreen should have died first, or with her. Instead, she'd survived. No use to explain she'd had three arrows in her body and been bashed on the head by a dwarven axe. Benalia was not interested in justice, but in rules. The crimes rolled on, with Norreen mentally filling the gaps: how she'd "fled to Estark" (unconscious in a wagonload of bodies) and "skulked in secret" (fourteen months in a charity hospital) without "reporting to her masters" (good trick—she didn't even know where Estark lay in respect to Benalia), had "debased her trade" by street fighting for the amusement of crowds (and food), had fought to the death in the arena "without compensation" (to save the life of her lover, Garth), and so on.

She waited for the end, and her death. She tried not to cry, thinking of her son.

The charges finally ran out. "How do you plead?"

"Guilty as charged." Had anyone ever pleaded innocent? Her voice was even. She could at least die with dignity. But oh, her child was so young!

"Very well. Await punishment." The Speaker was trying not to smile. Norreen only glared at him. Of the hundreds of men in Benalia, she had to stand defenseless before Sabriam, the man she'd refused to marry. But then, she could count: she should have known this season his caste was ascendant. Not that staying away had been a bad decision: Sabriam looked even more wasted, dissipated, addicted than ever. As ruler, he was feted by the leading clans of one of the largest cities in the Domains, and nightly parties were taking their toll on him: wine, feasting, and orgies would probably claim him before the year was out. She hoped.

Sabriam wiped his chin, couldn't resist nattering. "Benalia is especially disappointed in you, Rakel. Alaqua was our finest warlord, you her most promising squire. But you let her down, and so the Red Iron Mountains are still outside our sphere. That's cost the city dearly in the time you've been away dallying." He almost licked his lips at the last word.

"Unchain me," Norreen grated, "and I'll show you how I dally."

A wet chuckle, and Sabriam had to wipe his chin again. "I must add, it was a severe disappointment to me that you refused my offer of marriage. An insult to me and my clan."

Norreen seethed. Being executed would be bad, but being talked to death worse. "*You* are an insult to your clan, Sabriam, and all of Benalia! That your warty hands control this city's destiny is like letting the jackals tend the graveyard! And as for marriage, I'd sooner lie with a pig in shit than with you; the smell would be sweeter, there'd be less chance of catching disease, and I wouldn't wonder when the pig would desert me for a bottle or a little boy!"

The crowd gasped, though many tittered. Even some of the elders flanking Sabriam wanted to nod: rivalry within the clans was as fierce as street fights among clans.

Noting the ridicule around him, Sabriam's voice quivered, and he sprayed spittle. "Prepare her!"

Hands shifted on her manacles, and the blond warrior stepped in front with a long white dagger in hand. The infamous dagger of Benalia, sign of a hero. They'll kill me right here in the chambers? Norreen thought. Ah, well, better than in the dungeons. Her son would remember his mother died with pride. . . .

But the knife at her neckline didn't seek her heart. Instead, it kissed her skin as it slicked down the front of her bodice, severing her ties. The blade continued on, slitting her clothes, leaving her naked.

The courtiers tittered. Norreen blushed crimson from head to toe, and they giggled more. She couldn't believe this colossal insult. A hero should be afforded a hero's death.

The blonde snorted when she beheld Norreen's naked frame; the broadened buttocks, the heavy legs, the protruding belly, the hanging breasts that leaked milk. Except for her face and arms, her skin was white, having lost its tan, while warriors trained naked under a broiling sun. Someone brought a bundle to Norreen's side, and the blonde picked something from it.

What, in the name of the Eternals, were they *doing* to her?

Dressing her. The blonde commanded she lift her foot, and amazed, Norreen complied. With help from one of the men, they jerked the leather breeches up her thick calves and thighs, grunting more than necessary with the effort. Over Norreen's torso they draped the leather jerkin of a hero and, despite her chains, laced it under the armpits. Finally, they slung on her war harness with its pouches and short sword and dagger and gauntlets, a round shield hung on behind, and they fitted her with boots. The blonde then stepped back, spitting to show her annoyance with mundane tasks.

But Norreen could only wonder. Since when did they dress the condemned in war garb?

"Things have changed," Sabriam answered, as if reading her mind. "Under our rule is a new policy. We no longer put criminals to death." (Criminals, her mind rang.) "We no longer waste—valuable resources." People hissed at the mention of money. Warriors were not cobblers and fishmongers.

Sabriam went on, loudly, as if to stifle an old argument. Arguments were three a penny in Benalia. "In a new show of mercy, we grant condemned felons one chance to redeem themselves. One. You have been chosen to act out the wishes of the Speaking Caste. If you perform well, you will be pardoned and readmitted to the society of heroes. Fail, and you will be put to death."

Still throttled, though feeling stronger in her warrior's garb, Norreen asked, "What is my assignment?"

"There is, in the eastern reaches, an army building. This army plans to expand from the east to the west and threaten Mother Benalia herself. You are to join this army, or sneak upon it, however you see fit, and assassinate its leaders."

"Who are they?" asked Norreen. It was automatic to get an order clarified. Her head was swimming at this reprieve. One moment she was dead, the next alive and loosed to the field like a hunting dog. She knew Sabriam must be lying: this chore was undoubtedly something to further his clan's power and hold.

"The leaders are a female wizard, one Greensleeves, said to hold great power over nature, and the other is the army's general, called Gull the Woodcutter. Capture their heads. Guyapi will call for you then."

"What about my son?" Norreen hadn't meant to shout, but it was torn from her heart.

Sabriam smiled, drooling. "Your—bastard—will be held here for protection, given to tutors to catch up his lessons. Though I imagine he'll be so far behind the other children will—test him—frequently. You might not even recognize the boy. So hurry back. Wizard!"

"No!" Norreen barked. The tutors were merciless: she knew that from personal experience. They'd beat every ounce of humanity out of her sweet boy, might kill him outright as an example to others. *"Noooo!"*

She flung herself against her bonds, wrenched them from her captor's hands. Leaning forward so as not to fall, Norreen charged the dais. With an old, sure strength, she vaulted it, then the table. Sabriam reared back, addled and slow in his responses. Norreen had time for one good kick—smashing the toad's nose so blood spurted—before she was toppled from the slippery table.

She crashed to the dais on her shoulder. Someone grabbed to roll her over, but she kicked, heard a knee snap. Then the blonde's hand descended, her dagger reversed, and the heavy skull-popping diamond on the hilt bounced Norreen's head on the teak floor, and she saw stars. Still struggling, she saw the wizard Guyapi stretch out both hands, sparks flying from his fingertips.

Her child cried, "Mama! Don' leave me!"

Then the sparks enveloped her, and she fell again.

CHAPTER
3

"L-LEAVE IT! IT'S NOT IM-IMPORTANT!" GREENSLEEVES tried to order her followers out of her tent, but they bumped bums and elbows stuffing odd shapes and bundles into four traveling trunks.

Greensleeves stooped to grab up her badger before someone stepped on it and was bitten. The gray- and brown-striped beast was scruffy to the touch, its fur as stiff as horsehair. One of its ears bore a notch from a long-ago fight. The badger wasn't a pet, or a familiar, merely another creature that followed her around. Like the chickadee on her shoulder that had flown down from a tree one day and simply stayed.

The girl wizard peeked out the open tent as she heard a loud flapping in the sky, like a mile of wash snapping on a clothesline. The tornado whirled in the distance, but came no nearer. So what could the flapping be? The badger in her arms growled.

All over camp, people gathered children and weapons and tools and ran for the woods. Greensleeves, responsible for them all, shrilled, "F-flee, everyone! And h-hide . . . " She gave up. No one was listening. And her stutter only got worse when she was excited.

"*I'm* going!" barked the practical Lily, tugging her cloak into place. "We need to get out and flee to the forest! Come on, Greensleeves!"

Yet the two men only stuffed the chest faster. Both were "students of magic," people who loved magic but could not themselves conjure. The smaller man was Tybalt, who was in nominal charge of the army's artifacts. He had a huge nose, scrawly whiskers, and ears pointed enough to suggest elven blood. The other was Kwam, a tall, dark, lean young man.

Greensleeves had four such students attending her: they sought to decipher a treasure trove of magic goods, booty from the lying conniving Towser, the wizard who'd tried to sacrifice Greensleeves and kill Gull. Chased off, he'd left behind four chests of geegaws and scrolls and toys and potions and junk. There was no way to know what was valuable, so the magic students packed it all.

Then, sudden as lightning from a winter sky, the attack arrived.

In seconds, colored heads rose above the low tree line, then dark-skinned warriors in glorious colors—on flying carpets.

The carpets were six feet long, intricately braided in all the colors of the rainbow, with fluttering tassels at the four corners, all achingly bright on this gray winter day. Greensleeves wondered how the flyers steered, for they only glanced down to make their quivering carpets descend. The carpets hovered a foot from the ground, as if to avoid being soiled by the earth and slush. The raiders wore flowing shirts in brilliant colors, baggy pants, and tall yellow boots with turned-up toes. Capes light as silk whirled around their shoulders as they moved with the grace of ballet dancers.

Deadly dancers. They shrieked some foreign name, drew scimitars with curved blades, and leaped to the attack. The first to die was a Muronian dervish,

who'd been spinning and singing his song of doom, ful-
filling his own prophecy, for a flying man cut him
down with a stroke of his sword. Still keening, the
dervish sank in his filthy robes, facedown in the slush,
until another invader severed his neck with a razor
slash.

Dark-skinned men and women—a score or more—
dashed about the camp, hacking down the few too
slow to flee. A cook died, a ladle still dripping gravy in
her hand. A cartographer only half drew his machete
before he was disemboweled. Denied a wealth of victims, a dozen raiders leapt to the gently rippling carpets, barked orders to their charges, and soared
above the cedars to seek victims in the woods.

In those first few seconds of the raid, a half-dozen
marauders zipped toward Greensleeves and her tent.
Goggle-eyed, the wizard spun to run inside. If she
could somehow shield them—if she could remember
how to do it—she might save herself and her charges.

But she'd barely yanked the tent flap closed after
her before Lily screamed.

The front of the yellowed canvas tent split. A dark
man, bony-faced and swarthy, with a black goatee and
plumed turban, had slit it from ridgepole to floor. He
jabbered at the women, probably to stand fast, and
then jabbered at his companions.

More scimitars sliced the heavy canvas to shreds.
Ropes parted, and the ridgepole leaned over and
flopped onto the tatters. Greensleeves and Lily backed
into Tybalt and Kwam as male and female raiders
exposed them like farmers tearing open a rats' nest.

In the wan sunlight stood two camp beds, four
ornate chests, a dirty braided rug, and nothing else.
The raiders held their scimitars pointed, a ring of steel
trapping the magic users and students. The name
"Karli" bubbled through their talk. Greensleeves noted
their breath steamed and their teeth chattered: the
excitement of battle temporarily dimmed, they noticed
the cold, and clutched their silk capes around their
shoulders.

"What are they after? Us?" squeaked Lily. "And what are they waiting for?"

Greensleeves didn't answer. For her life, she couldn't remember how she'd once shielded herself.

For the hundredth time, she wished she knew how to properly cast spells.

The answer came as another figure appeared in the sky: a woman dressed brightest of all, surrounded by four more raiders on flying carpets.

This wizard flew through the air without a carpet, as if standing. On her feet were bright pink slippers, so curled the toes folded onto themselves, that sported tiny wings buzzing like a hummingbird's. Raising her arms, the woman landed as lightly as a butterfly amidst the ravaged camp.

She was short, delicate as a cactus flower, skin dark as mahogany, hair white as milkweed fluff. She wore a heavily brocaded jacket and long thick pants, with a cape of yellow feathers so fine they looked like mohair. Most curious, her jacket was lined down the lapels and around the middle with a myriad of buttons and medallions. Her smile was triumphant and smug.

Greensleeves recognized the smile. She'd seen it on Towser's face, usually at the height of a new betrayal. The badger in her arms growled again, and the chickadee Cherrystone hopped behind Greensleeves's head.

Mincing delicately, like a cat afraid to wet its feet, the woman alighted in the slush and approached the ruined tent. She arched an eyebrow at the occupants: Lily in white wool and fur, her clothes embroidered with yellow and blue and red flowers, all travel-stained; and Greensleeves, who always looked a ragamuffin—tattered wool skirt, a ragged jacket with the green sleeves cut back, a plain cloak held with a brass shoulder pin, a ratty shawl over that, and a hat to cover her tousled brown hair.

The wizard, who must be Karli, addressed the two women in a fluting language like oil bubbling up from sand. Her tone was condescending: she could recognize

the wizardry in each of them, but had only contempt for
their plain clothes and manner. She frowned when they
didn't answer, tried another language unsuccessfully.
Shaking her head, Greensleeves thought; She's from far,
far away in the Domains.

Irritated, the wizard cast a covetous eye past Tybalt
and Kwam at the four carved chests standing on the
rumpled camp rug. Lily harumphed. Greensleeves recognized the glance: greed for another wizard's possessions.
Karli touched a crystalline button on her lapel and
flicked two fingers in the direction of the magic students.

Tybalt and Kwam grunted as if they'd been kicked
in the stomach. Hoisted off their feet by an invisible
blow, they were knocked back a dozen feet until they
smacked into the line of tangled cedar trees. Snapping
branches enfolded them.

Karli fingered another medallion, a round lion's
head, and spoke to her raiders in a singing tone. They
hastened to fall back and dash off, leaving only two
guards safely behind Karli with swords drawn. The
other raiders set to looting and vandalism with a
shout, dumping out bedrolls, emptying crates and
packs, even kicking over the cooking gear.

That left only Greensleeves and Lily to face Karli.
In a flash, Greensleeves guessed this wizard believed
they already had some shield spell in place
(Greensleeves wished she did). And some horrendous
spell was about to befall them to breech the non exis-
tent shield.

Greensleeves uttered one first, one she was sure of.

Snarling, a pack of eight huge timber wolves
appeared in a circle around her and Lily.

A giant ape.

Gull recognized it from an old book of pictures
he'd once seen. A monkey as big as a big man, with
glossy stiff hair like a boar's. Monstrously strong and
ferocious.

Or so it appeared. It was still just an animal, and

Gull had neither the time nor bent to battle a dumb beast. He had to get to camp, which was beseiged by the flying-carpet riders.

The gorilla raised its arms high above its head and shouted. But didn't attack. An old farmhand, Gull guessed the ape was posturing, pretending to attack, seeking to be king of the barnyard by bluff.

So rather than attack, he copied the beast. See if it understood its own actions mirrored.

Raising his axe over his head in both hands, Gull howled back.

The gorilla reared to its full height, taller than Gull, shot up its arms, and roared again.

Titans' fire, thought the woodcutter, the thing was huge! It must weigh as much as a bull! One of those fists could probably drive his head into his torso!

Still, it hadn't rushed him.

Gull shook his axe, roared again. From the corner of his eye, he saw Tomas and another soldier circle around him, bow and crossbow raised. Gull didn't need that help; it might panic the ape into attacking.

Stepping forward, he hollered again until his throat hurt. He was within striking range of those impossibly long arms, and he kept a tight grasp on his axe. He might need it. The ape smelled of dung and rank sweat. Gull screamed his throat raw.

The gorilla blinked, rolled thick lips in a snarl. Abruptly, it turned and slunk away among the cedar trees. For something so huge, the only mark of its passage was a jiggling branch tip.

Tomas started to say something, but swore. He pointed. A half-dozen more black hunched shapes, smaller, scurried off through the forest. Lesser males, or females, Gull guessed. There would be legends about demons in these hills forever, if anyone ever came to live here.

For that matter, there was one more weird story about Gull the Woodcutter for the soldiers to tell around the campfire.

"Co—" Gull coughed, throat sore. "Come on! Form

your troops. We've got to get to camp, drive off those—carpet riders!"

Flying carpets, he thought bitterly. More wizard madness. Was there no end to it? Why couldn't wizards channel their powers for a good cause, improving fields for sowing, healing the sick, draining swamps, or collecting butterflies? Why attack some wizard's party in the middle of a wilderness?

Because they lusted for power was why. The way dragons ate other dragons and so grew stronger. Life came from the death of others, and wizards sought to be chief among all living things.

Brushing these morose thoughts aside, Gull checked that the soldiers were with him and pressed through the cedars for camp.

They had not gone a hundred feet before a Muronian dervish came thrashing through the trees toward them, shrieking, hood back, blood streaming down his face from a head wound. Panicked, the man ran smack into Gull, clawed at him for protection. The woodcutter had to shove him aside to get by. One of Tomas's soldiers shouted and pointed.

Zooming from the direction of camp came a flying carpet. Astride, intent on the prey she'd nicked, the raider saw the soldiers too late. A long arrow slammed into her upper chest. At the same instant, a crossbow bolt zipped through the carpet and transfixed her leg. The double blow caused the woman to reel. Gull expected her to pitch from the soaring carpet, but it stayed attached to her feet even as she slowly turned and fell from the sky. Magic glue, thought the woodcutter, a handy spell.

Like a wounded eagle, the colorful raider flipped twice before crashing amidst the trees. Gull wondered what kind of loot she might sport, then berated himself. He was growing as mercenary as his soldiers. But these days, he had tremendous expenses.

He rushed on and heard a woman shrieking orders, men shouting foreign curses, a snarling like a dogfight. Bursting free of the trees, shedding itchy needles, Gull glanced quickly around the camp and took in the bodies and vandalism, the brown-skinned, white-haired sorceress and twin guards threatening Greensleeves and Lily, and the pack of wolves leaping to their defense.

What to do? Protect his sister and her friend? Protect the innocents in the forest? Kill raiders? Who knew what was best in a battle, the most insane act people indulged in? He wasn't even a soldier, let alone a general!

Behind him sounded roars to Torsten and Ragnar and Jacques le Vert and a dozen gods of war. Tomas's twelve soldiers burst from the woods, hot to attack. The colorful raiders, thralls to that white-haired wizard, left off their looting to shout back a challenge.

His actions were decided, anyway, thought Gull. He hefted his fearsome felling axe and charged.

Axe swinging, he charged the first marauder. But the woman was fast, incredibly so. Skipping to one side, perfectly balanced, she aimed her scimitar point at Gull's oncoming face. With a yelp, the woodcutter slewed to one side and flailed with the axe rather than striking properly. He missed the raider, but made her jump aside, and he just missed impaling himself on the sword point. Thrown off balance, Gull stumbled in slush and loam.

By the time he'd regained his feet—expecting an icy stab in the back all the while—Tomas had engaged the raider. Lunging with his shield, the older veteran tricked the fighter into going for it, then neatly dispatched the woman by severing her windpipe with one quick thrust. By the time she died, Tomas had moved on.

Stumbling on roots and stumps, Gull entered the battle. Battle cries had brought most of Neith's and Varrius's companies running from the trees, so they matched the raiders in numbers. But these desert hawks were doughty fighters. In one corner, Gull saw a bird-bright man drive back three of his fighters. A slashing saber cut down a female fighter with a pike. It would be touch and go to defeat them. If they could.

Hoisting his axe, he ran at a knot of raiders harrying Neith's company. Shouting "Follow me! Let's go!" and other inanities, he charged their right flank. Neith's soldiers—mostly men and some three women—tried to keep their ragged ranks as they paced forward shouting.

The desert dwellers braced for Gull's clumsy attack. But the woodcutter had sense enough to halt outside of sword range, but well within throwing distance. Too late, the foremost desert raider realized his error. The axe-head slammed into his side just below the armpit, killing him outright, smashing his corpse into his companion.

Pressing the attack, crowding, Gull ripped the axe from the dying man's ribs and immediately whipped the haft straight across into the next woman's gut. She whoofed and toppled over. Grunting, hating his work and himself, Gull slammed her under the chin, breaking her jaw.

Damn wizardry, he thought, and all this unnecessary dying. These folk were compelled to fight, slaves to magic, forced to battle to the death for a wizard's vanity.

The only good here, he thought, was that while his and Greensleeves's army must fight and die, each soldier was a volunteer. No one was pressed into service.

All around him, fighters howled, shrieked, cried, and died. Individual battles raged all over the mucky camp. The defenders, Gull's people, were holding, not retreating. How his sister fared with her wolves he couldn't see. It was a mad tangle by her tent. Gull wondered how he might turn the odds, drive off the desert fiends, when, with a thrum of hooves, Helki thundered into the clearing.

"Gull!" called the female centaur. "Cavalry comes! Two tens or more!"

Events spun faster than Greensleeves could fathom.

Karli's two guards jumped at the sight of the

wolves. Both, either through loyalty or compulusion, braced themselves to protect their mistress. One man instinctively slashed at the pack's leader, huge and black and shaggy-haired, clipping its nose as it flinched.

The big animals normally wouldn't attack unless struck first, but they were confused and panicked, and snapped and snarled fit to shake the heavens. Protecting his pack, the big wolf lunged. Instantly, it and four more swarmed onto the man, growling, biting, tossing their heads to shear flesh to the bone. The other guard slashed at the wolves, only to bring the remainder upon herself.

The wizard Karli ignored the slaughter her guards suffered. Clasping a dainty brown hand to a medallion at her waist, she barked a word. Fire blossomed at her feet, as if she were a witch being burnt. Flames flickered as high as her waist, their breeze stirring the yellow feathers of her robe, yet Karli paid them no heed. Greensleeves and Lily could feel the heat, smell the resin of burning cedar twigs and the hot dusty canvas.

Impatient and hot-tempered, unable to speak their tongue, the woman stabbed fingers into her palm. Imperiously, in sign language, she first indicated a round shape, then walking motions with her fingers, then waggling like an octopus's tentacles.

Genuinely puzzled, Greensleeves strove to understand. Muzzy-headed most of her life, her brain awhirl with a thousand random thoughts an hour, the girl still had trouble concentrating on a single idea for long. Ignoring the snarling and yelling and crackling of flames, she shook her head repeatedly. "Wh-what d-do you *w-want*?"

Greensleeves saw Lily too was confused, but her friend edged closer, trying to interpose herself between the druid and the ill-tempered witch.

The hot-eyed wizard struck her fist in her palm, a final demand for the box-walking-wiggling thing. Pouting, she stabbed a finger at Lily and grabbed another medallion at the hem of her jacket.

Lily gulped and collapsed like a burst balloon.

"N-no!" Greensleeves said, panting. "Pl-please! I d-don't know wh-what you w-want!"

But the wizard was wroth. The flames around her feet crackled so high her face was distorted by heat waves. Pointing at Greensleeves now, she grabbed another medallion.

Greensleeves suddenly felt felt airy and light, as if she were floating, though she knew she was earthbound. She watched, detached, as Karli frowned at the failure of her spell (which spell?), grabbed another button, and pointed again.

This time, Greensleeves felt a stab like an icicle to her heart, a shriek at the back of her mind. An overpowering urge to run swept through her, to snatch up her badger, to escape, to hide, to bury herself in a hole if necessary. Yet something held her rooted.

The spell hit the wolves. Yelping, the bloodied animals pelted for the cedars. Two were dead, cut down by scimitars, but both guards were down and unmoving. Lily lay flat on the dirty rug of the ruined tent, her face as pale as her clothes, limbs at odd angles, like a dropped doll.

Greensleeves tried to think of something to hurl back. But fighting was not in her nature. Her normal reaction was to run and hide, as an animal would. Only humans killed each other without reason. But she must remain here, defend the camp and her followers if she could. How could she combat this aggressive monster who lusted for unknown curiosities? And how could she fight a wizard who knew *real* spells when all of Greensleeves's were blind instinct?

Wreathed in flames, hissing like a desert adder, Karli touched a pair of gold buttons at the corners of her jacket.

Smoke billowed as if from a fissure in the ground, yellow this time, and a pair of huge ugly women took shape.

Taller than her brother Gull, the women sported boiled-red skin, with black hair that jutted straight up in a

topknot from sharply defined widow's peak. Thick
through the body, the massive sagging bosoms were
speckled with hairy warts. Their faces were not human:
low foreheads, noses long as hound dogs', thick lips protruding because of huge saber-toothed fangs that reached
past their chins. They were dressed in a grotesque par-
ody of yellow and green dancing girl outfits, with their
horsey ears sporting tasseled earrings big as foxtails.

Ogres, she thought. Or ogresses. Giants known for
their cruelty.

Karli gabbled orders, and the ogressess advanced
with red, warty hands reaching to grab the girl. They'd
break her arms if they seized her, Greensleeves
thought in panic, crush the life from her. Unless Karli
got—whatever thing she desired.

Help, the girl thought, I need help. Yet she was a
natural wizard, untrained, only able to summon things
she'd touched in the past, unable to control them.

The ogresses raised fearsome hands like
meathooks in the air—

Greensleeves waved her hands frantically, as if
shooing them away.

Then, under and around her, the dirty rug was
punctured in a dozen places. From below.

Gull was counting his diminishing forces, trying to
reckon how to repel incoming cavalry, when Holleb,
the other red-haired centaur in fluted painted armor—
now spattered with blood—thundered into the clearing as if shot from a ballista.

He carried a feathered lance longer than his horse
body, bloodied to the grip. He shouted something to
Helki, who whirled and cantered toward him, only to
spin around again as she caught his meaning.

Not good, thought Gull. Holleb had been tracking
the cavalry to the east. If he was here, it meant . . .

"Tomas!" Gull yelled. "Form a square! We must—"

With a shriek like a desert windstorm, blue-robed
cavalry soldiers burst into the clearing.

*   *   *

All around Greensleeves there shot up, rippling green-brown, white shafts of stone as pointed as swords. Some were no bigger than knitting needles, some shoulder-high. They were stalagmites from some distant cave, a place Greensleeves had never seen.

Sharp as fishhooks, the stalagmites formed a wall of swords around the young wizard. They stippled the ground, rent holes in the dirty rug, leaving her only a six-foot clearing within twelve-foot deep walls. The girl wizard had to drop her kicking badger and snatch Lily's hand to pull her within the circle, lest she be skewered from below. Her nose wrinkled and eyes watered from the stink of ammonia, for the imported cave floor was inches thick with bat guano and writhing black insects.

Yet if Greensleeves hoped to stop the ogresses, it didn't work. Momentarily stalled by the swift appearance of the deadly spears, the ferocious monsters backed off, then rammed ahead like mad bulls. Stone pinged and tinkled and crackled as they bashed through the barricade. Greensleeves flinched as stone fragments flicked against her face. The ogresses shrieked as their warty bare feet crunched on the stone stumps, but they came on doggedly.

Something *else*, Greensleeves thought, she must conjure again! Yet it was hard to think over all the thunder and shouting, for more horse soldiers had charged into camp.

What could save her from rampaging ogresses?

A tawny lithe shape came to mind, one that ran like the wind and leapt rock cliffs like a mountain goat. Something with teeth and claws.

With the thought and wish came the conjuring.

Spitting, a large mountain lion shimmered into being at her feet. A white-whiskered muzzle snarled, soft round black-rimmed ears laid back. And the cougar charged the enemy before it.

With one bound, the big cat left the ground as if

winged. Claws like razors raked one ogress's face,
gouging an eye, slitting a long nose, slicing red slob-
bery lips into shreds. Blinded, howling like a demon,
the ogress toppled sideways, smashing into the sharp
stalagmites, impaling herself. The smell of hot blood,
like sheared copper, filled the chill air.

Yet like any animal, the cougar only fought to
escape. It bounded off the huge fallen body like a
springboard and vanished amidst the enveloping
cedars. A flicker of a tufted tail, and the big cat was
gone.

The other ogress howled at the outrage done to
her sister, and smashed ahead to crush Greensleeves.
Far behind, Karli shrieked encouragement like a mad-
woman.

A bigger barrier, thought the wizard. I need something more solid. Vaguely, she recalled an artifact far
off in the Domains, on a tropical island, an oddity
dropped from somewhere else farther off.

Fetid breath that reeked of rotten meat washed
into Greensleeves's face as the ogress smashed at the
last of the stalagmites. Greensleeves fluttered her
hands wildly, for her life depended on her actions.

Shimmering as if in a heat haze, then solidifying,
an ancient and exotic clay statue nine feet high suddenly rippled into being and snapped stone spears by
the dozens by its weight.

Greensleeves could feel the warmth of the thing,
drenched in tropical sunshine. She knew nothing
about it, except it had been found lying askew on an
island where her brother had been banished. Placid as
a saint, the statue sat cross-legged, hands in its lap,
almond eyes closed. Imprints, scratches in the clay,
chased down its middle like a row of buttons. A dull
bronze color, its skin was hardened like terra cotta,
yet it looked supple enough to get up and dance at a
command. Perhaps it could, given the right command.

Whatever its purpose, it made a fine barrier.

The ogress trumpeted in rage as the statue
blocked the way to Greensleeves. She hammered a

horny fist on the thing, stamped on stone spears to get around.

But Greensleeves was erecting a wall of wood—branches, roots, and trunks—all queerly curved back on themselves, impassable even to a rabbit, plucked from deep in her homeland, the Whispering Woods. Even the heavy clay statue was rocked by the wood wriggling under its rump. Gesturing, Greensleeves raised the wall all around—ten, twelve feet high—until she stood in a small circle of deep gloom. Listening to the ogress rage and tear at the wall, she felt safe. At least until she could think of some other defense.

Unless she'd woven a trap. Inside this wicker cage, she couldn't see what Karli might conjure. She did hear the desert wizard scream in rage and frustration.

Across the clearing, Gull could see the wizard Karli grab a bronze medallion set with a purple stone. From the stone, billowing like smoke, arose a purple shape shot with glowing green. The woodcutter saw the cloud rise and loom over the well of wood with the girl at the bottom. Then Greensleeves could see it.

Purple, naked from head to toe, with green glowing eyes, reared a devil.

CHAPTER
4

NORREEN HAD SPARKS BOTH INSIDE AND OUTSIDE her head from the blow to her skull and from being conjured elsewhere.

When the sparks subsided, she knelt in mud and slush. The smell of cedar resin filled her nostrils. Her shield, slung wrong, dug into her back. Her hands were free, she noted: the wizard had contrived to send her without her bonds.

A chill struck, and she shivered. All she wore against her skin was a leather jerkin. Her breasts were damp with milk, and her breath formed great clouds in the air.

And through the steaming vapor, she saw a raid in progress.

Gull the Woodcutter, a general not by choice, was soon to lack an army.

The phalanx of cavalry were dressed much the same as the flying-carpet folk. But these riders waved scimitars long enough to split a man from head to toe.

The line of horses exploded from the evergreen forest, each rider expertly peeling left or right so as to make room for the next invader, offer the widest attack, and kill the most targets.

So swiftly did they come, Gull was caught flat-footed in the open, hung between wanting to aid his sister—as female giants in yellow and green pressed her flimsy stone barrier—and needing to encourage his troops, the backbone of their defense. But where was everyone else? Where was Liko and his massive strength? Why had the centaurs disappeared back into the forest: to head off more cavalry? And were Bardo and his eagle-eyed scouts fighting somewhere? How could this army be so huge at suppertime and yet have everyone disappear in a battle?

He noted in the hustle and bustle and dead and dying, a strange, armed woman in black leather had entered the camp. She stood poised, taking it all in. Was she a scout sent to study their defenses from the rear? There was little enough to scout: they had no defenses.

Tomas, the oldest veteran, cool no matter what the odds, had formed his male and female fighters into a wedge. Two ranks deep, they'd backed against the cedars with pole weapons and swords out. There were perhaps twenty of them, with Tomas at the point of the wedge and Neith and Varrius on the ends. Besides opposing the oncoming cavalry, the red sergeants kept their querulous troops from breaking and running.

But despite the wall of steel, the first pass of the horse-borne raiders cut the line as if they were lopping heads off dandelions.

Tomas had either misjudged his defense, or the riders were crazy, for they slipped along the line as if skirting a harmless fence. Flicking their long thin sabers expertly, they struck at half a dozen soldiers, splitting skulls and faces and arms, then skipped away as if their horses had wings. By the time three riders had scourged the line, the ranks were crumbling. Tomas was down, helmet gone, blood welling from his bald head.

Gull swore and ran, his bad knee shooting agony up his thigh. The last he'd seen of his sister, she was being threatened by a purple cloud. Lily had dropped earlier as if poleaxed.

And if she died? And they never resolved whatever stood between them?

Damn all wizardry! And damn him for being brother to a wizard, and a lover of one! And as for *fighting* wizards, he might as well take up pig farming, for all the good he did!

A thrumming under his feet made him turn. Lost in bitter recrimination, he'd forgotten the first rule of the battlefield: pay attention.

From behind, fast as the wind, two cavalry riders bracketed him with sabers poised to strike.

Greensleeves yelped as the purple devil swelled into the air, the tallest object for miles.

Wrapped in ropy purple muscle, its head was long as a horse skull with a bulbous top, with smoke issuing from a hole like a whale's spout. Blank eyes glowed green, and an open mouth formed a green maw. Naked, shaped like a man, it wore only huge gold hoops in its pointed ears. Spikes on its elbows glowed white, flickering with hellish fires.

As the thing rose, the dark wizard Karli shrilled in her gurgling tongue. Spreading hands wide, the efreet's fingers began to grow, lengthen. In seconds, they were longer than its body. As easily as shrugging, the devil slid the elongated digits into the wood woven around Greensleeves and tugged. The entwined trees rent into splinters and bark. Tossing the kindling aside, the creature plunged purple digits deep into the earth around Greensleeves and plucked up a scoop of dirt big enough to fill a wagon.

Greensleeves and Lily and the contents of the tent were perched atop the mass.

Rising into the sky, tumbled on the shifting mound of earth held together only by the ratty tent rug,

Greensleeves sobbed out of sheer frustration—fighting gained nothing, yet she had no choice. Again, she sought for something to help her, something that might cause the least damage.

Her first most natural reaction was to conjure something familiar. The badger at her feet, a constant companion for all that it lacked a name, reminded her of another. Framing the beast in her mind, she imagined it flying through invisible miles—

—flickering to her in a rainbow of earth colors: brown for the earth, flushing green for plants, fading to blue for the sky and clouds, and finally yellow for sunshine, giver of life, it soared to her, landing—

—square on the efreet's chest.

It was another badger, but a giant one, with a body as big as a horse, weighing half a ton or more. Its very weight gave the efreet pause, caused him to sink to no more than a dozen feet in the air.

Startled to materialize in the air, the giant badger latched onto the solid surface under it.

Claws sank six inches into the efreet's purple chest. Snarling, the badger scrambled for footing, raked furrows down purple skin, which split to spill green blood. The scars healed in an instant, yet the efreet twisted in surprise and pain.

With both elongated hands full of soil and two young wizards and their trappings, the devil could only attack with its toothless green jaws, and did. The cavernous mouth snapped closed on the badger's head.

Greensleeves recoiled from the sickening crunch as the badger's skull was crushed. Four paws spasmed and lost their grip. The efreet spit out bone and blood and fur. Greensleeves wanted to scream for her poor lost giant badger.

The efreet carried her higher, so high her brother looked like a mouse. His upturned face was almost swamped by blue-robed riders swooping around him. Off in the distance, standing knee-deep in evergreens, was the giant Liko, hunting for enemies that were

probably right under his big feet. He finally spotted
Greensleeves's dilemma and came running, too late.

The bundle of earth shifted under her, and Greensleeves squatted to steady herself. With one hand she
hung onto Lily, with the other her small badger.

Karli rose, hovering alongside on her pink flying
slippers. White hair wafting in the wind, she folded
dark arms within her yellow feather robe, a smug
smile on her face. Greensleeves wanted to slap that
smile off. She was astonished at the depth of her sudden hatred.

Very well. If she must fight, she would.

She'd attack with something to drive the woman
insane.

Chased by twin riders, Gull grabbed his bloody axe
close to the head and ran for the nearest evergreens
like a rabbit for a hedge. Behind came the cavalry, so
close Gull imagined he could feel the horse's hot
breath on his neck. Any second he expected a sickle
sword to split his skull to the jaw.

Then a flicker of black cut across the path of the
nearest horse.

The strange woman in leather.

Quick as a ferret, lithe as a panther, Norreen
dashed toward the nearest horse. Watching her target
and the slippery stump-covered ground, she flicked
out her short sword at arm's length, nicking the
horse's sensitive nose.

Stricken, spooked, the horse flinched and veered
so hard—away from Gull—the rider almost lost her
seat. Using the pause, Norreen ducked around the
beast and pinked the animal on the withers to force it
farther away from Gull.

Shouting, "Drop!" Norreen belted Gull's shoulder
to knock him straight back. He crashed heavily on turf
and cedar stumps.

Norreen didn't look as she hopped over him.
Slipping sideways to present a narrower target, she

executed a perfect over-the-head slice that exposed no part of her arm to the next oncoming rider.

His aim thrown off by the shifting target, the raider tried to change his slice to a backhand swing. He never completed it.

Norreen's blade snipped his arm off neatly at the elbow. So sharp was the Benalish blade, the charging raider felt only a cold kiss along his joint. When he raised his sword arm to find where he'd been struck, he found it instead missing and bloody. In another three strides, he'd pitched from the saddle.

Norreen braced herself back and yanked Gull upright, surprising him.

"I seek Gull the Woodcutter, general of this army!" She held on to his hand to keep his attention.

"Bah!" spat Gull. "It's a fool's in charge of this mess!" His army was long gone. The remnants of Tomas's line had disintegrated, leaving dead piled up around the dying Tomas. What good can come of all these people dying? he thought.

Norreen could have screamed with frustration. "Then where is—"

Gull shrugged free of her grip and grabbed his huge axe. "No time! We must—" He looked for his sister, then saw her twenty feet in the sky and rising on a crumbling mound of earth lifted by a purple demon.

Norreen gazed at his axe, a huge double-headed tool such as a woodcutter would use. Was this the man she was looking for?

A thrumming underfoot woke her warrior's instinct. She grabbed the man's arm again and searched for the source of danger.

Four cavalrymen had swerved in their direction.

Hissing like a frustrated cat, Greensleeves channeled her fury at the woman who kept her captive in the air and hovered not twenty feet away on her pointy-toed slippers.

Once Greensleeves had trekked into a swamp for a

rescue, wading thigh deep. To their horror, she and
her brother had been covered with—

Glittering in green and brown ripples, the wizard
Karli was suddenly dotted with scores of fat leeches.

They peppered the dark woman's skin, greasy
slugs like blobs of snot, long as fingers, latching onto
her dark skin with rasping, drilling mouths hungry for
red blood.

Hovering beside the efreet, Karli was first confused. Idly, she touched her cheek where she had felt
a touch of dampness. With a gasp, she plucked at the
slimy thing, failed to pull it away, tugged frantically,
and ripped it from her skin. Blood spattered.

She shrilled like a pig at slaughter. Panicked, wailing, she tilted sideways in the sky.

Confused, the purple efreet wavered, sank back
toward earth. Greensleeves hung tightly to her friend
and pet, prayed the wizard didn't unsummon the
efreet and drop them dozens of feet. If only—

But Karli's wrath knew no bounds. Clutching
wildly for a medallion at her waist, one marked by a
spiral, she uttered a hoarse cry through her screams
of revulsion.

Dropping from the sky like a thunderbolt, the tornado ripped into the camp.

Gull planted his feet, hefted his long axe behind his
head, and faced the oncoming four riders. If he must,
he could probably cleave through a horse's throat and
kill a rider. That would be one foe slain.

The warrior in leather had to fend for herself.
She'd shown herself competent in battle. More than
he.

But what was . . . ?

A roar like a thousand screaming madmen filled
Gull's mind: noise so loud it seemed to come from
within him, not without. The ground rocked as dirt
and wood chips and cedar twigs and ashes exploded
into the air. Invisible fingers plucked at his wool cap,

the hem of his cloak, the ties of his leather jerkin, his hair. The roaring intensified until he felt his skull would burst and his guts turn to jelly.

The sky went dark. Above him loomed a twisted shape like an inverted mountain, a swirling dark mass with the power and whimsy of a god.

The tornado struck.

The woodcutter couldn't know that tornadoes don't travel along the ground but spin in the air dozens or hundreds of feet high, then drawn to the earth like lightning, touch down with winds of five hundred miles an hour, then bounce off the earth again, hovering and touching, like a stone across water, until the tug of the earth slows and dissolves them.

Thus the funnel storm, summoned by Karli, reappeared in the air a hundred feet above the camp—

—then tagged them, playful as a puppy.

People in the camp were tossed like ants. Gull was lifted and kited straight at an oncoming horse.

He grunted as he struck the rider, a man spiced with cinnamon and tobacco smoke and honeyed tea. As if by magic, Gull slammed into the man's chest and sank onto the saddle of the brown horse. Gull had time to notice the reins were set with jewels and real gold leaf.

Then both men and the horse were flung, sailing, spinning, through the air.

The horseman fetched into thick wiry cedar branches like an arrow into a straw target. Gull went with him. He felt his boot torn off. He hung onto his axe, though he could feel twigs gouging his skin. The smell of cedar oil overwhelmed him. I'll smell like the forest forever, he thought dizzily.

Mashed under Gull, the horseman gasped and shuddered. Gull smelled fresh blood, felt a point dig into his breastbone. The rider had been impaled on a snapped tree trunk.

Then the horse, flung after the two men, crashed onto both of them.

Gull felt the beast slam alongside him into the trees, so close the mane filled his mouth with rank, sweaty hair. Horseflesh crushed the wind from his lungs, and he panicked. The dead weight kept dropping, half burying him, crushing him into the bracken even as the horse kept kicking. Vainly, he strove to push himself clear—panic gave him the strength to move a mammoth, he thought—but he could only grasp twisting, tearing twigs.

Drowning in horseflesh and cedar, his head slammed into something hard-soft, and he knew no more.

Greensleeves clutched Lily—who lay as limp as a sock, barely breathing—and her badger, and the dirty rug that propped them on a crumbling pile of dirt.

Yet everything was being tossed like winnowed wheat. She might as well have snatched at the giant dead badger, or the efreet, which shimmered like a candle flame being snuffed by the tornado looming over everything. Or grabbed at Karli, who cartwheeled above the forest, shrieking and plucking at her skin to claw off the leeches, doing as much damage with her long fingernails as the bloodsuckers.

Then Lily and badger and rug and dirt trickled through her fingers, for she was falling.

No time to conjure . . .

She struck the cedars.

Only her thick wool clothes saved her from permanent harm. Her cloak had tangled around her head, and she felt a hundred woody fingers tear at it instead of her skin. Her head banged against something and ached. Then she forgot that as her foot dropped into a hollow and her body wrenched the other way. She shrieked as her ankle snapped, pain ripping through her like a wave, stunning her.

Only Norreen saw the end of Karli's raid.

The ferocious zephyr had wafted the warrior

woman off her feet and set her down as light as thistle-
down fifty feet away. Still, the experience of flying on a
killer wind left her weak-kneed, and she groped for the
support of a nearby cedar.

From that place, she saw the desert wizard land.
Other folk—both Karli's and this army's—crawled
about the camp, or sat with their heads in their hands,
or lay quiet, never to move again, their breath sucked
from their bodies, their hearts stilled. Even a huge
ogress in tattered clothing lay facedown, moaning, her
back broken by an errant tree stump.

Karli was a tousled red-splotched horror. She'd
gouged her skin, ripped out hair, and rent her clothing
to get the hideous leeches off, though in fact they had
started to die the instant they were plucked from their
distant swamp water. Furious, almost hysterical with
loathing and a desire to get away, the wizard kicked
through the spillage from Greensleeves's tent.

Around a fresh gaping hole, the carved chests lay
cracked or broken. Dirt covered everything. The small
woman kicked and dug, tossing things haphazardly,
growing more frantic.

Unmoving, Norreen watched and wondered. The
wizard seemed to have a definite target, some treasure
she coveted, for she didn't pause to analyze anything,
just pitched it all aside and dug deeper. Then she
stopped, aghast at her good luck.

Norreen held her breath.

The wizard had found a pink box the size of a
skull. It was curiously banded all about, or—it was difficult to tell—else carved with buckles on most faces,
some square, some oval. Karli laughed gleefully as she
clasped the artifact to her bosom.

Then the thing dropped through her fingers.

Norreen gasped. It looked as if the woman had
fumbled it. But that wasn't true. The warrior had seen
with her own eyes.

The thing had slipped through her fingers like
smoke.

Dumbfounded, Karli stooped, grasped at it, but

failed to lift it. Her hands couldn't touch the box any more than they could lift water. Frantic, she paddled her hands through the image of the box again and again. But it was no use.

Battling magic with magic, Karli touched the buttons on her now-shabby jacket and mouthed spell after spell. Each time, she strove to pick up the box, each time failed. Frustrated tears came. She'd found some magnificent treasure, Norreen knew, and now she couldn't take it home.

But . . . had the box not *wanted* to go with the wizard and made *itself* intangible?

Furious, Karli stamped her feet, kicked at the ghostly artifact, put back her head and screamed. Then she recalled her plight. Many survivors around the camp, both defenders and raiders, looked at her. A couple of local soldiers conversed quietly, hunted for a crossbow. . . .

With a final look at the box, part scorn, part longing, Karli shuffled her feet, wrapped her tattered yellow feather cape around her shoulders, and rose into the sky to fly off.

Norreen, an old soldier, noticed she left her troops behind. They had failed her, so she deserted them.

Damn all wizards, Norreen thought.

Then she sighed, picked herself up, and crossed the clearing. She should find that big man with the axe. He seemed to know what was going on, could probably take her to Gull the Woodcutter.

And find that small wizard, she added. Despite her ragamuffin outfit, she must be the famous Greensleeves.

With luck, she might kill both Gull and Greensleeves before the army could recover.

And return to Benalia.

And win back her captive son.

CHAPTER
5

"HEY, WAKE UP, SOLDIER! *WAKE UP!*"

Groggy, his skull splitting, Gull climbed out of a dark pit into wan winter sunshine. The edges of the pit still loomed above him, ragged-edged and quivering, until he remembered they were cedar trees. Oh, yes, there'd been another battle. Had they won or lost? Gull would like to win once, just to see how it felt.

Then he recalled Greensleeves being spirited away. And Lily. Were they . . . ?

Norreen shook him again, tugged on his single boot. "Hey, big guy! You alive in there?"

"I don't—" Gull coughed, spat out cedar needles. Sitting up, he felt a thousand scratches like insect bites. Brushing his face clear, he slid down more cedar branches, banged against something cold and stiff.

A dead horse.

Clumsily, stiff as the dead mount, Gull clambered free of the entwining cedars and climbed over the brown horse. Under the horse lay a blue-robed rider with a blood-soaked tree stump spiked through his chest. All of them were propped up by a nest of crushed cedar trees. The woman in leather had woken him. Now she offered her gloved hand and hauled him free of the tangle. "Thanks," he muttered. "Have you seen my sister? And the woman in white? And my boot?"

Ah, thought Norreen. This big lug is the wizard Greensleeves's brother. That was why he held some minor command or bodyguard function. He probably carried a felling axe in imitation of this army's famed general. He looked big and tough but clumsy—he had dozens of scars and lacked three fingers on his left hand. It was good she'd saved his life: it might ingratiate her to Greensleeves, let her get close. "Yes. She's deeper in the forest. I pulled you out so we could pull her out."

"Oh, thanks. You're very kind," the woodcutter mumbled. His lips were scraped and mashed and puffy. His whole face, in fact, was scabby and scratched—and itchy as the devil, with cedar pitch and needles down his shirt. More than anything, he wanted a bath. But Greensleeves and Lily came first. "You saved my life back there. My thanks. You're a fine warrior, too. You practically danced among those horses and never came close to being nicked. How is it you speak our tongue, when none of that dark wizard's other folk did?"

Norreen felt a surge of pride at the compliments, even though she wasn't a fine warrior but an average one, and fat and slow at that, with muscles shrieking and quivering throughout her body. But for the rest, what did he mean? Ah! He thought she'd been summoned by the wizard. Very well, let him think that. "Uh, I was taken on the fringes of her land, at the edge of the desert."

"So you're stranded, too?" Gull scouted for his axe and boot, found them under tree rubbish. Pressing through the cedars, he aimed for the camp's clearing. Norreen noted he limped on a bad right knee. He called over his shoulder. "Well, I'm sorry for that, but you're not alone. We're all victims of wizards, all trying to get home."

The word "home" pinged in Norreen's heart. Crunching along behind, she called, "I need to speak to Gull the Woodcutter."

The man before her snorted. "Why?" He stomped clear of the trees. Almost everyone was busy at the far side of the clearing, where the soldiers' line had been so savaged. Camp followers wailed over their dead husbands and a few wives. Bitterly, Gull said, "He's doing a piss-poor job of generaling. He should have stuck to lopping branches."

Without another word, the big man walked to the largest knot of people. Norreen trailed behind. Soldiers and camp followers dragged bodies into long straight lines. Both men and women wept or cursed or worked silently. Amma, a Samite, leader of a ragtag group of healers, gave orders as to which wounded should be taken where. The big man stood with his axe, until the healer in white beckoned him over.

Lying on the ground was Tomas, once a proud sergeant in his red cohorts, then field leader of this motley army, now dying. A gaping head wound shined red at his hairline. His eyes stared up at the sun, for he was blind. Yet much of his native strength remained, enough to grab Gull's hand and drag him close.

"Gull!" shouted the dying man, as if he were already far away. "General! Can you hear me?"

Norreen's eyes bugged as the big man bent over the soldier. Red hands stained his leather tunic, groped at his tanned face. He, too, shouted. "I'm here, Tomas! Right here. I'm sorry you were hurt, Tom. This is all my fault."

The blind man half rose, clinging tightly to Gull. "No! No, not true! You're trying! Fighting for the good! Never forget! You're helping, helping us all get home! We need you, Gull, and your sister, too! Your cause is good—"

His strength and spirit escaped in one long sigh, and he fell back on the mucky soil. Gull closed his blind eyes.

"I'll remember, Tomas. I promise."

Norreen gaped. This young, gentle, considerate man was the army's general? The famed and feared Gull the Woodcutter? Brother to Greensleeves?

The one she must assassinate?

Greensleeves awakened to a gentle nudging and calling of her name. She opened her eyes to find a dark angel hovering over her. It had a lean face, dark long straight hair, and a serious worried look.

"Oh, K-Kwam. It's y-you."

"Aye, just me," came the gentle reply. Just one of the magic students, a helper around camp, tugging branches off her.

"How is she?" asked a rough voice: Tybalt's. Together he and Kwam hauled Greensleeves from the tangled nest of broken cedar branches. One of the healers was helping Lily rise from another heap a dozen feet away. But Greensleeves shrieked when she tried to gain her feet. Her ankle wobbled and bent under her.

"Broken!" bleated Tybalt. "I'll fetch a healer, make a litter—"

"I can carry her," offered the gentle Kwam. Greensleeves was too preoccupied with not moving her leg—and taking another stab at standing—to object. Carefully, the tall student gathered her in his arms, surprisingly strong. Cradled against his chest, Greensleeves felt like a child again. But she was careful not to jiggle her leg. Her badger snuffled among the branches, then scuttled after them. Her chickadee, Cherrystone, flew from some hidden branch and alighted on her shawl. The sight of her animal friends warmed the girl, and she smiled. Kwam kept a straight face, concentrating on his footing.

Tybalt cleared a way through the broken trees, already talking. A raid and tornado and brush with death were not going to silence him, nor distract him from his passion. "I took a quick look at the artifacts! They're all still here! Someone said that the dark wizard pawed through them, but she didn't take a thing! Strange, huh? Oh, and I found another—no, two!—more uses for things! Do you want to see?"

Bobbing in Kwam's arms, woozy with pain, Greensleeves stammered, "C-can't you j-just tell m-me for now?"

"What? Oh, surely! First off, that sausage grinder? Or what looks like a sausage grinder? You won't believe what came out of that when we stuffed some pork in it! And that tin dog? It started yapping . . . "

Greensleeves didn't hear much of his blather. She hurt too much. But Kwam, she noted, was very careful not to jostle her. He should be a healer, the girl thought idly, not a student chasing after magic.

Wincing against the pain, Greensleeves saw they'd stepped out of the tree line. Greensleeves's heart sank as she beheld the long line of dead bodies in the clearing. But she tried to be polite. "Y-yes, th-that's fine, T-Tybalt. I'm g-glad I f-found those th-things." And she was, in a way. "I-it was th-thanks to y-you, T-Tybalt, we could bring T-Tomas and others here—"

She was interrupted by the sight of her big brother approaching. Behind him walked a strange woman in black leather and war gear. Gull's deerhide tunic was smeared with fresh bloody handprints. His face was grim.

"If we hadn't dragged Tomas here, he'd still be alive on that island. Now he's dead, along with many others. Let's face it, Greenie. We're accomplishing nothing."

The campfire at the center of the circle crackled and popped and smoked, for their firewood was green. People squinted or ducked out of the way as the breeze blew ashes into their eyes. Dozens of soldiers and camp followers, cooks and healers, cartographers and librarians and clerks ringed the fire in circles, as well as many hangers-on whose purpose Norreen couldn't fathom. But there was much she didn't understand about this motley crowd.

At the center was the army's council, a most informal group: Gull as its general, Greensleeves and Lily as its wizards, the centaurs as scouts, the red sergeants Varrius and Neith—minus their comrade Tomas—Bardo the Paladin as chief of scouts, even Stiggur, the boy who rode the clockwork beast.

An improvised dinner behind them, the leaders of the army sat and discussed their plans and strategies for all to hear, even took comments from outside the council. Coming from a strict military background, with fierce discipline and coded orders and nonfraternization between officers and soldiers, Norreen couldn't imagine how anything got accomplished, nor how orders got carried out. It was incredibly sloppy. No wonder they lost all their battles. And where were the pickets, for the love of Typhon? Didn't these people know the best time to forge a second attack was a few hours after the first, when the survivors were tired and scattered and picking up?

"I kn-know," stammered Greensleeves, "I kn-know we're n-not doing we-well. B-but we-we're trying." She noted her chickadee was cold and tucked a fold of shawl around its tiny body.

Her brother scratched his face and winced as he tore off scabs. "Well, our father used to say, 'As long as you're still trying, you're winning,' but I'd like to truly win once in a while, triumph instead of just trying. We had—how many?—killed today for nothing. We might as well paint bull's-eyes on our armor and call the wizards to take their shots." But he fell silent, remembering his promise to the dying Tomas.

It was quiet throughout the camp, with only the crackling of the fire and groans of the wounded at the hospital tent breaking the still night. Norreen resisted shaking her head. Such defeatist talk, even if true, coming from a general? Unthinkable. A general was supposed to say he won, no matter how bad the losses.

In the silence, Greensleeves asked, "How m-many d-did we l-lose?"

A clerk, a thin man in dark robes named Donahue, looked at a slate marked with chalk. "It's hard to say. We had six soldiers killed outright by their cavalry, including Tomas. Two of the dervishes died, one trampled, one from a saber wound. A cook and her daughter were cut down. Two children were stabbed, but we cant't find their parents. At least five camp followers are missing, probably lost in the forest. We're hoping they see the campfire."

Gull sighed, then asked, "Wounded?"

Amma, dressed in a powder-blue robe and white hat, referred to a slab of bark with charcoal marks. "Three of our soldiers will probably die, four may recover. A student was severly burned falling into the fire and will probably die. A cook has a broken leg and internal injuries, trampled by a horse: him I don't know about. An old man was brained—no one knows who he is—and will probably never awaken. One of my healers lost a hand trying to stave off an attack: she should live. One of the scouts has a shoulder wound that may go septic . . . " There were other, minor injuries she totted up before finishing, "And our Greensleeves has a broken ankle and can't walk. Plus half a dozen foreign cavalrymen and those carpet riders lie wounded: four should make it."

"If they do, sign them up." Gull sighed again. "We need all the help we can get."

"No!" shrilled a woman from the outermost ring. Disheveled and weepy, she wailed, "They put my Hassel to death and *you* want them to *join* us? They'd cut our very throats and you'd *feed* them? That's not right! It's an insult to my poor dead husband!"

Gull peered across the ring of faces, his own lit red by firelight. His voice was mild. "It's not that way. Atira, isn't it? I'm sorry about Hassel, but you must remember we're all in this together. These desert soldiers were compelled to fight by wizard's magic. They had no choice. We do, and we're out to change things. Though I'll admit we're not changing much. . . . "

Norreen couldn't believe her ears. A general

argued with a harridan, a whorish camp follower? A
real leader would have her flogged and quartered. And
admitting failure and shortcomings? This was no
army, it was a rabble! She'd do the world a favor by
beheading these fools.

Why did nothing they say make sense? Change
things? What things? You couldn't change the world,
you could only survive it.

However, she remembered, her lover Garth had
single-handedly turned an evil city on its head, toppled its most corrupt and powerful houses, improved
the lives of thousands . . .

The council heard the other reports. The head
cook reported the food, mostly iron rations, was
mainly unspoiled, though they'd need fresh meat
soon. The hunters reported there was no game at all
in this forest except small birds. Perhaps if the army
swung closer to the bluff in the east, they could find
deer and goats there. The clerk reported many of the
tents had been slashed beyond repair, though they'd
recovered most of the horses and mules: Liko the
giant, and Stiggur, atop his clockwork beast, were
expert at herding. Kamee, head of the cartographers
and librarians who mapped the territory, reported
many scrolls had been burned or trampled, their work
lost. Tybalt, the magic student, reported some magic
artifacts had been smashed when they were dropped
by the purple devil, but most were still intact.

Gull and Greensleeves heard the reports, none of
them encouraging. People muttered. A child cried it
was sleepy and wanted its papa. Finally, the woodcutter mulled, "So we survive. But are we any closer to
our goal? Who can say?"

Norreen couldn't contain her curiosity any longer.
"I don't understand! What *is* your goal? What can you
hope to accomplish driving through this godsforsaken
forest? What is there to conquer out here?"

People hushed. Gull and Greensleeves and Lily
and the rest looked at Norreen curiously, until she
damned herself for drawing their attention. But the

woodcutter was as mild as ever. "Yes, you're new. Later, we should gather the other converts here and tell them, too. Let me see if I can explain. . . . "

Quickly, he told of how he and Greensleeves had lived peacefully in an eastern valley called White Ridge . . . until one day, when two wizards and their wagon trains appeared from nowhere. Instantly the wizards had fallen to fighting, conjuring soldiers and monsters and disasters from all over the Domains, out to slaughter one another. Gull and Greensleeves's village was caught in the middle, as if gods had built a campfire on an anthill. Within hours, soldiers and barbarians and trolls and rain and stone rain and an earthquake had devastated the village. The wizards eventually vanished, but within days their legacy—lack of water, plague brought by rats, vampires, infection— had wiped out the rest of the village. The survivors had walked away, all except Gull and Greensleeves, who stayed more from stubbornness than anything else.

Or Gull did, for in those days Greensleeves had been simple. Camping in the woods, they'd met stragglers from the wizards' armies, abandoned by their leaders: the giant Liko, who'd lost his right arm to a rock hydra, the centaurs Helki and Holleb, the clockwork beast, even a useless goblin named Egg Sucker.

"Useless?" piped a voice. The belt-high gray-green thief popped up from behind a stack of firewood. He waved a cooking spoon at Gull. "I'm not useless! Who's the one drove off the wolves—"

"Hey!" interrupted a cook. "That's my spoon!"

Egg Sucker bleated and turned to run, knocked an iron tripod over, and dumped an entire cauldron of soup into the fire, extinguishing it. Hopping and rubbing his shin, he ran off into the dark with the cook in pursuit.

Normally folks would have laughed, but they were too tired. Gull only sighed. "Maybe that's our problem. Our good luck charm is bad luck. . . . Where was I? Oh, yes . . . "

In time, Gull had signed on to a wizard's wagon

train—for, he now knew, the man could hypnotize and lie like a cobra. Later, almost too late, they learned the wizard Towser, actually recognized Greensleeves as an unrealized wizard, and plotted to sacrifice her. Lily, too. Ultimately, his scheme had backfired, for the two unschooled wizards, and Gull's misfit companions, had trounced the wizard and sent him fleeing.

Albeit after many, many innocents had died.

"So, you see, other than Lily and my sister here, we've had nothing but grief from wizards. They're like sharks, or jackals, or dragons. They battle their own kind and eat their magic to grow stronger. We mortals are just cattle to be used, the way the gods use men. But we cattle decided to fight back.

"This army," he raised his hands to take in the motley collection, "is made of victims of wizards' ravishments, and we're all dedicated to finding wizards and stopping them.

"And while we're at it, we're trying to find the way to our homes if we can. Wizards think nothing of plucking people or animals from their homes, throwing them into a battle hundreds of leagues away, then abandoning them and fleeing when the fight goes sour. With the Domains, so vast that no map could hold them, it might be years—or never—before some of us find our true homes. And many, like poor Tomas, never will. And that's why we have cartographers, who map where we go and question everyone we meet, and librarians, who sift through the stories and rumors and tales and try to piece together a complete map.

"But it's not easy," Gull continued, as everyone listened raptly to the story of which they were all a part. "We've traveled for nine months, picking up lost souls everywhere, seeking other wizards so we might control them, stop them. Kill them if necessary, though we don't know how yet. And we seek our homelands. Or most do. Greensleeves and I have no home left.

"So far," Gull concluded, "we've blundered into two other wizards and beaten down their armies or monsters, but each time they got away. . . . Still, we're all volunteers, putting our hearts into it, so we have the advantage in battle over compelled troops. We might be disorganized—more so now that Tomas is dead—but we fight hard. And we keep trying."

He paused for breath. "Does that make any sense? Or are we mad?"

Absorbed in the tale, Norreen blurted, "What? No. But . . . I've never heard of wizards seeking to help folk, not without demanding a king's ransom in return. In my land, even the healers accept only gold for even the smallest wound."

Gull laughed easily. "What's gold? No one in this army is even paid! We share what loot we find, but it's precious little."

"No *pay*?" Norreen shook her head. "I've never heard of an army that sought to help and not hurt . . . It's like, a . . . crusade."

People murmured at that. The noble word hadn't been voiced before. Norreen felt like a fool: she was supposed to infiltrate this army and assassinate its leaders, not gain attention and broadcast her opinions.

"Wh-where is y-your land?" Greensleeves asked. "And what y-your name?"

"Huh? Oh, uh, Rakel." Her true name, unused for years. "Of . . . the Southlands near the back country of Gish. My, uh, people grow grapes and press wine." Or Garth had, until magic took hold of his soul and whisked him away. He was a victim of magic, too.

As was everyone gathered here. But they'd united in a cause, a crusade to help common folk, not to empower or enrich themselves but to help the innocent.

Like something from a story, she thought, an ancient tale told to children about the glory days of Benalia, when it was a fabulous city determined to better the lives of everyone. Not an intrigue-plagued maze where everything was for sale, including loyalty and honor. Including fighters such as herself, and their souls.

And if she were to assassinate these two gentle

folk, put this crusade to an end, the evil in the world
would howl in triumph.

But if she didn't kill them, she'd never see her son
again. . . .

"Well," asked Lily, who'd so far been silent. "Will
you join our—crusade?"

"Y-yes," said Norreen, now Rakel. "Y-yes, I will.
Thank you." But tears ran down her cheeks.

CHAPTER
6

"HERE IT IS!" GLOATED TYBALT, HOLDING UP WHAT looked like a simple sausage grinder. "Wait until you see what it can do!"

By the next morning, the camp had settled into a semblance of order, and Greensleeves had a chance to get back to her magic entourage. Tybalt, their nominal leader, was bursting to show off their latest discoveries. He fiddled with the sausage grinder, stuffing a mash of things into the hopper atop, blathering to himself as much as to his audience.

Greensleeves sat before her tent on a chair of hastily lashed cedar boughs and branches. Raised above the slushy root-ridden ground, it made a fragrant if pitchy seat. Her splinted ankle was propped up on a box. It throbbed mightily, despite Amma's brew of feverfew, fennel, rose hips, and other herbs. Cherrystone, the chickadee, hopped up and down her leg as if it were a tree branch. The badger slept, grumbling at phantom enemies.

As Tybalt and two other students fussed, Greensleeves reached out a grubby calloused hand

and touched Kwam's. Curiously, the tall quiet serious student jumped. "I'm s-sorry, K-Kwam. I only w-wanted to thank y-you for y-your help. C-carrying me."

The magic student could only blush and look away. Greensleeves wondered at his reaction. Did he dislike her? He muttered that it was nothing, then walked off to fetch something.

Greensleeves sighed. She was so clumsy with people. She was seventeen now, but in many ways she felt herself to be only one or two years old. Since her birth in the village of White Ridge, so overshadowed by the mysterious Whispering Woods, she'd been a half-wit, a simpleton. Her family—all dead now, except for her brother, and never properly thanked for their patience—had said she was "gifted with second sight" and accepted her, tolerating her nuisances and bumblings and mischief with soft hearts. It was her brother Gull who'd borne the brunt of her meanderings, for he'd taken her along to the forest when woodcutting, both for her company and to keep her from disturbing the village. Often she had been found opening the rabbit hutches and bread ovens, springing traps and pulling babies from their cribs, or untying the dogs and stealing pies.

Little had anyone suspected, or she herself known, that the curious magic of the Whispering Woods had invested her soul and spirit with magic so strong it overpowered her mind. Once they'd left the woods behind, for the first time in her life, Greensleeves began to think clearly. Yet so much mystical energy remained in her, she could move magic as a child can stack mud into mud pies.

But like a child, her control was erratic and unschooled. Ignorant.

She was a bow fully bent, with no way to nock an arrow nor any target at which to shoot. And what good was power with no control? A lightning strike could destroy trees, but who wanted their trees shattered?

Alone in the woods, wandering for miles, with no more brain than a possum, she'd befriended timber wolves, dryads, badgers both big and small, bears, elves, cardinals, cougars, bees, tree-folk, and dozens of other creatures.

But as for getting along with people . . . She loved them dearly, but didn't always understand them. And now she had so many friends—Lily, Tybalt, Kwam, and now this new Rakel—yet she never knew what they were thinking.

Or herself, for that matter.

"All right!" Tybalt's boisterous voice interrupted her thoughts. "We're ready to start!"

Tybalt was a mystery to them all, for no one knew if he was truly human, elven, part elven, or dwarven—or something else. He'd heard of their crusade in months past and trekked across country to join them: big nose, wiry side-whiskers, purple cap, outlandish clown clothes and all. When he explained (whether true or not) that he was an "expert in magic artifacts," Greensleeves had gladly turned over to him the chests and jars and gee-gaws she'd culled from Towser's wrecked wagon train. In time, Tybalt had found more students of magic, like Kwam. Together with two women, Ertha and Daru, the four spent every moment experimenting with the contents of the chests, although they were unable to conjure magic themselves.

So far, they'd discovered precious little.

The erstwhile sausage grinder sat atop a chest where Tybalt had clumsily nailed it. Tybalt waved an arm theatrically. "This looks like a simple sausage grinder and, indeed, you could grind sausages with it! Stick meat and spices and meal in the top, slip the casing over this exit hole here, and you'd get sausage! But, there's more! We've spent hours and hours experimenting—"

"Can we get on with the demonstration?" asked Daru, older and broader and peppery. "You're making me hungry."

"Oh, surely. Uh . . . Oh, so we've mixed and matched and stuffed the hopper with everything we could find! Now, we've got—let's see—salt pork and deer brains and burdock leaves and dirt and cedar twigs and candle wax and a pinch of salt—"

Greensleeves leaned forward in her twisted chair. Perhaps by her looking expectant Tybalt would get on with it.

"Anyway," he concluded, "watch and be amazed!"

Vigorously, he grabbed the handle and began to crank while Daru used a stick to mash down the mess in the hopper. As the machine cranked, Greensleeves watched the exit hole. She expected sausage stuffing to ooze out and spill on the ground—except it came out solid, as if already cased.

The girl wizard gasped.

What oozed out of the steel hole was the head of a snake.

A twin-nostriled snout popped out, then the wide pit-viper cheeks of a rattlesnake. The head was green shot with yellow: the color of cedar twigs shot with candlewax, perhaps. It looked for all the world as if the serpent had accidently climbed into the machine and was fighting to get out. But Greensleeves could see that was impossible—

"Look out!" bawled Kwam so loudly the wizard jumped. The badger disappeared in a flash at the noise, and Cherrystone zipped away.

Tybalt was so intent on turning the handle, and Daru in seeing she didn't get her fingers caught, they were both oblivious to the serpent. With a shiver and hiss, the five-foot reptile thumped to the slushy ground. Furious, perhaps at the coldness of the earth, perhaps at the noise, or perhaps at the rude conjuration itself, the snake instantly curled itself into coils and prepared to strike. Its long fangs were as white as shaved bone and glistened with dripping venom.

The thing centered its short-sighted vision on Greensleeves's wounded leg. As Tybalt and Daru hopped out of the way, the snake rattled once, an angry buzz, and prepared to strike.

Friend of animals though she was, Greensleeves squeaked, shrilled—

—and Kwam interposed himself between her and the snake.

The rattler exploded, uncoiling, striking as hard as a club. The magic student grunted as the head hit his knee and the fangs sank like needles through his woolen trouser leg. The snake wiggled to free its teeth, snapping one off. Its powerful gyrations made Kwam sway like a tree in a gale.

Then Tybalt, recovering his senses, raised high the sausage grinder and smashed the rattler's back.

The venomous creature whipped back to bite the prodigal sorcerer, but its back was broken and it could only half turn. As it did, Kwam stamped down with his sturdy shoe on its head. The long strong body flexed and flailed, snapped like a whip, then gradually fell still.

Tybalt pushed back his purple cap and wiped a bald pate. "Whew! Wow! We never created a poisonous one before! They were always little, like garter snakes! I wonder if we put in too much pepper—"

He bleated as Kwam toppled onto him.

After the hurly-burly—when Kwam's leg was tied with a tourniquet and he was bundled to the hospital tent, Amma slit the wound and sucked out the poison, healers kneaded his arms and legs to diffuse the poison throughout his body, and it was pronounced he would live—Tybalt had a hard time interesting anyone outside in another magic artifact.

"This one, here." He held up a clockwork tin dog on a small pedestal like a music box. He didn't expect anyone to look and spoke quietly for once. "We cracked it out of a box with a magic lock. When you wind it up and hold it near a magic user, it . . . "

He wound a key in the thing's back, and instantly it swiveled on its base, aimed its tin muzzle in Greensleeves and Lily's direction, and barked. *Yipyipyipyipyipyipyip,* it went, for long nervewracking minutes, before its spring wound down.

Tybalt looked around at the circle of unsmiling faces in the pale morning light. "Isn't that great?"

Greensleeves eased herself into the wicker chair and tried not to sigh. Cherrystone returned, and she caught him on a finger. "Y-yes, T-Tybalt, it's f-fine. L-lovely. P-please t-take it a-way." Tybalt nodded dolefully and slunk away with his tin toy. Daru and Ertha worked quietly deciphering some scroll. They had no wish to share in Tybalt's shame.

Gull had run over when the magic student had been stricken, and Rakel had followed him like a shadow. (If Gull noticed, he didn't comment.) Idly, the woodcutter mused, "I wonder if that's how Towser knew you and Lily were unrealized wizards. But why didn't you hear any of that yapping?"

Greensleeves put both hands in the air, let them drop. "I d-don't—" She gave up. Talking was too difficult, and her stuttering wore her out. She'd liked it better before when, she only made animal noises: snuffling like a badger, chittering like a squirrel, whistling like a blue jay.

Idly, casually, Rakel lifted a gloved hand and pointed to the pink banded box sitting atop another chest. "What's that ugly thing?"

Everyone looked. Lily, who'd been sitting quietly embroidering a shirt, said, "That's a mana vault, we think. Towser had it dug up from the bottom of a crater. It fell from space. It's supposed to store mana, magical energy, but we haven't been able to find out how. Towser wore it on his head, tied with a scarf, when he tried to sacrifice Greensleeves, but we don't think that's how to use it." The ex–dancing girl looked closely at the warrior woman. "Why do you ask?"

"Just curious." Rakel shrugged. She knew it had been that single object the raider Karli had coveted yet couldn't carry away because it had turned intangible. But Rakel kept the knowledge to herself: it might prove useful. "It's hideous."

Lily nodded without agreeing and returned to her needlework. Without looking, she noticed when Gull left, and the warrior Rakel followed in his tracks. She sighed loudly and jerked a thread through the cloth, tearing it.

Greensleeves sighed as well. "You too, Lily?"

Lily put down her work, and stared at the sky. "What are we going to do, Greensleeves? What can we do?"

Greensleeves got up, hobbling on her one good foot, and turned her chair to face her friend, who was sitting on a camp stool. Though the early winter air was chill, bundled in their woolen cloaks, it was pleasant enough in the wan sunshine. The work of the camp went on around them: hustle and bustle, shrieking children chasing one another, the sergeants hollering drills at their new charges, the smell of a meal simmering, a father singing to a baby slung on his back as he pounded a small anvil. Cherrystone pushed further under Greensleeves's cloak and went to sleep.

Yet the two women were uneasy, and it showed. Greensleeves began, "P-perhaps i-if we g-go over wh-what we kn-know . . . "

"We've done that! A thousand times!"

"I kn-know, I know! B-but p-perhaps we m-missed s-something."

Lily stifled another sigh. She was tired of feeling sorry for herself. "Very well, let's try. What do we know? Well, in fact, we don't *know* anything but what we've seen and done ourselves. So what do we know for sure, based on that?"

Lily went on, enumerating. Wizards, it seemed, had an ability (from whence, no one could say) to conjure things from one place to another. When, by traveling, wizards could touch things, they could "tag" them (Tybalt's word). Thus they formed a catalog of animals, plants, natural features such as stalagmites, magical sources such as black lotus plants, enchanted meadows, and all sorts of creatures. These things contained "mana," mystical energy wizards could "tap"(no one knew how). A wizard, having tagged something, could later manipulate the mana (from the land they stood in? or the land they were tagging? from inside themselves?) and summon the object to his or her side.

Somehow, they could also force the thing summoned to fight on their behalf.

After they'd been schooled in magic-making.

Neither Greensleeves nor Lily had had schooling. They could only work magic by guesswork. Sometimes, not at all.

They guessed Greensleeves had been infused with magic since childhood by the Whispering Woods, and could, under stress, conjure a thing she'd touched in the past. But she couldn't move herself through the void ("shift"—another of Tybalt's words), as had Towser and other wizards they'd seen. Why not? How to do it? Why did Lily's conjurings glow white, while Greensleeves's rippled in earth colors? How did other wizards control hordes of demons? Had they ventured to demon lands and touched each one? No one knew, though everyone—Greensleeves and Lily and Tybalt and the librarians—had a hundred ideas and notions and snatches of stories and old legends.

Yet for all the confusion Greensleeves suffered, Lily was even worse off. They knew she possessed magical ability, for under stress, when Greensleeves had been about to be sacrificed, Lily had wished for Gull and summoned him from a distant island where he'd been banished. That one time, her hands had glowed white (the ex-prostitute laughed bitterly at the idea she possessed any whiteness). Since then, she'd had no success with spells in any form.

Except one.

So Lily and Greensleeves were wizards, with no way to harness it very well. True, Greensleeves could conjure cougars and wolves and walls of swords. But neither quickly nor easily. And one had only to see her bruises, and those of her followers, and the line of fresh graves at the edge of the forest, to know how flukey her magic-making was.

In fact, if it weren't for Tybalt and his students,

there might not be an army at all. They had fiddled with a silver hoop set with coral and triggered a shimmering portal to the tropical isle where Towser banished his prisoners. Stepping through the portal onto the island had let them rescue the red soldiers Tomas and Neith and Varrius, Bardo, and a handful of orcs—and discover other oddments such as the oriental clay statue. The fighters had become the core of their army, since Gull knew nothing of armies and their organization. Yet, as Gull had pointed out, Tomas had come here to fight and only found death. Magic, he'd muttered, was a blessing and a curse, usually the latter.

To Lily, magic had proven a cause for soul-searching. A dancing girl and prostitute since childhood, practical and hardheaded, with small ambitions and no illusions about life, Lily had been astonished to learn *she* was a wizard—with but a single spell. She both gloried in and was terrified by her unknown abilities, as unwilling to test them as a baby bird to leave the nest. And so she'd become hesitant about every aspect of herself: magic, life, love, loyalty.

"I used to be so *confident!*" she wailed. "I knew what I was about, my duties were clear, I had only to dally with Towser and collect my pay! I was going to travel to a city and open a *shop*, for pity's sake! But now . . . What good am *I* doing this army and its crusade? You protect us with conjuring, Gull organizes the fighting, Amma heals, the cartographers map, the cooks cook—I can't even cook, by Xira's Wings! I'm not even a *whore* anymore! Or even 'the general's girlfriend'! Here I was, in love with your brother—or I thought I was, and he with me, though how he could love a whore I don't understand—yet I'm not even sleeping with him these days because—because . . . "

Sobs stopped her. Tears of frustration and rage and anger and confusion ran down her cheeks. Greensleeves hitched herself forward and held Lily's wrist. Lily almost laughed: she, supposedly the crusty woman of the world, took comfort from the tiny stuttering Greensleeves. But today even Greensleeves's natural buoyance was at a low. Perhaps her broken ankle fatigued her.

"Oh, L-Lily." The smaller woman sighed. She shifted her thin legs, wincing as her splinted ankle ached. "I-I'm not m-much g-good as a w-wizard, either. All I d-do is m-make a t-target for other w-wizards. Wh-what's the g-good in th-that?" Her stammer made her speak slowly. "I h-hate to f-fight. Wh-why can't p-people just get a-l-long?"

Lily picked up her embroidery, alternately scrunching and smoothing it. "I don't know, Greenie." She used Gull's nickname for his sister. "I fear the magic itself changes a person. Once they learn they can manipulate it, they must, as a child must have a sweet they've seen on a shelf. But can someone learn magic and not become a parasite, a vampire living off commoners? Is that what we'll become?"

"Even to c-call them c-commoners is to d-denigrate them," said Greensleeves, sighing. "Oh . . . w-would it j-just be better if we'd n-never l-learned we knew m-magic?"

Lily reached out her hand in the dark and touched the girl's thin shoulder. Comforting Greensleeves encouraged her again. "One way or another, it's done and can't be undone. If there's one thing I learned in a life of hard knocks, it's that there's no use mourning the past. You must look to the future and hope it will be better. We'll keep trying, as Gull does. I know we will. And somehow we'll learn how to control magic not for ourselves but in aid of others. And we'll learn how to control ourselves, too."

Greensleeves touched Lily's hand in reassurance. "All r-right, then. T-together. One b-benefit of all th-this, I-I've m-made a g-good fr-friend."

And at that, the ex–dancing girl smiled and squeezed her friend's small hand.

They were an unlikely pair, one too-worldly, one unworldly, but they had much in common and had come to depend on each other, confiding their secrets and doubts.

To change the subject, Greensleeves asked, "C-can you sh-show me your sp-spell? I-it's someth-thing I c-can't d-do."

Smiling, Lily put down her work againg. "All right. I like to show off my spell. My only spell."

She moved away from the tent and chest and bundles, and stood in a clear spot a dozen feet across. Closing her eyes and ears, shutting off outside sight and noise, the girl groped to find the magic for her one spell. She didn't know how to articulate it, only that she "rummaged around in her skull," hunting the spell like a quail in the recesses of her mind. Then she found it, but now she needed to feed it. For that, she sent her thoughts upward, higher, reaching for the clouds. Slowly, she felt her hands and feet tingle, then burn. The glow—and she knew her hands glowed white now—spread down her legs and up her arms, from her wrists, into her loins and belly and shoulders and torso, finally lighting her head like a candle. Then—

"You're d-doing it, L-lily! Y-you're f-f-flying!"

The ex–dancing girl opened her eyes and found herself looking down at the tops of nearby cedar trees. She was tilted so her dark hair hung around her cheeks, dangling in thin air. The glow was all through her, but cool now, and she felt as hollow as an eggshell. Greensleeves was ten or twelve feet below her. Clumps of mud rained from the soles of her stout shoes. Tentatively, her belly tight with fear and wonder, Lily spread her arms like a bird, rose higher . . .

"Wonderful!" boomed a voice. "That's fab—"

With a jolt, Lily lost her hold on the spell and plummeted to the ground. Below her came a shout, then she grunted as someone caught her around the middle and by one leg.

Gull shook his head as he lowered her. "Are you all right? I just barely caught you! Was it me who stopped your spell? I'm sorry! I—"

"No, it's—it's fine." Gently, Lily pried herself from his arms and stepped to the ground. It felt hard and cold and unfriendly after her brief flight.

She wished, she was surprised to find, she could fly forever—fly away and away, away from herself and her cares. To a place where she wouldn't need dreams, or love, or hope. A place where she could be as pure as the air.

But she couldn't tell Gull that.

Gently, she distanced herself from the man who'd been her lover. She noticed the hurt look on his face, like a lovesick puppy trying to understand her, to not blame her for withdrawing. They no longer slept together, or even talked much—Lily spent her time thinking, these days, wondering. But she couldn't explain about what. Not to him, or Greensleeves, or herself.

But how could she love someone else without loving herself?

"Well, you look fine, flying like that, Lily," said Gull, not stiffly but no longer friendly. "Keep it up. Flying would be a valuable skill we could use."

"Oh, Gull . . . " said the girl. But he turned and walked off, busy as always. After him went the new warrior woman, who'd only yesterday dropped from the sky. Over her personal frustration, a streak of curiosity made Lily mutter, "What's *her* game?"

"What?" asked Greensleeves. She looked after her brother, not understanding.

"Nothing," said Lily. "Come. We'll visit Kwam and the others, see how they are."

"All r-right." Greensleeves rose painfully, and Lily offered her a shoulder. Cherrystone protested being pushed off his shawl and hopped around indignantly. Lily went slowly: she knew what it was like to be helpless. She'd broken an arm and leg in the final battle with Towser.

As they stumped along, Lily was preoccupied with her own thoughts, but did hear Greensleeves ask, "It's v-very st-strange, b-but every t-time I t-turn around, K-Kwam is th-there."

"Hmmm . . . " murmured Lily, but said no more. Greensleeves would figure out why Kwam "hung around" soon enough. Until then, her life was complicated enough.

The girl sighed. "Th-there are s-so many th-things I d-don't understand. . . . "

But Greensleeves was to learn all she wanted, and more, beginning that night.

When a voice awoke her.

A voice in her mind.

A command.

"Greeeeeennnnnnsleeeevvvves . . . "

The girl awoke with a start, snapping upright so fast her ankle was shot with pain. Hissing, sweat-browed, she grabbed her throbbing leg, listened again for the voice.

She'd been having another nightmare, as she did most nights.

She'd been walking through a forest, knowing she was lost, unsure which way to go—and that was scary because she'd never been lost in a real forest. But this one looked the same in all directions, and the bark on the trees resembled brains ripped from skulls and wrapped around the boles. The brains talked to her, whispering, but she couldn't understand what they said. Only their threat came through, a menace that she'd never understand, that all she knew was wrong. Then the whispers grew louder, drumming into her mind, until her own head throbbed, and ached, and finally exploded—

But the most terrifying part was she knew what came next. Her brains burst from her head, leaving her skull empty. She was stark raving insane, madder even than when she'd been an idiot, mindless as a baby bird, never to think clearly—

—at that point, she always awoke, shaking and sweat soaked.

But this voice, calling her name, was new.

Not heard, but felt.

Though her body was sweating, the voice wafted

through her mind like a cool spring breeze. It hinted of spring water, and crisp freshets bubbling over rocks, and mossy glades, and the tang of tannin and oak leaves.

"Greensleeves. Come."

The girl pressed her hands over her ears, but the voice would not stop. Gently, she nudged Lily, to ask if she heard it, but she couldn't wake her friend. Bespelled? Or just exhausted?

"Come now."

Greensleeves had no choice. She had to go.

Wriggling on her thin legs, dislodging the badger sleeping under her and the chickadee sleeping above, she kicked open the tent flap with her good foot and slithered outside. As she lay there, panting in pain, she saw a guard walking the periphery of camp. "H-help me, p-please!" Though how he might help she didn't know.

Yet the man didn't hear her. "H-hello! P-please? Oh . . . G-Gull! W-where are y-you?" But it was no use. Three fighters rolled dice by the campfire, not thirty feet away, but never turned in her direction. She'd become a ghost, yet the soil was cold underneath her, and the dew was wet. She shivered and tugged her cloak closer.

"Come now."

She had to go. The lure was hypnotic, a gentle but insistent demand. Lurching to her one good foot, hopping from tent to tent, then to the line of picketed horses, she selected a dappled cob, threw her belly across it, and swung her agonized leg over its back. The badger had followed her, anxious to be with his mistress, but Greensleeves couldn't reach him from her new height. Cherrystone hip-hopped around and around, unused to night traffic.

The horse stamped and snorted at being disturbed by night, but still no guard turned or noticed. One female fighter with a crossbow passed directly behind the horse and kept walking.

Sobbing at her forced mission and the pain, the

girl tugged at the horse's hackamore. More by natural instinct and animal affinity than training, she coaxed it to back from the picket and stumble from the camp.

Into the evergreens.

Toward the north, to the end of the taiga and past, up a grassy slope she could picture in her mind, then onto a plateau of oaks.

To the voice.

And its source.

CHAPTER
7

"YOU WERE ASLEEP, YOU BASTARDS! OR DRUNK!
Or blind or stupid!"

"We wasn't!" countered the bleary-eyed guard.
"None of us was, though I wish I was now! I could use
some sleep——"

"Never mind that!" Gull roared in the woman's
face. "My sister is spirited away from her tent in the
middle of the night, and you fifth wheels don't even
know about it! I know what *your* word is worth!"

The whole camp listened to Gull's tirade, the first
time he'd ever shown a temper, but they all knew how
he fretted about protecting his sister. Just as they
knew magic must have been involved.

Lily voiced the thought. "Some enchantment was
afoot, Gull. I never woke once, and you know what a
light sleeper I am." Unexpectedly, she blushed in front
of the whole camp. "I mean—she had a broken ankle.
She had to crawl over me to get out. It must have been
a spell——"

"Save it!" he snapped. "You're as much to blame! If
you'd been more careful——"

But he halted as he saw her blink back hot tears. "Oh, never mind! Bardo! Saddle the best horses. Bring three of your scouts. And get some food! I'm going after her and *not* coming back until she's safe. Varrius, you're in charge. Soon as you can, fold up the camp and follow us. We'll build up fires every day at dawn, noon, and dusk so you can track us. *Don't* let me down, like this load of walking tripe!"

The guards snapped their heads up, but only glared rather than answering back.

Gull ignored them. Grabbing supplies from the cooks—a wineskin, a canteen of water, a ham and some potatoes—he hurried to his tent, slung his quiver and longbow over his back, and grabbed up his axe and mule whip.

Stiggur came running. The boy was growing, but still small. These days he wore his hair pulled back in a queue like his hero. "I can come with you, Gull! I can bring Knothead"—the clockwork beast, named after one of Gull's dead mules—"and can see over the trees—"

"No. They need the beast to carry the heavy stuff. Stay here and guard the camp." He couldn't be harsh with the boy, who was as inoffensive and eager to please as a puppy.

Yet no sooner did Gull turn to his horse than he faced someone across its back: a young man, his height and age, but lean, dressed in black. Gull knew who he was, a magic student, but not his name. What did he want?

"May I accompany you? You might need some magic—"

"No," pronounced the general. Adun's Shield, did everyone think this some lark into town for cakes and ale? And why should an inept student want to pursue his sister?

Rakel trotted up, her war gear hung around her, a battered leather helmet on her head, a borrowed cloak around her shoulders. "I'll go. I've had scout training."

Gull frowned as he saddled his horse, a wide-

chested dapple-gray. "For the last time, no! I don't
need—"

"I'm going."

For the first time, Gull looked at her. Now why
should *she* tag along? Didn't anyone have proper work
to do? Yet she was a trained soldier. Her military bearing and that garish seven-pointed star on her forearm
said so. "Can you use a bow?"

"Better than you."

The woodcutter frowned, but something in her
demeanor made him believe her. "Then borrow one.
Quick!"

She was saddled and ready to go before him, for
there were a thousand details to be dealt with around
the camp. He finished with a challenge to the guards:
"And you lot can pull double shifts until Greensleeves
is back safe and sound!"

The guards spun smartly, showed their backs.

To Bardo and the three scouts, all ready to go,
and Rakel, he hollered, "Let's go! Find her trail and
plant your noses in it!"

The woman was old, old. She'd been old for a long time.

She sat on a flat stone where the lichens had been
rubbed off. It lay before a cave set into a hillside
bright with yellow winter grass. Overhead rustled the
dead leaves of pin oaks. The hollow was in the midst
of an oak forest, and the forest covered the top of a
wide highland plateau.

Greensleeves felt only mildly tired. Riding through
the taiga, she'd seen the sun climb the sky, set, then
rise in what seemed only an hour. Yet not once had
she to needed to step down to eat or drink or relieve
herself. Another abbreviated day followed, the taiga
ending, then another three climbing a slope to the
plateau, sometimes dismounting and crawling where
the way was too steep to ride, then another three days
penetrating the oak forest. All in no more than a
"day's" ride.

As she rode, the horse never tiring, the badger scurrying along easily, the chickadee never leaving her shoulder, she'd reflected that her brother would be pleased to see this forest, for it abounded with boar and deer and elk, raccoons and possums, beaver in the creeks. Even in this early winter, there were mushrooms and teaberries aplenty. The sun shone brightly up here, and Greensleeves knew it was not just because of the altitude.

It was because of this woman.

She wore only a white robe, miraculously clean but made of plain wool. She was barefoot, unadorned, and her long white hair hung down her back in an old woman's kinky cascades. Her eyes were closed, but as the girl drew close, she said, "Greetings, Greensleeves. I'm glad you came."

The girl had had no choice, but didn't say it. She studied this magic user, obviously one of great power.

She must have power to still be alive.

The right side of the woman's face was frozen, the lip hanging in a half-grimace, she drooled. She reached across with her left hand, craggy and blue-veined, to wipe it away, for her entire right side was dead. Her arm hung limp and withered; her leg was twisted, the foot curled. The shoulder was hunched upward. Yet the left side had not much more strength, for it was all the old woman could do to prop herself up on the rock to soak up sunshine like an old dog.

As if reading her thoughts, the woman said in a whisper as raspy as last season's corn husks, "I apologize for my appearance. I've been fighting death, you see, for a long time now. He visits regularly, like an unwanted suitor, but each time I drive him from my door. Like many suitors before," she added with a chuckle. "But each time I die a little. Like a tree, losing a limb at a time. The rot hasn't stilled my heart yet, but it takes much magic to keep it attentive." Again, the dry chuckle.

Greensleeves slipped from the saddle, careful to land on her good foot, wincing at the bad one. She let

the horse loose, and it fed, cropping lovage at the edge
of the hollow. Both badger and bird took off after food.
Unafraid, the girl perched by the old woman on the
rock. "Y-you're a dr-dr—" She took a breath. "Druid!"

"Aye. And you're a magic user. But untrained.
Would you learn?"

Greensleeves's eyes went wide. "Y-yes! Y-ye—" For
a moment, she could only stammer, and had to
breathe again. "Yes! I w-would! C-can you t-teach me?"

"Aye, I can. If you care enough. If you can make
the sacrifice."

"C-care? I d-do c-care. But wh-what s-sacrifice?"

"Any. All. The final sacrifice."

"M-my l-life?"

"That and more."

Greensleeves grew puzzled. What bigger sacrifice
could anyone make than her life? "A-anything. I h-hate
being h-half a p-person, knowing I h-have p-power, b-
but can't u-use it."

The druid's hand fluttered off the rock and came
to rest on Greensleeves's. It felt like an errant feather
but cold as an icicle.

"I am Chaney," came the whisper. "It means 'Oak
Wood.' You see, even when I was born, my family
knew what I would be. And so it was with you, given
your name because your hands were always stained
green from rooting up flowers and plants. Are we
agreed, then? I the teacher, you the student?"

"A-anything, mistress."

"Call me Chaney. You are young and take oaths
lightly. You'll learn otherwise. But let us start. Prop
your ankle up here, child, and undo the splint."

The druid worked quietly, easily, while Greensleeves watched and waited. Finally, she would learn
how to wield magic.

Now if only she didn't lose her mind doing it.

"It's be'vitching, and no doubt," said Bardo.

Four men faced tiny gaps in the taiga, urinating

into pockets they'd kicked with their heels. Rakel and the other scout, a woman named Channa, squatted at the opposite side of the trail. "Trail" was a misnomer; their route was nothing but squeezing between the interlocked branch tips of the endless evergreens.

The scouts were all dressed alike, in green or brown tunics and trousers, dull gray woolen cloaks, and low-brimmed hats that shaded their faces. Longbows jutted upward from saddle cases. Wide-bladed short swords, called falcions, that could dismember game, branches, or enemies, hung low on their hips.

"How could she be bewitched," Gull asked, "if no one saw any strangers come into camp and Lily was right alongside her?"

Bardo shrugged, hitched his belt. "I don't know. But ve've got a lame girl on a cob fit for dog food, no canteen, no food, no blankets, just moving at a valk, vhile ve've ridden hard until our bladders should burst, yet ve see no sign she's dismounted."

The paladin, a tall man with a slow way of moving, squatted and parted more branches. The dry needles underneath showed hoofprints. "Your sister is either a clockvork animal like Stiggur's hatrack, or she's under a spell. Even paladins on crusade don't ride for six hours at a time."

Gull wanted to shout in frustration. "But she's just walking and we ride like hell! When will we overtake her?"

Bardo shrugged again. "Ve may not. I'd say she's under a compulsion, and von't stop till she reaches her destination. I've heard of such spells, a geas on horse and rider. Time collapses so days pass like hours. So for catching her . . . ve're not vitches, so must rest our mounts."

"But—"

Bardo didn't bother to argue. He told his scouts, "Vun hour. Dinos, camp ahead; Channa, vatch our back trail. Vater your animals before yourselves." By example, he poured water in his hat for his white warhorse. The horse's breath steamed as it slurped. "Rakel, your name is? You know scouting? Ve'll see. I'll assign you same as the rest. Build that signal fire."

As commander, only Gull was given no duties. Which meant he could fret more. For something to do, he chopped down a cedar tree and lopped off its branches while Rakel struck flint and steel. The warrior woman was impressed with the efficient way he worked, using his great strength without wasting it.

She asked, "You worry about your sister a great deal, don't you?"

"Huh? Oh. Yes, I do." He stacked the driest branches on her fire to get it crackling, then added the green top to make gray smoke. "Yes. Though she's no longer a simpleton, she's still an innocent."

Rakel hid a smile. His sister wasn't the only innocent in this forest. She couldn't get over the naive way the man answered any question—nothing like the men of Benalia, who guarded their every thought and action lest someone use their strength or weakness against them. As Garth had acted lately. She plied Gull with more questions, telling herself it was to learn more about her enemy—a target for assassination.

"Is Greensleeves your only relative?"

"Aye." Gull leaned on his axe handle, stared at the flames as if the answers lay there. When Rakel ate some of her iron rations, Gull belatedly remembered to also eat. "All our family was killed when two wizards destroyed White Ridge. My mother's heart gave out to some life-draining spell. My father was killed when stones rained from the sky. The same killed my brothers and sisters, or else plague carried them off. My little brother, Sparrow Hawk, disappeared. I reckon he was seized by soldiers, made a slave, or else he died and I couldn't find his body. We'll never know. Greensleeves is all I have left, and I was charged with caring for her. I take my charges seriously."

Rakel sipped wine from a skin and watched him surreptitiously. "Surely she's not all you have. What about Lily? Isn't she your—ladylove?"

A shrug. "I don't know. She was for a while, but she's obsessed with magic now. As my sister is becoming. There's something about it; it's addictive. Magic users pursue it more than food or sex or friendship or anything else. I hope I never learn what it is that draws them. It robs you of humanity. And it's taken my sister, again, damn it!"

"But what about the army? You have their loyalty. They look up to you."

"A collection of misfits. Half seek their homelands, half signed on because we pay a little and they crave adventure, or they have no homeland at all. I'd rather there wasn't any army, and Greenie and I and my family still lived happily in White Ridge and had never heard of magic. But that's all gone. And wishing wizards away is like swearing at horseflies in Harvest Month. You must live with them." He poked the fire with his axe head, careful not to let the blade heat up and spoil the temper.

Rakel ate in silence. She didn't ask any more questions. His answers shot too close to her heart. He didn't want fame or glory or adulation or riches. He wanted only a home and family and quiet days to till a farm or tend to household chores.

That had been Garth's dream, so he'd said. But magic had seduced him away. And she'd been plucked from her hearth to pay old debts. Why did the gods deny the things you wanted, even the simplest things?

Gull, she thought, would never leave his family to go running off after magic and fame. He was a man after her own heart. . . .

" . . . Everything is a web, you see. We're part of it. Some wizards would believe we're the *center,* but anyone with sense can see there are no centers, only interlocking spheres—the way snowflakes, with six points, lie together in a snowbank, touching yet apart, united yet separate. . . . "

Studying, concentrating from dawn to dusk, never idle, the days passed quickly for Greensleeves.

Chaney gave her no rest. The old druid talked
incessantly, for she had a world of knowledge to
impart and not much time left. The woman never tired,
nor did Greensleeves, though they ate only mushrooms or acorn bread or strips of willow bark or fiddle-
heads or teaberries. Nights passed in an eyeblink, and
Chaney was already talking when Greensleeves awoke.
Or perhaps, nights passed without her even knowing it,
so that darkness came and went as if a cloud had
passed before the sun.

But she had no complaint, for she learned more
every minute, and the knowledge piled up on itself,
each bit of lore adding to the others, heaping high
over her head until she thought she'd smother. But
she listened, and experimented, and learned, and daily
grew more confident.

" . . . Oddly, the *easiest* thing to do is conjure something from one spot to another," Chaney explained one
day. The old woman was as wasted as ever, only her
hoarse whispery voice alive, and she seldom strayed
from her warm rock. Yet Greensleeves felt they'd
explored the universe and all its planes, even touched
the stars, all while sitting in this one clearing. "It's no
trick to bring an object from one place to another. It's
harder to get out of a chair, walk through a door, and
fetch a candle from another room. Conjuring moves
things through *space*. You choose an object *there,* and
make the space around it the space *here*. . . . "

Vaguely, Greensleeves expected snow any day, for
it had been early winter when she left the camp, and
now they must be approaching the turn of the year.
Yet every day remained as balmy as winter could be,
and every day she learned more. Occasionally she
wondered when Gull would arrive, but then brushed
the thought aside. She had more important things
than food or companionship or sleep to marvel about.
She was learning how to move the universe itself.

Yet some nights, the dreams came back. Dreams
of insanity. And the more magic she learned, the
closer she felt herself drawing to the precipice. . . .

Yet always there was Chaney's gentle raspy voice, dragging her back to safety, coaxing, cajoling, prodding, praising. Like Greensleeves's mother, Bittersweet, whom the girl, then a simpleton, had only known in a vague way. Perhaps, by attending Chaney, Greensleeves could pay back her dead mother for all that loving attention. Certainly she felt warmest when Chaney called her "child."

"You called me a druid, or above that, an arch-druid," Chaney was saying, "yet druid is just a name for a magic user steeped in nature magic. Sorceress, warlock, witch, thaumaturge, wizard, planeswalker, magic-maker, shaman, priest—all just names. People name a blue jay, but it's only for themselves: it doesn't change how the blue jay lives, or thinks of itself. . . . "

So the lessons ran on, Greensleeves feeling she'd learned a lifetime of knowledge in a short time. Yet one morning, she found Cherrystone tucked into her cloak, stiff and cold. When she commented on the bird's death, Chaney replied, "Chickadees only live for two or three years at the most, dear. . . . "

Gull's search party left the taiga on the second day and mounted a yellow-grass slope toward another plateau. Often, they dismounted and climbed using their hands, half-dragging the horses. Nights they pick-eted the horses securely and posted a guard, Gull insisting on taking a watch.

The scouts were in a world of their own, reading the sights and sounds of the forest, guarding by night, talking little. Dinos and Channa were lovers who shared blankets at night. Bardo rode ahead or off to one side, lost in his own thoughts, communing with his god. So Rakel rode alongside Gull, and they talked.

They talked of many things, though she was care-ful to guard her words. She let him think her a simple wandering soldier swept up into Karli's service. But she spoke of her family left behind in Benalia, and Gull's casual questions made her remember things she'd forgotten long ago: stories and memories and incidents from her childhood and youth, things floating to the surface lately because now she had her own child, Hammen. Thoughts of her child made her heart ache. Yet it was a sweet ache, and she felt herself growing closer to her family, though they were far, far off.

She swore, though, she'd get back her child and see her lost family again. And if Garth returned, she'd demand he harness his magic for good, helping people, not conjuring monsters and killers to fight killers and monsters.

But to free her son, she must bring the heads of Gull and Greensleeves before the council, present them to the odious Sabriam . . .

Could she do that now? Would it be better if she never went back? Could she hide from that "shifting" wizard, Guyapi? Could she disappear into the wilds of the Domains, stay here?

But, oh, her son, to never know his mother . . .

Evenings, under the frosty stars, Rakel lay in her blankets and listened to Gull pace the campsite, breathing not five feet way. After days of aching, her breasts had finally dried of their milk, and her soft body toughened to the trail. Now, as she lay alone, missing her son and Garth beside her, she found herself aching to be held.

And one night, it was not Garth, more distant in her mind, that she thought of hugging, but Gull.

More lessons . . .

"There's magic in everything, though some more than others. Humans carry some. Elves are so steeped in it, as a fish is steeped in water, that they can't separate it from their daily lives. Some humans call themselves lucky, but luck is just using magic without realizing it. So there are no magic users and non-magic-users. All are magic. But only a few have learned to tap the power within. . . . "

One morning, Greensleeves reached to pat her badger, and the creature bit her. Surprised, she studied the animal and found its eyes had gone blind with cataracts, so it snapped at everything in defense. And its fur was mostly white now, not gray, and it moved stiffly, as if arthritic. Badgers, she knew, lived six or seven years. This one with the notched ear had been a yearling when it began to follow her. How . . . ?

"Magic is all mixed up, like a giant hash or stew. It comes in all colors, all flavors, all species. Druids deal with nature magic, but even that's composed of earth magic, water magic, animal magic, and wind magic. Some wizards like only magic-magic, that is, manipulating magic: spells for determining how much magic lies in an artifact, or how to make an artifact invisible. I suspect your friend Lily, since she can but conjure some and fly a little, taps cloud magic, or sky magic, or the magic of whatever lies about the sky, if anything at all. I've been to mountaintops and found the air is thin and cold, and suppose as you rise higher there's nothing at all—except some untapped kind of magic, perhaps. . . .

"The trick is to know what type of magic you tap and purify it. If you seek to fly, then you want *only* cloud and sky and sun magic: if you drag along iron-red earth magic, you'll tote an anchor on your feet. Yet you must learn to *see,* to pick out one leaf on one tree in a vast and unending forest. . . . "

Slowly, the girl learned, absorbing, asking questions. Hundreds of questions.

"Planeswalking? I used to planeswalk when I was young. But no more. I've moved beyond that. In time, I learned it's best to let nature take its course. You'll learn that someday, I suspect. It's all refinement, always learning. That's why I no longer carry a grimoire. I've reduced everything to a song, you see, so it's easier to remember. . . .

"Compulsion? Ah, yes, the laying of the geas, forcing whatever you summon to fight for you. Yes, many wizards employ that in their quest for power. It's usually the second spell they learn, for they reason, what good is it to conjure unless you can control and direct what you conjure? Yet a blade has two edges, and if you live by compelling, expect to be compelled. But you're not interested in forcing others to your will, are you, girl? No, I thought not. Only volunteers, like your soldiers. Good, that's best. Because I wouldn't teach it to you even if I knew it. . . .

"You didn't collapse when that desert wizard pointed at you, yet Lily did? Perhaps you're so infused with magic it acts as a natural shield. Have you a shield spell? There, then. Normally it takes years to master that skill, to form a wall of pure mana, yet you deflect magic as easily as a duck deflects rain. . . .

"Nightmares? All wizards have them, dear. When you conjure, you're sending your mind, part of your spirit, after the thing you conjure. There are tales of wizards who sent too much of themselves into the ether and never got those parts back. . . . "

That scared her.

"Tagging? Oh, yes, some call it that. It simply means if you've seen an object or creature, handled it, smelled it, you *know* it with the *vision,* the sight. Any commoner, for instance, given a horseshoe nail, would recognize it. But take that nail and fling it into a foundry where lie a thousand such nails, and that poor blind soul couldn't find it again in a thousand years. But a wielder of the way, a manipulator, could merely summon the *image* of that nail—the single one they'd touched—change the space around it, and pull it to their hand. . . .

"Lower wizards, hedge wizards, can only tag something and let it lie and hope it's there when they need it. Higher wizards can tag a thing or creature— without it knowing it's tagged—and lock the tag to prevent others from tagging it. Thus they protect their treasure troves and chests, and sense when someone disturbs them. A good thing to remember, too, for fools who lust after artifacts. Finger an object of great value, and risk the instant wrath of someone so high you cannot conceive of them. You don't own things, remember: they own you. . . .

"Tapping, on the other hand, is gathering mana to you from surrounding lands. You can tap the mana of the land and air and water, or you can tap reserves inside yourself. But not too deeply, lest you be left a nut with no meat. You might die. Or worse. . . . "

"But you try it, dear."

"What?" asked Greensleeves. She blinked, trying to concentrate. While she understood all the teacher taught, she was always ten steps behind, always trying to catch up, as if Chaney galloped on a horse and Greensleeves ran afoot.

"Summon something."

"Uh, what, Chaney?"

"Anything. Anything you can imagine." The druid's one good hand fluttered in the air, a butterfly with tattered wings that had to fight to stay aloft.

"Oh. All right." Greensleeves rubbed her brow, tried to imagine something. Something in camp, perhaps.

Then suddenly she knew, as if the object had sent her a signal.

Frowning, the girl stood up from the rock. A cool breeze swirled from out of the oak forest, wiffled the yellow grass dotted around, made the curled pin oak leaves shiver. Greensleeves was sure it was colder these days, that winter must be here, that the breeze was tinged with ice. But then, perhaps it was tinged with ice melt, was a spring wind, and winter was behind her. Or several winters. She couldn't know.

She frowned deeper, put out her hands in a vague gesture. Her movements had gotten clumsier lately. She suspected the motions she'd once made—in her untutored, ignorant attempts at magic—had hindered rather than helped her. But she couldn't know why. Now she just paddled her hands in the air, clumsy as a child learning to walk.

Briefly, a whiff of nightmare slid through her mind,

like an oiled snake, coming from darkness, returning to it, but leaving a dark trail behind. Sweat beaded on her brow. Was the power worth the fear of insanity?

But the object she wanted was there, singing to her like a siren.

Chaney leaned on her rock like a frozen lizard. Greensleeves made a pass at the air with her hand, then back, and—far more easily than ever before, created a flicker along the ground.

A brown square appeared on the grass, not much bigger than a man's hat. Then it rippled upward; green, not the muddy green she'd always conjured before, but a pure living green, like the first breath of spring. Then a square of vivid blue, bright as the sky after a storm. A hint of sun-yellow and—

—the mana vault lay at her feet.

It glistened, pink and shiny like a polished seashell. Greensleeves picked it up. She explained, "I don't know why I chose this. . . . It more chose me, I could almost believe. It's a mana vault that a wizard named Towser—"

"Mana vault?" husked Chaney. "Oh, no, child. That's not a mana vault."

"It's not?" Greensleeves juggled the box as a child might a stone. "But it fell from the sky. The wizard who dug it up was very excited. He said it was a mana vault."

"Then he was a fool. That thing is alive. Alive as you and me."

Gull pointed. "There she is! Halloooo, Greenie!"

For three days, the scouting party had traversed the oak forest on this plateau. The scouts were laden with all kinds of game: turkeys, moorhens, beavers, a haunch of mule deer. They almost couldn't resist shooting at game, shooting until they had more than they could eat, for after the desertlike taiga, this forest was a cornucopia.

Now the woodcutter reined in at the edge of a

hollow before a small cave and hill. At the center was his sister and, seated on a rock, an old woman in white who looked more dead than alive. Gull hopped from the saddle and limped on his bad leg down into the hollow. Greensleeves handed the pink mana vault (but shouldn't that be back at camp?) to the old woman, then ran toward her brother. Gull grabbed his sister around her waist, scooped her up, and hugged her so hard she squeaked. "I was so worried! Why did you run off? Was it some spell?"

"Oh, brother! I've so much to tell you! I've been learning all about magic from Chaney here! Her name means 'Oak Wood,' and she's a druid, and I'm a druid, too! She's taught me about all kinds of things! Interpreting astrological signs, chakra points—those are magic centers in your body—how to listen to crystals . . . "

Gull set her down, smiling, and looked her over to see she was safe and sound.

She was different, he thought. But how?

She looked hale and fit, slim as ever, tousled and sunburnt. Her gown and shawl were more tattered and threadbare than ever, as if she'd spent the last several winters living out of doors. And . . .

"Your ankle is healed!"

The girl looked down, wiggled one foot. "Oh, yes! Chaney fixed it, made the bones knit overnight! She can do all sorts of wonderful—"

"And . . . you're . . . bigger!"

"Eh?" The young woman stepped back to study his face. Her big brother didn't seem as tall as before.

Gull saw even more. She was a couple of inches taller. Her bosom and hips had filled out, too, and her face had more flesh to it, her cheeks padded and soft, her neck firm. Gone was the coltish, half-starved look. His sister had come to resemble their mother, Bittersweet.

The girl had become a woman.

Older than her big brother Gull, perhaps.

As if years had passed overnight.

"And . . . your stutter's gone!"

"What?" The young woman put a grass-stained hand to her lips. "Oh! You're right. I never noticed . . . "

Rakel stood on the lip of the hollow and watched the brother and sister chatter. Unconsciously, one hand rested on the pommel of her sword.

They're together again, ran her thoughts, with only a few retainers. Tonight, I could slay them easily and collect their heads. By tomorrow, I could be in Benalia, deliver my prizes, redeem my son, journey to the farm, and wait for Garth, should he ever return.

But she couldn't. Gull was a decent man fighting for a good cause. Greensleeves was an unselfish wizard, out to help others with her magic: something unique in Rakel's experience. She couldn't snuff out these people, their dreams, the hope they embodied and promised the world.

Yet it was them or her. And her son.

Which? she wanted to cry out. What to do?

CHAPTER
8

"I DON'T UNDERSTAND." GREENSLEEVES POKED AT the pink mana vault, as she had for days now. The thing fascinated her, especially since Chaney's pronouncement. "How can you tell it's alive?"

Leaning on her good arm, Chaney gave a one-sided shrug. "It's a way of seeing, dear. You'll learn it. Have you noticed it feels warm to the touch?"

"Well, yes," said the girl. "But I thought that was just warming in the sun."

"No. Nor could an untutored person sense it. Here, set it by me."

The girl propped it on the rock by the woman's pale blue-veined hand. This was another balmy winter day, with no snow despite the altitude. Wan sunlight warmed the yellow grass and rustling leaves of the hollow. Now that the others had arrived, her brother and Rakel and the scouts, hunting and seeking a spot for the army to encamp when they arrived, the days passed more slowly and yet more quickly. It was normal time, Greensleeves decided, where hours sped by if you were occupied, or dragged if you were idle. Not that Chaney gave her a moment's rest: if anything, she talked faster now, threw ideas and notions at Greensleeves as if pitching hay to hungry horses.

"But, to be alive—I can't imagine. It crashed to earth like a falling star. It made a pit you couldn't throw a rock across, so deep the layers were yellow sand. How—?"

"With magic, as with life, all things are possible," Chaney interrupted. "You must come to understand that, above all else. For magic is only limited by the mana available *and* the wielder's imagination. That's why Towser didn't see the life in this box. He took one look, decided it was a mana vault, and so it remained."

"You mean—it *thinks*?"

What would it be like to have your mind trapped inside—this thing?

Chaney chuckled. "All that lives thinks, some things more clearly than others. Now hush. I wish to speak with it."

Gently, like a feather alighting, she set her white hand on the pink box. She closed her eyes and sat still so long Greensleeves thought she'd dozed off. But then the druid shook herself. "It's guarded. By others and itself. Help me lean here, dear."

Wondering, Greensleeves eased Chaney down until her forehead rested against the box, as if on a stone pillow. The druid mused, "You'll learn this, too. Sleep on a skull to discourse with the dead. . . . Ah, there it is. . . . A spark, deep inside. . . . Hello . . . "

The old woman suddenly yelped, a dry croak.

Chaney's head snapped back as if kicked by a mule. Groaning, shuddering, she flopped on her back against the mossy stone. Groaning, drooling, her eyes rolled white in her head.

Grabbing for the druid, Greensleeves brushed the pink box.

And recoiled in horror.

The pink mana vault squirmed and sprouted a half dozen thick and green and pointed arms. The writhing appendages, different sizes, forked or truncated, popped from the box on every face, some from depressions, others from corners, with no rhyme or reason. The pink box flushed green dappled with brown spots, like a frog's skin. Amidst the twisting tentacles there bulged three stalks exposing round bulging bloodshot eyes that swiveled in Greensleeves's direction. A corner split into a mouth with a red lolling tongue.

All this happened in seconds. Then, with a lurching hop, the vault hoisted itself on a handful of speckled tentacles, hopped off the rock, and scuttled away across the dry leaves.

Stunned, Greensleeves watched it go. Oddly, she realized now that she understood Karli's demand for a "magic walking box".

Then she remembered Chaney. Feeling the woman's chest, she found she was not breathing.

"Oh, Chaney," she whimpered. "Oh, Gull! Oh, *help!*"

"Gull," said Rakel, a hand on her sword pommel, "I've made a decision. I'm going to join your army."

The woodcutter looked at her curiously. The two of them had spent the morning riding in a wide circle, hunting a clearing for the army to bivouac in when they arrived in a few days. It was pleasant work, bobbing to the easy gait of the horses, threading among tall oak trees over a brown carpet of leaves, the sky white-blue overhead, the sun warm on their necks. Gull told himself he was working, but in fact, he was relaxing. Running his makeshift army these past months had exhausted him: having found his sister, he had a wonderful excuse to loaf.

He didn't understand Rakel's comment, but then he didn't understand most of what women told him. Women, to him, thought on some higher plane. While men blundered about, seeking a stone to sharpen an axe to cut a tree to plane into beams to make a new ridgepole, women sent their hearts to the stars, seeking— well, whatever they sought. Happiness? Contentment? The secret of existence? He couldn't guess, and had no time to ponder. He had trees to fell and an army to command, and that was work enough.

He told her, "Fine. But I thought you already had. You can fight, and we need fighters—"

"I can fight," she interrupted, "but you can't."

"Huh?" He stopped his horse, a dapple-gray he called Ribbons for its trailing mane, and squinted at her.

"I know how to fight," she explained, "but you're hopeless. The only thing that keeps you alive in a fight is your brawn and reflexes. And the fact you've swung that axe since you could first lift it, I suppose. But if you ever go up against real fighters, they'll make mincemeat of you."

"I suppose." Gull was too mellow to be insulted. Besides, she was right. "I've no training in fighting, only woodcutting. I do the best I can."

"Not good enough." Antsy, Rakel dropped the reins and hopped off her horse to the scrunch of leaves underfoot. Stepping away, she wrapped her arms around her chest, hugging herself unconsciously. She gazed into the oak forest without seeing it. Off in a sunlit clearing, browsing elk lifted racked heads, glanced at the two humans, and returned to cropping brush. Gull slid down and stretched, eyed the distance to the elk in bowshots.

The man asked, "Well, I could train with—no, Tomas is dead. Bardo, perhaps. But there's so little time in the day—"

"No!" Rakel whirled, found him uncomfortably close. She noted again how handsome he was, skin tanned to mahogany by a lifetime outdoors, his brown hair tousled and tied back in a queue, his eyes a vivid green. Smaller and darker, Garth, handsome despite his star-shaped scar, was fading in her mind, until she could barely picture him. Flustered, she went on. "No. I need to train you. It's a—gift. Before I must—"

Gull waited. "Before what?" Odd, he thought, how vulnerable Rakel looked once you got past her leather armor and soldier's tattoo and weapons. Her short-cropped black hair had grown almost to her shoulders. Her face was hard, a warrior's face, but retained a woman's softness deep in her eyes.

The woman turned away. "Before I must—leave."

Curious now, Gull followed her. "Why leave?"

She waved a hand, a fluttery feminine gesture she didn't know she possessed. "I can't stay with your army forever. That's why I want to train you, and the others. I've been schooled in military thinking since before I could talk. Your sergeants, Varrius and Neith, have some skill, but no officer's training. They've no sense of logistics and tactics."

"What are they?" asked Gull, curious about anything that could improve his army's fighting ability. And the woman who wanted to change it.

She whirled, found him close enough to kiss. She snarled instead, "See? Logistics and tactics are the two sides of an army, its most basic functions, and you know *nothing* about them! Where I come from, every *child* is taught—"

But the words stuck in her throat.

Gull was obscured by a picture of her laughing son, Hammen. Whom she'd never see again. For by training Gull and Greensleeves's army, her gift to keep them alive and fighting wizardry, she'd decided to throw away her life and all she loved.

Her son would be raised by a cruel and unfeeling state, and never see his mother again.

And suddenly she was sobbing.

Gull did the instinctive thing, for he couldn't abide his own helplessness when a woman cried. He pulled her to his chest. How women could turn on tears in seconds he'd never understood. Nor why so many carried some secret sorrow in their hearts. This one— tough, sad, sweet Rakel—seemed to carry more than her share.

Rakel clung to the man's chest, her tears running down his deerhide jerkin. He was so kind, so sensitive, so attentive. How long had it been since Garth held her? kissed her? She turned her face up: he seemed as tall as the oaks he'd once felled. Ruthlessly, she caught the back of his neck, pulled him down to kiss her.

Gull kissed back. He was surprised, but then again, not very. Briefly, he thought of Lily, who'd come to love him, then had quit loving him (or had she?) to explore magic. He'd probably fall in love with Rakel now. Though he didn't know why, women clung to him, and when they clung he returned their embraces, fell in love with them. But that was more mystery, as mysterious as how women could be so tough and so soft, so hard and so yielding, so gentle and so savage.

Older and wiser, Rakel knew this wasn't love, or even lust. It was simply sadness and heartache and a desire to hold someone close. She'd hold Gull, love him with her body, use him for comfort and solace, try to quench her sadness while her heart crumbled inside her.

Because she'd be dead before the next moon.

Panicked, alone, not knowing what else to do, Greensleeves laid the old woman flat on the stone—she weighed no more than a basket of flowers—clamped her mouth on Chaney's, and blew hard enough to inflate the woman's chest. After four lusty blows, Chaney sobbed and shuddered, and breathed on her own. Greensleeves sat back, wrung out from worry, and mopped her face with both hands.

And that's how Gull and Rakel found them some time later.

Greensleeves noticed her brother failed to look straight at her, but rather over her head, while Rakel looked calm and peaceful for the first time since she'd arrived from thin air. Greensleeves immediately thought of her new friend, Lily, and what she would think—or whether she would notice. Lily, too, was distracted lately, bewitched by magic, frustrated by her inability to control it. As Greensleeves was frustrated by the fear of insanity.

But for now Greensleeves brushed personal

concerns aside. She ran up to her brother and took his maimed left hand. "Gull! You've got to help us! The mana vault—only it's not a vault, but a green brain with tentacles—it ran away!"

For a second, all Gull could think was for sixteen years his sister had been mute, and now she made up for lost time. "Slow, down, Greenie. What—brain? tentacles?"

Hurriedly, the girl explained the strange transformation of the vault. Rakel looked to Chaney and saw the old woman was fine, if exhausted. The old druid was chagrined at being taken unawares. She mumbled, " . . . but it's a powerful artifact, no doubt about it. The most powerful one I've seen. . . . "

Greensleeves pushed past her brother. "I have to find it! It's—"

Gull surprised her by grabbing her wrist. "Hang on! I don't think you should chase it. If it's powerful enough to coldcock this druid, it can make worm fodder of you in an eyeblink."

Greensleeves pulled at her wrist, but stayed fast in his viselike grip. "Let go! It's not dangerous! It's probably just frightened! I—"

Her brother hung on. Having suffered at their hands, Gull hated all wizards in principle and still had mixed feelings about his sister practicing the art. For some time, he'd wanted to talk to her about using and misusing magic. Now, he decided stubbornly, was a good time. "No, I don't think so! Better it stays lost for now. You can't just—"

But she wasn't listening either. "I said, let go, brother! I want that artifact! I know what's good for me, not you!"

"I've taken care of you every day since you were born! You've been *my* charge and *my* worry since I can remember. And I don't—"

Gull's temper rose, but so did his sister's. Greensleeves gave one more tug and shouted, *"Let go of me!"*

Gull got out a single "No!" before—

His hand flew off her wrist. A lightning shock, or

blow, or charge, bowled him over backward so he cannoned into Rakel, bounced off her, and slammed his head into a tree. Sprawled on his rump, he rubbed his sore head and cursed in a muleskinner's jargon.

He stopped because his hand hurt. Opening his palm, he found the skin burned raw, as if he'd touched a stove. "What did you *do* to me?"

Greensleeves only stared at her wrist. Her skin was red where he'd grabbed her, but over that lay a green glow like a bracelet. Chaney pushed off her rock, hobbled on one good and one stiff leg, and examined the fading green ring. "Hmmm . . . Another variant of a shield spell. Soon you'll be able to wrap your whole body. No one will manhandle you then." She sniffed at Gull and tottered crab-fashion back to her rock.

Gull stood up, licked his palm to sooth the burn. "So. Greensleeves joins the ranks of the true wizards, using magic to brush mortals aside. What will she learn next, and how will she control us, now that she's no longer a pawn?"

Greensleeves stared at her hands as if at a stranger's. "That's not true. I haven't changed . . . "

But deep down, she knew she had.

It frightened her.

Spooked, she jumped a foot, as did everyone else, when from behind came a squeaky echoing voice like nothing they'd ever heard.

"Ran did I because thoughts mashed mine mind scared but see are not bad good so came back did I what is it want you from I?"

The people stared in shock.

Balanced on the winter leaves, not a foot high, was the green brain propped on writhing tentacles. The voice came from its tiny red mouth.

Like Greensleeves, once it began talking, the green brain wouldn't shut up. Not that night, or all the next day, nor the night after that. It only quit when its listeners, eager as they were for knowledge, grew so weary they dropped to sleep on the spot.

It didn't help that the talking brain's babble was almost incomprehensible.

" . . . mines every hand with tall towers above big holes below ivory tower all white and cave like mouth with eyes atop dwarves ride inside carts go down deep fetch mana use Mishra against Ashnod ask why green sign fall from sky I put in cage bars of rust press against eyes cannot see long time cold in space not cold but empty no food see stars turn white purple blue red blow up bang put in box and sent into space everyone wants I no can have council decided Sages ran screaming big one fall down eyes burst blood knife fly make noise like splat running in dark sunshine hot big birds eat wizard pull arms belong to me sun bake us dark woman smell of sand come no want to go with her make ghosty find . . . "

Greensleeves rubbed her aching eyes and put out a restraining hand. "*Please* slow down! What was the story? Someone stole you and ran out in the desert? Or was it the woman named Karli who tried to steal you just this past month? When are we talking about? And how did you get into the sky to come down and make the big pit?"

" . . . Sages said if one has all would want and make all others do what says so said no one can have I so put in box and cannot see it dark inside box but feel great weight and pushed rushed smushed through sky and find it cold not-cold and floaty arms go all over no hold so take box shape . . . "

"Arms of Axelrod, Greenie!" groused Gull. "Would you make the damned thing *shut up* so we can sleep? It must have been a *torture* device where they locked you in a room and it drove you mad!"

"You're babbling, Gull," teased Rakel.

All of them, Greensleeves and Gull and Rakel and Chaney and the scouts, save for one pacing guard, occupied Chaney's cave cut into the hillside. The eight of them were crammed head to toe in blankets on the sandy floor. Rakel and Gull shared the same blankets, and the woman never took her arm from across her new love's broad chest all night. Chaney catnapped, for she never slept longer than an hour, but Greensleeves strove to stay awake to decipher the squeaky voice's nonsense.

The box sat on a rude table next to a tallow candle. The tiny flame flickered and glistened on its wrinkled skin. The fleshy and forked and truncated tentacles never stopped wriggling like a nest of snakes. Yet the young wizard woman sat with her head propped on her arm not a foot away, transfixed.

"Wait, wait," she pleaded. She needed sleep desperately, but her need for knowledge was greater. "Why did everyone want you? What can you do, besides turn into a pink box and back?"

" . . . pink box shape of box hold I squished into pushed squashy into space when sent away box not true shape any shape good—"

"Wait, wait. You took the shape of the box they encased you in, correct? You have no true shape? You can look like anything? How about—a frog?"

She reared back as the wriggling mass sucked in its tentacles, wriggled some more, squished and squashed itself, and became a frog the size of a cat. It changed in an eyeblink, but never once did it stop talking.

" . . . make wizards do what wizards want do Sages say not good make anyone do what do have to send away cannot destroy because made by all for all . . . "

Greensleeves started again as a ghost materialized by her side: Chaney, white and dessicated as a corpse in the rushlight. The woman put out her hand—Greensleeves swore the light shone through it—and touched the not-frog on the head. The bulgy spotted eyes neither blinked nor retracted, as a real frog's would.

"Child of the Sages," said the druid, "say that last again."

" . . . not good to make anyone do anything anyone wants so I must go but cannot be destroyed because made by all . . . "

"Ahhhh!!!" breathed the druid, and Greensleeves

feared she was suffering another attack. But it was only wonder and awe that moved the druid. "You see, child? This is a construct of the Sages of Lat-Nam! They—"

"The who?"

"Oh, dear. It's been so long. The Sages of Lat-Nam. An ancient college of magic users, founded by Drafna, dedicated to codifying magic, but also to understanding the even more ancient devices left from times untold—*and* to stopping the brothers, Ura and Mishra! I'll tell you more later, but there isn't much. The Sages were the largest conclave of wizards ever convened, and they worked for—decades, it's thought. They sought to harness magic and fabricated many, many wonderful and deadly gadgets. Most were destroyed when Urza and Mishra found them in the Brothers' War. But never mind that.

"This," she patted the artifact, which kept on talking, "is one of their constructs! And if I'm hearing it aright, *it* had the power to compel one wizard to obey another! I don't know if it was designed to be a controlling device, a punishment the conclave could use to bind other wizards, or perhaps some linking device so they might pool their power. But take note: it says it couldn't be destroyed because it was too powerful, made by so many wizards working together. So they had to send it away."

Dawning awareness struck Greensleeves, no longer sleepy, and she sat bolt upright. "You mean—"

"This bauble," Chaney concluded, "is the single most powerful artifact in all of history."

Mind awhirl, Greensleeves fought to fathom the ramifications. Gull and Rakel had left their bedroll to study the artifact.

"It was too powerful," the young woman panted, "because it can control—any wizard . . . "

"And we control it!" Gull interrupted.

"What?" asked the crowd.

"Don't you see?" The woodcutter stood tall and

banged his head on the low stone ceiling, but didn't notice. "Don't you see? It was too dangerous to keep around, because a wizard can use this to compel other wizards to do their bidding! As wizards compel pawns now. It's the answer to our prayers! With this—thing—we can finally catch those rampaging wizards and strip them of their power. It's the key the army needs to succeed."

It was almost silent as people absorbed this fact. Almost, because the frog blathered on in a whisper.

"It can't be that simple," muttered Greensleeves. "Nothing's simple in magic-making."

Rakel said, "Gull, I thought you hated magic!"

"I do!" protested the woodcutter. "But this ends the careers of those who abuse it! Finally, some *good* magic!"

"Or bad," croaked Chaney. She leaned on the table with her good hand and stared deep into the frog's eyes. "So powerful a device will be a magnet for every magic user in this sphere. You'll be plagued every day with someone out to steal it."

Rakel gasped. "Yes! *That* was the thing Karli sought when she attacked your camp. She tossed all the other artifacts aside without studying them, only to pick this one up. But as soon as she grasped it, it turned intangible, like a ghost image, and fell through her fingers. She cried when she had to leave it and flee."

"Why didn't you tell us that earlier?" asked Greensleeves.

"Eh? Oh." Because, back then, Rakel had been an enemy to them. "I forgot."

"Never mind," said Gull. "Greenie, what say you? Can you and Chaney figure out exactly how to use this babbling thing against wizards?"

"I—I don't know. It's all so new, so sudden. Chaney?"

The old druid mused, "Given time, we can figure out anything. But—"

"We need to learn how to use it," said Gull, "and soon. Before some other wizard comes and takes it and uses it to control *us*."

CHAPTER

9

"FOR THE LOVE OF LADY EVANGELA, WILL YOU get that handle *up*?"

Gull took a new grip on his axe haft and held it sideways across his chest. "I don't see—"

He flinched as Rakel's sword blade flew at his face. With a wrench and twist, he batted the short blade upward, but the warrior woman skipped back, whipped the blade underneath, and thumped it against his chest. She'd encased the tip in birch bark, but still he grunted.

The two practiced in a clearing remote from Chaney's cave. Here winter's bite was more intense, their breath frosting in the air, their feet shuffling over fallen leaves.

"You're slow." But she puffed herself. Working on the farm and vineyards had kept her in good shape, but for farmwork, not fighting. Her legs felt like lead, her arms and stomach soft. But she felt tingles of the old strength, the old power returning. Now she must hone her body as she'd honed her sword.

Exasperated, Gull lowered his axe. "I never claimed

to be a hero from some legend that slays hydras and medusas before breakfast! I'm a woodcutter, by the Eternals! Trees don't dodge when you slash at them!"

Staring straight into his eyes, Rakel snapped up her sword to lunge again, but this time he knocked the blade down. Following, he snapped the axe handle at her face, and she had to duck. But she squatted, dropped her left hand to the ground, snaked her blade behind his outthrust leg. "You're hamstrung. By the teeth of the gods—in one hour, I've killed you a dozen times, crippled you twice that. And I wasn't even counted a master swordsman in Benalia, just average."

Thoroughly disgusted, Gull dropped his axe, grabbed her by both arms, and threw her over his head. She landed on her back, but flipped over with one hand, ready to attack again. He asked her, "Can you tell me why, please, you're so hot about training me? I was doing perfectly well—"

"Oh, Gull. Can't you see? You've been lucky so far, going up against blue barbarians and trolls and pig-men, or whatever they were, but a real fighter will drop you in pieces on the ground before you can lift that plowshare!"

Gull frowned. She hadn't answered his question, but he let it be. She had more secrets than a box of boxes. He shook his axe. "I've wielded this axe since I forged it at twelve. I won't put it aside for some cheese slicer like yours. I've survived so far—I've replaced the damned handle six times because swordsmen keep whittling it!"

Rakel couldn't hide a slow smile. Dropping her sword, she came close, pressed a hip against him. "Well, as long as no one whittles down your other weapon, you'll be fine."

Scoffing and laughing at the same time, Gull dropped his axe and squeezed her so tight she squealed. Yet he wondered why her moods changed like summer skies: happy one moment, crying the next. And why she wouldn't tell him.

Then his arms were full of melting woman, and he forgot everything else.

*   *   *

A winding horn fetched the two fighters back to camp.

The ragtag army had finally reached the plateau. Bardo's scouts led them straggling to a clearing in the forest where the oaks were stunted, no more than thirty feet high, and soon had then hewn down. Everyone walked or rode or led pack animals, for one of Gull's first rules was no wagons. Soldiers were loaded with packs on their backs and spears across their shoulders. Wives and husbands were laden with sacks of food and camp gear. Samite healers carried satchels of unguents and bandages and herbs. Liko wore his long strapped-on club and toted another. Stiggur drove his clanking whirring clockwork beast, hung with packs and tents and cooking gear and spare weapons and oddments, topped with children like a pier with gulls. Helki and Holleb, tripped like horses on parade, armor and gear strapped across their glossy roan hides. Tybalt and the three other students of magic dragged a travois heaped with battered boxes and chests and bags full of magic whatnots and junk. Cooks with burn-scarred hands carried cornmeal in the folds of their shirts. At least one drunk hung askew on a mule. The goblin Egg Sucker was perched in a nest above the clockwork beast's tail, asleep. A mad Muronian dervish walked with bare feet, arguing with himself. There were assorted dogs, half-wild, three red-brown cows on tethers, chickens in upside-down bundles. Six cartographers and librarians hauled a travois laden with scrying tubes on tripods, leather rolls of maps, and sheaves of scrolls and parchments wrapped in oilskin. And on the perimeter rode the rest of Bardo's scouts.

This motley mob ambled into the clearing, dropped their bundles, erected tents, lifted their skirts or unbuttoned their trousers to relieve themselves, dug firepits, hewed down trees for firewood, butchered game bagged on the trail, explored the woods or played pranks on their friends, and bustled with the hundred other tasks the army needed to survive another day.

Rakel stood on a low rise, gloved hands on leather-clad hips, and shook her head in disgust. She said to Gull, "What a shameless rotten lousy bunch of scarecrows! A *real* army would eat them alive and leave nothing but their screams!"

Miffed, Gull defended his charges. "We did all right against Karli's flying-carpet folk and those blue riders."

"What?" Rakel stared as if he drooled. "You lost ten fighters: a *third* of your force! That's a defeat no matter how you tot it up! Another *victory* like that, you won't have a lame dog to command!"

"Fine, you teach 'em! That's what we agreed, isn't it?" Actually, he wasn't sure what they'd agreed, except she claimed she'd reorganize his army into a potent fighting force. It suited him: he couldn't organize a wood detail. "Give 'em time to settle in, then we'll—"

"No. There isn't time. That green slimy thing is a trouble magnet, and any second the sky could drop on your heads. We wouldn't have enough left to bury the bodies. No. We start now. Right—now."

Gull only waved a hand.

Rakel shifted her sword at her belt, her hero's dagger on the other hip, and strode down to meet the army.

Her army.

Rakel ordered the trumpeter to blow a blast on her ram's horn, a good loud one. *Ta-roo, ta-ta-tarooooo!* Rakel cupped her hands and hollered, "Gather round, everyone, and be quick about it!"

Gull had to admit no one came running smartly. People looked, shrugged, put down their tasks, ambled over. The warrior woman stood on a cook's box. The crowd whispered, talked, joked, wondered what was transpiring. One female soldier with a long blond braid called, "Who are you? I don't remember hiring any dancing girls!"

The jest drew guffaws until Rakel leveled a gloved finger at the joker. "You'll find out, once you shut up.

For now, you're docked half a day's wages for wasting our time. Where's the clerk? What's your name? Donahue? Well, now you're quartermaster because that's what an army calls its head clerk. Mark that woman's name. Because from this moment forward, you're an army and I'm its commander!"

People whispered, poked one another. One woman asked, "What's that make Gull?"

For answer, the woodcutter stood beside Rakel, though not on her cook box. He was tall enough for everyone to see. "I'm commander in chief, or general, or whatever she calls me. The figurehead, anyway. Rakel will be in immediate command. She's better at it. I'll watch for now."

"Hey!" said the big joker, her yellow braid wagging. "What makes her so special? *I* could do a better job! Any of us could!"

For answer, Rakel hopped off the box. The crowd let her pass to stand before the blond woman, a full head taller than Rakel, big-bosomed, wide as a barn door across the shoulders. Her leather armor was scarred in a dozen spots, as were her bare arms. With her ragged black hair and neat black leathers, Rakel looked like a child before this amazon. She told the joker, "I'm in charge because I'm the best fighter in this army. I can lick any one of you bastards. Care to try?"

The big woman stepped back. Wary, she reached across, laid a hand on the pommel of the huge sword by her side—

—and Rakel exploded into action.

Dipping, whirling, her booted foot swung around waist-high and kicked the woman's elbow so hard she half spun. Roaring in pain and sudden rage, the joker lashed out with her other hand. Rakel ducked underneath, shot upward so her shoulder rammed the woman's elbow from below, crippling that one also. Rakel's fingers rapped the joker in the throat, stifling a cry. Gagging, she fell back, and Rakel whacked her knee with a fist to help her fall. She crashed on her back—

But another man, a friend, ripped his sword from

its sheath. Shouting, he slashed overhand at Rakel—

—until Rakel's sword flashed and they struck with a tremendous *clang*. Hands numb, the attacker fumbled his sword. Rakel stepped inside his weak defense, smashed the heel of her hand under his chin. His jaw clacked shut. Rakel knocked him back four feet with a horrendous slam to the breadbasket that made the crowd groan.

Both fighters down, Rakel grabbed the joker's arm and wrenched it backward until she howled. The warrior jerked as if lifting a bale of hay and slammed the blond alongside her male friend. When their vision cleared, both soldiers were sighting down the length of her shining blade.

"Now," she puffed, "I say I'm commander of this army. Any more arguments?"

The two shook their heads, careful to move nothing else.

"Right then. Get up. We've work to do." She sheathed her sword and raised her voice. "I want every fighter, armed with his or her choice of weapons to assemble here in one hour! And when that horn blows, you come *running*! Understand?"

There were mutters of agreement, murmurs. "Yes." "Aye aye." "Sure."

She raised her voice higher. "When I ask a question, I want to hear 'Yes, Commander!' loud and clear! Is *that* understood?"

"Yes, Commander!" shouted a dozen folk.

"What?"

"YES, COMMANDER!" shouted half a hundred.

"Good! One hour! And come *running*! The last to fall in works for free today!"

This time when she turned, the crowd jumped back. The two on the ground were helped up by friends. People noted that, for all they'd been abused, they had neither bruises nor breaks.

Rakel caught up with Gull. "Come. We'll eat dinner."

"Yes, Commander!" the woodcutter shouted.

She glared and he grinned, but his grin faded. "Uh, surely. This way, uh, Rakel. Commander . . ."

*   *   *

After the midday meal, Rakel sounded the horn, and soldiers ran pell-mell. Camp followers, male and female, came to see the new commander at work.

Rakel wasted no time. She counted nineteen soldiers, eight female, plus four of the desert cavalry who'd been captured in the battle of the taiga. Though they spoke no common language, they made their wishes known with sign language. Everyone assumed they were members of the army now and accepted them as such. If any of Gull's people held ill will against the soldiers for the attack, they had yet to act on it.

Rakel paired the soldiers off at random, three pairs at a time, and had them fight with their chosen weapons, warning them not to shed blood. Beside her stood a clerk, borrowed from Donahue, a young woman named Frida, with a quill and parchment and inkpot. With a practiced eye, the new commander watched the fighting, studied strengths and weaknesses, saw where they excelled and what they tried to hide. After each battle, she got the fighters' names, rated them on a scale, gave them a rest, and called up two more. Gull stood behind the whole time, and watched and learned. By midafternoon, she'd paired winners against winners and rated everyone from the rawest recruit with delusions of grandeur to the oldest toughest smartest veteran. Yet even these she was able to teach a few tricks, which gained her a grudging respect.

Well before sunset, she called off the fighting, and folks eased up with a groan. They groaned again as Rakel took on the next responsibility.

More than half the soldiers had camp followers: wives, husbands, children from those in swaddling clothes to teenagers. Many were artisans, selling their goods and services to the army: blacksmiths, cooks, leatherworkers, tinkers. Some men paired up as blanket mates, and the big blond joker had not one but two wives living in her tent. Some fighters were plain mercenaries after loot, some were boys and girls who had run away from dull farms, many were displaced families pushed out by wars or wizards or plagues or harsh rulers. Rakel didn't care why anyone had joined the army, except to know they came freely. She told Gull, "Volunteers can't complain about orders they dislike, because they've no one to blame but themselves."

And her next orders were to tear the camp apart and reset it.

Men and women had set up tents any way they chose, willy-nilly, to catch the sun or face the dawn or front to a neighbor or whatever. Cooking fires were everywhere, as were dungheaps and trash heaps and refuse. Rakel undid all that.

She walked around jerking up tent pegs and kicking aside bundles, then borrowed a rope from the horse wrangler. Putting her clerk Frida at the other end, she stretched it taut and drew a line in the leaves and dirt and low bushes of the clearing. All tents were to be erected along that line, one pace apart, and not any pace either, but a military pace, thirty inches. With new groans, but grudging admiration, the camp reset their tents.

There was more. Exactly one hundred paces away from the last row, in the woods, would be latrines. They were to be dug just so, with a shovel and dirt to throw over waste. Anyone caught not using the latrines, squatting in the bushes or behind a tree, would be draped bare-arsed over a pile of cordwood and caned until their buttocks bled, no exceptions for man, woman, child, soldier, camp follower, or officer.

They were allowed one hour for supper. Everyone had settled down to rest and gossip and knead their aches and relax at the end of the day, when the horn sounded again. People groaned, but ran. The commander's clerk, Frida, read out the new assignment of officers.

Not counting the scouts and cavalry (cavalry? they wondered), there were to be three companies: red, blue, and green. Captain Varrius would head the Red Company, Captain Neith the Blue, and Captain

Ordando the Green. Ordando was more surprised than anyone, for she was the big blond-braided joker Rakel had trounced that morning. When Rakel offered her congratulations, Ordando could only stammer like a schoolgirl at a dance.

Rakel had more announcements. Until uniforms were more uniform, each soldier was to wear a colored cockade on his or her hat. She expected the cockades to be in place at assembly (assembly?) at dawn tomorrow.

She finished by telling them she was proud of her fighters, that they showed great promise, but the whole army had far to go to be up to snuff. Lights out was in one hour, and no talking after that. Her clerk read the picket watches, not one picket, as Gull had put out, but four on overlapping routes. Dazed, folks crawled off to their tents, except for one crowd that gathered around a fire to sip brandy and speculate on their new commander and their future in the army. An hour later, they found her word was good, for she walked up with a brimming bucket of water and dashed it on their fire, smothering them with hot ashes and dirty steam.

Rakel finished her night by going over tomorrow's orders with her clerk, then dismissing the exhausted girl. On silent feet, she patrolled the perimeter of the camp, startling at least two guards. She caught a young couple writhing in the bushes, tore them apart, and hurled the boy ten feet to land on his naked rump. They scampered for their parents' tents. She caught a woman lifting her skirts. The woman wailed that it was too far to walk to the latrines, and too dark, but Rakel gave her a stripe where it hurt with the flat of her sword, then watched the woman scurry off limping.

Finally, when night was darkest, she stumbled up the slope to her own tent. Before it sat Gull, honing his axe with a stone while watching the winter stars wheel across the sky.

"You're amazing, Rakel," he whispered. "You've accomplished more in one day than I've done in six months."

She didn't stop, only shucked her baldric and crawled into her bedroll, laying her weapons within handy reach. "I've accomplished nothing. But I will."

Then she was asleep, out cold as only a seasoned soldier can be, leaving Gull to wonder what it was that drove her so.

Then he crawled inside and lay beside her, and slept himself.

The next days were the same: orders coming so fast and furious it put everyone's head aspin. But Rakel never let up; in fact, as the army grew more efficient, she tightened the strictures even more, until soldiers asked permission before spitting.

The three companies—Green, Red, and Blue—were small, only six or seven in each, but Rakel assured they would expand in time. (How, no one could see, but they didn't argue.) She formed ranks within each company, putting the most veteran fighters on the outside and staggering the raw recruits in the middle, so the veterans might keep them from running in battle. She did recruit right away, offering any camp boy or girl over thirteen a cadetship at half-pay, and got six right off. Furthermore, she put all of the adult camp followers on half-pay, arguing they helped sustain the army and deserved to be recompensed, endearing her to everyone.

Rakel changed the fighting tactics. Recalling how they'd been butchered by the cavalry charge in the taiga, her first act was to make every soldier a lancer. Poles were cut in the forest, and the army's two blacksmiths were given old swords and scrap iron to reshape. To Rakel's specifications, they fashioned detachable spear heads to fit on poles. Every soldier was to carry a pole when traveling, hanging gear on them if necessary. When called to combat, they were to attach the heads and create a wall of tilted spears, butts planted firmly against the ground. No horse, she assured them, no matter how well trained, would breach such a line of steel. Then she demonstrated by driving a warhorse at the line. The horse locked all four feet, and Rakel pitched headlong from the saddle to slam on the turf. To her amazement, and everyone else's, a score of fighters ran to help her up. Everyone laughed, and the cement in the army bonded tighter than ever.

There was more. Every fighter must carry either a short or longbow. Crossbows she deemed too slow and heavy and consigned them to a bonfire. All soldiers must wield a shield unless they could demonstrate they were more effective without, such as the axemen, and these were paired with partners to protect them as they clove through imaginary enemies. Simple horn signals for advance, retreat, charge, and more were created and memorized and tested in hours and hours of drill. When the companies were up to snuff, Rakel set them drilling and training against one another, and the competition and jibes and banter pushed men and women to excel more than ever.

Culling through the fifty or so horses in camp, regardless of whom they belonged to, she selected several and created a cavalry. Into it went the four desert cavalry riders, three men and a woman, who were slowly learning the local language, their spokesman a squint-eyed man named Rabi. For the rest, Rakel mounted two men and one woman who proved they could ride well, and outfitted them with boots and sabers. For more, she stole away two of Bardo's scouts, Channa and Givon, and gave Bardo the service of Holleb, the male centaur, intead. Helki, his centaur wife, was made captain of cavalry. Sloppily sentimental as ever, Helki ran crying to Gull that she was separated from her lover, but Gull refused to countermand Rakel's orders. The cavalry were given yellow cockades and armbands, and they chose to wear them long so they fluttered in their own wind. Accustomed to military discipline, Helki bit her lip and drilled her small troop all day and half the night, until they could charge and wheel as tightly as a flock of starlings.

Bardo and his remaining four scouts, and now Holleb, were given no special uniform, for they were to blend in with the forest. Instead, Rakel ordered them to embroider black feathers on either shoulder of their clothes; the sign of the raven, they were told. In fact, she only wanted them to have something special to show off, for the disparate units of the army had fallen into friendly rivalries that Rakel knew only encouraged unity.

As further incentive, she created a pay scale based on shares of loot. Gull had simply let loot be divvied up equally—when there was any. Rakel changed that. Recruits received a share a day; veterans two or three, depending on years of service; captains five shares; the commander ten; and Gull, as general, fifteen. When Gull protested he didn't need that much, Rakel explained. Soldiers were by nature lazy and needed goals, even modest ones. If a soldier drew the same pay as a sergeant or captain, there was little incentive to advance, to campaign to be appointed an officer. Unused to anything military, Gull had to agree, because soldiers did come forward offering hitherto unmentioned skills. Yet no one complained that all this extravagant "pay" existed mostly on paper, for the threadbare army often went months without seeing real coins.

Rakel went further. She explained to Donahue, now the quartermaster, and to Gull, that there were two aspects to war: logistics and tactics. Tactics involved fighting: how to find the enemy, how to engage and destroy it, how to follow up. Logistics covered the thousand tasks required to refit an army so it *could* fight, not lack for food or tents or arrows or candles. In his glory with numbers to juggle, Donahue hired three more camp followers who could write and cipher to track supplies. He also assigned hunting and foraging details to bring in game and mast.

By the end of one week, the camp was neat as a pin, clean and healthy and brimming with food and camaraderie. People talked of nothing but Rakel's ideas and skills and abilities, and new ideas they could propose. They vowed they'd never seen anything like it, how she was a wonder-worker.

Yet Gull, holding her in their blankets at night, knew how frail and solemn this woman could be. Sometimes she cried, for no reason he could discern, refusing to give him answer or clue.

Except once. Spent with exhaustion, Rakel asked him how many days until the Mist Moon was full.

"Why do you care?" he asked. "Is there some appointment you needs keep? Or is this a private goal, to whip the army into shape by a certain date?"

"Just tell me," she said, sighing. "How many?"

Gull peeked out the tent flap, counted on his fingers. "Perhaps . . . eight days. Or seven. *Why?*"

But she only rolled over, back to him, and sobbed quietly before drifting off.

Gull was left to walk the silent camp, and stare at the moon, and ponder at the strangeness of women.

Having spruced up the soldiers and camp and camp followers, Rakel moved outward. Guards herded every person in camp before a phalanx of clerks who noted their name and job. This census yielded some astonishing results.

For one thing, there were five half-wild orphans in camp. Unbeknowst to anybody, these children had infiltrated the army from villages and towns and formed their own clan. They lived half by stealing and half by helping at needed tasks: toting firewood and water, tending fires, earning a dish of food here and a coin there. Rakel put an end to that. The two smallest children were given to families who requested them. Two more were assigned to the cooks' crew. The oldest, the leader, a girl not yet ten by the name of Dela, was assigned to help Stiggur and his clockwork beast.

For even the clockwork beast was put to work. Stiggur's tall strange animal had been used haphazardly to carry supplies, like some giant mule. It was hung like a moving bazaar with iron cauldrons and nets of onions and spare weapons and chests and sacks of clothes and drying laundry and other junk.

Stiggur took pride in bearing the load, for the clock-work contraption never balked or slowed. But Rakel didn't like it. She asserted the beast was too valuable as a war machine to serve as a clothes rack. Blacksmiths and carpenters were called in to refit it. Modeled after a war elephant, Rakel ordered a plat-form built atop the beast's neck and back. It protected the driver from arrows and allowed for a half dozen archers. Stiggur, bursting with ideas, proposed mount-ing a ballista, a giant crossbow, over the beast's rump. The boy reckoned that, considering the spinning gears and pulleys within the beast's frame, it would be sim-ple to work up a strap and hook, then add another pul-ley to draw the heavy bowstring to full cock.

Rakel went one better, and assigned Liko to the beast squad, as it came to be called. If a ballista were built, the giant could simply yank back the rope. In the meantime, Liko was trained to work in tandem with the beast. He was to fight along its right side, thus pro-tecting his good left arm and leaving his right club-arm swinging free. Stiggur and Liko trained faithfully, a wooden horse and wooden-headed giant, both clumsy as walking trees, but Rakel didn't care. She figured just the sight of a giant wooden horse and a two-headed giant would shatter any line of soldiers. Liko was also fitted with a leather smock of dried bullhides after the three oxen were butchered. Tests showed the hides would turn most arrows, and possibly save his life.

Moving through the camp, Rakel checked on other groups. Some functioned so well Rakel did no more than inspect and approve. The Samite healers, in blue robes and white hats, under the woman Amma, knew their trade and could handle any wounds or disasters with a combination of gentle attention, herbs, knowl-edge, magic, and prayer. Itinerant healers, they had joined the army, Amma explained, because they agreed with its mission.

So too had the cartographers and librarians, under a serious young woman named Kamee. Invited by Gull, and under the army's protection, they were often absent for days, surveying, investigating ruins and caves and towers, drawing charts, interviewing shepherds and crofters, sifting details of the folklore and geography of the land. As far as anyone knew, they were fashioning the first maps and histories ever made of this continent, searching for clues to the lost homelands of so many of the army members.

Now, however, the librarians were off with Greensleeves, collecting stories by the dozens, along with Tybalt and his magic students. Rakel mentally assigned them to Greensleeves's command and forgot about them.

The cooks, under the direct control of the quartermaster, prospered by the assignment of extra help and the streamlining of the hunting and gathering. Rakel only insisted the campfires and butchering and cooking be neat and orderly.

Everyone worked, carried a weapon, or contributed somehow, and finally Rakel got down to the dregs. Her census had exposed one old man who was simply a lush, drunk all the time on bought or begged liquor. Tied to a tree and doused with water, he refused to stay sober, so he was finally marched before ancient Chaney, who conjured him to a distant city where wine was popular. The sole surviving Muronian dervish was quieted long enough to learn that his "occupation"— shrieking about the end of the world, damning sinners, lamenting their lack of faith and hope, promising the army would perish in horror and holocaust—was not work. He was warned to find a job or else await the final cataclysms elsewhere. He settled for picking up fagots in the woods while muttering dire predictions.

Left to the last, because he was so good at skulking and shirking, was Egg Sucker, the gray-green goblin who lived by thieving. Rakel wanted Chaney to banish him to another plane, but this time, Gull interceded. Egg Sucker, he argued, was their "good luck mascot." He'd been with them since the first raid on White Ridge, was now the only survivor of his clan, and deserved a chance to seek his homeland. Relenting,

Rakel "assigned" him to the scouts, which meant he skulked in the woods by day, raiding bird's nests and anthills. By night, he slept atop the clockwork beast's tail in a nest of his own making.

The only ones who suffered were the camp dogs. Rakel argued that they bit the children, stole food from the kitchen, shit everywhere, and kept folk awake with their nighttime fighting. Since no one could train them as war dogs, they were nothing but trouble. People were shocked when Rakel had them rounded up, slaughtered, and stewed, but the larger lesson was clear: everyone contributed who wanted to stray.

The lesson was reinforced one day when Rakel ordered everyone in camp—everyone—to lay their possessions on their cloaks for inspection. Merciless, she ordered a bonfire built, then picked through peoples' goods and hurled into the flames anything that was "excess baggage." Tattered clothing, ragged blankets, spare tools, worn boots, trinkets, even one child's doll (she'd owned two) were burned. This army, she announced, would move fast by carrying nothing extra.

Throughout the reorganization, Gull followed and watched in awe. He did his share: soothing hurt feelings, dispensing advice, smoothing things over, making decisions when Rakel was busy. He even apologized to the guards he'd accused of sleeping on duty when Greensleeves disappeared. Rakel said that was fine: a general should be a fatherly figure with human flaws, while the commander could be the cold-blooded ball-busting machine that pushed soldiers to the grindstone to polish and toughen them.

But mostly Gull was amazed at his new freedom. Without nitpicking details to steal his days and plague his dreams, he actually had time to think of their larger mission. He could plan their next move, whatever it might be, once he'd talked to Greensleeves and Rakel and Chaney.

And Lily.

CHAPTER
10

GULL FOUND A CROWD SETTLED INTO CHANEY'S hollow before the hill. Besides his sister, Lily, and the druid, all the librarians were gathered. There were four of them, led by Kamee, an older woman of severe lines, her blond hair shining with silver. The librarians dressed much alike, in plain jackets of solid colors with many pockets for quills, inkpots, rolls of parchment and vellum, and baggy skirts or breeches. Their fingers were delicate, strong, and inkstained.

Greensleeves greeted her brother with a hug, and Gull was surprised to learn he'd been gone—no more than a half-mile away—for days.

He noticed something else new, too. She'd always worn the same ragged green shawl, knitted by their mother for Greensleeves's twelfth birthday. But now it was studded with tiny objects of all shapes and sizes. Some he recognized: a periwinkle shell, a chunk of dried oyster mushroom, a pine seed, a twist of vine, a wisp of gray horsetail, a flitch of cornhusk, a spiderweb. Other things he wondered how she'd gotten: a bear's tooth, a lion's claw, a pin shaped like a dagger, a pearl, a green-blue gemstone. Lifting a tattered corner, he asked, "What's—"

"Oh." She shook her brown, twisted locks, peeking at her shoulders. "This is my catalogue."

"Your cata—"

"My grimoire. My book of magic. Every wizard needs one in the beginning, Chaney says. Remember Towser carried a little book chained to his belt? And Dacian, the brown wizard, had a bag at her shoulder? Well, these help me recall my catalogue of beasts and spells. See, this is a mushroom for the fungusaur. And this pin——" She stopped, following his gaze.

Walking away, alone, into the winter forest, went Lily.

Greensleeves led her brother to the crowd. Chaney kept her place on the sunning rock, but she shared it with the green brain, today looking like a box turtle. Gathered around it were the four librarians, consulting in whispers, listening and scribbling to the never-ending stream of babble from the living artifact.

"How can you stand to listen to that thing?" Gull asked. "I'd go mad."

"We all would," Greensleeves agreed. "We take turns, then move off to discuss what we've heard. Then we form questions to see if we can steer it to a specific topic. But it's hard. It has a mind like a parrot's. It can tell you what it's seen and heard, but can't tell you what it means. We—"

Gull held up a two-fingered hand to stop her. "Have you got anything sensible from it yet? Anything we can use?"

Greensleeves bit her lower lip. "Well . . . part of its power is to change shape, perhaps so someone could hide it. It had been stuffed into a stone box for so long it took that shape. Remember how the box looked banded and buckled? Those were old straps around the box, Chaney thinks. And it has some sense of its audience, because it won't perform for some wizards. It stayed locked for Towser, and turned ghostly so Karli couldn't steal it. But is that because it *likes* us?

We learned the Sages of Lat-Nam fought over who should possess it. At one point, someone stole it and ran off into a desert and was eaten by vultures. But we don't know who. But finally, the conclave of Sages, we think, enclosed it in the pink box and sent into the heavens."

"What? How?"

"We don't know. It was dark in the box, it says, but it went past the sky. I never thought of the sky having a ceiling, but it must. It was out amongst the stars, where it's cold, or not cold, just . . . empty?" She shrugged.

"But how do you use it to control other wizards? Do you just point it at them and say, 'I command such and so'? Or have it turn into chains and shackle somebody?"

Another shrug. "We haven't discovered that yet. We're hoping it will tell us."

Gull shook his head. "I'm glad you're working on it and not me. Have you learned any new tricks? Has Chaney taught you how to pull a rabbit from your sleeve yet? Or turn chalk into cheese? Or how to blast people with hellfire so they let go of your arm?"

His sister frowned at him, but she was contrite, too. "I know. You're still smarting because I gave you that—lightning blast. But that was an accident, and you shouldn't go grabbing people's arms. And anyway, magic can do good, too. I was telling Chaney all about you, how you used to take care of me—"

"Used to?"

"Don't interrupt. And how you were the village woodcutter, and the strongest man in the village, but got a bad knee—"

"Why should she care?"

"Hush! *Because* she can *heal your knee*!"

Gull piffed. "Not bloody likely. I got this three years ago. If it hasn't healed by now—"

Greensleeves didn't argue, just took his hand and led him around the librarians and the thing on the rock. "She fixed my broken ankle overnight. And

ankles are trickier to set than knees: they've many
more bones, and smaller. So just listen. Chaney?"

The old druid opened her eyes slowly, like a cow,
and took a moment to focus. She drew a shaky breath.
Gull suppressed a shudder. This woman was more
dead than alive, and without magic would have been
worm food—what? Years ago? Decades?

But her tone was cheery. "Ah, yes. Big brother the
woodcutter. Greensleeves told me about you."

Gull felt like a boy again. Chaney was so old a red-
wood would feel like a seed.

"She mentioned your hand. May I see?"

My knee, Gull corrected mentally, but he gave his
maimed hand into her one good one. His three fingers
were severed clean at the palm: when the fingers had
been smashed by that jumping tree stump, his
mother, Bittersweet, had lopped them off cleanly at
the joints with a paring knife before folding over the
skin, which had hardened into white scar tissue that
wouldn't tan. Gull had stopped being self-conscious
about his deformity years ago. Still, it gave his stomach a queer feeling to see the druid pore over it so. As
if the horrendous pain of the wound would come back
at her snake-dry touch.

The old woman murmured, "Easy enough if you
know how. Yes, I can encourage them to grow back,
though it will—"

Gull involuntarily snatched his hand back. "Grow
back? Are you daft? You can't make—"

The old woman smiled her lopsided smile. One
rheumy eye fixed on him, the other squinting. They
were so clear a blue they had almost no color, Gull
noticed. "No, I can't make them grow back. But you
can. With my help. Never heard of such a thing? A
salamander can grow back a tail, can't she?"

Gull kneaded his stumpy hand. "Of course. But a
man's not a salamander."

A lopsided shrug. "True, only cousins. Still, if you
wish—"

Greensleeves interjected quietly, "Perhaps you

could address his knee, Chaney. My brother's, uh, skittish around magic."

Like a stupid horse, Gull thought. But he presented his bad leg. It looked normal enough. But once broken, by a tree again, it had healed stiff and wouldn't bend very far backward or forward. It also ached in bad weather and tired easily.

Again the snake-cool hand touched his brown skin, making him shudder. The druid closed her eyes to better feel, digging her hand, surprisingly strong, deep into the muscle. "Ah, yes. Broken by a tree. A black oak with a lightning-stricken top, which put it out of balance and made it jump." She chuckled at the astonishment written on his face. "This could be made almost good as new. The bones have grown horns deep inside. We need to dissolve them, then relax the tendons . . ."

Whispering, she chanted something simple, repetitive, in some ancient tongue. Gull waited, patiently, then impatiently when it droned on and on. He hadn't come here after mumbo-jumbo, he'd come to talk to his sister. And Lily . . .

A wave of fatigue suddenly washed over him, and he swayed, almost fell. Chaney stopped her chanting and nodded. Greensleeves looked puzzled, "Are you all right, brother?"

Gull put a hand to his head, swayed more, had to sit down. "No, I'm—weak." A flitter of panic stirred. This felt like the same deadly weakness that killed so many of his family.

"Normal," rasped Chaney, "perfectly normal. You must surrender strength throughout your body to heal what's broken. Eat hearty and sleep, and you'll be fine."

Gull didn't believe a word of it. Gods, how he hated magic and all its filthy dealings! He staggered upright, found his bad knee as shaky as ever, but burning deep inside. "No. I'm fine now. I'll go see . . . Lily."

He stumbled off after her. The two druids watched him go. Greensleeves asked, "Will he be all right?"

Chaney nodded. "Yes, both in the head and the body."

"Head?"

"Aye. He'll have healed a rift between magic and his beliefs. But now, back to work. Tell me, how would you encourage a tree to hasten its growth?"

Limping worse than ever, and aching with weariness, Gull caught up to Lily. She shuffled along through yellow-brown leaves of oak and beech. She still wore the hard-traveled winter gown and jacket, embroidered with yellow and blue and red flowers, and a white cloak with edges embroidered with more flowers, but sensible oxhide shoes. A white hood covered her dark curls.

At Gull's approached, she stiffened.

"Uh, how are you, Lily?"

"I'm ignored," she sulked. Dark eyes flashed under long lashes. She wore her hood up, and Gull had to stoop to peer into her face. "Chaney has no time to teach me, Greensleeves is busy with her, the students study the green brain, the librarians scribble, you train by day and arm wrestle your amazon by night, and I . . . do nothing."

"I, uh, I thought you were practicing magic. Learning to fly."

"Do you see me flying?" She waved her hands at the ground. "Conjuring anything? Shifting? I may never be able to truly fly, or conjure a fig. Chaney took a minute to scry me, but only said my and Greensleeves's magics are different. Greensleeves taps nature magic, and I—tap little. Chaney thinks I use sky magic, or cloud, or mist, or sun magic. That's why it's so hard to grasp, she says. A tree is solid and chock-full of magic, but sunshine spilling over clover is scattershot, just dribs and drabs. And I'm down here and the sky is up there, and how am I to tap that? Make a pilgrimage to some mountaintop? Just when I think I'm ready for a breakthrough, I piffle away the mana. I needs be a honeybee, collecting acres of mana like nectar for a dollop of honey. I—"

She stopped abruptly, for she detested whining, especially her own. "Chaney calls me Lily the White. Can you imagine? The symbol of purity for a bastard and whore! 'White' suits me no more than 'Lily.'"

Gull realized yet again he didn't know if she had another name, had never asked.

The woodcutter rubbed his aching, burning knee. He was bone weary and ravenously hungry. "I never thought of you as a whore, Lily, not even when you worked for Towser. Life is hard, and you were just surviving, as was I. I made a sacred vow to slaughter wizards and ended up working for one. If anything, you were more honest than I. And lilies are beautiful and pure, no matter where they spring from, even a manure pile. I know you're pure of heart—"

"Hush." She stepped close, put a finger on his lips to quiet him. But when he reached for her hand, she backed away.

Despite her self-imposed gloom, his kind words cheered her. But compliments wouldn't solve her problem. She changed the subject. "How are you, Gull? How does your man-eater treat you? She has more hair on her chest than you, I bet."

Gull ignored the teasing. "Rakel's rife with some secret sorrow. She's dying inside, I think, desperately lonely. It's not lovemaking or even love she wants, just—contact, affection. You were that way once; you needed me. Then you found magic . . . "

Lily looked away, but Gull saw tears fall from her lashes. He reached out his hands, and this time she slid into his arms, weeping silently against his chest. "I just don't know what to do, Gull. I've got magic inside me, but it doesn't work right. As if I'm an improper vessel, old and cracked, and it leaks out . . . ."

The woodcutter pushed back the white hood and stroked her scented hair. "You're neither old nor cracked, Lily. You're young and strong and sweet. If anything, magic won't reside in you because you're *too* pure. Magic spawns evil and trouble, and corrupts everything it touches, from all I've seen."

She sniffed, shook her head, but smiled. "You know that's not true, for your sister has magic and does good. I wish I could, too."

Gull sighed. How had life gotten so complicated? "I'm keeping an eye on Greenie to see she's not corrupted. And I still don't think you must practice magic. Just because someone is good at—I don't know—slaughtering hogs doesn't mean he must become a butcher. You were going to open a shop once, remember?"

"Yes, but I'd find precious few customers out here." She chuckled. "Oh, you make me feel better, Gull, if only because you're as mixed up as I am. But at least your path in life is clear."

"Is it? Sometimes I wonder. . . . I'd like you to be on my path again, someday, when you're ready. You're still here in my heart." Though lately, Rakel was there, too. Did women understand love any better than men?

Lily sensed the struggle within him. Gently, she pushed away. "Well, I'm glad for that. But it's *my* heart that needs deciphering. I still don't know who I am, or what my destiny is, or my purpose." He made as if to speak, but she stopped him with a quick kiss and gave him a brave smile. "Don't argue. I argue enough with myself. You tend the army, and I'll tend my—flying. And we'll see where we end up. You came to speak to Greensleeves about leaving, didn't you?"

"Well, yes." He gazed into her eyes. "But how did you know that? Are all women magic?"

"That's a secret." And taking his hand, she led him back toward the hollow.

Greensleeves was eating soup and biscuits, talking quietly with others about the green brain and its weird pronouncements, when a whooping shout made her jump.

Gull bounded out of Chaney's cave as if shot from a ballista. He'd returned to the hollow exhausted, yawning and droopy-eyed, and had crawled into the cave and fallen asleep curled on a bearskin like a child. Now he hooted, laughed, waved his arms in the air, danced a jig.

"Look!" he gasped. "Look! Chaney, thank you!" Before anyone could blink, Gull ran forward, caught Chaney's white head, and kissed her on the lips. The old druid laughed, dripping spittle, but Gull didn't care. Gull guffawed with delight as he swung his right foot backward, forward, from side to side. "This is wonderful! There's no pain! And it's so supple! A little tight, perhaps—"

Chaney kept smiling. "All normal. Your muscles have gone unused for years. In time, a few months, t'will be good as new."

Laughing at her brother's delight, Greensleeves said, "See? I told you! She's a miracle worker! And if I keep studying, someday *I'll* be able to perform such wonders. I hope," she added.

"I believe you, Greenie. I'm converted. There are good uses for magic!" He tousled her brown hair, as when she was little, and they both laughed. "I'll be good from now on. I'll no longer accuse all magic users of spreading evil and seeking only power."

Chaney muttered, "We'll see about that." But she smiled nonetheless.

The good mood spread over the party as they talked around the campfire into the night. The weather had remained as balmy as early spring. Greensleeves knew this was some doing of Chaney's, that she'd enchanted the plateau—or as she would put it, "encouraged the weather to stay mild," for she never forced anything. Greensleeves loved the notion of always dispensing magic gently, but sometimes she worried—could she stick to it?

"There are four stages to conjuring, Chaney tells us—"

"I *think,* dear. Others might speak differently," interjected the old druid, who sat with her eyes closed as if asleep. She chuckled. "Surely many would. Nothing provokes an argument more than codifying magic."

"Yes, well . . . " continued Greensleeves. "The first stage is to conjure from far away something you've touched directly, handled and gotten to know. The next is to conjure *yourself* there, where you've walked before: what you students call shifting. After that, you might learn to conjure something you *haven't* touched but can imagine. Finally, you can conjure yourself somewhere you've never been: this is called planeswalking."

She looked around the ring of fire-bronzed faces. Chaney, Gull, Lily, Tybalt, Kwam, Daru, Ertha, Kamee, and one of her librarians. Rakel, not a student of magic or folklore, sat by herself at the edge of the firelight, staring at the glow in the sky. While the others were ruddy-faced near the fire, the full moon shining on her face made her pale, as if she were a ghost sitting amongst them, unseen, unheard.

At their center, on a rock, sat the green brain, currently mimicking a green-brown mottled lantern. It rattled on, of course, but in a whisper. Tybalt had asked for the shape. He delighted in testing the brain's possibilities. Poking the lantern, he said, "Sword." Hissing like a snake, the lantern shape melted, as if too close to the fire, elongated, and flowed into the shape of a sword. At the end, though, was a tiny red mouth whispering. Tybalt chuckled. Everyone else mostly ignored the show.

Greensleeves finished, "I can conjure familiar things. Lily conjured only once, but she can fly, too, something none of us can do. Or can you, Chaney?" The old druid only shook her head. "Chaney thinks I'll be ready for the next step . . . conjuring myself elsewhere, soon. I'm not so sure about that, but . . . "

"But what?" asked Gull. "You're drifting, Greenie. What're you not sure about?"

Greensleeves went quiet. The uncertainty, the fear, never far away, returned. She was afraid to send her mind out because she feared to lose it. Insanity hovered at her shoulder like a harpy.

And she had learned enough about herself and magic to know that unless she conquered that fear, she'd never be a true wizard.

"Greenie?" prompted her brother.

Greensleeves shook herself out of her reverie. This was not the time to air her fear of insanity, not with everyone counting on her. Yet she often felt like a fraud, offering hopes that might never materialize. "Uh, anyway, if my . . . studies go well, I'll be able to shift . . . the whole army elsewhere."

"So?" asked Gull, "how will that help us trap wizards? Don't forget our goal. When you shift, could you plunk us down alongside some iron-fisted bastard we can then thump?"

Greensleeves didn't bristle at the implied criticism. She was used to her brother's plain speaking. "Perhaps. Sometimes, if you have an object a wizard has tagged, you can trace the tag through it and find him or her. But let's say we do find a wizard. Then, if we can use the green brain to capture them—"

"How?"

Greensleeves huffed. "Would you stop interrupting? We . . . don't know yet. We know the thing is powerful. It could pull down the moons if you find the right command. But we've yet to discover exactly *how* to subdue wizards. . . ."

"That's like finding a ten-ton rock sitting on a catapult without finding the lever. What good—"

"Gull, shut up! We'll find the lever! We need time! Magic is a very imprecise science!"

Her brother gave a big sigh, but moved to the next topic. "Consider. Even if you can take us anywhere *and* we lock up a wizard, it's still like stomping one cockroach in a privy. We'll have stopped one while a hundred are still out ruining folks' lives."

"We have to start somewhere." Greensleeves sighed.

Tybalt picked up the green sword, examined it in

the yellow torchlight, put it down. "War hammer."
Folding, flowing, the brain became a long-handled,
square-headed hammer with a spike and a red blab-
bing mouth. Tybalt hefted it and made a swipe at an
imaginary enemy.

The silence dragged. The council's jubilation evaporated as they realized the hopelessness of their task.
They could blunder along, leading an army, hunting
wizards, until they were old and gray, the night
seemed to whisper.

In the silence, Greensleeves asked, "Tybalt, what
are you doing?"

"Huh? Oh! Just experimenting!" The big-nosed student bubbled enthusiasm. "Maybe it's a weapon we
need. A sword or a—spear, maybe! Perhaps if you
struck a wizard with it, or threw it at them, that would
compel them to obey you. There are legends like
that."

No one could think of any, but no one argued.

Gull flexed his right leg, still toying with his new
freedom of motion. "Well, we can't wait for you to
planeswalk, or whatever, Greenie. It's time to move
on. Marching."

"Move on?" asked several people.

"Aye. Rakel's pulled the army together fabulously.
It's sharp as a sword, tight as a drumhead. All we need
is to drill every day and build up our numbers. But
we're the match for any group our size, or bigger, she
says. And she should know. And we've eaten or salted
or jerked every scrap of meat on this plateau. So it's
time to move on. You can do your studying on the
road. But we need to decide which way to go."

"No choice." Chaney's raspy whisper startled
them all. "You came from the south. The mountains
west are too high to traverse, and the plateaus east
offer nothing, so you must continue north. The land
there drops off slowly and turns to badlands."

"Badlands?" asked half a dozen.

"Aye. Ravines and steep hills, some half a mile
high. Unexplored for years now, probably teeming

with mana. Greensleeves and Lily can tap it for future use. And there are ruins and caves to explore. They'll give up many a secret."

Crouching over the brain-turned-war-hammer, Tybalt said quietly, "Helmet."

Gull said, "May I ask, what is our final destination? Do we even have one? How long shall we travel, collecting mana and hoping to pound a wizard?"

Greensleeves pursed her lips. Gull stared at her, continually surprised at how she'd grown and matured since coming to this enchanted plateau. Like a whole other person, yet the same. She was his knee was both old and new. "Ultimately, we must find a home, a place to ensconce ourselves and build a following. If we settle in a populated area, build a castle or fortress, we can get the local people behind us and spread our—"

"Are you mad?" Gull waved both hands. "That would make us *warlords,* by the Eternals! Are we to enslave folk, as other wizards do? How can it be right if *you* do it, but wrong if *they* do it?"

Greensleeves rolled her eyes. "Bro-ther, think! We can't wander forever. You said so! And if we find people to *welcome* us, not as conquerers but as *friends,* we can pacify a valley or even country, impose peace and make it stick."

Gull gave up arguing. He rubbed his face with both hands. The scar tissue of his left hand felt cold on his face. Could Chaney really regenerate his fingers? He'd been so long with seven, he'd feel clumsy with ten.

Tybalt chuckled. The green brain had formed a helmet, round and plain, though crinkled on top as if it were still a brain. Idly, he picked it up, looked inside, slipped it on his head.

He failed to notice it lacked a red mouth and, for the first time since they'd discovered it, was silent.

Gull stood up. "All right, let's drop the far-future plans for now. Tomorrow we can get the army moving. Rakel—Where's Rakel gotten to?"

The party looked around, but didn't see her. She'd slipped away like a wraith.

Then all jumped as Tybalt screamed, a piercing blast that ripped his throat raw.

Holding the helmet on his head, he thrashed, howled, kicked so hard he almost knocked Gull down. His mouth frothed, his eyes rolled in his head. He screamed and screamed and screamed.

Cursing, Gull slapped Tybalt's hands off the helmet, grabbed it by the rim to pull it off. He yanked, yanked again, and cursed anew—this time in fear.

"It's stuck! It won't come off! Greenie, help me!"

But the young woman wizard sat shaking, paralyzed with fear. There it was—raw insanity, her greatest fear. Visited by the most powerful artifact ever. And she had handled it, touched it!

Gull yanked, cursed. "Rakel, then—damn it! *Where's Rakel?*"

The warrior woman wasn't far, not a quarter mile off. She knelt on the sodden winter leaves, drew her short sword, and inverted it. Taking a firm grip on the handle with both hands, she set it against her chest just under the ribs on the left side. Her arms tensed as she readied to drive the blade home into her heart.

Through the trees, a rising full moon lit the blue sky.

"My work is done. Good-bye, Hammen, my son. Grow strong."

She plunged the blade into her chest.

CHAPTER

11

SHARP AS A SERPENT'S TOOTH, THE SWORD TIP
split Rakel's leather jerkin, sliced her skin, bit a rib—

—and went flying through the trees from a swift
kick.

Gull had sheared leather from his boot toe. Rakel
was cut to the bone on her left forearm and bled like a
stuck pig.

But she was alive. For now.

"Are you out of your mind?" Gull grabbed her by
both arms and hoisted her into the air. Livid with rage,
he shook her like a puppy; she hung limply and took it.
"What are you *doing*? Are you trying to *kill* yourself?"

A foolish question, thought Rakel. Her thoughts
spun. What would Garth say if he knew? Where was
he, anyway, and would he even care? He had magic.
But why should Gull care? Oh, yes, he claimed to love
her. But what was love, anyway? She loved her son,
but here she was leaving him alone in the world—

"Answer me! Why are you doing this?" Gull shook
her so hard her head wobbled. When she didn't
answer, he dropped her to flop like a fish on dry land.

Slowly she wiped her cold forehead. She felt cold all over. She should. She should be a corpse.

But the hand she raised ran with fresh hot blood. She was bloody everywhere—down her arm, her face, bubbling under her ribs.

Gull hovered over her, quivering with anger. One word crashed down on her. *"Why?"*

Her answer was also one word, the key to her existence: "Duty."

"Duty to what?" In the darkness, he looked like some tree giant among the trunks, tall and brown and craggy, with hands outstretched like entrapping branches.

"My duty—as a mother." Idly she wiped her bloody arm across her breast. Her brain was fogged, as if she had already passed on to the Darkness.

"Mother?" The word galvanized Gull. He fell beside her on his knees, used a belt knife to hack ribbons from his tunic and wrap her arm. She had a child. Did she also have a husband?

"I've a son, Hammen. He's held hostage by the council. He'll be killed if I fail my mission. I had till the full moon, and I've failed. But if I'm dead, if the shifting wizard couldn't find me, they might assume I died attempting my duty." Suddenly there were people fussing all around her as she babbled. Greensleeves and Lily cut more strips of cloth and bound the wound under her ribs. She tried to push them away, but they only moved her hands aside and worked busily. "If I were killed fighting, they might not pass the shame of my failure onto Hammen. The tutors wouldn't hector him to death. My baby would be allowed to join the ranks of warriors. He'd be alive, unlike me—"

"I don't understand!" Gull snapped. "A *council* sent you here? You said you got swept up by Karli's army! What's this benighted *mission*?"

Rakel laid on her back, staring at the darkness as people worked. The sky overhead was black except for the bright gray-white Mist Moon. "I was to kill you and Greensleeves and bring back your heads."

The three looked at one another, stunned.

Gull stooped, caught Rakel under the back and knees, lifted her to his chest. No one had carried her like this since she was a child. As she'd carried her child, so very long ago, and laid him in his crib, and lied that his father would return soon.

Maybe, if she dwelt on it, she could die of a broken heart. . . .

A hour later, Rakel was propped up on blankets and a cinnamon bearskin in Chaney's cave. The fire, a simple pit in the middle of the floor, had been built up so yellow light and shadows danced on the walls. She nursed a flagon of spring water to which Chaney had added rose hips and feverfew and some red powder. She talked, but only with her head. Her heart was far away, questing after Hammen and Garth.

Tybalt, still screaming from the helmet locked on his head, had been bundled in blankets and toted away to the hospital tents.

" . . . and so I found myself transported into the middle of your battle with that wizard. I helped you to ingratiate myself, to get close to you, to kill you both . . . "

Greensleeves leaned forward on her little three-legged stool. Her white-haired badger poked its head from underneath her skirt, and she idly scratched its snarly muzzle. "But, Rakel, why didn't you just ask for help in the beginning?"

The woman stared at the fire. She took another sip of water: she was terribly thirsty after losing all that blood. "My duty was clear. I was to kill you. I thought you were like any other army: cruel and callous and rapacious. But almost immediately I learned differently, that everything Sabriam and the council said was a lie—though I'm a fool to be surprised. Every council of every clan lies these days. Benalia is so wrapped up in intrigue and fabrications, she couldn't recognize the truth if it came naked before her. Or decency, or justice. The very cornerstones of your crusade. I had to fulfill my duty, yet I couldn't, and I didn't know what to do, and I decided to help you, but that meant my death no matter what. . . ."

It was silent a while, only the fire crackling.

Lily, raised in hardship and always practical, spoke first. "I don't see much of a problem. We journey to this city, Benalia, and take your son back."

Rakel snorted, a tired laugh. "You've never seen Benalia. It's a city of more than two hundred thousand, the largest city in the Domains, or so they claim, and every person in it a trained soldier. We've grandmothers who could take Gull's axe from him with one hand and spank him with the other." She sipped more water. It was bitterly cold and sent shivers clear through her. Or maybe she was just empty of blood. She felt empty.

Gull said, "Lily's right. We've enough fighters and magic users to jump straight into this council and force them to release your son."

Rakel shook her head, infinitely tired. "The council meets in the Grand Hall, with the pride of the army standing shoulder to shoulder around them. You can't shift in. There are wards against any type of magic, unless they've been suspended by yet another wizard. Benalia is not a place, you see, it's a giant machine to churn out war. It's layers and layers of lies and muscle and steel and gold—"

Chaney wheezed, "Where humans dwell, a wizard can go, wards or not."

"Yes," said Greensleeves. "If we take only a few, get our hands on the council—"

"On their throats," growled Gull.

"Blink out of there," added Lily. "But who should go?"

"Me," said Gull. "Rakel here. Let's see . . . archers. Liko, perhaps?.."

Rakel felt cold all over. "You people talk—you're discussing—you—you're serious! You'd take on the whole *city*? Risk how many lives? Just to fetch out *my* son? When I was sent to *assassinate* you?"

"Of course," said Greensleeves. "You're our friend."

Rakel was surprised as a loud sob broke from deep in her breast.

Then she was crying uncontrollably, and all of them comforted her.

Yet their plans soon hit a wall. They didn't have enough information to make a decision.

Rakel reported that Guyapi, the shifting wizard, was to fetch her at the full of the moon, her and her prizes. But the moon was full with no sign of the wizard. Why the delay? Had he shifted here, shadowed her, seen Gull and Greensleeves still alive, and departed? No, replied Chaney in a calm voice, she would have known if anyone shifted close by. Still, why the delay? And what could they do when he did arrive? Could they capture him, force him to return them to Benalia? (None of them knew where it lay, even Rakel, except in the west somewhere.) Could they then grab Hammen and run? or shift out? They didn't know.

So they must wait. Chaney could tell when Guyapi arrived, then they'd proceed as best they could.

And they had to move on. Surprisingly, Chaney was going with them. She would leave her cave and enchanted plateau, suffer as only an invalid could, travel with the army. She had, she said, still much to teach Greensleeves. Then she would "move on," but not through this world.

So it was decided, at dawn around the fire, to go.

Into the badlands.

The badlands were well named.

At the rim of the plateau, where the oak forest ended, the band could see them in the distance. A scrubland sloped to a bottom land Chaney reported had once been a mighty river. The badlands looked carved by water, rippled like the bottom of a streambed. They extended as far as the eye could reach, merging to the still-jagged sierras on the west, leaving behind the plateaus to the east.

Now, from the riverbed, the army officers and magic users could study them up close.

The badlands were almost two lands: tall spires, ridges, mesas, all riven in a thousand places by ravines, gulleys, and arroyos, some a mile wide, some too narrow for a horse to pass. Directly before them was a single valley a half-mile wide, but splitting off it were scores of wide and narrow exits. The upper reaches were some sixty or seventy feet high. There was no point in climbing, unless one wanted to see more badlands, for some tops were only big enough for an eagle's nest while others were razor-sharp knifebacks. Some mesas were perhaps a quarter-mile square, but isolated from their neighbors, so one would climb up only to climb down again. The army must thread the ravines, the gulleys, the rills. Gull was heartened by his decision to stay on horseback and afoot, for wagons would find the terrain impassable. There was no flat ground wider than a tabletop: everywhere the land tilted and sloped, up and down and up again, often cracked deep enough to trap a leg, all littered with rocks and boulders skull-size to barn-size. We'll be mice creeping through a gravel pit surrounded by ragged stone walls, thought Gull.

If they entered at all. "If there's no water . . . "

"There is," said Greensleeves.

Gull looked at his sister and her tutor. Greensleeves rode a tan mare she'd named Goldenrod. Old Chaney rode a small horse, almost a pony, in a hammock seat fashioned from lathes, rawhide, and canvas. The pony didn't mind the burden: Chaney was a light as a sparrow. Gull asked, "How do you know?"

She blinked. "You can smell it. And greenery."

Gull chewed the inside of his cheek. "If you can, that's sufficient."

Puzzled, Greensleeves glanced at Chaney, but the druid only smiled and shook her head at the denseness of nondruids. Greensleeves was surprised no one else could detect the water. Since leaving the plateau, she'd found all her senses heightened. She knew the water ahead was in small pools and tiny freshets, laced with lead and alkalai, but potable. The greenery was scrub oaks and chestnuts and yellow grass growing in cracks and on narrow shelves. She could hear jackdaws sleeping in nests on the ledges; sense the forward mules, smarter than horses, were restless at some alien presence miles inland; knew a storm brewed on the horizon to the southwest; heard prairie dogs hiding underground; knew the rocks were mostly limestone and feldspar and quartz. She told Gull these things.

Gull grunted at his sister's new talents and went on, "If there's water, the next problem is fodder for the horses. Can you and Chaney conjure a field of hay?" He wasn't sure himself if he joked or not.

"That won't be a problem," Chaney told him. The withered dame sat perched in her hammock seat like an old owl, with only a thin cloak around her shoulders and a woven reed basket under one arm: all her possessions.

But one thing bothered Gull most of all. The land was so still. Aside from soaring birds, hawks or vultures, there was no sound. Not even the hiss of the wind, for the ridges shut it out. The air was cool and dry: Gull's breath didn't steam in this early afternoon.

"I want to think this over," Gull told the assemblage. "Where's the trumpeter? We can—" Beside him Rakel cleared her throat. Oh, yes, Rakel was commander, in charge of details, while he attended strategy. "Uh, order a rest, please, Commander. I'll talk to the scouts."

Rakel just nodded at Gull's new pomposity. Lines of worry were etched alongside her eyes and mouth, for she slept little these days. But she knew how to command. Barking, she ordered the trumpeter to sound Rest.

As the notes trilled out and echoed back, soldiers and camp followers and cartographers and librarians and cavalry and cooks and one giant slid off their horses or dropped their packs, rubbed their rumps, called to neighbors, dug in pockets for jerked meat or dried fruit, wandered off (joking, "I need to walk a hundred paces") to piss down a crack. Rakel ordered Varrius to post pickets from his red company and forbade the cooks to light fires.

Pleased at the smooth efficiency, and his own freedom to ponder, Gull turned his horse, the dapple-gray named Ribbons, toward Bardo and Holleb, captain and sergeant of scouts. Their scouts, all four, were already ahead in pairs, dispatched at dawn. The paladin wore his mail coif over his ears, with a brown brimmed hat over it. The centaur had donned his helmet and breastplate and held his feathered lance pointed at the ravines. They're expecting trouble, Gull thought, but haven't told me yet. Interesting.

"What do you make of it?" he called.

Bardo frowned and patted his horse's neck to calm it. The animal was nervous. "I don't like it. Something out there. I need more than five scouts. I've seen lands like this before. A broad avenue can turn into a box canyon, or squeezing through a crack can reveal a green valley. There's no sense to it except for animal trails: they trip from green to green. But vith these clouds, you can get turned around and vander, have to vait until the stars come out."

They looked up. Cloud cover had rolled in, stacked thick. It had the look of permanance. Gull turned and looked toward the distant oak plateau. The clouds parted over it to spill wan winter sunshine. Chaney's magic, he wondered, or just an enchantment on the plateau?

Holleb growled, "This land like our steppelands. Biggest enemy is weather. One moment sun, then rain like pitchforks, or hail that can kill, or snow belly-deep. No way to tell until too late."

"Unless the druid warns us," said Gull, then corrected himself. "Druids. We'll have to guard against becoming separated. That's paramount. We'll need to fashion bundles of rushes, something that will burn smoky, tallow perhaps, and see that each group has one, and flint and steel. Anyone who's lost will—how shall we do this?—send up two columns of smoke, staying put until we find them."

"Good if someone could fly," mused Holleb. "Can your lady friend there, in white?"

Gull shook his head. Lily couldn't do more than float. Magic was damned imperfect and impractical stuff, he mused.

"Why did you say something is in there, Bardo? Greensleeves said the same, said the mules could sense it. How do you know?"

A shrug of powerful, armored shoulders.

"But what? One rattlesnake or a horde of orcs on war mammoths?"

Another shrug was the answer. "You could hide a herd of mammoths behind that ridge. But not feed them. Still . . . "

"He is right," rasped Holleb. "I sense perhaps only one big thing and many smaller. More than that, I cannot say."

Gull stifled a sigh. He hated making decisions on scanty information and hunches. "Very well. We'll be on our guard. Bardo, use Ordando's greens for more scouts—"

Greensleeves trotted over on Goldenrod. "Someone's coming!" She pointed at tiny jigging dots in the distance. Everyone squinted, surprised she'd spotted them first. Bardo was miffed.

The scouts were Givon and Melba, in their colorless gray and brown clothes with raven-feather insignia, on geldings of the same muddy hues. The two were brother and sister, dark, with curly black hair cut short. Melba reported, speaking to Bardo. "We went about four miles. No sign of people. Some antelope trails skirt a mesa and then split. Four possible routes may open up. The land shelves steeply, perhaps a hundred feet in a mile. We won't make more than eight miles a day in there, more likely six." She hesitated, looked to Givon, who nodded. "And we saw a flying horse."

Bardo snorted. "A pegasus? Vas anyone riding it?"

"No. It was very high up, but definitely a horse. Dirty white with yellow tones. Wings cut like a vulture's, but white. And a crest of feathers, we think."

Greensleeves trotted away to see how Tybalt fared among the healers. Rakel joined them and asked, "Did it do anything when it saw you? Bank away to warn someone, or come closer to investigate?"

"No. It disappeared north. It's hard to track something in the sky with these walls."

"Ve know. Good vork. Vait." Bardo asked Gull, "How long vill ve remain here?"

Gull craned around in the saddle. It was midafternoon, and the army had settled some. "Let's camp here. T'will give us time to adjust to these walls and to figure out marching orders. Plus we'll water up. You take Ordando's people and explore, Bardo. Chart a course by dawn. I'll see the cooks gather wood—"

Rakel cleared her throat, and Gull shut up. "Uh, carry on, Bardo. And you, Rakel, if you please."

Chagrined, he turned his horse, clopped away, then realized he had no place to go, nor anything to do. He was the only idle dog in the army. But his job was to think, he reminded himself. So he'd think.

He handed his horse to a boy and girl appointed officer's grooms by the wrangler. He accepted a wineskin from a cook. Wandering, he found happiness in his "new" right knee, almost as strong as the other, which let him walk without limping. He settled against a sunny rock, sipped wine, stoppered it. He stared at the walls to think about how to assault them.

And promptly fell asleep.

The first attack came three days into the badlands.

By day, the marching order gave them confidence. Far ahead, usually out of sight, were Bardo's augmented scouts. In the army itself, first went Helki's cavalry, spread out where possible. Next came one company of soldiers. Behind them trooped the clockwork beast, lopsided on this sloping terrain, driven by Stiggur and his ten-year-old "squire" Dela, and Egg Sucker sulking near the tail. Liko stumped along on the beast's right side, one head watching the scenery, one head daydreaming. Then came the officers and wizards, placed where they could see but remain protected. Then followed the bulk of the camp followers, artisans, knowledge workers, and more. Finally came the last company of soldiers, for an attack might come from any of the hundred ravines around. The companies rode line-abreast, spread out for room and to discourage idle chatter, for their job was to watch the land and heed the shouts of officers.

But they weren't attacked by day.

This night found them camped in a vast bowl with thirty or forty cracks splitting sixty-foot-high walls. The companies and cavalry were dispersed at the four compass points of a circle, with the nonfighters at the center. A tall staff and banner marked the officers' tents, and in the nearest tent to that was a girl appointed trumpeter and a boy drummer.

The night was old, the fires died low. By orders, almost everyone was either in a tent or their blankets. Only Gull was up, for Rakel couldn't sleep and so he couldn't. The two stood at the biggest cooking fire nursing mugs of herb tea with honey. Gull hoped Rakel would calm soon, banish her nightmares, so he might get some sleep. It was tough to nod in the saddle.

He had his own worries. Givon and Melba, the brother-sister team of scouts, had failed to return at dusk. They might be camping in the wilderness rather than lose a promising route, or might be navigating by the stars. But still, Gull worried about any of his charges out by themselves. He fretted about fretting, too, wondering if too much personal interest in his soldiers was bad. But he knew no other way, and so he lived with it.

He jerked his head up as a blazing star streaked across the night.

No, not a falling star. Too close.

Just above his head, a yellow-red blur sparkled, rocketing by so fast he barely saw it.

It landed in the cook fire and exploded.

Hot ashes and coals dashed in Gull's face, singed holes in his clothing and skin. Batting at chars, deafened by the noise, he clawed at his eyes to clear them. The first thing he saw was Rakel's hair burning as she swabbed cold tea in her eyes. He batted out her flames.

People screamed all over the camp, but not as many as expected. Mostly he heard the shouts of officers—Varrius, Neith, Ordando, Bardo, and Helki. Rakel, one eye still blinded by ashes, shouted at the camp followers to belt up, screamed at the trumpeter and drummer to sound To Arms. But every fighter in the camp had already tumbled from blankets and tents, weapons strapped on before boots and hats. Gull felt a surge of pride. This army, small though it might be, was ready for any foe.

Or so he thought.

Someone shouted, pointed straight up.

High on a cliff wall, backlit by a red glow, was a huge armored figure. He glistened all over, silver and steel chased with gold, and giant horns projected from his closed helmet past spike-studded shoulders.

His arms were spread wide. Conjuring.

"Balls of Boris!" Gull barked. "I know that bastard! He hit us in the burned forest by the star crater! He sent a horde of—"

Gibbers, shrieks, wails, howls. A cacophony welled all around them. Skipping, hopping, leaping, skittering from the darkness of every ravine around the bowl came a horde of scampering demons. Foremost among them, held aloft on sharpened stakes, jogged the heads of the missing scouts, Givon and Melba.

"Bastards!" Gull cursed. "Lousy sneaking bastards!"

"Shut up!" Running for their tent, jerking out her helmet and baldric, Rakel shrilled, "We'll take 'em! Finally! Something to *fight*!" She gave a glorious war cry that made Gull fall back. *"Ye-ha-YEEEEEEE-HA!!! COMPANIES! TO ARMS!"*

CHAPTER
12

"FORM UP!" RAKEL HOLLERED. "CAPTAINS! DRESS your lines! You! Don't you backstep an inch or I'll have your guts for garters! Form up! Don't worry about those demons, worry about me! Form up, I said!"

Rakel turned from the oncoming wave of demons to glance at the camp. Gull cast a look that way, too. The camp followers were performing their duties: rather than gawking or screaming or running to hide, most were striking camp. Blacksmiths and cooks and clerks and mothers with babies slung in sacks or toddlers at their knees stumbled in the dark, dropped the tents, stowed cooking gear, saddled horses and pack mules. The army's new commander had decreed that, when action came, every nonfighter was to strike camp. Her purpose was twofold: one, so the army could move quickly, either in advance or retreat; two, to keep folks busy to prevent panic.

"Tighten up! They can't hurt us! They're just demons, by the spirits!" Rakel shouted more to distract her charges from fright than to give them information. From their four compass points, Rakel had

drawn her meager force into a thin ring around the
camp. But the ring bristled like a porcupine. Almost
fifty warriors wore shields slung at their backs, axes
or swords on their belts, and bows and quivers over
their shoulders. In addition, each held an oak lance
tipped with a wicked steel head. The cavalry and
scouts champed at the bit just inside the ring, and
Rakel had by her the young musicians. Waiting at the
center, ready to go in any direction, were Stiggur atop
his clockwork beast and Liko wielding two clubs.

A small but potent force.

Facing hundreds of shrieking demons.

It was hard to see them by the wan firelight—fading
fast as cooking fires were extinguished—but the
demons seemed much alike. They were no bigger than
chest high, so Gull wondered if they were another
species of goblin. Some had tall pointed ears, some
none, some twisted horns like a goat's, others smooth
bald heads. Yet each looked dried out, as if mummi-
fied, their guts shriveled and their skin shrunk tight to
the bone, so every rib could be counted, every joint
picked out in skeletal detail. All went naked, with dark,
wrinkled skin like burnt snakes, and all had long white
fangs that glistened. Most hideous, they had round
red glowing eyes like coals kicked up from hell.

And there were so many! Gull wanted to shout
from sheer surprise. They spilled from cracks in the
canyon walls like ants from a rotten tree, leaping,
bounding, hopping, and shrieking.

Then he had no time to think, for the demon wave
struck.

Immediately before Gull was Captain Ordando's
Green Company. The men and a few women stood flat-
footed and bent-kneed, lances leveled, braced as if
ready to fight an undertow. Gull wondered why Rakel
hadn't made them string their bows and shoot, but perhaps she thought the light too poor, or that the demons
came too fast, or that missing might damage the army's
morale. Whatever, the line looked pathetically thin to
Gull, but the fighters didn't waver. This was partly due

to Rakel's training and stern discipline, partly to her standing just behind them with short sword drawn. All knew she'd cut down the first soldier who ran. But though some knees wobbled, no one bolted.

Howling, yipping, gabbling, shrieking, the leather-skinned demons flung themselves upon the line. One leaped high, only to be spitted on an iron spear blade. The demon's yowling mouth shut with a *clok*. The blade was wedged deep in the squirming body, which looked dry and scaly both inside and out. The fighter hefting the long lance shook it and flicked off the leathery body, losing the detachable blade. Immediately there was another demon to spear, and it too died, pointed green wood piercing its dry guts.

One demon scuttled as low as a cockroach, mouth open and white teeth exposed like a bear trap, going after a fighter's leg. They had no weapons, these monsters, only long claws and sharp teeth, like giant rats. The fighter, a dusky female stippled with tattoos, snapped back her lance, as she'd been taught, and smashed the butt on the fiend's head. Dazed, it bit the stony soil, and she stomped its skull out of shape. Without looking, the she-fighter speared another demon, and one behind it.

Ordered to keep back by Rakel, to watch the battle line for gaps and to study the enemy, Gull noticed a second line of foes creep from the canyon clefts.

Orcs. Gull had seen some on the tropical island where he'd been banished. These were not dark, but light skinned. Firelight flickered on their bodies with a greenish hue. They were all bald, with tusks jutting from their lower jaws and pointed ears sticking above their naked pates. Despite the winter chill, they wore only harness straps and ratty leather or fur kilts. Most carried clubs studded with obsidian, or short flint-tipped spears. Yet a half-dozen lugged long tubes like hollow logs. One balanced a log across his shoulder. The mouth of the tube belched fire, and a screaming arc of flame shot overhead. Though it scared the horses, the missile only hit a far canyon wall, hung there sputtering, and fizzled out. Rockets, Rakel called them, filled with some black powder, exploding like lightning, killing the shooter as often as an enemy. Such must have been the fireballs cast into the campfires.

The woodcutter counted roughly, decided on at least a hundred orcs hanging back there, then trotted over to tell Rakel.

She didn't turn, but watched her soldiers fight demons. "Orcs! They're nothing! Ignore them! Close up that line, Captain Neith!"

Feeling foolish over worrying—a hundred armed orcs were nothing?—Gull fell back, swinging his axe idly.

Bodies piled up along the line. One fighter had three demons strung on his lance, twitching like trout, and could no longer hold them. He pitched the lance at more monsters, then drew his sword and dragged his shield around. With a shout, he batted one demon back while he split open another's skull. Similar scuffles raged up and down the lines.

More lances were hurled down amidst twitching bodies. An axeman shouted to his partner, a stocky woman with four red braids below her steel helmet, and they set to in tandem. Two-handed, he slung his parrot's-beak war axe high and mowed into a trio of demons while his partner ducked and slashed at demon bellies and throats, protecting them both with her shield.

From the darkness, into the dim light, fiends kept coming. Their weird bloodcurdling cries, like the shrieks of enraged eagles or wildcats, echoed and ree-choed. One knot of demons broke through the line immediately before Gull, bowling two fighters aside. One fighter was down, a demon latched onto his arm with razor teeth. To the man's credit, he didn't shriek in panic, but tried to roll out from underneath to regain his feet and keep fighting. Gull couldn't stand by and watch, so he hefted his axe and charged.

But someone shouldered him aside so hard he almost fell: Rakel. She shouted, "Stay off the line! Watch from the rear!" Then she thrust out with her short sword, not hacking blindly as Gull would have, but delivering quick surgical strokes that severed a demon's neck, arm, or spine, deft as a fishmonger gutting flounder. Yanking the bleeding man from the ground by sheer strength, she barked, "Brave soul!" and made sure he was back in place. Then she was gone, dashing where needed.

Miffed, feeling helpless with inactivity, Gull backed up, his axe a weight dragging in his hands. He tried to do his job, to watch the overall battle. But it was hard to sit on his hands.

He cast about. Demons came at the lines from all around, but thickest up here where Rakel worked. She'd signaled the cavalry forward in pairs, and they leaned down from the saddle and sliced fiends with their long sabers. Stiggur shunted the clockwork beast forward to plug a gap between the Red and Blue Companies: shifting levers, driving the contraption forward and then backward, the tree-trunk hooves stamped demons to pieces, preventing dozens of others from breaching the line. Close by, Liko hammered demons with two clubs as if swatting flies. At the center, camp was disassembled and packed, leaving only smoldering campfires. Camp followers quieted frightened horses and children. The cartographers and wranglers and some cooks had drawn their own swords, forming a second ring in case it was needed. Healers, Samites and others, lugged wounded to a makeshift hospital. Another rocket sailed into camp and exploded next to milling horses, knocking over two and terrifying others, so the wrangler and his child helpers were hard put to hold them.

Not a hundred feet off, Gull saw his sister. Her tent and gear had been struck and wrapped by two young girls hired as maids. Chaney the druid sat on a box, propping up her withered frame with her good hand. Lily watched Greensleeves. But the new druid stood unmoving, bareheaded, brown hair asnarl, arms wrapped around her shoulders as if she were cold. She stood so still, gazing at the cliff where perched the armored wizard backlit by eldritch fire, Gull thought she was paralyzed with fright.

Should he run to her rescue? Stay here and *not* fight? What?

Greensleeves was not frightened. Indeed, she was probably the calmest person in the other patchwork army, discounting ancient Chaney.

The woman wizard was concentrating. She needed to conjure something to get at the other wizard, high as he was, and few things in her grimoire would make an impression.

And she wanted to impress herself.

Among Towser's belongings, Tybalt had discovered a blue gem that felt icy to the touch even on the hottest day. Tybalt had tinkered with the stone for days. Finally he'd decided what it might be.

Whether Greensleeves could use it, no one knew . . . but if she were to conquer the fear of losing her mind, this might be the place to start. For the thing tagged by the stone was alien to her, something untouched. But she was determined to try.

Her right hand touched the stone, stitched to the ragged green shawl knit by her mother. The gem's cold burned her fingertips, but she hung on. The being it represented was far, far away. So far, it dwelt on a plane where humans could not go. A place of intense cold and whirling winds, with no place to stand. . . .

Come, she told the ancient nonbeing. Come. We need you. For our cause. For goodness . . .

Greensleeves shivered as she sent her mind into the vast blueness of the gem, sent her spirit soaring along an arcane trail, sent her heart zooming into the ether. Her very life seemed to hiss along invisible lines, scuttle on spiderweb strands over incredible heights, skitter along the edges of steep mountain trails. She might have been a bird flown too high, or a beetle blown too far out to sea, or a fish too far up an icy river. With her mind—tenuous as a bird's breath— she reached for the being, far, far out in the blue void where even the air seemed to freeze. . . .

And touched a hand colder than buried stone.

Shuddering, shivering, Greensleeves felt her hold on her mind slip.

The hand, incredibly powerful, tugged, seemed to yank her brain from her skull, like a tooth from its socket.

No, she cried in the silence, no. I'm . . . staying . . . here . . . and *you* must come! Now!

Grimly, she hung onto her mind and the earth below her. It was warm, while the ether was cold. It was loving, full of life, eager to grow, while the distant reaches were ugly and silent and dead. No, the woman fought. No, you come *here!*

The tug came, harder. Deep inside her body, she felt her heart skip a beat. Then another.

Wanting to scream, but needing her strength, she dug her heels into the warm mother-earth. Magic flowed into her: mana she tapped from all around— warm, flowing, like a bath of hot lava. Teeth grinding, she hung on and *pulled* on the chilling hand.

And suddenly it slipped, and she had it.

A rush, a scurry, a howl, and the ice-being zoomed at her like a comet from the sky.

Greensleeves opened her eyes: even they ached from the strain. She was back in the dry canyon in the northern badlands lit by dying campfires. The winter weather was crisp, but tropical compared to where she'd been. Now . . . where was . . . ?

"Ah," breathed Chaney behind her. "Very good! Aim your bolt!"

"Oh, my!" gasped Lily.

Yes! sang a voice inside Greensleeves. She'd conjured something from the farthest away ever! And she wanted it to land—she scanned the bluff, spotted the armored wizard—there!

Up high, where he supposed himself safe, the armored wizard found the eldritch light around him flickering. A simple light spell outlined his body like fox-fire to instill fear in an enemy. But now his light guttered like a candle stub as alien winds howled around him.

The armored wizard heard a whistle like a hurricane descending. Turning, he saw an inverted cone wink into being, brown at the bottom, then green, then blue, then yellow.

Then a blast like a tornado struck him.

A woman of ice, it seemed at first: naked, long bodied, all white, with flowing lines of water or ice. But this creature was pure air, chilled by the upper atmosphere until its very breath could kill. The air elemental looked female, whirling, flowing, a tornado from its waist down, a mermaid made of air, yet it had neither gender nor soul. The being hummed across the top of the plateau—and spotted the armored wizard.

Playful, with no more brain than a puppy, the air elemental whirled close to the armored wizard to see what he was. Boring through the air, dragging a frozen hurricane after it, it swirled under one of his massive armored arms, slithered along his back, spun alongside his shoulder.

Greensleeves could see it all clearly from below. She took pride in her risk, in conquering her fear, in choosing aright. The stubborn elemental, once fetched here, would delight in a big warm silver plaything.

The wizard staggered at the elemental's touch, stumbled backward to avoid the hideous cold. Already half-paralyzed, he shuffled too close to the edge of the bluff and only just recovered in time. Spinning, almost toppling, he beat the air to keep the elemental back. But it slithered closer, friendly as a dolphin. Teasing, it slid between his legs, dirt and dust whirling into the air. Chilled in the codpiece, the armored wizard jumped, fell to his knees, agony slicing like a knife. Yet the elemental returned to churn across his chain-mail belly.

Desperate, the armored wizard staggered upright, uttered a quick spell, and raced for the edge of the bluff.

Greensleeves gasped as the wizard soared off the bluff, high in the sky, like a bird taking flight. But he was not flying, only jumping, and his path arced down to touch another bluff across the canyon. He'd gotten away for the moment, Greensleeves whispered to herself.

But he ran for his life. And Greensleeves's air elemental pursued.

Demon bodies were stacked knee-deep before Captain
Ordando's Green Company, and Gull could see that it
was the same all around the camp. Yet their lines still
held, thanks to Rakel's sound judgment and occasional
sword thrust. And the demons' charge had failed. Many
fiends lay whimpering, skulls smashed, jaws broken,
shoulders or arms cleft. Above them stood the fighters,
panting, drenched in their own sweat, spattered with
dark red demon blood and their own and their comrades'. Yet they grinned fierce warriors' grins, and they
lusted for another chance to prove themselves.
    Farther out, the demons had halted, stalled.
Behind them cowered the orcs in a wavering, cringing
line. There were no longer hundreds, only perhaps two
hundred demons and orcs to speckle the darkness.
The monsters feared the army they'd failed to rout.
    Rakel gave her warriors what they wanted—a little
more action. She ordered the sweating trumpeter to
sound To Arms, raised her voice and shouted with a
cracked throat, *"At the slow march . . . advance!"*
    Gull shook his head. To advance in the teeth of an
enemy was a charge, although his commander
wouldn't call it that. But advance they did. With a collective grunt, Rakel's army stepped over dead and
dying demons and charged at a snail's pace. Ordando
shouted, "Ho!" and someone shouted back, "Ho!" Soon
they were all shouting, "Ho! Ho! Ho!" Then "Hooooo!!!!!"
Chanting put them out of breath, but they did it anyway, marching toward the dark horde with swords
and axes ready. Not waiting for Rakel's approval or
disapproval, Gull jogged to the line and fell in beside a
warrior. She glanced over and grinned at him through
blood-spattered lips.
    They'd marched fifty paces, unconciously increas-
ing their pace, thinning their line, stamping down hard
on the tilted rocky soil, when the demons broke and

ran. The orcs were long gone, back into clefts and cracks like scattered rats.

Men and women bellowed, laughed, howled like the fiends had earlier. They shook their weapons in the air, wept for joy, shouted obscenities and taunts and threats.

Gull shouted along with them, but part of him was sad, for he'd done nothing to win this victory. This army, he thought, needed everyone but him.

High on the bluff top, the armored wizard landed with a jolting crash. The air elemental swirled right after him, faster than he was, sending chills through his armor. Desperately, the wizard batted at the thing, but it was nothing but air, frigid as hoarfrost. Finally, he shoved a gauntleted hand into a chain mesh pouch at his belt and pulled forth a stone that glowed red-orange. Holding the stone high, clenched tight in his fist in front of his armored face, he blew across the stone at the air elemental.

Its inhuman face a mask of frost and fear, the elemental spiraled into smaller and smaller wisps, and disappeared.

Far below, Greensleeves saw the wizard whirl back to the attack. Yet his right arm went limp and hung straight down, still clutching the stone. The ancient Chaney rasped, "The Mightstone of Urza, found again. I wondered where it had gotten to. Yet he's not strong enough to use it. See his arm droop? One spell too many t'will suck the very life from his heart. I doubt he wants to win that badly."

Indeed, the wizard used only one hand to conjure. In the valley below, Rakel stopped her cheering troops from pursuing the retreating demons, even tripping a couple of fighters to get their attention. Shouting, ordering trumpet calls, she reformed the whittled-down circle around the camp. She trotted from captain to captain, hurling compliments here, warnings to dress the line there. She barked that the camp followers had done well in striking camp, but should build up the fires for light. The battle wasn't over yet.

Feeling useless, Gull trailed behind her.

When a man shouted, the two turned.

Greensleeves felt the chill first and smelled rot fresh from the grave. Then she saw them.

Shambling from the darkness came a line of zombies. Of Scathe, Gull remembered. He'd seen them before, in the burned forest. Wretched things, cheated from death, freshly plucked from their graves, most in the shrouds they'd been buried in, many naked. Some were whole, a ghastly gray, but many lacked limbs or patches of skin or even heads. They shuffled, stumbled against one another, lurched ahead, dead and mindless, things of unspeakable horror and abject pity.

Some of the army whimpered and whispered at the sight. Rakel stood white faced, trying to think of an attack: she was trained to fight the living, not the dead. A few fighters in the line backstepped, and when Rakel spoke to still them, her voice was a small croak.

But Gull knew what to do. He bellowed across the circle, "Greenie! The wall!"

But his sister was ahead of him. With scarcely any effort, she touched a twig woven into her shawl. Hissing under her breath, making sounds like the wind in treetops, she pictured the Whispering Woods she knew so well, and a spot where nature had run riot, and trees grew so thick they bent upon themselves and their neighbors. Reaching with her mind, she urged a strip of forest to appear—*there*.

Men and women sighed as a living fence of tightly woven wood rippled green-brown-blue-yellow before them at a stone's throw. Unlike Greensleeves's previous efforts, this wall of wood took a graceful curve, matching the line of her army, extending clear across the canyon from wall to wall, thick and deep. All sight of the zombies was blotted out, and the army breathed easier.

Greensleeves smiled to herself and relaxed. Chaney allowed a satisfied sigh to escape her parched throat. Greensleeves would one day be a legend among wizards, if she survived.

Atop his clockwork beast, Stiggur hollered. Yanking at the controls, he spun the wooden creature, wheezing and clumping, in a circle. The slab-iron sides shoved Liko the giant around to face a new menace. Helki the centaur, captain of cavalry, also spotted the danger from her greater height, and let out a caterwauling whinny—a shout of delight, for now the cavalry would have their turn. All the riders, yellow ribbons fluttering at their sleeves, stood in their stirrups with whoops and yells. Rakel laughed to see their enthusiasm.

Down the canyon flickered what looked like a wisp of ashes. But the swirling gray fog coalesced into a company of cavalry, and Gull remembered them. All black, from their horses to their beards, the riders carried long sabers and big kite shields with a split blazon of a half-silver devil's face, their only color. Javelins hung across their backs on narrow straps, and Gull knew they carried grapnel hooks on saddlestrings. He'd fought these folk last spring when they attacked Towser's wagon train, had chased down three men who carried off Lily, and—by the grace of the gods—killed them.

There were thirty or more on stamping, snuffling horses. Their captain raised his saber and bellowed in a rough tongue, evidently exhorting them to strike hard.

But his harsh command sputtered when he saw what was forming against him, and Gull laughed out loud, then cheered.

The black knights faced equals now: Helki, in fluted painted armor, with a feather lance long as her roan body, their captain; four desert hawks who were almost centaurs, so long had they lived in the saddle; and more cavalry speeding to catch up—scouts in dull clothes marked with a raven's feather, Holleb even bigger than Helki, Bardo their armored paladin on a warhorse the color of smoke, the clockwork beast with Stiggur cheering atop and Liko stumping along-side with his two clubs.

Rakel's cavalry was hot for battle, shouting and yipping as they thundered the length of the canyon, lances leveled. They were fourteen against thirty, but they charged the harder for it, hot to prove their worth to the rest of the army.

The black mercenary captain howled orders, swept his saber to the right and left to signal line-abreast, and put black steel spurs to his black mount.

Closer the two lines thundered, one ragged with hot joy, the other so precise the animals' noses were even.

The noise when the two lines struck was deafening.

Sabers crashed onto shields, steel lance heads pierced breastplates, blades tore across horses' throats, riders were unseated to crash on their backs like a crate of dishes. A scout went down, decapitated by a saber. A black cavalryman gasped as Helki's lance cut through her chest, and toppled, stealing the lance. Bardo the Northern Paladin let his shield flop behind him as he hoicked himself up in the stirrups and struck two-handed with a bastard sword almost as tall as himself. He clove through a man's thigh and a full foot deep into the horse, so it jackknifed and hurled the dying rider a dozen feet. Caught between two attackers, for with dou-ble the numbers the black horsemen could pair off, Holleb raised his bloody lance sideways. The thick bar in his hairy horny hands smashed across the windpipes of both riders, but not before one slashed the centaur's rippling biceps to the bone. So grievous was the wound, Holleb dropped his shattered lance, clutched his arm, and wheeled from the fight lest he faint and tangle his friends' feet. The desert hawks in the blue robes were a blur, their smaller ponies skipping and dancing almost in circles; the cavalrymen pinked a thigh here, a horse flank there, a woman's face there. From their foursome's attack alone, six black riders were dead or crippled in the first minute of the clash.

Carried thundering along by their own weight, the horses split the two lines into a dozen fierce struggles.

Two desert men locked in wheeling combat with three black riders. Helki plucked a bronze-hilted sword from her war harness and struck stinging blows right and left. The lines disintegrated into snorting, spinning hooves and shouts and spouting blood.

Then the black riders found more trouble.

Nearest, Captain Varrius's Red Company got permission to advance. Shouting, "Hoo-ooo! Hoo-ooo!" they crowded the black riders, denying them space to wheel properly by threatening with oak lances.

Into their midst stamped the clockwork beast, which panicked the black horses, as did the sight and smell of the foreign giant. Liko had time to strike once, his great tree-club pulping a rider and horse, before the black lieutenant—as the captain had died on Helki's lance—ordered a retreat. Wheeling, swinging wildly to hold back the enemy, pestilential as a swarm of wasps, the black riders reformed a skittish line and cantered away south.

Greensleeves saw them flicker into ashes, as if invisible fire consumed them. She glanced aloft to see how the armored wizard had unsummoned them, but the bluff was bare, backlit only by the gray light of false dawn.

Gull and Rakel joined her, Chaney, Lily, and the rest.

"What does it mean?" asked Gull. "Where's his next attack?"

"There isn't one!" Rakel shouted. "We won!"

Behind them, that realization came to the army, which sent up a rollicking cheer that grew in strength until it shook the walls of the canyon.

"But we didn't capture him!" Greensleeves piped. "That's our goal!"

Rakel sighed, a soldier unthanked for her trials. "We stopped him, defeated him, and are whole and hearty! Be grateful for that! And work on one thing at a time, will you? That armored bastard's still out there. We'll get him! And roast him in his shell over a slow fire!"

CHAPTER

1 3

THE ARMORED WIZARD CAME BACK, AS RAKEL had predicted, but not the way she'd assumed.

The army mended and moved on. Not everyone went under their own power. Holleb the centaur's arm had been so badly slashed the Samites wanted to amputate it, but Helki refused. Chaney fussed and clucked over it, poking with her one good arm, muttering spells, and ordered it bound close to his chest and left to "must"—to fend for itself. Knocked for a loop by pain and herbal medicine, Holleb clumped along in a daze, supported by his doting wife Helki. Rakel shuffled the companies, for losses were four dead, two grievously wounded and likely to die, and four walking wounded. A desert cavalryman was counted among the dead, and his comrades keened a high wailing song all night long to send his soul to the paradisial oasis they pictured as heaven. One enemy, a black knight, had been left behind by his fellows, wounded in the head. Surly and superior, he vowed he would never serve in such a mockery of an army, so Rakel ordered him beheaded, whereupon he relented and joined the cavalry. His name was Terrill and, like many in his company, was a mercenary from a plainsland

called Wrenna. He knew nothing about the armored
wizard except that he paid in gold nuggets whenever
he summoned the Black Knights of Jenges.

So the army wound deeper into the badlands, and
the attacks began.

The canyons grew deeper and wider, and one
morning, threading a shadow-dark rill, an avalanche of
rock crashed upon their entourage. A cook and librar-
ian were killed, a dozen others hurt, including one
healer whose leg was smashed and had to be ampu-
tated. Four horses and mules with broken limbs had to
be put down. The army had to retreat to open space
and wait until dark before negotiating the rock-strewn
passage, and blundering in the blackness lamed two
more animals. Someone had glimpsed gray-green bald
heads grinning down at them—sneaking orcs under
the armored wizard's command. The cowardly and
unanswerable attack only fueled the anger of the fighters, their families, and the rest. A young couple took up
ropes, and in the darkness, with only short swords at
their sides, scaled the heights to seek the enemy. They
found nothing, but won praise for their efforts.

After that, the army stuck to wider passages and
camped more in the open. Yet the following night,
another rocket hurtled down from the sky. Fortunately,
everyone knew this presaged an attack and scrambled
away from the cooking fires in time. The resulting explo-
sion—red and yellow shot with green flecks—blasted
iron cookware twenty feet in the air like deadly hail. The
army braced for an attack, then spent a sleepless night
waiting, only to see a peaceful bleary-eyed dawn.

One morning a party of scouts was set upon by
huge tawny cats. One woman had her leg raked open,
though she was lucky the beasts mauled her horse to
death instead. Gull knew the animals' names—lions—for
he'd seen them conjured by the armored wizard when
they'd attacked his horse and mule herd months ago.

Another scout, Dinos, wandered into a cave. His
partner, a woman, reported hearing odd music and
warned the man not to go. But he ignored her, as if

mesmerized, and by the time she reached the cave, he was dead, the back of his skull crushed by a stone club, his body hacked to gory bits.

Soldiers growled for revenge now, and Gull and Rakel were sympathetic, yet there was little they could do but remain on guard. To run off singly or in groups would only cost lives and weaken the army. Once, when another rocket slammed into yet another camp- fire, a half-dozen soldiers spontaneously leaped up and dashed off into the dark. This time they returned limping but grinning, bearing the gray-green flat-nosed heads of three orcs and their wooden tube of a rocket launcher. Gull could commend their work, while Rakel had to discipline them for disobeying orders.

"Actually," she confided to Gull in their tent one night, "I'm glad to see them fighting mad, eating nails and breathing fire. After that big victory, their morale is high: they're hot to fight. If only we could *engage* an enemy and crush them!"

"We will," said Gull. "Have faith. 'All things come to one who has patience.'"

Rakel rolled her eyes. "You're becoming quite the doddering grandfatherly old duffer these days. Any more wisdom, graybeard?"

Gull chuckled and hooked her waist with one arm. "Come closer, child, and I'll give you more than advice."

All along, Greensleeves continued her studies with Chaney. The two would retire to some semisecluded spot, under a tree along a canyon wall, or into a shel- tering overhang, or beside a rock pool. Chaney would whisper some chant that, while giving no outward signs, kept the others away, and together the two would converse, memorize folklore and uses of plants, histories, and rhymes and chants for hours on end, though they never seemed to be gone for very long. In these lessons, Greensleeves learned of Urza and Mishra, of the Mightstone and the Weakstone, of the Brothers' War, of Ivory Towers and mile-deep mines, of entire continents laid waste to produce war matériel, of the monsters conjured or created in the darkest days of the war, of doomed slaves formed in Ashnod's Transmograts, of the cursed rack and the Su-Chi, of the all-healing Amulet of Kroog, a city destroyed so thoroughly that no one knew where lay its ruins, of the grinning Atog that burrowed through graveyards, dragging along the sins of haunted souls, and much, much more. It was thrilling, learning of the glorious and dark days of ancient history. Yet every story elicited a hundred questions for which neither Chaney, nor anyone living, had any answers.

After each lesson, Greensleeves stumbled to her tent and collapsed on her bedroll, wrung out both physically and mentally. She'd awake, her mind bursting with knowledge; sometimes she confused people's names, even her own, and she'd lose track of the day and their destination. She was drunk with learning some days, and Lily and her maids would have to shepherd her around the camp.

And as for picking one spell from the hundreds she learned, she often felt like a starving man at a banquet, paralyzed by the sheer number of choices before her. "How," she asked Chaney, "can I decide upon a spell to use in a wizards' duel, when there are so many?"

Chaney only chuckled. "It will all come clear. Filling your mind with facts is like filling a basket with grain: it takes some jolting and thumping and time to settle into place. You'll know when the time comes, be able to read the surroundings and the mana and your foe and your resources, the same way a bard knows which song of hundreds a king wishes to hear."

"But when will I be able to shift?" Greensleeves returned. "You said that was only the second stage, and I've never even tried it, or have a clue how to proceed. For all the things I've learned, I find a thousand questions with no answers, a thousand gaps unfilled."

And secretly, part of her dreaded trying the experience. If anything could unhinge her sanity, it would be dissolving herself and flying in shreds through the ether.

The druid startled her when she patted Green-sleeves's hand with an ice-cold paw. "All in time."

One morning Amma announced that Tybalt was recovered. Joyously, Greensleeves, Lily, Kwam, and the other students hurried to his bedside, a simple mat in the shade of an aspen tree.

The elf-man's nose appeared larger than ever because he was so pale and hollow-eyed. The green stone brain helmet, Amma reported, had simply dropped off last night. It now lay propped on a rock not far away. Yet Tybalt's sunken eyes were clear enough.

"Welcome back," Greensleeves tried to joke, though she felt as cold as the rocks around them and kept one wary eye on the stone helmet. "How—what—happened?"

Tybalt closed his eyes, still wrung out from his ordeal. "The helmet . . . must be the object we seek. The weapon . . . to use against wizards . . . to compel them. Notice, as I failed to . . . there is no mouth, no whispering."

They all looked. It was true. The thing looked as lifeless as a stone and was just as silent.

"When I donned it . . . I could feel, hear, a clamor of voices. Scores of them, all demanding I surrender, desist, stop practicing magic. But . . . I *have* no magic, no spellcasting. Oh, it hurt!"

People nodded in sympathy. Tybalt and Kwam and Daru and Ertha were "students of magic" because they loved it, were fascinated by it—and had no magic themselves. Their hope was, by long study, they might somehow *learn* to conjure.

Tybalt creaked on, "It was the voices of the Sages of Lat-Nam, dozens of them, shouting me down. Without any shields, any protection, any way to isolate my mind, I ran shrieking, hiding in a dark corner of my own skull." He shivered uncontrollably, and Amma pulled his blanket higher. His voice was a whisper. "I thought I'd never come out. . . . "

Greensleeves's own hands shook as she took
Tybalt's. "But you did. You were very brave to sustain
such—a bombardment of commands. Very brave to
seek to return to—" she couldn't say "sanity" "—yourself. All's well now, and you should rest."

"Aye," said Tybalt. "I think I will." He immediately
began to doze, but then snapped awake, grabbed
Greensleeves's hand. "But you know! There's more!
There *are* secrets inside the helm. There are tales and
stories in there, and spells, hundreds of them. As if
you could read the minds of the gathered wizards.
Imagine what you can learn . . . !"

Greensleeves shook her head and gently disen-
gaged her hand. "You'll never stop questing after
magic, will you, Tybalt? Yes, we'll investigate the
secrets. But not today. Now rest."

Exhausted, drained, Tybalt's eyes shut and he slept.

"Well," huffed Lily, looking at the stone helmet.
"Now we know how to use it to compel wizards. But
do we dare?"

Greensleeves had no answer.

A scout galloped into camp the next day, right past the
pickets, straight to Rakel's tent. Vaulting from the saddle, he wheezed, "I found it—Commander! A—spire—
hollowed out—like a—a bat cave! Not three miles—east
by north! It's the home—of the armored wizard!"

Rakel smacked a gloved fist in her palm. "I knew it!
His sneaky little attacks have been increasing. He's
growing more harried because we're close to his
home. Keep talking!" The commander grabbed up her
leather helmet and a drab cloak. "Hie, you! Fetch me
rope! Summon the general and round up any stray
scouts! You, show me!"

The stronghold of the armored wizard looked like
nothing as much as a potato masher stood on end.

Like many of the strange, wind-carved spires

they'd seen in these canyons, it was wider at the top
than the bottom, a single upward-tapering column of
red stone that stood alone in the center of a small valley. Chaney had explained that the spires were flint or
chert, veins upthrust from the center of the earth,
harder than the layers of limestone around them, so
that, over centuries, wind and water had carved them
free. The spire's top was as flat as a table, perhaps
fifty feet across. The spire was shot full of holes, like
some birds' rookery, and indeed, large bats with
yellow-spotted breasts flapped dismally in and out of
holes. But many holes had been enlarged enough to
accomodate a big man—one in armor and wide horns.

Besides the natural protection of the isolated
stone—the holes began thirty feet off the ground—a
moat had been dug around the column. A single flat
stone walkway spanned the moat; a chain ladder hung
from the lowermost hole.

Lounging in the valley, sleeping like lizards, squab-
bling over food or booty like buzzards, littering like
rats, were a hundred or so orcs, the wizard's standing
army. Caves dotted the canyon walls: hovels for the
creatures to shelter in. The lack of pickets or guards
showed how useless and slovenly the orcs were.

"When shall we attack?" whispered Gull.

The spies crouched in a high rocky cleft overlooking
the valley. Rakel had taken most of the day to bring them
here, crawling over scree with dull blankets draped over
the watchers. The commander had made the scouts
shuck any items that might jingle and had ordered soot
rubbed over anything shiny. They'd taken two hours
alone to crawl through the cleft, careful not make a sil-
houette against the skyline. There was Gull, Rakel, Bardo,
Kamee the chief cartographer, and two scouts.

Rakel answered, "The armored wizard always
attacks at night, so we'll attack by day. At dawn, when
these night creepers are most tired. T'will give us the
whole day to campaign."

She then asked Kamee, "You say three clefts enter
the valley?"

The dark woman nodded. "Four, counting this one, but it's too high to drop without ropes. The other three are all negotiable by horse, though we'd have to be careful of landslides."

"We'll come in too fast for those." Rakel thought for a while. "We'll use all three. More elbowroom to attack, and we'll keep them open as boltholes if things go wrong."

"They won't go wrong," Gull told her. "Our soldiers are champing at the bit and you're in charge. We'll win this one—a good clean victory to take home to our families."

But his casual phrasing stung him. His parents were dead. Victims of wizardry. He'd do well to remember that in the battle ahead. It would lend him strength against the armored wizard.

"The dawn after tomorrow, then," said Rakel. "No fires till then, and no noise. We'll move into position tomorrow, turn in early and rise at midnight."

Despite herself, she chuckled with glee. If only her old instructors in school could see her now, commanding an army and planning an attack deep in hostile territory.

And if only Garth were here. And Hammen, to watch his mother work and win glory.

For once, the army of Gull and Greensleeves made the sneak attack, and they tackled it with hearts afire.

The three entrances to the wizard's valley were at the north, east, and southwest. Rakel's forces had ridden into position the day before, jingling weapons tied down, horses' hooves muffled with rags. The camp followers had trailed along and set up camps under overhangs and in caves where possible, and the children carried on their chores and games in whispers. Finally, in blackest night, the infantry padded forward, and horses were led into line.

Rakel watched the sky and listened for the army's preparedness. Then, sending up a prayer to her war god, she ordered a charge.

The ram's horn's blare shattered the dawn.

Hooting and hollering and screaming, the army poured into the valley as the sun rose bloodred across the badlands, splintering the lands into long red and black shadows. From the north rode the cavalry and scouts, lances couched alongside their mounts' heads, yellow ribbons fluttering. From the southwest, the shortest route, came the Reds and Greens running, while from the east, the longest route around, ran Rakel and Gull before Neith's Blues. Though they numbered only thirty, they screamed like three hundred, and the thunder of hooves and boots in the three narrow canyons was tremendous.

The sleepy enemy was caught flat-footed. The treacherous orcs, who'd struck from above and behind so often, found themselves trapped among three phalanxes of enraged warriors. Olive-colored orcs screamed, ran, crashed into one another, tripped and fell, dove into their tiny caves so fast they bashed their heads on rock walls. Two fought to cross the single stone spanning the moat around the wizard's spire, and their tussling toppled both into the moat screaming.

But they weren't discommoded for long. Most died in minutes.

The combined cavalry and scouts had permission to lead and, under Helki's command, formed a double wedge that sliced through the orcs like scythes through wheat. Lances spitted the orcs, and when the shafts splintered or became too heavy, sabers split green heads, clove through banded arms. Foot soldiers plied their bows. Strings sang and arrows hissed, and orcs died transfixed. The terrified creatures dodged this way and that to avoid the death all around, but the exits from the canyon were blocked. Green-black blood soaked into the stony floor of the valley as the screams became fewer. It was horrible slaughter, but Gull and Rakel and all the rest had agreed the army deserved it. The orcs' sneak attacks were returned with a vengeance.

Half his standing force was dead before the armored wizard appeared. Greensleeves and the students, including the tottery Tybalt, had followed hard on the heels of the officers and the Blues. They glimpsed a brawny naked figure at an upper window cut from the rock, but the man ducked back. He reappeared minutes later, only half his formidiable armor strapped on: the breastplate, horned helmet, gauntlets, and girdle. For the rest, he wore only a dirty wool smock.

From his high window, the wizard waved both hands, scattering white chips like seeds. These rained from the window, and where each landed, curly wisps of ash spun upward and formed three score or more skeleton-goblins, tiny jittering shapes of old yellow bone. Gull and Greensleeves had seen these long ago in the burnt forest and had been terrified. But by day the skeleton-goblins looked like old chicken bones dumped on a midden, and the first blow of a cavalryman's saber scattered the bones like kindling. The skeleton-goblins were crushed along with the dying orcs.

Greensleeves laughed aloud. For once, another wizard was cut short. Conjuring took time, she knew: some spells only seconds, others minutes. But the half-dressed and flustered wizard would get no more time. Greensleeves saw to that.

Slipping off Goldenrod, the new druid raised a hand, pointed at the high chamber where the wizard struggled to conjure another spell, and thought of some of her oldest friends, who this moment slept the winter away in the highlands of the Whispering Woods. "Help me, my friends, and I'll see you rewarded. . . . "

Even above the noise of slaughter, she heard an echoing squawl from the half-armored wizard. He lurched to the window, spilled over the sill, hanging desperately by two hands, then slithered into another window just below. From the chamber he'd just vacated, a huge grizzly bear jammed out its head, growling and coughing and casting about, looking for the man who'd invaded its den.

Greensleeves saw the gauntleted hands project

from the lower window. Idly, she wondered what the wizard wanted to summon. She'd have to ask later, once he was captured. . . .

Hitching her skirts, she squatted and placed both hands flat on the ground. She'd talked to the earth yesterday, listened with an ear to the ground, read its pulse and mood. Now if she could tap it . . .

The slaughter in the valley was all but over. Green bodies splashed with dark blood lay everywhere, at all angles, like shattered dolls. Male and female fighters chopped the throats of wounded orcs, and teams yanked more from caves by their ankles before stabbing them. Others wiped their blades clean on the orcs' ragged kilts. Rakel ordered the trumpeter to sound Assembly: the officers had agreed to pull back from the spire and let Greensleeves work. The army reformed, but at arm's length, so as to make a scattered target in case of rockets. They laughed with delight at their easy victory. The cavalry spun their horses dramatically, tripped in pairs and trios to guard the exits to the valley. Many shielded their eyes against the dawn light to see what happened next.

What happened was the partly armored wizard raised high a clenched fist that glowed red between his fingers. That was the Mightstone, they knew by now, a deadly if mysterious weapon. Involuntarily they shrank back, and Rakel had to bark at them to keep still.

But Greensleeves stayed hunched, squatting, palms flat on the dirt. Her eyes were closed as she concentrated.

From his high balcony, the armored wizard shook the Mightstone, shouted an ancient curse that echoed and reechoed from the walls.

And slowly, the canyon walls began to flow.

Soldiers gawked, pointed, as huge drops of solid rock oozed from the walls and spilled across the stony soil. Rust-red and ochre and dirty white and shale gray, the drops puddled like molten steel, then slowly reformed.

From the center of the globs rose a knob, then a neck, then a torso that sprouted arms. The tall shapes coalesced into men and women, giants made of clay, soft and featureless, yet seemingly as powerful as the earth itself.

The flush of victory evaporated, and soldiers panicked as they were surrounded by scores of these clay beings. Rakel's captains shouted themselves hoarse to keep the lines dressed, whacked soldiers in the back and shoulders with the flats of their swords. The puddling shapes loomed all around, as tall as Liko the giant. Such monsters, the army knew, could crush them underfoot like ants, and there'd be no way to strike back. Boots shuffled as men and women cast wildly about. Some called to Greensleeves to save them. Even the magic students gibbered.

All the while, Greensleeves pressed against the earth.

Down, went her mind. Down, went her spirit. Like a blind mole, like a swimmer, she reached deep with invisible fingers of mana, hunting, searching, sensing strengths and faults. Frightened voices came to her dimly, and folks called her name, but she was lost beneath the soil.

Forgotten, off to the side on the swaying saddle on a pony, sat the ancient druid Chaney. Rasping, hacking, she cleared her throat and sang in a voice like a crow.

Rakel jogged toward Gull. Doughty she might be, but giants of clay were too much for thirty soldiers. She was ready to order a retreat, mentally searching for the quickest route out. And cursing. Why weren't the damned useless hand-wavers stopping this magical menace? Past Gull, she could see the clay creatures take their first long steps from the puddles that birthed them, raise great earthen fists over their heads, poised to crush the life from the living . . .

Chaney's wild weird song rose, rang from the walls . . .

. . . and slowly, slowly, the clay men slowed, then stopped, frozen. When all of them had halted, having gone no more than three strides, the druid's singing stopped.

In the silence, soldiers sighed and giggled with relief. Tybalt, recovered from his mind-sickness, tiptoed forward. With a war club he'd picked up, he crept toward the nearest clay giant, which towered like a copy of the stone spire. His club at arm's length, Tybalt tapped, then rapped on an outthrust frozen leg.

Like a sandcastle, the leg crumbled and collapsed, shattering on the ground.

Soldiers roared their approval. Rakel laughed, too, and waved an arm, dismissing the ranks. Foot soldiers ran to raise their weapons and whap the clay men. Recovered from their fright, they laughed uproariously, like children, as they knocked the clay men to heaps of dried mud.

Then the earth jumped under their feet.

Reaching deep into the unseen earth, Greensleeves had found a fault, and traced it to a spot close by the surface. Driving magic fingers into the crack, shrugging magic shoulders, she'd irritated the earth enough for it to react.

The shock snapped the canyon floor like a carpet.

Rocks jiggled from the walls to clatter on the ground. Soldiers swayed to keep their balance. Cavalry riders held their reins close to keep skittish animals from bolting. The trumpeter dropped her instrument. Someone screamed. Off to one side, Chaney smiled.

The wizard's stone spire shivered, shifted.

Greensleeves watched, fascinated by her success. The pinnacle of stone supporting the spire, not a dozen feet thick, snapped. For a second, it stayed upright, but slowly, slowly, gravity fought to bring it down. Unbalanced, the stone spire tipped, toppled.

Straight at Greensleeves.

The druid's eyes went wide. She scrambled up from her dirty knees, hiked her skirts to run. As the shadow of the falling spire engulfed her, she saw her sturdy brother running to rescue her. But he was too far, too late.

Then a heavy tread sounded to one side. She heard someone panting. Strong but slender hands snagged her waist. The mysterious someone hoisted her against his chest and kept running at an oblique slant.

Both were lifted off their feet, then slammed to the ground, when the great stone spire struck the canyon floor.

The sound was a tremendous *whump*. There followed a crashing growl as the chambers and internal walls smashed together and crushed flat. Rocks shot through the air, felling more than one person. Choking dust billowed in waves that blinded.

It was minutes, the stone dust settling heavily, before Greensleeves identified her rescuer.

As the stone spire had careened downward, Gull saw a flash from an upper window. The partly armored wizard leaped, a long magically augmented bound.

But it couldn't carry him to the canyon rim, or even to a high ledge, and he slammed full into a stone wall twenty feet up. Armor and magic partly protected him, but he bounced painfully and slid in a heap to the canyon floor.

He scrambled to his feet, fumbling at his belt for a charm.

And Gull caught up to him.

Squinting in the dust cloud the wizard had raised, Gull swung his double-headed axe high over his right shoulder. Before the wizard could duck, the axe blade crashed into his breastplate, knocking him back against the wall. Another well-aimed blow dented his helmet, then the returning blow tore it from his head so it clattered amidst the rocks.

Gull swung the axe overhead in two brawny hands, ready to cleave the wizard like a hardwood log. He was clearly dazed, so Gull shouted, "Do you yield, you bastard?"

The wizard raised empty hands. "Yes, yes! I yield! Don't kill me! I'll not conjure!"

The woodcutter lowered his axe to his shoulder, then grinned. "So. I guess I'm still useful after all."

Behind him, the army cheered and cheered.

But it was a while before Greensleeves noted the capture or the cheering, for she was wrapped in a man's lean arms, and he only now let her go.

"Kwam?"

The tall youth rose awkwardly, brushed at his clothes without answering. He was tongue-tied. But his eyes shone with pleasure: he'd risked his life to rescue her and had succeeded.

For the first time, Greensleeves took note of this man. He'd hovered around her or nearby, she realized, for months. She'd always thought he was merely enthusiastic about learning magic. But now she realized why he stayed close.

He was enthusiastic—about her.

Tongue-tied herself, she could only smile at him. He smiled back.

No one saw the man who winked into being atop the canyon rim. He was a dark man, bearded, wearing a practical and plain dark jerkin ornamented with a star-and-moon motif across his breast and ribs. A black, red-edged glyph on his jerkin glowed softly, a ward of delusion, an aid against detection, for he sensed two powerful wizards were nearby.

It was Guyapi, wizard of Benalia, who had shifted Rakel to her assigned targets this past moon.

No one saw him, but he saw Rakel. He watched her order fighters into ranks, saw her consult a tall man who carried a woodcutting axe and a small tatty woman in green with a lumpy shawl. The man and woman looked alike, no doubt brother and sister.

They were alive, and Rakel was aiding them.

Having seen all this, the wizard winked away.

Back to Benalia.

CHAPTER

14

"YOUR NAME IS HACK-ON?"

"No, it's Haakon! *Hay-kon* the First, King of the Badlands! What's your name, Wax-in-Your-Ears?"

Gull let the insult pass. Confident they wouldn't kill him, the no-longer-armored wizard had grown surly and petulant, like a spoiled child.

The army had relocated to another canyon a mile from the wizard's ruined home. Vultures and rats and coyotes had already arrived to feast on the orc bodies left behind. Also left behind had been the wizard's armor, for Chaney considered it too dangerous to keep—it might compel someone to don it. They'd pitched the pieces into the moat around the shattered spire and tumbled rocks after them. The Mightstone they'd kept.

This valley sported grass where a small cataract spilled from the rocks on the north side. Chaney reported the badlands were softening, that Haakon's spire was a sort of gateway to arable land farther on.

While the sounds of dinner and laughter and songs of victory rang around them, Gull, Rakel, Greensleeves,

Bardo, Helki, and the other officers tried to interrogate Haakon, self-proclaimed "king of the Badlands," who sat on a rock like some ugly desert toad.

The "king" was a big man, powerful but gone to fat, with a jowly chin, huge gut, and soft hands. The crown of his head was bald, and lank graying hair hung around his ears and dirty neck. He stank from wearing armor and missing baths. Gull judged he'd been a bully once, important somewhere, but now he was just a bloated, smelly prisoner in a filthy wool smock.

And recalcitrant. Gull had asked him several questions and gotten only snipes so far. He tried once to appeal to the man's vanity. "How long have you reigned in these badlands?" Gull asked. "I know you showed up near the star crater—"

"Stop prattling, pig!" snarled the wizard. "We'll tell you none of our secrets! All we'll lend is a warning— watch your back! You won't keep us long!"

Rakel scoffed, drawing a black glare. She dangled her short sword by the pommel. "If he won't talk, he's no use to us. Let me carve some fat off him and stake him for the vultures. At least he'd do some good for them."

The wizard glared, but sweat popped out from his furrowed brow. Gull moved upwind. Their real concern was that this wizard had to be guarded at all times by at least two people, lest he mutter and hand wave and shift away, disappearing into the ether. They'd finally caught a wizard, Gull reflected, but had no way to hold him.

To keep the man guessing, he said, "That might be best. We surely can't lug him along. The big tub of guts probably eats more than any three men. Summon an execution squad. But take him up the canyon a ways. I don't like to hear buzzards croaking." He winked as he finished.

But before the bluff could unfold, Greensleeves approached, bearing the green helmet. Behind her came the other magic students, including the still shaky Tybalt and the quiet Kwam.

More and more, the woman found herself studying Kwam with sidelong glances—when he wasn't aware of it. He was tall and dark and slender, with mild brown eyes as deep as a well. Greensleeves even liked the smooth unhurried way he walked, how his long strong hands could work so gently.

For the first time in her life, she felt fluttery in the stomach about a man. And chagrined, and awkward, and happy. Kwam must have admired her for a long time without her realizing it, but she'd been too busy to notice his—special attention. She couldn't frame the word "love" yet in her mind.

Gull frowned at the helmet. Rakel tapped her sword pommel and her foot, impatient for results. The other officers were curious but unexcited. Mostly they wanted to sleep, having been up all the previous night in a war council and having fought half the day.

The fat wizard squinted at the helmet. Still a curious brown and mottled green, it looked more like a brain than ever, with crinkles running along the top. Clearly, he didn't know what to make of it.

Without preamble, Greensleeves nodded at the seated wizard. "Hold him, please."

Used to taking orders, Bardo, Rakel, and Helki clamped powerful hands on the wizard. Only Gull balked. "Greenie, what—"

Greensleeves plopped the helmet on Haakon's head. *"Yaaaahhhh!"* The wizard jerked as if he'd been stung by a rattlesnake. Surprised, Helki let go, but Rakel and Bardo grimly held him down. The man's whole fat body spasmed as he grabbed at the helmet, tugged on it, writhed, hissed, moaned, shook.

"Greenie, what in blazes are you *doing*?" barked Gull.

"Experimenting. Studying." The young druid stepped back from the kicking squirming Haakon. "We know what it did to Tybalt, so we—"

Gull waved his long axe in agitatation. "We surely do! It damned near killed him! It drove him stark raving mad for a week!"

"I—" Greensleeves paused. The word "mad" tolled

like a bell in her own mind. "I—we know why the helmet was crafted, and how to use it. So we'll use it. That's our goal, isn't it, to put wizards under our compulsion?"

Flabbergasted at her casual cruelty, Gull sputtered, "Well, yes! But—we didn't mean to—make people suffer!"

Greensleeves sniffed. Her tone grew pouty—proof she argued on shaky ground. "Haakon's made people suffer! How many of our charges did he kill in his sneak attacks? Poor Dinos was lured by a siren's song and had his skull smashed! Lahela lost a leg in a rock slide! So if he suffers, so be it!" Yet her voice shook. "And he won't suffer, much! Tybalt has no magic in him, none he can tap, so the helmet near drove him—never mind. But Haakon's charged with mana, and it will protect him. That's why the commands are so strong, Chaney and I reckon, to break through any personal shields a recalcitrant wizard might erect. *And* if we're to stop his depredations—and that is our goal!—we must take some chances!" she finished.

"If the helmet is so harmless," her brother said slowly, "why haven't you put it on your *own* head?"

"I—" But the druid had no reply.

Gull walked away. Rakel let loose of Haakon and followed.

Greensleeves and the students waited. Slowly, gradually, Haakon's defenses were broken down, and he ceased to struggle. With a grunt and gurgle, he let go of the helmet, went limp, and slid off the seat onto the ground.

Greensleeves bit her lip. This was the crucial moment, the final test. If it failed, she might have driven a man insane for nothing.

And insanity, to her, was worse than any death.

Leaning over the flabby prisoner, Greensleeves asked in a quavery voice, "Can you hear me?"

"I hear you." Haakon's surliness was gone. He stared straight ahead, at nothing, and spoke in an empty tone like a dead man's.

"Whom—whom do you serve?" asked the woman.

"You, mistress."

Greensleeves closed her eyes and sent up a silent prayer of thanks to the spirits. She turned to the magic students, who watched uneasily. Even Kwam looked shocked. "See? We were right! Tybalt, isn't this grand? We've got a way to control wizards at last. We can add his power to our cause, or just turn him loose, impose a geas for him to pursue only good ends. This is what we've been fighting for all along!"

Tybalt only pulled on his long nose with one bony hand. "Well, mistress . . . if you say so. . . . "

Greensleeves frowned, puzzled, growing angry, but no one would look at her. When she turned to Bardo and Helki, they picked up their weapons and walked away.

"What is *wrong* with you people?" Greensleeves asked. "Two victories in one day aren't *enough*?"

The only one to answer was Haakon sprawled on the ground. "Yes, mistress." It sounded like a moan of pain.

Greensleeves sighed and pointed at the prisoner. "Fetch Amma's healers to bundle him to the hospital tents. See they don't dislodge the helmet. Tie it under his chin with a rag, if need be."

"Yes, mistress," said Tybalt absentmindedly.

Greensleeves snapped, surprising everyone, *"And don't call me that!"*

She blinked, surprised herself. And horrified at the fright in Kwam's eyes.

Turning, her vision blurring with tears, Greensleeves stamped off toward her tent.

That night, despite general exhaustion, the camp hummed like a hive of bees. Talk of victory over the orcs, the destruction of the spire and appearance of the clay giants, the capture of the wizard, the compelling helmet, and plans for the future ran round and round.

Gull and Rakel sat on a frayed rug before their tent, crosslegged, gazing at the campfire. Rakel honed her sword to remove a notch gained that morning. Gull polished his axe handle. They talked in low tones that kept others from intruding.

"She worries me, Rakel. No two ways about it. She was born with great magical powers, and she's learned scads of tricks from Chaney. Now she can even put other wizards under her spell, so she's a wizard over wizards. If she can use *their* powers, too, she'll be like some wolf that eats weaker wolves and becomes a god-wolf or something. . . ."

Rakel stroked her blade with a whetstone, harder than necessary. She barely heard Gull. She'd been thrilled today by their victory, by the cut and thrust of battle. But once she settled down, as every night, she thought of her son, and a lump grew in her throat.

Hammen's mother prayed that somehow her son hung on, resisted the brainwashing of his tutors, kept faith in his mother, awaited rescue. *Don't give in,* she willed to him across the miles. But why, she fretted, hadn't Guyapi come to fetch her? Chaney said she'd know when a wizard shifted nearby. The full of the moon was past, so where was he? Was this more deviltry of Sabriam's, making Rakel wait before recalling her to Benalia? And once Guyapi arrived and found she'd collected no heads, could they truly grab him, force him . . .

Gull's thoughts rambled, too, as he continued his monologue to Rakel. He neglected his polishing and simply stared into the fire. " . . . And do you notice how she uses that royal 'we,' same as that fat wizard? Greenie used to be so sweet. A bunch of daisies would keep her happy for hours. Now she quests after power like any evil wizard. This quest of ours turns sour— What is it? We don't wish to be disturbed."

He said this to a trio that marched in from the far side of the campfire. Having gazed at the flames so long, Gull couldn't see them well. Greens? They wore tight-fitting leather jerkins and trousers and floptop boots, wrong for winter weather.

They picked up their feet, came at a half-trot. Gull grabbed up his axe.

Rakel saw the tattoos on their left forearms: the seashells of Clan Deniz.

"Gull, watch out!" Rakel snapped her legs under her and hopped up like a grasshopper. Without another word, she shrieked a battle cry and swung her short sword.

Foremost of the trio was a tall woman with blond hair braided down her back. She and the rest wore short swords at their hips, but carried wooden staves in their hands that were four feet long with rope loops at either end. The blonde brayed a laugh and snapped the staff at Rakel's head. "Ha, Norreen! Fat and slow as ever—"

Her words died as Rakel feinted. Having acted deliberately slow, she reversed a weak thrust, then whipped it faster than the eye could follow. The blade's tip slipped past the blonde's stick defense, just far enough. Six inches of blade split the woman's liver. The cruel stab wound would take days to kill her.

"Fight, don't talk!" snarled Rakel.

The blonde gasped and stepped back, instinctively defending, but too late. Horrified, she began to cry. "Oh, no! Not me! Oh, no!"

The two males had skipped around her, flanking Rakel. With her free hand, the warrior woman grabbed the blonde's stick and wrenched it left as a partial shield on that side. Barking "Ha!" and stamping, Rakel flicked her blade at the rightmost man, forced him to drop back. She'd remembered a lot in the days since being abandoned in this part of the Domains. She shoved the dying blonde in the leftmost man's direction. "Ha! Gull, move!"

In the three seconds since Rakel jumped up, the woodcutter had just gained his feet. He raised his axe handle across his chest to halt a swipe from the rightmost hero's stick. The wood rapped Gull's axe handle, and Gull had the irrelevant thought that he'd just polished out the dings.

Barking, using Rakel's training, Gull snapped first one end of his axe, then the other at the man's upper chest, an awkward place to defend. The hero, surprised to see a Benalish defense used by a stranger, dropped back. Gull kicked, his boot crunching the man's knee sideways. *Use everything in an attack,* Rakel had lectured him, *and never hold back.* Gull followed his feints with a direct blow, driving the thick hickory haft straight at the man's face, popping him between the eyes, knocking him flat.

But the warrior woman was beset. The blonde, switching from sorrow to white-hot anger, threw herself at Rakel, disdainful of her own death. The wooden stick and its ropes—a capture noose for taking slaves, Rakel knew—looped the steel pommel of Rakel's sword. Having snagged her foe, the blonde clawed for Rakel's eyes. Frustrated by the darkness, in danger of being blinded, Rakel lost a precious second trying to free her sword. At that moment, the leftmost hero bashed her across the head. Stunned, Rakel tried to keep her feet, couldn't find the ground. Head spinning, she fell, still trying to free her sword.

Gull heard the thunk, heard his lover groan. He latched onto a blond braid shimmering in the firelight and yanked the hero off her feet and away from Rakel.

The last standing hero had snaked a loop over Rakel's throat and cinched it tight. Hoisting her in front as a shield, he dragged her backward. "Guyapi, I've got her!" he hollered into the darkness.

Who? Gull wondered. And where had these assassins come from? Dressed like Rakel, they had to be Benalish heroes. But how had they gotten past the pickets? Too late, he realized—

Just beyond the firelight lurked a dark figure decorated with stars and a moon. The man extended both hands, and sparks flew from his fingertips.

Gull shouted, "*No! Rakel!*"

But his lover, and the hero holding her, and both heroes on the ground, suddenly crackled as if on fire. Sparks engulfed them all. Gull leaped, stumbling in the darkness and blinding light, and grabbed for Rakel. His hand passed through.

Then they were gone.

* * *

Gull's shout roused the whole camp. Guards and soldiers ran from the four points of the compass.
Greensleeves staggered out of her tent pressing down
the folds of her skirt. Helki clattered to her feet and
grabbed up her lance.

And in the confusion, the guards watching Haakon
turned away.

The fat wizard sat slumped against a rock, as
before, near the hospital tents, the helmet still on his
head, wrapped in a blanket provided by a healer. His
blank face shone greasy in the light of the guard's fire.
He looked dead to the world, with less mind than an ox.

Yet he wasn't mindless, nor idle.

Voices shrieked in his skull, demanding, commanding, ordering he submit. And he had. No single
wizard could stand up to that cacophony of demands.
But amidst this turmoil, this mind-storm, Haakon
retained a tiny part of his sanity. He couldn't disobey
the orders, couldn't shift, couldn't even move. But he
could send a message, could reach out along thin,
invisible threads, could summon a potent force, one
perhaps strong enough to battle even this many
voices.

The two guards were distracted by the firelit hurly-
burly over at the officers' tents. They argued whether
one should stay, or both. If it were another raid—

Haakon muttered an old arcane incantation.

At every hand, whiskery shapes whispered from
the ground, like ashes swirling in a dust devil. The
shapes hopped up, hip-high, and took on solid spindly
forms, with red glowing eyes and long white teeth.

Demons, dozens of them, overran the guards,
spilling one to the ground, biting her flesh away with
sharp snaps of their pointed fangs. The other guard
cried out once as the fiends climbed up his body. He
tried to run, but got only three paces before he died.

Deep inside, Haakon laughed as dozens of hungry-
eyed demons capered around his feet. Let them try to

keep him prisoner, he gloated. He'd overrun this camp, spill the army's blood, and somehow work off this helmet and make his escape—

Triumph turned to confusion, then horror, as the small demons suddenly swarmed over Haakon like rats over a dunghill. Trapped, unable to move, Haakon swore, screamed, whimpered. But the demons scrabbled their way up his body.

One and all, they lusted for the green helmet atop his head.

A dozen claws ripped and scratched at Haakon's head. A razor-sharp talon split his ear, another his cheek. A finger gouged his eye, the claw jiggling inside the socket; he screamed and was pricked in the tongue.

Then his bald pate felt icy cold, for the green helmet was plucked off.

The guards were long dead, so there was no one else to see the demons pluck the helm from Haakon's blood-streaming head. The beasts bobbled it, clutched for it, batted at it, while the blind, fat wizard screamed and bled.

But Haakon's screams had been heard. Greensleeves and Gull and several others ran up just in time to see the helmet and the demons shrink to wisps of ash that curled on themselves and sank away altogether.

"Gone," breathed Greensleeves. "Just—gone! And we need it so! It's the answer to everything! But where's Rakel? Who were those fighters in black?"

"Bastards, that's who!" Tears of rage ran down Gull's face. "Heroes, they call 'em, a warrior rank from her city, Benalia! But assassins is more like it! They've enslaved her, dragged her back to their benighted city! We've got to go after her!"

Greensleeves shook tousled brown locks. "No, we've got to get back the brain. It's the most powerful artifact ever. We need it, or we're nothing!"

"We're *not* nothing!" Her brother's bark startled her. "You've grown too attached to that thing. It's just a—geegaw! We can do without it. We need Rakel back."

"*You* need Rakel back. *You've* gotten too attached to *her*."

"I have not! I mean—She's the commander of this army, by Gabriel's Fire! We need her to win any more battles!" Rakel was, in fact, more than an able commander to Gull, but he couldn't blurt out the word "lover" in public.

Healers fell to tending Haakon, gasping when they saw his ruined eye and torn face.

"All right, you're right," Greensleeves panted. "We need them both. But how will we find them? We don't know where Benalia lies, or where the demons have gone."

A crowd had gathered, scores of people, who listened raptly. A raspy voice sounded, as if an owl hovered overhead to add to the conversation.

"If I might interrupt." Chaney leaned on Kwam at an angle. She had to raise her voice about the whimperings of the blinded wizard. "I believe I know where the demons have taken your green toy. Phyrexia."

"Phyrexia?" asked Greensleeves. "What's—"

"You are impetuous as your brother these days, Greensleeves. Listen and learn. Phyrexia is a plane so distant most wizards don't know it exists, let alone visit there. Many thought it destroyed in the Brothers' War. A plane of demons, like Ashtok and others. Yet Phyrexia's demons serve a purpose, a geas leftover from the war. They steal sentient artifacts and rip them apart, dismantle them utterly. A living horde to kill living artifacts. Another war machine that backfired, no doubt, for they still seek out and destroy such artifacts, which is why so few are left. Poor Haakon summoned the wrong horde this time. If your green brain remains in Phyrexia—the 'Hell for Artifacts'—for more than a day, there will be no way to reconstruct it."

"Then," said Greensleeves, "we need to go immediately."

"Are you mad?" countered her brother, waving his axe, making folks flinch. "Didn't you listen and learn? She said there are nothing *but* demons there, and they pull magic junk apart! How long do you think *you'll* last? And meantime, thugs in Benalia will be pulling *Rakel* apart, because she failed to assassinate us. Does that penetrate your skull, or have you reverted to a *dunderhead* again?"

People hissed, and Lily, behind Greensleeves, gasped. Gull had even shocked himself. But Greensleeves didn't blush or cry. Stubborn as her brother, she just shouted back, "Do I need to take advice from·you? You've been mooning over Rakel so long your brains have turned to mush! How long—"

"Mooning? I'll tell you who's mooning around here! Who's got big brown cow eyes and his tongue hanging out, following you around like a lovestruck puppy." He pointed at Kwam, propping Chaney, and the youth flushed scarlet. "And that reminds me! Stay away from my little sister!"

"You leave him alone!" Greensleeves went deadly quiet, coldly furious. "Are *you* the only one allowed *love* around here? You can't even make up your mind who to tumble into the blankets; poor neglected Lily here, or your sword-swinging barmaid!"

Gull snorted, spat, waved his hands. Greensleeves had pinned him, and he had no retort. His little sister glared back at him, her eyes hot enough to melt his axe head.

"If I may interrupt," came the soft rasp. Chaney paused until she was sure they were listening. "Thank you. You're both forgetting something. You two speak of 'going after' either Rakel or the green brain. As I understand, *I* am the only wizard here who can shift. Lily's done it but once and has no clue how to do so again. Greensleeves, for her own reasons—or fears—has yet to reach that stage.

"Yet *my* planeswalking days are over. I find it difficult enough to sustain myself in this plane, let alone any other. So no one, in fact, is shifting anywhere.

"Unless," she added, "Lily and Greensleeves are prepared to learn how. Tonight . . . "

CHAPTER
15

ONCE AGAIN, RAKEL WAS TRUSSED, A PRISONER IN the small stone anteroom hung with tapestries. She was left there, chained facedown on the stone floor, for hours. Then, once again, come late morning, she was hauled choking before the Benalish council presided over by the smirking Sabriam.

But this time, it was she who was different.

The Norreen hauled here before had been a farm wife and mother, growing fat and soft, her breasts heavy with milk, her mind filled with gardening and tending livestock, cooking and childrearing.

Now, as Rakel, she was a warrior again, concerned with killing strokes, logistics, tactics, ambushes, training, discipline. She could feel the spring in her legs, the might in her sinews, and despite the choking slave rope around her neck, her back was straight, her carriage proud.

But she couldn't help shifting her eyes, hoping her son was here. Little Hammen, she worried, how have you fared at the hands of these dissipated thugs?

Only two heroes, the two men, held her, for the

blonde with the liver wound had been taken to the hospital to await death. The two men were strong, as Rakel was strong, yet she concealed her strength. As she'd taught Gull and Greensleeves's army: Never show your full strength to the enemy until it's too late—for them.

The long room was the same, for little changed in this city—it was smug in its decadence. The crowd of hangers-on waited for entertainment, the long blue runner with pink seashells ran to the dais with its glossy table and seven stone-faced council members, all mortal her enemies, all of the Clan Deniz. The exchequer stood with a scroll etched in red, as if he hadn't moved in the last fifty days, and centermost was the Speaker for the Caste, the pasty-faced Sabriam, looking more worn-out than ever. The parties he was staging nightly—at the city's expense—must be legendary. The man's nose shone glossy white, and Rakel allowed herself a smile. Sabriam had had his nose regenerated after she'd broken it with that kick, the best blow she ever struck.

She was surprised at her own smile, and heartened. She'd found an odd peace. Weeks ago she'd tried suicide, and part of her soul still floated in the ether with Garth and Hammen like a lost balloon. In the meantime, she'd done her best. No matter what, these pigs could only kill her, and death was not as cruel as some fates. She'd returned to the ways of the warrior. Now if she could only take a few enemies with her to the Darkness.

"Rakel of Dasha of Argemone of Kynthia," droned the exchequer, beginning his list, "you stand accused of the highest crime; treason against the city-state of Benalia. Having been ordered to fetch back the heads of Gull the Woodcutter and Greensleeves, general and wizard of the army assembled in the east, who threaten to make war on the city-state of Benalia, threatening its borders and its sovereign people—"

"Bullshit!" Rakel barked, loud and clear.

The exchequer's voice stopped with a bleat.

Retainers buzzed. Council members frowned and whispered.

Speaking during charges was against the rules, as was pleading anything but guilty, but Rakel was no longer a hero of Benalia. She was a commander of a distant army, ragtag and rebellious for sure, but dedicated to a worthy cause.

These toadies should learn that right away.

"Your charges are a pack of lies! Gull and Greensleeves are good and decent folk. They've dedicated themselves to ridding the world of wizards' predations. And they've got scores of followers—volunteers, not slaves! So while this cesspool of a city fouls its nest ever deeper, wreaking havoc and destroying the good, *someone* is out to make the Domains a safer place for *common folk*. There's—ack!"

At the lifting of Sabriam's bony hand, her captors had twisted the noose around her throat. No matter. People murmured and scowled, but Rakel might as well have shouted into the wind. No sense or reason or decency would flower in this ashheap.

Sabriam arose painfully from his seat behind the council table—he was crippled by some foul illness— and signaled to the exchequer. "Enter a plea of guilty. Rakel, await punishment." Then he tottered around the table and stepped to the chamber floor, an old man at thirty.

Sabriam came before Rakel and stood just out of lunging range, assured the captors held her tight. He wiped his chin where he drooled. "Rakel, you have failed again, and this time there'll be no saving grace. You'll die at the next rise of the moon, an example to others who would fail our mother city. But the pain you suffer in body will never match your spiritual pain. We've a small surprise for you." He smirked, but a cough broke the smile. He waved his bony hand again.

Rakel would have spat on him, but that was beneath her. There was no way to hurt her now—

She gulped as a small boy was brought forward by a state guardian. Though he was barely more than two years old, the boy's head was shaved, and he wore black leathers from head to toe, the spitting image of a hero, even to the small dagger at his belt.

"Hammen," she breathed, ashamed at the sob in her voice.

"No!" snapped the boy. His eyes glittered ice-blue at her, Garth's eyes. "That not my name! I S'briam now! Like him!" He pointed up at the smirking Speaker. "My parents were bad, and died because they were bad. Now I a hero, a winner! I grow up strong and kill my city's emenies!"

People chuckled at his mispronunciation, applauded his spirit and dedication.

So they've taken even my son, Rakel thought. Perverted him, taught him to hate his parents and his upbringing.

So there are fates worse than death.

But the boy's mother drew herself up straight and spoke in a calm, though shaking, tone. "I understand—son. I'm glad to see you're—well. I want you to know that—no matter what—your parents will always love you."

She dropped her voice, so the child and Sabriam and even the retainers along the walls leaned forward. "And I want you remember something else, child. A strong image, a lesson to carry with you forever. Something your mother did."

The boy's eyes glittered still, but now sparkled with curiosity. Inquisitiveness was beaten out of Benalish children, for it made them less apt to take orders. She was encouraged by this sign of native intelligence. She told him, "Remember this—"

Her captors had relaxed their hold a fraction, and it was all the new, revitalized Rakel needed. Hollering, she lunged and smashed the crown of her head square into Sabriam's face.

The man howled as his still-healing nose exploded in bone fragments and rich red blood. Then Rakel was beaten to her knees and choked almost insensible, as folk ran hither and thither around the council hall.

She rasped to her son, "Never stop fighting, Hammen! No matter what they do to you! Or me! There are decent folk out there, who fight for the good—"

She got no farther, for the rope ripped skin from her neck, cut off her air. Hoicked to her tiptoes, she was towed backward from the hall.

"To the dungeons!" slobbered Sabriam. "Take her—"

Dragging Rakel by the throttling rope, the guards whipped aside a tapestry at the end of the room and half threw her down a stairwell.

Yet she'd seen her black-clad, bald son lock his gaze to hers.

He would remember.

The officer and magic users stood stunned by the old druid's words.

Greensleeves murmured, "Me? Shift somewhere? That I've never even visited? But—I can't!"

Lily just shook her head. "Nor can I."

Chaney hobbled forward and put out her one good hand like a dry leaf. Hesitantly, the two women took it.

"You can, and you will, for different reasons and the same ones. Come with me, children, and we'll talk. In private."

Meekly, the two young women walked with the old, shuffling one.

The women sat in a circle of rocks some distance from the camp, in semidarkness, where the breeze was cool and whistled around their ears. Lily's flower-embroidered skirts and cloak, through now travel-stained, glowed luminously in the firelight. Greensleeves looked tousled and leaf-strewn and childishly messy as always. Both felt like children, too, as they sat before this woman, who was as ancient as the rock walls.

Chaney carried her woven basket hooked on her good arm, and it squeaked as she leaned forward. "Now listen carefully, for time grows short: mine and Rakel's and our army's. These are things I've tried to tell you all along, but neither of you were ready to listen. You were both too afraid."

"Afraid?" asked Lily. "I'm not—"

"I am," said Greensleeves, "but I don't—"

"Hush and listen," Chaney cut them off. "Conjuring and shifting are two faces of the same tree, opposite sides of a leaf. With one, you summon the item you want to you. With the other, you summon yourself to a place you know or sense."

"But we don't *know* these places!" bleated Greensleeves.

The druid raised a withered hand. In a dry whisper, she said, "I've thought long on your problems and believe I know part of the solution.

"Greensleeves, my child, you have a very strong sense of *place*. You live in the here and now, in tune with the soil and sky around you. You have a hard time imagining being elsewhere. And so should a druid feel at home—must—but it makes for hard shifting, which is why I no longer play with it. Lily, you have never loved yourself, never felt at home since the day you were sold into slavery. As such, you have always wished yourself far away—anywhere, as long as it's far. While Greensleeves knows her surroundings to the depths of the earth and the center of a leaf's veins and the gut of a hawk overhead, you touch your surroundings no more than a butterfly in a breeze. This is why you tap the magic of the sun and clouds and sky. Yet still we have balance: one of you wishes to stay, one to go. Two sides of the same leaf, again.

"And you have fears. Greensleeves fears losing her mind, her self. She had no mind for her first sixteen years, her thoughts as scrambled as a baby squirrel's. The idea of sending her mind questing into the ether, and perhaps losing it, terrifies her—and keeps her rooted. Lily has always dwelt too much in her mind, for it's all she's had. Nothing, not her clothes, not her food, not her money, not even her body, have ever belonged to her. As such, she's always sent her mind questing. Yet she can't grab hold of the magic around her to lift her away.

"Is it happenstance, children, how your magic powers have manifested themselves? Haven't I told you both that magic comes not from without but from within? Can you see why Greensleeves can summon a thing to her side, here where she's comfortable and happy, yet not remove herself? Or that Lily seeks to fly far away, never wanting to touch down?"

In the darkness, staring at the druid's craggy face, the young women were silent.

"There is only one solution, and that is to cut yourselves free. Once you were babies and could not move at all. Then you learned to roll over, then crawl, then walk, then run. Now you must both learn to fly. But you'll never shift, never fly, dragging the weight of fear with you."

Slowly, Greensleeves nodded. It made sense. To recognize fear was not hard. But to overcome it might be impossible.

"Not impossible," Chaney stated, and Greensleeves jumped. "No, I'm not reading your mind. Your face says enough. I have here . . . with me . . . Help me open this basket, dear. Thank you. Something for each of you. Things I've carried for some time. A time which has come. . . . " She groped in the basket, and Greensleeves had the frivolous thought that she'd pluck out an apple for each of them. Chaney was never one to fiddle with artifacts, she knew, but she'd never asked what Chaney carried in the basket, her only traveling gear besides a worn cloak.

"Lily," the dry voice scuttled around them in the dim light, "hold out your hand."

The ex–dancing girl, ex-prostitute did. Into it the druid placed something small and cold as the tip of an icicle. Holding it up to catch the distant light, Lily saw it was a small pendant on a rawhide chain: a tiny egg, pale blue with darker speckles, like a robin's egg, yet as hard as a rock.

"It is a rock," said the druid. "Or rather, an egg so old it's become a rock. The teacher who gave it me called it a dingus egg, for even he couldn't fathom its age. Think you of how long an egg must lie in the ground undisturbed till it turns to stone."

Lily held the thing by the thong, as if afraid her hands might soil it. It was no bigger than an acorn. "But . . . how do I use it?"

"This 'dingus egg' was to hatch a creature from long ago, a flying beast covered in leather, but not a bat, for t'was older than bats, even. This creature, and all its ilk, lived before mankind had been fashioned by the gods. Yet the egg failed to hatch. So the creature's spirit is trapped inside forever, never dead, but never to come alive. Through the millenia, it has amassed power, mana that predates man and all his works. As such, it can undo anything man can do." She smiled at her own long-windedness. "One effect is it can allay all geases, and magic screens, and spheres. In short, it could let you travel to any spot guarded against shifting."

"Oh," said the girl. She'd forgotten Rakel's warning, that the council hall of Benalia was warded against shifting and other magic. Otherwise, Greensleeves could probably just conjure Rakel back again.

"But those are only details," continued the druid. "More important than your rescuing Rakel is you rescuing yourself."

"What?" Lily shook her head, unsure she'd heard correctly. "I must rescue *myself*?"

Chaney's hand closed around Lily's and the ancient stone egg. "You keep your secrets close, Lily, too close. But I can see them, for I have eyes. This artifact can undo all the works of man, by which I mean, of course, men and women. It was a woman, your mother, who sold you into slavery. It was a woman who bought you and trained you in pleasuring men. It was men who came to visit you, to use you, to keep your body from yourself.

"This egg, White Lily, was of a female bird-animal that could fly long before humans walked the Domains. Her power, gathered over the ages, can undo all the harm men and women have done to you. Do you believe that, child?"

Lily nodded. The egg no longer felt cold in her hand, but hot as a burning iron. "I—I guess so, mistress." Lily slipped the rawhide thong over her head, freed her hair from it, let it lie against her chest, pulsing and warm like a second heart.

Chaney sat back with her crooked smile. "Believe it so, daughter, and t'will be so."

"But," Lily went on, "what—"

Chaney tut-tutted as she fumbled in the basket. "Greensleeves . . . Ah, here it is." She put something in the woman's hand. "Druids, you know, generally eschew artifacts as human-built toys. Yet some prove useful, such as this."

Greensleeves received a clunky thing, a star as big as her handspan. It was made of different materials, with an ant at the center. Even the chain was of two materials: small copper links threaded with linen string.

Chaney explained, "A delicate thing, so don't drop it. Almost impossible to fashion, I imagine. Note its makeup. The arms of the star are wood. Binding them is a ring of metal, and inside that is a ring of red gemstone, and at their center, a once-living creature. Wood from a tree root, silver mined from a mountain, a gemstone from the desert, an ant plucked from underground. The elements of the earth, encapsulated, tightly bound unto themselves, then tightly bound together into a single piece. Many into one. As are you, my child."

"What?" asked Greensleeves. She'd been almost hypnotized by the ringed star.

"You are like this pentacle, Greensleeves. Possessed of great power and strength from deep within, composed of many facets: joy and love and madness and spirit and fear. Yet bound by fear. Now, fear not. This nova pentacle will bind you from now on, without hampering. T'will lock your mind and spirit inside you so they cannot escape. Yet with it, you can travel to the stars."

Greensleeves shook her head. The artifact seemed flimsy to her, offering little protection. Yet she had to admit her mind often felt flimsy, no more anchored to her body than a feather that had touched down when the breeze died. Her heart thumping, she worked the pentacle's chain over her head and laid it on her breast.

Chaney took a deep shuddering breath, as if she'd run ten miles. "That's all I can give you. It's time to go."

"But . . . " both women objected. Lily said, "You haven't shown us how to shift!"

Chaney sighed. "I talk and they don't listen. Those are but details, I said. Wrap your minds around what's important and let the rest go. Look to your hearts, for there lies the truth.

"Now come, my little birds. Time to fly."

No one found it odd that Chaney took charge. With Lily and Greensleeves propping her on either side, she tottered back to the main campfire where Gull and his officers waited. The druid sent the trumpeter scurrying to fetch Rakel's gauntlets, left behind at her tent. Chaney saw that the gloves were put into Lily's hand.

But Lily balked. "I—I can't do this thing! I can barely fly three feet off the ground! I can't—"

Chaney said, "Child—"

Gull, usually so deferential to elders, cut the druid off. His voice was gentle. "We're not ordering you to do it, Lily. We're asking you, please. We need Rakel to command this army. I can't do it, and neither can anyone else. It was thanks to Rakel we won our first victory against Haakon."

Lily said nothing, only picked at a thread on the hem of her shirt. She wondered how much Gull really loved Rakel, if that's what it was. "I just don't want—to get us all—hurt." Or worse, cast into some void.

Lily looked at the ground, but snapped her head up as Gull dropped to his knees. She was so small, and he so large, he was still at eye-level. Gently, he took her small hand in his huge gnarled maimed ones. The girl protested, "What are you doing? Get up!"

"Lily. I beg you. Be brave and help us rescue Rakel. Not just for the sake of the army, or my sake, or even for her child held hostage. But for your sake, too."

Flustered, the girl pulled her hands away, pushed at his shoulders. "Stop it! Get up! This is embarrassing. What do you mean, for *my* sake?" Why was Gull suddenly talking like Chaney? Did everyone know her innermost secrets?

Gull took her hands again and and she let him keep them. His back to the fire, she couldn't see his face well. But his tone was that mild gentleness she'd first seen in him long ago, when she came to love him. "Lily. I know you carry a great burden in your soul. Even I, clumsy and blind, can see it. You hurt inside. I know. I know that's why you won't get close to anyone, why you think you can't love, that you're unworthy of love. But you are. You're kind, and sweet, and considerate, if only you don't let your skittishness take hold—like a sweet horse that's been abused, you're afraid to run again. But that's why I ask you to do this, to help us. Because you need to help others, and to be loved, and respected, and cared for."

Lily felt a tear betray her and run down the side of her nose. How could Gull be so stupid and clumsy, then so sweet and understanding? Yet Gull and Chaney were right. It was herself keeping people at bay, shunning them, not them shunning her.

And perhaps, finally, she could help the army and her friends. Her friends who accepted her for herself.

As if in answer, the dingus egg glowed warm against her breastbone.

She sniffled. "All right. I'll try. But get up, get up!"

Around her people laughed, then *oohed* as Gull kissed her.

Lily snuffled her nose clear and wiped it with her wrist. "But I warn you. I might shift us a mile in the sky."

Gull laughed and bearhugged her until she squeaked. "Then we'll fly together."

The army cheered.

Finally it was time to go.

Preparations were finished, and everyone had satchels of food and sharp weapons.

With Greensleeves would go several volunteers, mostly female. Helki the centaur had donned her armor, put fresh feathers on her long lance, daubed on war paint in swirls and runes and handprints. With her wraparound helmet, her long face looked fierce, her hooded eyes stern. She had insisted on going, despite the fact that Holleb still ailed from an injured arm. Knowing the extent of their attachment, Greensleeves was impressed. Also in attendance was a female scout, Channa, a stocky woman with pouty cheeks, dressed in blue shirt and trousers and tall boots, a gray cloak with raven feather around her shoulders, and a curved sword in her fist. She had been the lover of Givon, another scout, who with Melba had been decapitated by the demon horde: she had a score to settle. The leader of the healers, Amma the Samite, in tightly belted blue robes and a white turban, had insisted on coming. The sole man of the party, Kwam, said nothing, but refused to budge from Greensleeves's side.

Greensleeves looked at her followers, all friends, and asked, "Ready?" They all nodded, serious, leery of being shifted. No one liked it, for it reminded them they'd been shifted before and lost their homes, perhaps forever. But no one balked.

Greensleeves asked Chaney, "We're ready, but how am I to find the stone brain?"

For answer, the druid put her one good hand on

Greensleeves's shoulder. The firelight on Chaney's old face made it ruddy and obscured the lines, so for an instant Greensleeves could see the young woman inside, looking much, she guessed, like Greensleeves herself.

"Think on it, as if you would conjure it. As you've tagged it, so it has tagged you."

Greensleeves blinked, adjusting to the idea that she was tagged. Then she searched her mind, and found it was true. They were all there, her tagged charges: the wolves, the grizzlies, the wall of swords, the rest. And far off, singing like a thrush in the wilderness, was the alien stone brain.

"Yes, it's there," breathed the young woman.

"Then close your eyes, gather your wits and your friends, and go to it. I shall assist."

Abruptly, the druid began to sing an ancient air that lilted on the night air and lifted the hair on the necks of the army. Up, down, around trilled the notes. Greensleeves closed her eyes, concentrating, one hand clutching the pentacle at her neck, her other hand visibly shaking.

For the first time, she felt magic flowing *into* her rather than *through* her. The mana of the land, possibly gathered by Chaney, possibly gathered by some facet of herself, flowed into her feet, her head, her hands, her heart.

Then Gull gasped.

The tattered hem of Greensleeves's gown began to glow: first brown, then rising green, then blue, then yellow for the sun.

By the time the party wore a halo of sunlight in the dark night—Helki's helmet the last, burnished as if gold, for she was tallest—the remaining army blinked to see them through the glare.

When their vision cleared, Greensleeves and friends were gone.

The observers let out their breaths with a collective rush.

Gull turned around, grabbed Varrius's hand, and shook hard.

"If we don't return, you're general, and may the gods help you." Gull tried to smile.

But the lean, black-bearded soldier wouldn't let go of Gull's hand, hanging on with the clasp of a black-smith. He stared up into Gull's eyes. "You will return. This army needs you and your sister and Rakel to do good, to stop the wizards, and to see us all returned home. You won't fail because you mustn't."

"Uh, very well. Thank you, Varrius."

Gull the Woodcutter toted his longbow and quiver over his shoulder, his mule whip and a black-handled dagger in his belt, his heavy double-headed felling axe in his hand. Beside him, Lily was wrapped in her white clothes and cape. Rakel's gauntlets hung limp in one of her hands. Bardo, a paladin of the north, his long face serious, was wrapped in chain mail from head to toe, so he resembled a giant snake. His gypon hung before him, the color of old gold, picked out by the red-etched winged staff. He carried a tall kite-shaped shield and his bastard sword, the blade so long he had to hitch the sword belt high on his hips. With them was Ordando, she of the scarred leather armor and bare arms and long blond braid, a bloodred cloak over her shoulders. She had a long sword and a round shield with a pointed boss in the center. She'd demanded to be in on the rescue, had dared to fight Gull for the honor. The woodcutter had only smiled and nodded.

Stiggur took his rejection less well. "*Please,* Gull, let me go! I won't be in the way! And I can help! Really I can!"

"For the last time, no," Gull tried to make it gentle, but he had to push the boy away at arm's length. "Lily will have enough trouble shifting the four of us, she says. Five is out of the question."

Stiggur blinked back hot tears. He wants so to be a man, thought Gull, but he's barely thirteen. And he was so likeable. Stiggur had aped Gull in every way—

pulling his hair into a ponytail, wearing a leather shirt and kilt, learning to wield a whip. But he didn't cry, only stormed off into the night.

Lily asked, "Are we ready, Gull?"

The woodcutter shrugged and smiled to cover his nervousness. "We wait on you."

Lily nodded and gulped. Of all of them, she still found it hardest to believe she could work magic. She had to shake her head. Though it was hard for her to imagine having power of any sort, she had to try. This was for Gull, she told herself, and for the army and the crusade, and for Rakel's child, for children shouldn't be separated from their parents. And for herself. It was time she stopped thinking of herself and considered others.

No one was really powerless. If anyone had taught her that, it was this tiny army that accomplished so much and represented so much more.

Chaney had given her the dingus egg, which she now held in one hand. The egg grew warm, and beneath its stone surface, Lily felt something kick.

Lily lifted the gloves. "I feel like some hunting dog, sniffing the scent off a rag."

Chaney put a hand on her shoulder. "It's not much different. They were manufactured in her city, and she wore them, put her sweat and blood into them."

Chaney took a rattling breath and sang. Lily thought of Rakel and called to her, as she'd once called Gull from across the Domains when she needed him so desperately.

Ordando was the first to notice, and she grunted.

Their hands glowed white.

The glow spread until they glowed all over, then it brightened. Lily found her face and hands glowing like the winter sun. Her eyes must have glowed, for her vision blurred, as if she had walked into a fog bank. They were really going, she thought—

Gull grunted as a weight struck his waist, clung. Stiggur had run and crashed into him.

"I'm going! You can't leave me now!"

"Damn it, lad, we can't—"

A roaring hiss filled their ears. They went white all over, clear through, then the world faded to white.

Then they were gone.

Neith, Varrius's oldest friend, and only contact with their southern homeland since the death of big Tomas, asked, "What now, Var?"

The lean man cast a glance around the elevated horizon, the lip of the canyon around them. "To start, you call me Commander, for such has General Gull made me and Commander Rakel would order. We'll carry on as they would wish and make them proud when they return. Since everyone's up anyway, and dawn's not far off, have the trumpeter blow Reveille. We can breakfast and get an early start on the day."

Neith wanted to protest: Why not get some sleep and move in the afternoon?

But he surprised himself by replying, "Yes, Commander."

CHAPTER
16

THROUGH A FOG OF RED PAIN, RAKEL HEARD THE heavy dungeon door creak open. As bad as things had been, they got worse.

The torturer turned from his portable bed of red-hot coals, a hot poker glowing in one hand.

This man, wide, squat, with powerful shoulders and forearms, had worked on Rakel steadily. Perhaps for a few minutes, perhaps for a few days. Rakel didn't know how long she'd hung here, the iron manacles cutting into her wrists.

The torturer was no sadist. More frightening, he performed his job with a bored detachment, like a butcher. He'd sliced off strips of skin from her ribs, flicked them on the floor, trodden them under filthy boots, stopped the rivers of blood by searing her wounds shut with a hot iron. The charred fatty smell of burning skin had made her retch, pain had made her black out, yet so far she hadn't screamed—so far. Somehow, she knew if she gave in, screaming and screaming, she might never stop, would lose her honor and mind with one stroke. So she fought back the only way possible.

Unlike most nightmares, there was plenty of light. Torches lined the blackened stone walls of the dungeon, for the torturer needed light to work by. She was naked to the waist, her leathers cut away along with her skin. She hung from the manacles, snakes of blood running down her forearms, so her feet barely touched the filthy floor.

She tried not to concentrate on her surroundings, but instead to escape in a fog. Perhaps she could will herself to death. . . .

A searing pain on her hip woke her. When it lessened a fraction, she heard voices far away.

No, right beside her. The nightmare writhed with new life.

Standing in the doorway of the dungeon, flanked by bodyguards with torches, was Sabriam. His face was swaddled in bandages, his voice muzzy from drugs or liquor to quell the pain of his shattered nose. He gabbled, muffled, " . . . something else! Make her hurt!"

The torturer spread beefy black hands. His voice was a subservient whine. "She is strong, a warrior used to pain. She won't cry out. Given a few days . . . "

"Days? Do something else!" Sabriam ranted. "Put one of her eyes out!"

The torturer shrugged. "You know the law. No marks where the crowd can see—"

"Damn the swine! I don't care about them!"

Rakel listened as if eavesdropping on a conversation between strangers. Even riddled with pain like a great burning weight, she noted the hypocrisy: the council would order torture, but not admit it. Anyone condemned to hang must walk to the gallows as if healthy and well-treated. So the torturers were limited as to where they could work.

Yet Rakel was suffering more than physical injury. Her soul was receiving scars that would never heal. She'd never let another person touch her again, would probably scream if someone came near.

The torturer bargained as if selling fish. "If I could

work on her feet, rip out her toenails, or shove slivers under the nails—"

"Not enough! I want her to suffer!" Sabriam's voice suddenly brightened. "What about rats?"

Rats. The word made Rakel shiver.

"Ha!" came Sabriam's laugh. "See? She doesn't like that! Fetch some rats! I want her to scream until her throat breaks!"

The torturer shrugged, shoved his poker in the fire, pushed past Sabriam to get out the door.

Rakel tried not to think of rats, or anything else. But Sabriam came before her, delicately picked up an iron poker and touched her breast. Her whole body shrank from the pain.

Sabriam laughed. "There's no escape, Rakel! You'll stay here, tortured beyond endurance, until you hang. Then the masses will laugh to see you dance on air. And I'll have your son beside me to show him what happens to traitors. Who knows? Maybe I'll adopt him."

Of all the torture she'd endured, Rakel found that hurt the most: her son perverted into something like Sabriam. So there were things worse than death. And death was her only escape.

She'd welcome it with open arms.

The torturer grunted, pushed into the tiny room steamy from blood and sweat and fire. He lugged two wire cages. The first was jammed with dozens of scuttling, squeaking, gray shapes. He set that one down and fussed with the second cage. One end was open, curved inward, fitted with stout leather straps.

Sabriam rubbed at the itchy bandages on his face and licked his lips. "How does this work?" He smirked at Rakel's uncontrollable shuddering.

The torturer pushed the open end of the cage against Rakel's naked stomach. "We strap this around her, then open the other end and drop in rats. They're hungry, so they'll gnaw at her flesh. To kill her, we'd build a fire under one end. Then they'd burrow all the way through her to escape. . . . "

Death, where are you? Rakel begged silently. Essa, Goddess of Death, take me. Now, please, before I lose what little honor I have left. . . .

A guard muttered, and Sabriam cursed. "I must go. The council meets. But I'll come back. Drop in only one rat at a time, see how they do. And for the love of the gods, don't kill her, or I'll do to you what you've done to her."

"Yes, master," intoned the torturer. He'd heard it before, amateurs telling him his job.

Rakel suffered new pain as the cold iron cage was hung on her middle. Every muscle in her body twanged, tense as the metal. Rats gnawing at her belly—what could be worse?

Her face, came the answer. She'd seen people hung with canvas sacks over their heads, stumbling up the gallows steps blind. It had been rumored they were nobility, the sack protecting their identity and family honor. Now she knew the truth. . . .

The torturer donned a thick leather glove and plucked a tiny slime-furred rat from the cage. Then he stopped, grunting. Out in the dark hallway, a light gleamed. Was Sabriam returning?

But this wasn't guttering yellow torchlight. It was pure, bright, white, radiant.

So bright, it penetrated Rakel's tightly clamped eyes. What . . . ?

Or who?

The torturer hissed, for the shapes were white. They must be ghosts, souls of folks he'd killed, for no one could shift into the council house—it was warded against magic and shift. Still clutching a squirming rat, the man fell back and reached for a hot poker.

Rakel gasped. Outlined in white, solid as the stone walls, was Gull. Around his waist clung Stiggur like a monkey. With him were Bardo and the Green Company's captain, Ordando. And Lily, shining white and pure as an angel.

The glow faded. The shifted party blinked in the gloom and smoke and yellow light of the dungeon.

Then a dozen things happened at once.

The torturer, better prepared for trouble, lunged with his red-hot poker for the nearest figure.

Gull focused and shouted, "Rakel!", the most glorious sound the warrior had ever heard.

Lily blanched and covered her mouth. Stiggur took one look and dropped to his knees, vomiting. Ordando barked an oath.

Bardo, trained since childhood in his religious order to fight evil, flicked his bastard sword high. With a *clang*, it hit the poker, which ricocheted off the wall. It clattered to the floor and sent up a smell of burnt dirt.

The paladin had attacked first, taken note of his surroundings second. Now he saw the man was a torturer, and his hot religious fervor turned to cold fury.

"The arm of the vun true god is long and mighty, and takes retribution on sinners!"

With that pronouncement, he batted the torturer with the flat of his sword, knocked the man sprawling on the filthy stone flags.

Gull swore muleskinner's oaths as he stepped over to Rakel and yanked at the chains fastened above her, inadvertently jangling her shredded wrists. Frustrated, furious, he ordered everyone back, then smashed his axe against the chains, severing them.

Rakel collapsed in a heap. Shaming herself, she wept openly with both relief and renewed fear for her child, for rescue meant a return to life and its myriad problems. She was more dead than alive and wanted only to crawl away into the darkness.

Gull tried to pick her up, but she was as limp as seaweed. Chittering, Lily chivied him aside and checked if any of the wounds were mortal. "You poor thing, you poor thing . . . "

Yet part of Lily's spirit was singing. They'd arrived in time to save Rakel, all thanks to her: Lily, a former prostitute.

Gull raged so loud ears rang. "Who did this to you? Who? I'll kill him! I'll kill everyone in this city!" He ranted on and on, uselessly. It was Lily who tore her petticoat to form bandages, Ordando who found the manacle keys hanging on the wall and unlocked them, Bardo who dispatched the torturer.

Shock and weariness had Rakel lapsing in and out of consciousness, but she managed to explain that Sabriam had ordered the torture, that he sat in the council room on the top floor, and that he held her son captive. "His nose—is bandaged. Sabriam's. Get him—kill him. But find—my son . . . "

"Mercy of Xira," whispered Lily as she bound Rakel's wounds. "You needn't fight anymore, Rakel. We'll save your son, get you out of here. I swear it."

"Can you take us to this council room?" Gull demanded. "Shifting?"

"I—uh . . . " Lily caught her breath. "Uh, no, no. I can't feel any magic. It's used up here, or else warded, or we're too far underground. Oh, I'm failing already. . . . "

"No, you're not!" Gull barked. "I've never been prouder of you! But we need—"

Rakel muttered, "Door—end of corridor—stairway straight to council room."

Ordando ran to investigate, ran back. "She's right! A spiral stair rises straight to heaven!"

"To hell, more like. But that's where we go."

Gull hoisted the bandaged Rakel in his arms, for she couldn't stand. She muttered to Hammen and someone named Garth. The woodcutter ordered Stiggur, "Stop puking and carry her! You wanted adventure, now you've got it!"

Awkwardly, the boy juggled the sagging woman, who for all her strength was smaller than he. He wrinkled his nose at her burnt, bloody smell, but didn't drop her.

They were ready. Bardo looked back at the dead torturer. With his sword, the paladin dumped the cage of rats so they spilled in a dirty gray pile. Then he yanked the door shut and snapped off the key in the lock.

Gull flipped his cloak free; it had made him sweat in the tight room. The woodcutter shoved his long axe into his wide belt, drew his bow over his shoulder, and tested the string. "Now we'll get this Sabriam. And the boy. Are you with me?"

Ordando wiped hands on her wool trousers, took a fresh grip on her sword hilt, and grinned without humor. "Take on a roomful of courtiers and their elite bodyguards? It'll be a pleasure!"

Single file, they trotted to the stairwell, and up.

At the top, Gull pushed open a well-oiled door and found a stone-lined room with a hanging tapestry. Through a peephole in the tapestry, he studied the council room as people shuffled in behind him: Lily in bloodstained, travel-worn white; Stiggur lugging the white-skinned Rakel, bloodied and dirty and wrapped in the boy's cloak; Ordando hot to avenge her commander's suffering; and Bardo, who raised his sword over their heads and waited for Gull's signal.

The woodcutter nocked a long arrow and nodded. Bardo's long steel sliced through the tapestry like cobwebs, and dusty folds collapsed at their feet.

Sun streamed through wide windows along one side of the room at the far end, making the blue rug glow with life. Gaping courtiers lined the walls. Startled guards stood flat-footed and bug-eyed in the doorway to the right. At the distant table on the dais, six council members rose to their feet. Only the seventh, sick with infection in his nose and too many drugs, stayed seated. Directly behind him, a two-year-old boy in black leather cried a single word.

All stared at the scruffy party that had appeared from behind the shorn tapestry, despite the best wards money could buy.

The scarred man in deerhide raised his longbow, and drew. And loosed.

Years of practice and a white-hot thirst for vengeance drove Gull's arrow straight and true. The shaft slit the air and lanced through Sabriam's shoulder, pinning him to the back of the heavy oak chair.

People gasped. Guards charged, but couldn't penetrate the drunken crowd staring at the double threat of Bardo and Ordando with shields and swords up.

Gull ran the length of the council room. Council members scattered. Snagging his bow over his shoulder, Gull hopped to the dais. With two hands, he caught the underside of the heavy glossy table, heaved, and pitched it aside. Nothing now stood between him and the shrinking Sabriam, who stared cold sober at the enraged giant.

"I am Gull the Woodcutter!" pronounced the man. He drew his long double-headed axe from his belt. "The man you sought to assassinate, along with my sister, and friend to Rakel!"

With that, Gull slung his axe high, as if for chopping firewood, and slammed it down with all his strength.

The heavy blade split Sabriam in two, shattered the seat of his chair. Blood, brains, gut, ribs, organs all slumped together in a slithering purple hash.

Jerking his bloodied axe free, Gull whirled to face the amazed courtiers and guards. "*There* is one of your own, and *see* what you people have done to her! Show them, Stiggur!"

The boy's arms were full of woman, so Lily lifted the cloak and showed the cuts and burns on Rakel's body to the stunned room. Slowly Stiggur turned in a circle to the dissipated dregs of Sabriam's clan. Some vomited, some fainted, some just turned away.

"See you?" thundered Gull from the bloodied dais. "There will be an end to this! Or this city itself will end! So swear Gull the Woodcutter and Greensleeves the Druid!"

Weeping, whispers, prayers answered him. In the quiet, Gull caught the arm of the trembling boy, shaven-headed, black-leathered. "Your mother needs you, Hammen."

The boy's blue eyes snapped cold fire at the tall man, but when Stiggur hopped on the dais with his pale burden, the boy's heart broke, and was rebuilt. "Mother!" He clung to her cloaked figure while Stiggur staggered under this extra burden.

Roused by the single word, Rakel opened blood-shot eyes, leaned and kissed her son's shorn pate. "Hammen."

Bardo and Ordando had fallen backward in lock-step, chivying the others toward Gull. The guards followed, halberds leveled, with no sign of attacking.

Then a captain of the guard jangled to the door and shrilled, "What are you waiting for? Seize them!"

The woodcutter glanced around, then stepped back to the open windows. He gasped at the sight from hundreds of feet high.

As far as the eye could see, to the base of distant blue hills, sprawled the city-state of Benalia. More houses and buildings and roads and people than trees in a forest, than snowflakes in a blizzard.

The guards came in a rush. Gull's comrades crowded onto the dais around Sabriam's splintered body. Bardo grabbed the heavy table to prop it sideways as a barrier.

Gull asked Lily, "Can you conjure us out? Or do we make a final stand?"

The wizard held her head. Things were happening too fast. "I don't know! I need time—"

Gull only nodded, strangely calm. They'd rescued Rakel and her son. If they died now, surrounded by scores of enemies, the legends would say they accomplished their mission, did the best they could.

Yet he had a thought as he stared at the city. "Might we fly?"

"Fly?" The woman stared wide-eyed. "Oh, no. Uh, I don't—"

"Now's the time." Turning, sweeping arms around Stiggur and Lily, calling to Bardo and Ordando, he stepped through the huge windows and perched on the wide sill. Wind whipped stray hairs around his face, tugged at his cloak. He put one arm around Lily. "Make us fly, Lily."

Lily wanted to scream. "I can't!"

Still with his odd, fatalistic calm, Gull leaned over and kissed the top of her head. "You can. I know you can. I have faith in you, Lily. We all do."

Wildly, she looked around at her comrades. Bardo and Ordando flanked them, held their swords poised through the open windows to keep back the flustered guards. Stiggur held Rakel and watched Gull, his hero, taking strength from him. Hammen held his mother's hand.

Lily bit her lip, held out her arms as if flying, and prayed. "I can't—"

Gull reached out both hands behind them and caught Bardo and Ordando's cloaks. "You can!"

Clutching them all at once, Gull leaned outward, and they fell.

The brown-green-blue-yellow mist before her eyes parted, and Greensleeves found herself standing in knee-high yellow grass.

She let out her breath with a whoosh, unaware she'd been holding it. "I did it!"

Eagerly she looked around, past her friends, around the horizon. Her brother and the army and the canyon and the nighttime were gone. Instead, there were rolling hills of yellow grass in every direction, the sun high overhead. "I did it!" she repeated, thrilled. "I conjured us all away and—" She needn't add, "kept my mind intact," so fell silent.

Her traveling companions looked around at the yellow hills, the empty sky. There was nothing else to see.

It was Helki who asked, "But where are we, Greensleeves?"

"Eh?" The wizard cast about once more, but there wasn't much to see. "Ummm . . . isn't this Phyrexia, plane of . . . demons?"

Helki pointed. "Some birds, high up, is all." The humans couldn't even see them.

Greensleeves bent and plucked a stalk of grass. It was timothy, with a fluffy grainy head, sweet smelling. The sun was warm, the breeze mild. Hardly a demon-plagued wasteland.

"What does this mean?" she asked the air.

Amma suggested, "Are you still in contact with the stone brain?"

Greensleeves frowned, concentrated. Deep inside her mind, she heard the song of the brain, its inane babble, a touch of fear. But it wasn't nearby, or even, she guessed, on this plane. "I don't understand. I should have gone straight to it."

"Perhaps," assayed Kwam, "we've reached some midpoint? Can you conjure it here?"

Greensleeves consulted the voice in her head. "No more than before. Those demons must have some lock on it. Chaney said a high wizard can do that."

She uselessly searched around. "I still don't understand. We must try again, I suppose."

This time, to be sure, she had her party hold hands: Amma, Helki, Channa, Kwam, and herself.

This time, the shifting was easier. Holding her nova pentacle (and her mind inside her), Greensleeves thought hard, called mana into her body and spirit from all directions, felt the glow ripple upward, envelop them.

They arrived on mud flats where salt water squished into and around their shoes and boots and hooves.

The place stank of low tide, the air so chilly their breath steamed. Far out, at bowshot, the ocean slapped a mudbank shore. Beyond, whales spouted plumes of fog into the frosty air. Behind them, the mud flat rolled for miles to salt grass. The oddest thing was the low setting sun tinged red: Greensleeves had no idea what that meant—nothing in her learning explained a red sun.

No one needed to say it: they were nowhere again.

Still, Greensleeves found the song. Was it closer?

Stifling a sigh, she asked that they hold hands, and

again she thought, and again summoned rippling waves of color to this gray landscape.

The first sensation after the rainbow mist left their eyes was of being stung everywhere.

The group could barely move for the thick fleshy leaves entwining all around them. They couldn't even see their feet, the fronds were so thick and pressed so close. Some leaves had sharp edges, like wooden shingles, that cut Helki's roan hide. But most immediately, they were beset by millions of huge brown-striped mosquitoes that drove stingers into every scrap of flesh.

"Quickly—ah!—Greensleeves!" bleated Amma.

Swatting and swearing with her brother's oaths, the druid took time to search for the stone brain. Not here still, but definitely closer. Hurriedly, she concentrated, muttered, summoned them away, leaving only their footprints and a few pints of blood behind.

Still rubbing and scratching, they found themselves in a desert of flat rocks, covered with green lichens and tiny yellow buds. The sky was overcast, threatening rain, and wind flailed their coattails and hems about their legs.

Helki pranced nervously, her hooves clacking on flinty rocks. Her tail snapped in the breeze like a flag. "Wind rises even more. It scours this land, pushes these rocks over. See you?" She rapped a rock with a hoof. There were healthy lichens on both sides, a sign they'd been flipped recently. And there was only wind to do it. A rock on a nearby slope clattered from its perch. A gust of wind knocked Amma over, and Kwam had to help her rise and stand in his lee. But then he had to anchor to Helki.

Greensleeves hunted. The stone brain was closer, but not here. The next plane, perhaps.

She'd have many questions to ask Chaney when they got home.

If they got home.

"Once more!" she yelled. "Hold tight!"

They vanished, Greensleeves with a prayer on her lips.

* * *

The whole world was black rock, burned and fused. Nearby was a blackened ruin of a stone building, no taller than Greensleeves, the walls smashed or melted down. There were more buildings at every hand, all destroyed, rolling up the walls of a vast valley. The sky was the color of steel, overcast, with no birds. The only smells were of rust and stagnant water and dust.

Despite the bleak surroundings, Greensleeves gave a little chirp. "I did it! This must be the place! It must be Phyrexia!"

The others congratulated her, patted her head and back, but then fell quiet. This place was so hostile, so inhospitable, they felt cowed. The ever-practical Helki asked, "Is perhaps bad question, but where are demons and stone brain?"

Greensleeves frowned. After the wind in the last place, this place was silent as a tomb: as if they'd been sealed away, dead and forgotten. Questing, she listened for the stone brain.

She swore. "It's not here!"

Channa had her bow half-drawn. She'd automatically moved a little distance from the party to scout. "This is not Phyrexia?"

Greensleeves sighed. "I guess not. Though it certainly looks like a ruined wasteland."

"Ruined by people," muttered Kwam. He held up a melted steel arrowhead.

"Take us away, will you, Greensleeves?" asked Helki.

"Of course." The druid clenched her fists, reached for the mana of this place to draw it into her. "That— stone brain must be . . . be . . . Oh, my . . . "

"What?" asked four people.

"Oh, my," Greensleeves moaned. "We shouldn't have come this way! There's no mana here! It's used up! Gone!

"We can't leave!"

CHAPTER
17

LILY'S FLYING SPELL CAUGHT THEM LIKE A PUNCH in the belly.

All felt grabbed by their chest and neck and crotch, caught in the air as if by a giant hand. Their legs were weightless, and they floated, as if in a dream, still falling, but slowly. Gull found the feeling both exhilirating and frightening, because he felt as free as a bird or a grasshopper, because he knew he was hanging in air on nothing at all—not a swinging rope, not a plank, not a tree branch—just magic. It was with both relief and disappointment he felt his feet touch the paving stones, felt his normal weight return with a thud as if someone had dropped twin sacks of grain on his shoulders.

"Lily! You did it!" Gull crowed.

Bardo, Ordando, and Stiggur, with his nodding and clinging burdens, landed. Lily lit, touching first one foot and then the other, like a deer hopping a fence. She smiled tentatively at Gull, who grabbed little Hammen's skinny upper arm and hung on. He didn't want the lad changing his mind and running out on them now.

"Now vhat?" asked the practical Bardo.

Behind them was the council house. The first four floors were stone and mortar, the upper stories yellow brick. High, high up, in a massive square tower was the room they'd invaded. Gull saw faces craning out and down at the fugitives. The woodcutter from White Ridge couldn't believe the size of the building: to him, a barn was huge, and this building could hold a hundred barns stacked like cordwood. For the first time, he appreciated the size and might of Benalia, for this was a single building duplicated a dozen times in the center of the city, with hundreds of smaller buildings surrounding them.

They were hemmed in. A wide stone-flagged plaza encompassed the council house. Along its outer edges was a marketplace, booths and kiosks jammed together selling everything: bright wares and polished weapons and heaps of food both common and exotic. People milled like ants, but stopped to stare, a crowd six and seven deep. Past them, both sides of every street were lined with three- and four-story houses. Gull knew the buildings ran to the horizon, for he'd seen it all from above.

So the country mice would have to survive in a city. With cats in hot pursuit.

From the council house charged a horde of council guards, elite soldiers of a city where everyone was a soldier. Wearing the black leather trousers and jerkins of heroes, they also bore close-fitting helmets and studded belts, all painted black. For weapons, they had steel halberds that gleamed from polishing, as well as short swords slung at their hips and round shields bouncing at their backs. They were both men and women, in mixed pairs, partners trained to fight together on the battlefield, to watch out for each other.

Fifty rushed Gull's party of four fighters and a wizard. Or three, since Stiggur had to carry Rakel. Or two, since Hammen needed looking after.

It was big blond Ordando who broke the woodcutter's reverie. Accustomed to cities, she whapped Gull in the arm and barked, "General! Go into the alley—that space between buildings. They can only rush two at a time, and it probably twists and turns. But get running!"

"Right!" Hoisting Hammen on his hip, spinning Stiggur around, Gull drove the whole party through the marketplace at a fast trot. Used to charging soldiers, and trained to get out of their way, Benalians jumped aside, then closed ranks again to see the quarry escape.

It was as Ordando said. Between two tall buildings was a brick-lined alley that bent at the end. It smelled rank, for people used it as a public toilet. Hollering, Gull half-tossed his followers into the alley. "Bardo! Take the boy and clear the way. Lily! See if you can get up a shifting spell. Stiggur, don't drop Rakel! Ordando, you go! I'll hold up—"

But the big woman instead pushed Gull into the alley with her rump, then backed into the entranceway facing out. Dropping her cloak, unlimbering sword and shield, she called over her shoulder, "You go! This was my idea! I'll slow them down!"

Gull grabbed at the woman's scarred shoulder. "But you said they could only rush two at a time!"

"That's still two! Go! I'll hold 'em! Kiss Rakel for me! And my wives!"

"But, Ordando . . . " Gull's voice trailed away like water down a drain. The rampaging soldiers were close enough to hit with a rock.

Ordando shuffled her feet, spat in their direction, and raised her sword. "Go on! And good luck to your crusade! Every wizard you stop is a dozen villages saved!"

Gull tried to think of something encouraging to say, but his mind went flat. Damning himself as a coward and failure, he turned and pelted down the alley.

Behind, he heard a shout and the slam of tempered steel on an iron helmet. And a laugh, loud and boisterous, as full of life as the north wind. "*Hy-ah!*

Come and take me, you bastards! Take *that!* Test yourself on a captain of the army of Gull and Greensleeves!
Hy-aah!"

"It's not good."

Channa, their scout, and Helki had ridden out
from the square while the others rested and
Greensleeves thought. The dark scout carried a short
bow in one hand with an arrow crooked alongside. As
trained, she'd immediately fanned out among the
ruined buildings to check for enemies, escape routes,
the lay of the land, and more. Helki tripped in from
another direction, but carefully. The ground, black
crazed glass like obsidian, was slippery under her
hooves.

"I find nothing alive. No plants, not even moss.
There may be water that way—I think it north—where
the land trends down, but I see no signs within a half
mile." She scanned the steel-gray sky again, searching
for birds or insects, shook her head. "I can't believe
any place can be so dead. . . . "

Her words fell flat in the still air, without echoes.
Even the air smelled dead, for there were no scents,
not even rust or rot. This place was gray all around,
stone and stony ruins and nothing else.

Devoid of magic, Greensleeves knew. The mana of
the land had been sucked away, siphoned off, when
the city died in some horrendous cataclysm. Was this
some spot where Urza and Mishra had battled? Could
any but the Brothers have caused such devastation?

Amma sat on the ground, folded her cloak over
her knees, waited patiently. Kwam unrolled a parchment and sketched the ruined buildings, trying to
make out the runes under the scorch marks. Helki fiddled with her war harness. Channa went farther, out of
sight, to scout.

Greensleeves wanted to scream. They were all
covering their fear so well, waiting for her to perform
a miracle. She wished desperately that she had one.

Questions rattled through her brain. Why had the trail of the brain led her here? Had the brain lighted here once? Been part of the final holocaust? Why did Greensleeves fail to arrive in Phyrexia near the brain?

And, most of all, how could she pry them out of this hole she'd dug?

What would Chaney say? What had been her teachings? Had she touched on the subject of what to do when mana was absent?

Magic comes from within, not without. She'd said that hundreds of times, and each time Greensleeves had nodded obediently. Yet she knew now she hadn't understood. It took knowledge to reveal ignorance. Hers.

There *was* mana here, of course. Inside herself, deep in her chakra points. A special containment of mana hummed in the nova pentacle on her chest. And within her friends, as with all living things, burned dull glows like fires banked in ashes.

So, if she must, she could use the mana here. Her own. And if she used too much? The answer lay all around her. A living thing sucked dry of mana would fall as dead and lifeless as this once-great city.

Conjuring and shifting were two sides of the same leaf. If she'd gotten in, she could get out. If she couldn't shift out, could she . . . what? Have something conjure them elsewhere?

"Oh!"

"Eh?" asked Amma.

Greensleeves began to understand. Perhaps, rather than gather mana locally, she could call to an object and use *its* mana to bring them along the trail. Wasn't the stone brain the most powerful artifact of all?

Shutting her eyes and ears to outside noises, Greensleeves sent her spirit roaming, hunting the cry of the stone brain. She found it, a tiny spark in the darkness. Gently, so as not to break the thread, she reached for it—

—and felt it grab hold of her, like a giant spider

from the depths of he forest. The power, the force of it, latched hold of her spirit and yanked.

Gasping inside and out, she called "Quickly! To me!" Greensleeves fought to hold onto her spirit-self lest she be wrenched apart. For here it was again, the old fear of losing her mind, going insane, descending into a fog of madness. Yet the nova pentacle helped her contain her mind with invisible bands, and more importantly, the gentle dry voice of Chaney whispered in her ear.

Her friends latched hold of her, fearful of being left behind. The pull was ferocious, an undertow sweeping her away, seeking to drown her.

Yet she remained anchored, for she had no mana to tap. Except the source inside her. Desperate, pulled in too many directions, thinking to save her friends even if it cost her life, the druid reached into her soul and snatched mana by the handful.

Her knees buckled, her heart skipped a beat, her brain lost its energy and humming flow. Blacking out, she detected ripples around her feet, rising . . .

With a rush, Greensleeves and company were pitched through the void.

Gull found the alley was indeed a rabbit warren of twists and turns.

Board fences, stone walls, tiny gardens, grapevines, dungheaps, garbage mounds, laundry on lines, all were crammed together until he could barely see the ground and walls. Stiggur hung back at the next turn, which Gull saw as if through a tunnel under the looming maze. Panting, he almost caught the boy, but he flashed down another alley, and so on, always out of reach. Gull wondered what he'd done with Rakel—had she died and they'd tossed her body?—until finally he glimpsed Bardo in the distance, Rakel's limp cloaked form cradled in one brawny arm, a bastard sword in the other. Beside him was Lily. The two conferred about their next move where a number of alleys converged.

Gull arrived with only one question. "Can you shift us out?"

"Not from down here, I don't think!" In her frenzy, the girl yanked on the tiny dingus egg strung around her neck. "There's little mana along the ground! I need to draw on my own sources!"

"Can you do that?"

"I th-think so."

Gull worried. Lily's eyes were sunken, her lips crinkled from tension, her hands shaky. She looked as if she could sleep a week. They might need to carry two women. "How is Rakel?"

"Alive but poleaxed," said Bardo in his plain way. "Lucky for it. Ordando?"

"Holding the alley."

Stiggur gulped. "Against fifty?"

Gull's nod was grim, though he panted from running. "We mustn't waste her sacrifice. We must get Rakel away, safe. And yourselves."

"And you," added Lily.

"I'm not important." But the woodcutter blinked. Even tired as she was, even successful in magic, Lily thought of others, as if responsibility had made her grow. She thought of his welfare. What had happened to the spark that had arced between them? Had it died, or merely been buried?

Bardo snapped, "Vhich vay? Lead, General."

Despite the enemies hunting them, Gull forced himself to think calmly. "Lily, what do you need to conjure us out of here?"

She cast about the dark confining walls. "Someplace high, where I can tap cloud magic, I guess."

"Can your flying spell get us—"

"It's the same problem! I need magic again, and can't get it from down here! And it's really more a jump spell." The girl wizard was calming, taking strength from Gull and the paladin. She tried not to think about capture, about suffering as Rakel had suffered. "It gives your feet wings, but dispels when you first touch down. Where we land better be safe—"

"Uh-huh . . . " Gull thought aloud. "Skipping over the rooftops doesn't seem useful, but we can't bull our way through the streets, either."

Bardo offered, "If ve break down a door, ve can climb to the rooftop . . . "

No one wanted to say it, but unless Lily could shift them away soon, their situation was hopeless. A whole city and a thousand soldiers only moments away were after their blood.

"Gull," said Stiggur, "I hear feet!"

Steps pounded in an alley, not from the direction Stiggur watched, but another way. Soldiers had circled around, or more had joined the chase.

Instantly, the paladin lobbed Rakel into Stiggur's arms, whipped out his sword, and faced the onslaught. Gull took up position to his right, the better to swing his axe right-handed. He grunted with surprise as little Hammen drew his hero's dagger and took up position to Bardo's left: he looked as harmless as a baby porcupine. Gull was shocked by the loss of Ordando. They were down to two real fighters and an exhausted wizard.

Their worries would be over soon. . . .

"Lily!" Gull drew his black dagger from his belt and tossed it at the girl's feet. "Don't let them recapture Rakel, or take you alive!"

"Gull!" barked Bardo.

There were six in this batch. Four men and two women in black leather, with short swords and round shields: a patrol that had guessed the right alleyway. They grinned, lucky to count a reward, they reckoned.

Or unlucky, for they faced Bardo the Northern Paladin and Gull the Woodcutter.

The patrol split, two pairs coming on, two young soldiers hanging back as reserves. The pair after Bardo closed warily, but the two before Gull smirked to see he had no shield.

Gull feinted, then lunged and batted his axe handle into the first smirk. Surprised, the man yelped and crashed on his back. Gull had hit him in the upper lip, smashing teeth and drawing a gout of blood.

But the woodcutter didn't leave himself open to attack. The second soldier, a woman in an iron helm, used the cover of the falling soldier to stab at Gull's thigh. Probably orders had been given for them to be taken alive, the woodcutter thought in a flash, saved for torture. If so, that gave him the advantage, because he could kill them.

And did. Using a move Rakel had taught him, Gull parried the sword blade aside with his axe handle and lunged close to his opponent. (Rakel's cool voice instructed, "Instinct warns us to back *away* from the attack. But you must move *toward* it, crowd your opponent, get *inside* his thrust!") He banged his hip against her shield, smashed the haft across her face. Stunned, blinded, the woman fell back. ("Always strike twice, two quick thrusts! Lightning has twin forks.") Yet Gull hung back from the killing blow. He never killed unless pressed—and if it meant he'd never make a good soldier, might die by a hand he'd spared, so be it. He settled for rapping her head again, knocking her senseless.

Bardo, better trained and armed, had laid out his two opponents bleeding, one from a stomach wound, one from a throat thrust. The boy Hammen held out his tiny dagger and stared in shock. Behind, the twin reserves gulped, nodded to each other, and stepped in to attack.

Gull yelled to distract them, hopped over his two prostrate foes, and—with no other way to attack—swung his axe with all his strength. Too late, the closer soldier, a woman, dropped her shield to parry the blow. But nothing could deflect that much scream-ing metal. The woodcutter's double-headed weapon spanked off the iron rim of her shield at the bottom, thudded into her hip, nearly severing her leg, and knocked her sprawling, falling when Gull wrenched the sunken blade loose.

The woodcutter watched her fall, drop her weapons, cry like a little girl. He tried to harden his heart, to recall these folk had tortured Rakel and

countless others, tried to assassinate him and
Greensleeves, all for their twisted triple-layered plots.

But as the soldier closed her eyes for the final
time, blood squirting out from under her red hand,
something went out in Gull's heart. A piece of him
died. How many would he kill, he wondered, before he
wasn't a man anymore, just a murdering machine?

"Let's go!" Bardo's voice croaked from battle rage.
He had killed his soldier long ago. "Ve've not much
time."

Stiggur, lurching under the weight of Rakel, shouted,
"More coming!"

Gull shook his axe, flicked gore from the steel. "We
can't stand here and kill all day. Lily, use your flying
spell. Get us on a rooftop."

"I can't pull down the mana—"

"Do it!" The harshness of his tone struck her like a
blow. Ashamed, he added, "Please, Lily. I've no ideas
left."

Lily nodded absently, clutched her dingus egg,
searched what patches of sky she could see, raised
her hands like a sun worshiper, and prayed.

"Hey, up!" yelled Stiggur as a dozen soldiers stampeded around a corner. Their swords and leathers
were spattered with Ordando's blood.

Yet they clumped to a halt as Lily yelled, "Jump!
That way!"

Gull noted the building she pointed to, so far he
couldn't have hit it with an arrow. But he flexed his
legs and jumped.

And didn't come down.

His body grew light, as if he'd jumped into water.
His feet dangled as if he'd stepped off a sandbar. The
soldiers grew smaller, disappeared behind. Others
rose with him. Lily's cloak billowed until she looked as
if she was covered in sea foam. Despite their predica-
ment, Stiggur grinned with sheer delight at the new
sensation—he hadn't had time to enjoy their earlier
fall. Gull was glad the soldiers of Benalia didn't carry
bows and arrows.

The building they'd aimed for, stone below, brick above, loomed like a small mountain. Lily made patting motions in the air, directing them downward, the first time Gull had seen her steer in midair. Behind a low parapet, he saw the rooftop was slightly peaked and covered with slates. Lead-lined gutters would channel rainwater out gargoyle spouts at the corners. Lily was the first to land, with a dancer's grace. Instinctively drawing up his knees, Gull landed hard, thumping as his full weight returned, almost wrenching his ankles. The burdened Stiggur flopped on his butt, but he kept Rakel's head from striking the roof top. The boy Hammen had latched onto the cloak wrapping his mother.

Immediately turning to business, Bardo wiped his sword on his cloak to squeeze off sticky blood, and shot it home in its scabbard. He jerked his longbow off his shoulder, tested the string, pulled out an arrow. He called to Gull, "Make ready to shoot."

Absently, Gull slid his axe into his belt, smearing blood down his deerhide tunic. He fumbled his longbow as he scanned their new defenses. The roof was bare, four planes of slanting slate shingles, with only a wooden trapdoor at the center. Four stories below, black figures converged on the building like soldier ants. "What are we to shoot?"

Bardo licked at the arrow fletching to smooth the feathers together, and nodded east, where the city was more spread out. The main barracks and training grounds must lie in that direction.

Gull gulped.

From that direction soared a flight of wyverns, small dragons as big as oxen, dark gray with dirty yellow bellies, pug-nosed, sharp, scaly faces, long scytheedged, sweeping wings. Astride the wyverns was the Benalish version of cavalry: nine lancers, all aimed in their direction.

Assailed from earth and air, he thought. They really were trapped.

*   *   *

"Love of the gods . . . " whispered Helki, and coughed.

Greensleeves squinted through an acrid fog that burned her eyes and lungs. She stood ankle-deep in ashes and bits of twisted, burned metal. When she moved, the heaps rustled as if infested with metallic rats. She couldn't see more than ten feet in any direction, for fog billowed all around, like the smoke of a forest fire. There was nothing but destruction at every hand, even in the air.

Channa coughed and cast about, overwhelmed. "This makes that last place seem a paradise." Others coughed in agreement. Squinting, Channa hefted her short bow and moved off to scout.

"But what this place *is*?" snorted Helki. She moved her long feathered lance in a circle, as if danger lay everywhere. Crunching trash underfoot, she peered down from her great height. Much of the litter was old splintered bones.

A shape scuttled at the edge of sight and Greensleeves started. Blinking against grit in her eyes, she'd just convinced herself it was imaginary when another flickered into sight: a small figure, just belt-high, dark all over, with gleaming white teeth and red eyes.

Then it was gone.

"We've arrived," the druid muttered. "The Hell for Artifacts . . . a plane of demons. Phyrexia . . . The brain is here . . . I feel it."

But that was all she felt, for her strength was gone. Blacking out, she toppled face-first into the ashes.

CHAPTER

18

GULL AND BARDO DREW AND SIGHTED ON THE foremost of the flying cavalry. The woodcutter asked, "Mount or rider?"

"Either," returned the paladin. "Vun's no good vithout the other. Hold until you're sure!"

"Now!" shouted Gull. He drew a breath, aimed for a dirty yellow breast so if he missed he'd strike the rider behind. Funny, he thought, they kept coming without any fear of missiles, no bobbing or evasion, aside from a ponderous up-and-down motion. Like bats and ducks, the wyverns found flying hard and had to pound the air to keep aloft, especially with burdens on their backs.

Air tight in his lungs, Gull loosed his arrow. Bardo shot in the same second.

Their arrows zipped through the air, struck the wyverns' scaly hides, and bounced off to clatter into the street below.

"Bevitched!" shouted Bardo. "Spelled against missiles!"

"Makes sense," agreed Gull, nocking again. "I'd not

climb on a thing that could fall to one arrow! But let's test the riders!"

He drew. The nine were close enough for Gull and Bardo to see gems studding the bridles across the mounts' pug snouts. Sighting, Gull watched yellow cat-slit eyes stare at him along the shaft of his arrow. Shifting his aim to the rider's lightly armored breast, he loosed—

—and the wyvern deftly interposed itself in the arrow's path. Again the arrow glanced off its scaly breast and ricocheted away, lost.

Swearing a blue string of muleskinner's oaths, Gull savagely jerked his bow over his shoulder and dragged free his bloodied axe. Bardo had already switched to his sword.

Gull wiped his hands on his tunic, took a fresh grip on his axe. He had no idea whether he could fend off an attack—seconds away—from those fearsome beasts and their riders with barbed lances. He scuffed his feet, which slid on the sooty slate roof tiles. Bad footing, a bad place to defend, four members of his party helpless . . .

Bardo ordered the nonfighters to crouch behind the parapet. Lily scooted low, catching the bloodied Rakel as Stiggur eased her down to the warm slates. The boy Hammen stayed with his mother, clutching her still hand. Bardo took up position over the huddled refugees. Gull was glad the paladin was here, for he knew what to do instinctively. The low stone parapet gave protection from one direction. The riders wouldn't dare spear them for fear of banging their points on stone and unseating themselves.

Gull took position at the other end of the party and grinned down at the fretsome Lily. "Work up what you can if you can. Get whoever's alive out, Lily. I know you can do it."

"Oh, Gull," said the woman in white, "I love you so . . ."

His death-head's grin turned to a gentle smile. "And I love you, honey. Always have . . ."

Bardo barked, "Stay down!" and the attack was on.

As Lily and the others crouched, the flock of nine split to circle the building. Instantly, Gull knew they were doomed. He couldn't watch everywhere at once. The monster-mounts beat at the air as they scattered like sparrows, yet their movements were timed together. Gull cursed as the wind of their passage buffeted him, tossing his tousled hair and tugging the hem of his cloak. Although the riders loomed large enough to shoot easily, the hurricane of wings would have sent any arrows spiraling. The wyverns thrashed not a dozen feet from the edge of the building, but the lance points reached far beyond their heads. The ends were polished steel, barbed like fishhooks. They would punch through a man like a giant knitting needle, then tear unholy wounds when wrenched loose.

And here came one now.

Idly, Gull wondered if these soldiers had orders to capture them alive. But he dropped that idea as, from two different directions, black-clad riders and their dark gray charges thrummed at him. Instinctively ducking, Gull swung his axe head to fend off one lance, then almost sprung his back lurching from the path of another coming the opposite way.

But ducking did little good, for another pair hissed through the air at him. Balls of Boris, but they were fast!

He chipped one lance shaft as it swept by, but the wood was so tough and so light he only knocked it aside without cracking it. Then he felt a shock as cold as a vampire's kiss.

A barbed lance head sliced along the top of his right arm, into the triangular muscle at the shoulder. Yelling at the chilly slice, Gull hopped sideways. His axe clacked against slate as his right hand went numb. His assailant flew on—a tail as thick as a young oak almost batted his brains out—but another dove in to spear at him again. Only by throwing himself backward against the parapet, and almost pitching over the side, did Gull avoid the swipe of the deadly pole.

They're like giant bees, he thought, and we're the flowers, rooted and helpless. He hadn't gotten in a blow yet.

As Gull fell, then kicked to regain his feet, Bardo shuffled amidst the huddlers and tried to protect them from all directions at once.

Fire licked along Gull's arm as he struggled to rise with only one hand, and that empty. "You're the . . . hero, Bardo—"

Bardo didn't hear. Shouting furiously, the paladin swiped at an oncoming lance, parried it aside with his shield. He slashed at a wyvern's leg and sliced tough scales on the underside of the thigh, their first blood—

Gull yelped, too late.

Bardo grunted as a lance head split his back and popped out his breast, square in the center of his emblazoned red winged staff. A jeering rider had nailed him from behind.

With a grunt from man and dragon, Bardo was hoicked off his feet and off the roof. His shield, on a leather trace, swung free as the paladin grabbed for the lance head in his chest—he would never drop his blessed sword, not even in death. But he couldn't find the steel head, for he was already dying. The rider, sagging in the air with the load, pointed his lance straight down. The paladin was ripped again as the barbed head tore through his lungs exiting. Freed of the deadly steel, he plummeted four stories.

All in seconds, before Gull could even shout.

Swearing, crying, threatening, the woodcutter kicked upright and grabbed his axe in his left hand. His right hung useless and bleeding, but that didn't matter now. He'd be dead soon, but so would some flying cavalrymen. Shouting *"For Lily!!!"* as a battle cry, Gull reared upright and flailed with his axe at an oncoming wyvern.

Yet the rider and mount deftly veered aside, well out of axe range, but not lance range. Gull watched the lance drive for his guts, tensed in anticipation of the shock.

Yet someone else reared up before him. Someone small, clad like Gull, even to a leather-tied ponytail.

Stiggur shouted, a high keen, and snapped his mule whip with a skill he'd learned from a master: his hero, Gull the Woodcutter.

The braided leather snagged the lance just behind the head, and the boy yanked. Gull saw the barbed head go wide, saw alarm flash in the rider's eyes under her small black helmet. If the boy hung on, she might be unseated, toppled from her mount to fall four stories. Heaving to drag up the tip, the rider hauled Stiggur off his feet.

And off the roof.

Bawling, Gull dropped his axe and grabbed with his good arm, snagging the boy's boot at the ankle. The rider above whipped back her lance, and the steel cut through the rawhide.

Stiggur plunged downward, over the side.

Gull tensed his belly against the parapet, braced for the shock. The boy's weight slammed Gull against the stone so hard ribs cracked. Gull's feet lifted from the slippery slates, and he looked straight down, forty feet, to cobblestones. Dangling, his kilt over his chest, Stiggur yet retained his shorn whip, which trailed below him like a limp kite string.

Gull was frozen, hardly daring to breathe lest he slip off the parapet. He knew his back was exposed, an inviting target for nine cavalry riders to fight over.

Red-faced, spotty-visioned, in searing pain from his arm, the woodcutter heard Lily shriek, felt her soft hands clutch his legs to pin him. He even heard Rakel croak. Below, Stiggur wailed that he was sorry. Bright pearls of Gull's blood fell into space.

The sky went dark as the wyvern-riders closed in.

Gray, they were, obscuring the sky. And brown, rippling to green, to blue, to yellow—

No, wait, thought Gull, that was—

The world faded away.

* * *

Greensleeves gave a sigh of satisfaction as her brother's party materialized in the acrid billowing fog.

Once her friends had roused her from a faint, she'd immediately thought of Gull and the rest, wondering if they'd succeeded in their mission. But when she'd sent out the tag, testing, she'd found something terribly wrong. Yet here they were, safe—

Her joy turned to confusion as she counted. It was the right number, but no, not if they'd—

She bleated at the blood and pain and suffering.

Gull clutched his shoulder as he sank to his knees. Stiggur, face red and clothing askew, held his head, then crawled on hands and knees to see if Rakel was all right. The warrior woman was half-naked under a cloak, Greensleeves saw, her body wrapped in hastily wrapped bandages soaked red. Lily was as pale as her namesake.

There was confusion and shouts and questions in the fog as everyone tended the wounded and tried to get answers. Ordando had "blocked an alley." Bardo was "dragon food."

In clear ringing tones that put everyone to work, Amma the Samite healer directed operations. Spreading cloaks over heaps of ash and twisted metal, the healer and Greensleeves and Lily set to work. They bound wounds, stanched bleeding, wrapped Gull's wounded arm tight against his chest and quivering ribs. Rakel got the lion's share of attention. Amma hissed as she cut off the rude bandages. Greensleeves looked, then wished she hadn't. Rakel's body was torn in long even stripes and burns, signs of deliberate torture. Amma sealed her wounds as best she could, but with no other help and the poisonous air, could not restore the missing skin. Rakel's body would be webbed with white scars forever.

Yet when Amma offered a large vial of painkiller to put her to sleep, the warrior woman refused. Blinking back tears of pain and joy, the Benalian insisted on staying awake with her son. Helki, the soppy sentimentalist, was so moved she allowed Rakel and her small son to be hoisted to her back, a very generous act, since centaurs were loath to act as beasts of burden. Rakel was propped there, with tiny Hammen in front, but the warrior woman needed her legs lashed with rags to the centaur's war harness lest she pitch off.

As Amma bundled up her supplies and Gull leaned on tall Kwam, the story came out bit by bit. The woodcutter finished, "All the wrong people keep dying! I fell down, useless as a dog turd, and Bardo took over and died saving us, as did Ordando before him. I lost two soldiers and did nothing!"

Lily, too, was sobbing. "It was the same with me! I stood by and hardly helped at all—"

From atop the centaur's back came a soft voice. The entire party turned to hear Rakel. "Lily only—breached the torture chambers of Benalia—whence no one's ever escaped. Gull only invaded the sacred council—split the Speaker like a cod—challenged the entire city to mend their ways, or else. Lily rescued my son and let us fly—saved all you see here. Only—that."

Both Lily and Gull looked sheepish. Greensleeves laid her hands on their shoulders. "Bardo and Ordando volunteered to rescue Rakel and her son, and did. To say they failed is, as you said, to deny their sacrifice."

The woodcutter was silent, until he coughed, then groaned as his ribs ached. "Never mind. I'll deal with it later. For now, where the hell are we?"

"One step from Hell," replied his sister. She coughed at the bitter, smoky air. Her eyes were inflamed and wept tears down her cheeks, making tracks in the soot. "Phyrexia, the Hell for Artifacts. The stone brain is here—close. Its pull is like a tidal wave. Once we arrived, I found the mana so strong I can taste it. And I conjured you."

Gull frowned. None of them could see fifteen feet. It might have been an hour before dawn or high noon, for all the smoke. "So where is the crawly thing?"

Greensleeves turned in a circle, her shoes crunching ashes. "A good question—"

All of them heard a pattering, someone dashing across ashes, harsh breathing. Channa, their scout, pelted toward them from the fog. She bled in a dozen places, yet strove to warn them. *"Dem—"*

The word was cut off as dark shapes jumped her, dragged her down.

With a howl, the demon horde boiled out of the mist.

There wasn't time to form a plan, circle for protection, or even to shout.

Dozens, scores, hundreds of demons swarmed over them like rats. The monsters latched onto clothes and skin, opened maws like bear traps, bit calves, knees, feet, hands. Their teeth sank like knives, punctured skin like needles.

Helki, with Rakel and Hammen strapped to her back, had dashed forward to rescue the fallen Channa. The centaur swept her spear in a wide arc, batted a dozen demons sprawling, jabbed and pierced two more, but a score leaped to take their place. Helki whinnied as a demon bit her in a rear hock, the sharp teeth cutting to the bone. Another scurried past stamping hooves and bit her in the loins, and another, her foreleg. The centaur crouched and kicked, leaped full in the air, jouncing her riders, but only shook one demon off. When she landed a body's length away, more creatures beset her. Half-blinded by fog and smoke, she struggled to find her direction, remember her goal. But Greensleeves's party was equally beset, and Channa was a scatter of clothing, a dark scalp, a rib cage glowing white. From nowhere, Helki thought of Holleb, and how much he'd miss her. . . .

Weary unto death, Rakel almost welcomed the onslaught, for death would end her suffering and torment. Yet she'd only just regained her son and didn't intend to lose him. Hammen, tied in front of her, huddled close, his bony back pressing against her breast and burning wounds. Yet the boy would make a hero of Benalia, for he'd pulled his tiny knife. Lunging, he stabbed between a demon's white-lined jaws, drove his blade out through the fiend's skull. Yet these demons were as tough as rawhide, stringy muscle and parched skin over bone, and the thing took a long time dying, clinging to the war harness until Rakel grabbed the handle and twisted to sever the thing's tiny brain. From then on, Rakel retained the knife, stabbing and jabbing expertly, aiming well and conserving her strength. She popped a red eye, drove the blade into a pointed ear, stabbed deep into a corded throat. But in her heart she despaired, for she felt the centaur faltering, her great strength stolen by a dozen wounds. Poor Hammen. She resolved to kill him before he was shredded by these fearsome teeth. Yet she'd have to do it soon. Oh, my sweet child, she thought, snuffed out so soon, and for nothing you did. Maybe it was better this way, she thought as she stabbed again, for the world was a cruel place. Or had been, until she'd met Greensleeves and Gull and their comrades. And Garth? Would he ever know? Or care?

At the first sign of danger, the hideous shrieking and gibbering and wailing like a windstorm, Gull instinctively hoisted his axe, but hissed as pain seared his right arm. With muscles severed and others stiff, he couldn't raise his arm above his waist. He shifted his weapon to his left hand, which lacked strength because it lacked three fingers. Funny he'd never had time for Chaney to regenerate them. Too late now. "Lily, stay behind me! Stiggur, you too! I'll seek—" He chopped down on a demon's head. They were so small, but so many! He stamped on another, crushing its chest, but three more swirled past it and attacked his legs. One caught hold of his deerhide kilt, punching holes with all four fingernails. Gull had to think how easily they'd penetrate skin. Then he learned, as a monster bit his left leg through the red leggings. The wound burned and itched and yet felt cool from bleeding all at once. And Lily? Could he save her? And the boy?

Lily hunkered by Gull's right side. Desperately she cursed her lack of control, her failure to learn protective or offensive spells. All she could do was fly, sometimes. But could she fly this lot—where? Was any place safe? She jumped as a demon leapt like a fox, latched onto her dark hair, snapped at her neck. Shrilling, she pressed against Gull as if he were a wall and tried to dislodge the monster. Teeth like splinters touched her skin, tore deeper. Panicking, but not wanting to shame Gull, she clutched at the fiend behind her, got her fingers bitten. Another leaped and caught her belt, dug in fingernails that cut her clothing and the skin of her belly. Oh, Gull, she wanted to say, I love you so. . . . But there was no time, and never would be, now. . . .

Stiggur had no time to haul back his whip, or draw his knife. Demons not much shorter than he bounded from every direction and latched onto his arms. He felt their teeth sink deep and couldn't help himself: he screamed. Stumbling backward, he fetched up against Gull's hips. As the woodcutter, his hero, flailed his axe one-handed at the onslaught of demons, the thick hickory haft reared back and slammed the boy alongside the head. Stiggur went down amidst a pile of lean dark hungry villains. . . .

Of all the party, only Greensleeves escaped immediate harm, for strong and silent Kwam grabbed her about the waist and hoisted her into the air. "I'll protect you!" he called, and she had the idiotic thought that his voice was very pleasant when he talked. But the magic student gasped as demons set upon him, biting, clawing, trying to climb him like a ladder after Greensleeves. He didn't know how long he could stay upright. Not long, for pain had him dancing, and it increased. . . .

Frantic, Greensleeves wracked her mind even while she struggled to breathe, Kwam held her middle so tightly. She would have to save the party, she knew, but how? Conjure what? Even a fleet of flying carpets couldn't aid them. A fungosaur? A badger? But the tendrils that linked her to her charges, her tags, were weak and thin, so far had they come from everything they knew. Yet there was one . . .

Strong as a silver-lit shining river, Greensleeves found the tag in her mind that twisted and turned but pointed unerringly to the stone brain. A pull like a whirlpool not far away. Yet she couldn't conjure it to her any more than she could swim up a waterfall. She must go to it. . . .

And abandon her companions?

Even with the thought, Kwam crumpled, flopped on his behind, still struggling to hold Greensleeves aloft. His strength had failed. Not far off in the haze, her brother swung at a dozen demons, but Lily and Stiggur were down under a pile of them. Even Helki had keeled over.

Any who weren't dead now would be in minutes.

Let my mind go. Let my sanity go, she thought. It was all she could do.

She shrieked as a demon bit her foot. Then she closed her eyes and went with the flow—threw her mind and body and spirit into the void.

Blinking, Greensleeves flopped in ashes and bones and dust. Alone, somewhere away from the demon horde, though not far off, she heard a piping like the squabble of sparrows. The horde, ripping her brother and friends to pieces.

But where was . . . ?

Something was digging into her back. A rock? A skull? Fumbling, she half rolled and got her hands on it.

The stone helmet: cast aside like trash, she knew not why. The most ancient, most powerful of artifacts. Jammed with secrets and mystery and miracles, yet so steeped in mana, so powerfully compelling with its order to obey, it could drive a practiced wizard stark raving mad.

Even her.

But her friends needed her. And there was no other way.

She could almost hear the gods laugh at her dilemma. She'd used the helmet on Haakon, but dared not use it on herself. And now she had no choice.

"Ah, me!" she panted. "Well . . . what's insanity but another state of mind?"

Biting her lip, her hands shaking uncontrollably, Greensleeves put the helmet on her head.

It was surprisingly light, weighed no more than a mob cap. It fit her perfectly, secure but not tight, as if molded to her head.

But the thoughts and commands . . .

Her mind swelled to bursting with the rancorous noise the helmet presented.

A hundred voices shouted at her to desist, to stop her evil ways, to obey. Voices of men and women, girls and boys, elders, and other, more alien voices. The bellow of a giant, the shrill of a centaur, a reptilian hiss. All ordered her to halt her magic-using or risk madness.

On and on went the commands, until Greensleeves felt as if her mind were dissolving. She'd only worn the helmet a second, she knew, but time stood still in here. The conclave would remonstrate until she submitted—an avalanche of threats to smother her.

No wonder Tybalt and Haakon went mad. A thousand voices shouting in one's head, threatening insanity . . .

But Greensleeves had been mad once. For the first time, as if a fog had cleared, or she'd turned some unknown corner, she could analyze that.

Most of her life she'd been an idiot. A thousand thousand thoughts had flitted through her mind every day. And what she disliked she could ignore.

These voices, she decided, were no more compelling or threatening than the hissing bubble of the Whispering Woods.

She could have laughed at the irony—she'd feared insanity by donning the helmet, only to find insanity had prepared her as the perfect wearer.

So, she thought, the last chains had been loosed from her mind, shattered forever.

And, as Tybalt had said, there was more behind the voices. The linked minds of great wizards lay open before her; she could read what she wanted. And take what she needed.

Visions stampeded through her skull like runaway horses, like a tornado, like a tidal wave. Pictures from long ago. Beings with dark robes and weeping horse skulls for heads. A long-fanged one-eyed goblin wearing a crown of red-hot nails. An ivory tower rearing above a golden autumn forest. A monster shrieking with a voice that shattered mountains. Women in blue that replicated themselves until they filled a mansion and spilled out the doors. Sprites dancing across flowers, together towing a patch of bleeding dog skin. A thinking being with a face like a melted candle. Phantasms with clocks in their bellies. Forges as hot as the sun, spilling forth treasure. Words. Songs. Battle cries. Sobs.

And spells. . . .

How to turn invisible. How to stop an enemy's heart. How to make trees dance by moonlight. How to calm a berserker, lure the leviathan from the depths of the ocean, pull a comet to earth, interrupt time, induce rust, charm a sanctuary, lock someone's spine, conjure visions, and many more. . . .

And deep inside the clamor, she heard the babble of the stone brain, a familiar voice, rushing on and on like a spring creek. And in its words a clue, a path, a way.

A hope.

Flooded to the eyes with mana, Greensleeves had only to picture her brother and friends struggling against the demon horde—

—and she was amidst them. From below the helmet she heard the shrieking and shrilling, heard an agonized cry as someone was bitten especially hard, someone still alive.

And there, in the swirling maelstrom, lay a tool. A shield spell, a second skin of mana to ward off danger, but magnified a hundred times. With a whisper she invoked its arcane name, plucking it from the whirlpool of sounds that rebounded in her head—

— then blinked as every demon was blown away as if by a giant wind. They landed sprawling, tumbling end over end, in litter and dust. Not one rose to the attack, but lay quivering as if lightning-struck.

There was more. In her mind's eye, Greensleeves saw blood bubbling from a severed throat. Kwam's. As easily as picking up a sewing needle—

— Greensleeves stitched the wound shut, erased all signs of damage, returned and recharged the blood in his veins, heard the man's heart stop fluttering and pump strongly again. Gull was down on one knee, his other under him, hamstrung when a demon had slashed teeth through the tendons. Winking, Greensleeves restored the leg. Lily had lost part of her scalp to a vicious bite, and Greensleeves reknit it. Amma's arm bled, but Greensleeves drew muscle and tendons back into place. And then she went all around, mending Helki and Rakel and Hammen and Stiggur. But not poor Channa, for there was nothing left of her but scattered bones and hair.

The voices in her head were a roar now, a deluge threatening to drown her. Her knees buckled. Try as she might . . . she couldn't grasp the clue to fix . . . herself. . . .

She had better move before she fainted.

She pictured their route, how far they'd come, and gasped aloud at the distance. They'd traversed a substantial part of the Domains, for she could see, far off, boundaries where the worlds ran out. It was all there, all the knowledge one could want, but it pulled at her, tried to pry her mind from her skull . . .

Oh, yes, they must shift. Funny she'd forgotten that. She must be . . . lightheaded. . . .

Striving to stay awake and upright, Greensleeves stretched out her arms and her mind, gathered her friends close to her skirts, and—in a heartbeat—whisked them to a place deep within her heart.

"Home."

CHAPTER
19

WHISPERING WOKE GREENSLEEVES.

Prying open one eye, she found herself looking up through naked tree branches at a wan winter sun overlaid with a tissue of clouds. A crow cawed close at hand, flapped from the tip of a tall spruce tree, leaving it swaying, alighted in the branches of a hoary oak, and cocked its head at her as if mimicking.

But whence came the whispering? Who was gossiping, or telling tales? Why did it sound familiar—

The druid sat up like a shot. Helki propped herself up groggily, struggled to gather four shaky roan legs under her. Lily lay curled like a baby, her cloak pulled around her chin, her mouth pouty in sleep. Rakel looked pink and rested and no longer like the walking dead. Hammen, her son, was tucked against her stomach with his thumb in his mouth. Amma and gentle Kwam lay nearby. Stiggur, dressed like Gull, murmured and reached for a blanket that wasn't there. And Gull, her brother, lay spread-eagled on the leaf-thick ground as if he'd fallen from a tree.

And by her hand, the stone brain-turned-helmet.

Then she remembered, and knew where they were.

"Gull! Everyone! Wake up! We're home! Back in the Whispering Woods!"

Within two days, Greensleeves had fetched everyone.

Under Varrius, the army had progressed out of the badlands and come to a long river that cut between high bluffs. That was as far as they got before Greensleeves appeared among them, shifting with ease, and waved her hands to ferry them to the depths of the Whispering Woods.

The lean, bronzed, black-bearded Varrius shook Gull's hand again and again. "I said you'd succeed and you did! And almost overnight!" Gull was astonished to realize they'd only been gone a day or two. How many lands had they crossed in that space of time? It was spooky. Magic would never agree with him. When Varrius clapped Greensleeves on the shoulder hard enough to stagger her, she only smiled.

Chaney's greeting was quiet, but just as lively for all that. She put her good arm around her two disciples and whispered, "I knew there would be losses. But I knew you would both succeed, too. Your hearts are too big to fail." Both Greensleeves and Lily blushed when the druid kissed them with dry withered lips.

With the organization and discipline that Rakel had instilled into them, the army set up camp in the woods and settled down to repair and regroup. Having lost Bardo, Holleb became captain of scouts, and selected two more soldiers to replace Channa and the lost paladin to bring his company up to snuff. With Ordando dead, Rakel promoted her sergeant, a stocky woman named Muliya, or "Muley," who'd shown herself adept at training. Despite the winter chill, the camp soon rang with shouts and laughter and song, and it was only in the afterglow of the evening's dying fires that folks talked of departed comrades.

Gull and Greensleeves consulted, rode far and wide, hunting landmarks, and decided they were probably north-northwest of White Ridge, yet still northeast of the star crater. But when her brother asked how they'd arrived here, and what came next, the druid was unsure.

"In the middle of that attack and that horrible place, I wished us home and we came here, back to my roots. And yours. You were more a part of this forest than White Ridge; you spent your waking hours here. We simply came back, as geese flock to their nests in spring."

Gull draped his reins over Ribbon's pommel and patted the dapple gray's neck. "But we can't stay here long. There was never enough game in these woods to sustain our village, let alone a hungry army. And no fodder for the stock. We couldn't live here in summer, let alone winter."

"We can." Greensleeves combed tousled hair away from her face and shifted her shawl with its charms. "Chaney has told me how to enchant the woods, not forcing them to grow, but helping them yield their utmost, as she did on her plateau under those oaks in the badlands. It won't take long for me to shift the balance and make us all comfortable. If we're frugal," she warned.

Gull shook his head. For a moment, he paused to listen to the whispering in the branches, the unending susurrus that babbled like a brook or a mob at market, or the stone brain, for that matter. The rush and hush were more muted in winter and seemed less sinister than before. It didn't disturb anyone in camp, but perhaps they stood only on the cusp of the whispering. Gull decided he needn't figure it out: it was magic, and he'd leave that to his sister.

Now he chuckled. "It's odd to see you sitting here, so in control, Greenie. When we lived here, the woods fogged your mind, controlling you. Now you're in control and can push the woods into whatever you need."

She shook tangled brown locks. "Not push, or

coax, even. Just help. But yes, once the magic overwhelmed me, but now I—can I say I overwhelm the magic?"

Before Gull could answer, a drumming sounded from the direction of camp. Turning, they saw Holleb and Jayne, his newly appointed scout, approaching at a fast canter. The centaur had been gone for four days, following a wagon trail through the forest, and here he was back, having donned his helmet and breastplate. The woodcutter groaned. "Uh-oh."

"Gull, Greensleeves!" gargled the harsh voice. "To west we find wizard! Dacian, she who enslaved I and Helki! And fought your Towser to ruin your homeland!"

Dacian the Red tossed in her bed of perfumed pillows. She was alone in the pavilion, a large and comfortable tent fastened to the side of her wagon. Since her entourage had been camped here for a fortnight, other tents had been erected to hold her many boxes and chests, so this tent was largely empty but for thick rugs on the forest floor, her huge folding cot, and her many pillows and quilts. Dacian slept in comfort, buried amidst piles of downy luxury.

Idly, she lay awake, though it was the dead of night and the rest of her camp was asleep but for pickets. She didn't know why she was awake, but she used the time to plan ahead. Another day or two would see all the soil in the star crater sifted and turned. Weeks ago she'd sensed mana in this direction and had pinpointed the crater as the source. It had been a vast disappointment to find that whatever had crashed was gone, yet she kept her workers busy digging. Such a place, so drenched in mana by whatever glorious object had eluded her, would make a fine source to tap—she could draw strength from this region forever. Yet the mana here was old, and strange. And why should a falling star be so empowered? But little matter. From here, her wagon train would trend east, close to that little village near the

white-streaked ridge that had been destroyed in a battle with that striped wizard, when she'd had to run
and abandon some of her choicest pawns. The woods
near that village whispered, she remembered. Much
mana there, surely.

Dissatisfied, she turned over, thrashed free of a
dozen quilts, turned again. Something bothered her,
something in the air. Perhaps she was just over-
wrought from driving her servants. Perhaps she
should summon one of the guards inside for a dal-
liance. Or two guards. . . . Or a serving girl to brush
her hair. Dacian was very proud of the thick glossy
hair spilling down her back. Yes. She could rouse the
camp, put everyone to work in the dead of night. If she
couldn't sleep, then no one should. . . .

Cross, frustrated, Dacian turned up a lamp, pulled
her brown and yellow robe over her shift, and drew on
soft boots. Lastly, she donned her satchel of artifacts.
She never went anywhere without it, not even to the
privy. Throwing the tent flap wide, she stamped into
the chilly air. "Guard! Rouse the camp! *Guard!*"

No answer. The brute must have sneaked away to
nap, she thought. She'd scourge him for leaving her
camp undefended—

No, wait. What was that noise? Voices, a man and
a woman's. Ah! The sneak dallied with one of the
scullery maids! Well, she'd teach them both a lesson!

Treading silently in soft boots over frost-nipped
leaves, Dacian followed the sound. There, by a tree,
silhouetted in the moonlight: her guard, Rida, and—
who?

A tall woman, long and sleek, naked as a baby,
with white skin light as birch bark and hair the color
of cornsilk, if the moonlight glow were not deceiving
her. Dacian pressed closer. Rida was a tall man, but
the woman was even taller. There was no woman that
big in camp. . . .

Then the woman retreated, slim back against a
stand of birch trees, and faded among them. Rida
stumbled after her, blundered into a trunk as if he

were half-blind, circled, blundered again, clearly bewitched. But how?

Then Dacian knew. She'd heard the legends. Shanondin dryads, mischievous tree spirits that could take any form. Even a beautiful impossibly tall woman. But how could there be *dryads,* some of the most enchanted creatures, without Dacian sensing them?

And what to do? By taking one form or another, whatever the viewer wished, the dryad could lure all her servants to the woods. In fact . . .

Dacian stumbled back to camp, almost bumping into a tree in her hurry. She found the cook's wagon and kicked underneath it. A surprised grunt and curse rewarded her. "Rouse, you lazy lice! Rida's bewitched by a she-sprite and you'll be next, skinned alive and eaten! Hurry!" Dacian kicked up the fire, too.

Her servants crawled out of tents, or tumbled from the backs of wagons. They hurried, fearing Dacian's short temper. Twice now the wizard had simply banished servants too slow to follow orders. One cook rubbed his face and swore softly, then let out a howl. "Look there!"

Approaching at a gallop, eyes gleaming red in reflected firelight, loped a pack of huge timber wolves. The shaggy animals bounded into the ring of firelight and scattered Dacian's sleepy staff like chickens. Serving women screamed and fought to clamber back into the wagons. Men shoved from behind, or climbed up the sides of the wagons. Dacian plastered herself against a wagon and fished desperately in her satchel for the right artifact. Fire would drive off wolves.

The wolves, as confused as the servants, merely trotted through the suddenly deserted camp and out the other side to disappear into the blackness. They wouldn't fight or fret anything that didn't interfere with them.

But Dacian missed their exit, for she'd plucked up a shard of flint sharp enough to cut a careless finger. Light, she needed light. She'd get it if she had to burn this forest to the ground.

Muttering, rubbing the flint against her woolen gown, faster and faster, she rattled off a spell, sent tendrils along a thin tag to the farthest reaches of the Domains, close to its fiery center, where dwelt—

With a *puff* and *whoop*, the fire elemental leaped from the flint full-bodied and alive. Formed of billowing flame, taller than the wagons, it suggested a female shape, but Dacian knew elementals were not human, or even really alive.

But she could control it. The elemental's flame scorched the night, reflected glittering off bare branches, steamed frost from the leaves of the forest floor. Half-blinded, Dacian circled her finger in the air. "Rise and reveal my enemies! Seek—"

But her words blew back in her mouth.

From the south, the direction of the crater, a rush of wind bowled her backward, made her stagger against the wagon. The gale flailed her long straight hair about her face, yanked at the hem of her gown, choked her with wood ashes plucked from the firepit. Batting her hair away, struggling to keep her feet in the frigid blast, she saw her fire elemental grapple with a similar being. White as a ghost, with a long twisting tail, the air elemental rushed for its comrade, playful as a puppy, dangerous as a tornado. Dacian caught her breath and shivered uncontrollably. The wind of its passage was chilled from the uppermost reaches of the atmosphere, with neither the warmth of the sun nor the earth in it. Dacian thought she breathed ice, was drowning in it.

But only for a moment. The fire elemental flickered and spun on its head, dashed for the air elemental. But when they met, the greater mana of the air-being extinguished the fire creature as a hurricane would snuff a candle. Dacian saw the fire elemental splinter into a thousand tiny wisps of flame, like the scattering of a campfire, then it was gone and the darkness returned.

Confused, missing its friend, the air elemental whirled once, twice, thrice around the camp, frosting the camp equipment and wagons and Dacian, then shot straight into the sky and vanished.

Teeth chattering, Dacian cast about in the dark. Where were her servants? her guards? Had they all run off? Damn them! She'd abandon the lot, leave them stranded in a winter forest!

Cursing, she reached into her satchel. Her hands were so cold she couldn't feel her fingers. Nor was there any light save moonlight to illuminate the contents. Fumbling, she pulled the first thing she could find: a seashell painted red.

Bitterly cold, Dacian mouthed an incantation to summon the beings associated with the shell. She'd need protection, lots of it, for whoever was out there had more mana than she. And she'd need time, if she were to escape with her wagons and booty. Completing the enchantment, she flicked the shell a dozen feet away.

A crackling sounded among the wind-churned leaves. A row of small shapes arose from amidst the leaves, no higher than mushrooms. But the shapes stretched and grew like dragon's teeth, so within seconds she had a line of soldiers between her and her mysterious attacker.

There were twenty-four, as she'd commissioned. All men, bronze hued, black bearded, in silver scale mail like lizard's skin and red kilts and cloaks. Each carried a round bossed shield and short sword, and two javelins slung on thongs over their shoulders. As the men blinked and peered around, suddenly wary in the dark, their captain—what was his name?— marched toward her in sandaled feet for orders.

He hadn't gotten six feet before a fireball lit the night, and war whoops sounded from two directions.

The soldiers crouched at the new threat, squinting at the bright light. Another sizzling fireball arced overhead, not fifty feet high, and exploded on the forest floor twenty feet away. An ash tree blazed like a torch as some pitchy substance ran, flaming, down its bark. Seconds later came another fireball from the same

direction, toward the crater, and this exploded even
closer, making men jump as it set the dry leaves alight.

The war whoops sounded again, many of them,
along with men and women's high-pitched howls and
shouts of glee.

Ignoring Dacian, the red captain hopped to the
end of his ranks and barked orders to file by twos.
Automatically, the men obeyed, though the enthusiastic whoops obviously made them wish they were elsewhere. A soldier on the end, a sergeant, barked back
at the captain that there were flankers to the side.

A line of cavalry thundered from the east. At the
forefront was a huge brawny centaur with a fluted
breastplate and closed helmet, one arm bound against
his chest, yet he hollered at the top of his lungs and
aimed a lance two armspans long. With him were
horsemen and -women, many with sweeping sabers,
others with axes and long swords. They had no partic-
ular uniform save for armbands of two colors.

No, thought Dacian, it wasn't possible. No one
could have conjured so large a force so quickly and
without her sensing a disturbance in the mana! It
wasn't possible!

The red captain made a quick count: he faced a
score in ranks of three. If the flankers had the same
numbers . . .

They did. Another centaur, leaner but still as tall,
led a line of men and women in gray cloaks stitched
with raven feathers. And behind them were more
ranks of soldiers with green armbands. Another score.

Veteran of a hundred battles, the captain knew
when to retreat. "Take cover, in pairs! Save yourselves
who can! Regroup north at dawn!"

Like pigeons scattered before a pride of lions, the
red soldiers paired off and dashed for the nearest
cover: behind trees, under wagons, behind tents and
then stands of brush. The cavalry fragmented to harass
them, whooping as they drove the men deep into shelter, horses snorting and blowing in excitement.

Dacian clenched her fists so hard her long nails

cut her palms. By the bloody brow of Shaitan, those were *her* centaurs! *She'd* recruited them in the Green Lands near the Honeyed Sea—*she'd* tagged them! And now they led an attack on her red soldiers and scattered them like mice! By the eyes of the gods, she'd *kill* someone for this indignity—

A chuffing and creaking and squeaking and clumping made her turn. The very earth shook underfoot. Grabbing at the wagon, she risked a peek. By the light of the burning tree, she saw two giant shapes stump toward her from the darkness. One had two heads— that stupid giant she'd recruited with a barrel of wine! The one who'd had his arm chewed off. Yet here he came with a long club attached to the stump. And with it was—curses upon curses!—the clockwork beast she'd found trapped in a canyon in the high plains. The two came to attack her!

But *how* had they been conjured? It was impossible!

Not so. For in truth, Dacian couldn't fathom that the troops were there of their own free will, not conjured and compelled, but cheerful volunteers.

Belatedly, Dacian realized she was alone. Her retainers were gone. The red soldiers had faded into the forest.

Time to go. Abandon the wagons. Get out while she could. She knew a spot to retreat, her favorite: a good-sized town in the lowlands where anyone with a full purse was welcome—

Digging in her satchel, she found a coin plucked from the town's fountain. Seeking to clear her mind, she stared straight ahead, made herself calm. It was only a short jump, and already she felt her feet tingle, her height begin to contract—

She gawked as something shimmered before her. Tree trunks, or branches, or simply a slant of moonlight, suddenly melted. Before her, gray-striped as the night, then suddenly blossoming with color, were a small woman with tangled hair and plain faded robes and a tatty shawl decorated with charms, and a huge man in deerhide and red woolens. He carried a massive double-headed felling axe. They appeared not four feet from Dacian. A camouflage spell, she thought. They'd been nearby and watching all along, and she'd had no clue.

The small woman, with the roughshod look of a druid, carried a stone helmet under one arm. Her free hand she laid gently on Dacian's shoulder. The wizard was too stunned to shake it off. And with that gentle touch, Dacian's shift spell dissipated like a pleasant dream.

Snarling, the wizard slapped off the druid's hand, but the big man grabbed her upper arm and hoisted her in the air, a prisoner.

As Dacian struggled, the druid plopped the stone helmet on her black glossy head.

A thousand images bombarded her mind, a thousand commands to obey . . .

Then she knew no more.

"So we win again," said Greensleeves. "It feels good! We're finally accomplishing something we can touch."

"I'm glad," grumbled her brother as he set down the rigid Dacian, "but not happy. This magic-mover tussled with Towser and helped destroy our home. It might have been she who loosed the stone rain and plague rats."

Greensleeves shook her head, amused. "You objected the loudest when I put this same helmet on Haakon."

"Well . . . " Now Gull was confused. "But I thought you were being arrogant and callous, risking someone else's sanity when you yourself hadn't tried the helmet."

"And so I was callous. And arrogant. And wrong. But the gods repaid me in kind, for later I had to don the helmet to save all your lives. A fitting punishment for arrogance, and a sure cure. No more of that."

"Still, we don't want to forget Dacian's crimes and show her any kindness."

"But kindness is all we have," Greensleeves disagreed. "If the wizards are bent on control and destruction, we must answer them with gentleness and cooperation. That's how we'll defeat our enemies and make the Domains a better place."

Gull nodded slowly. "You must be right, for surely bashing folks in the head can't help—much. I'm just glad you haven't become like them. That's been my biggest fear—that in learning magic you'd lose your soul."

Greensleeves laughed, a merry sound in the chilly night. She put a hand on her big brother's forearm. "Don't fear. Before I'd become like them, I'd turn my flesh to soil and feed the grass."

Gull grinned and mussed her hair. "Father and Mother and all the rest would be proud of you. But what do we do with this one?"

"Bring her to the right path, or at least put her on a short leash." Greensleeves turned toward the dark and called, "Kwam?"

Like a shadow, the dark student came to their side. He was never far from Greensleeves's side now. Gently, the druid placed Dacian's limp hand in Kwam's. "Take her to Amma, please. See she's bundled up. Take good care of her." The student smiled and nodded.

But Gull arrested him with a hand on his arm, then a reluctant smile. "That order goes for my sister, too. See you take good care of her. Or else." Kwam's smile crinkled, embarrassed. He couldn't answer, so he simply led Dacian away.

They were interrupted by a horsewoman trotting up. It was Rakel, again the commander, but wrapped in all wool and no black leather. She bounded from the saddle. "Hola! Did you see them run? And not a one spitted!"

Rakel laughed, happy to be working again, to be whole and well. Happy, too, that their plan had worked flawlessly. Realizing it was Dacian the Red they must attack, Greensleeves had insisted on as little bloodshed as possible. For, certainly, Dacian would conjure up her red soldiers—old comrades of Varrius and Neith and the late Tomas—or even centaur scouts, friends and relatives of Helki and Holleb.

And after all the blood and absences the army had suffered lately, no one wanted any more.

"You did well, Rakel, as usual!" said Gull. "I'm glad you're in command and not me. I'd have driven half the army into the crater and lost the other half in the woods."

Rakel leaned on tiptoe and kissed Gull on the cheek like a sister. "You'd have done fine. We all have our tasks to perform, and mesh like—"

Her voice stopped. Not ten feet away, a black cocoon formed from nothing. Like a silken ebony spiderweb, the spinning mass grew from a single dark line to the height and bulk of a human. Greensleeves fingered her shawl, Rakel her sword. Gull lifted his axe.

The cocoon steadied, then rent down one side as if spilling out a giant butterfly.

But what stepped forth was a lean man, oddly dressed in shabby wool breeches and an embroidered shirt of black with blue thread. A tattered leather cape hung from his shoulders, an ornate dagger and tooled satchel at his hips.

His face was bony, bronzed by summer suns. His eyes were a deep turquiose blue, but the left was framed by an old scar like a bright star. Both eyes blazed as he beheld the scene. His mouth was an ugly slash of anger.

Rakel found her breath locked in her chest.

"Garth!"

CHAPTER
20

"NORREEN!" DEMANDED THE DARK STRANGER. "Where is my son?"

"Who's Norreen?" Gull asked Rakel. Instinctively he moved in front of the women. "*You?* Who's *he*?"

"My husband," whispered Rakel.

"Husband?"

"You!" Garth pointed at Gull. "Get away from my wife!"

"Garth!" snarled Rakel. "Behave yourself!"

"Silence, traitor!" roared the wizard.

The man's arrogance sparked Gull's anger. Another damned magic user, he thought, who thought he ruled wherever he trod. Gull snapped back, "I've *carried* your wife out of stinking hellholes, and she's carried *us* to victories! Where have *you* been all this time?"

"Gull . . . " warned Greensleeves.

"Garth . . . " warned Rakel.

But both stubborn powerful men had taken an instant dislike to one another, and both exploded into action before they could think it out.

Garth flicked a hand to his satchel as Gull raised his axe and charged.

Before the woodcutter could strike, Garth swirled a black cocoon of pure mana before him and snapped it like a stick. Immediately before him, as if spun from the black cloud, stood a lich, a wizard long dead, so wasted only knots and strings of muscle still clung to its moldering bones. It wore a long blue robe, surprisingly supple and clean, that rippled in the torchlight like an ocean swell. The thing raised a green withered hand spotted with cankers and rot, conjured a fireball of a sickly green.

But whatever spell it sought to spin went unfinished. Greensleeves touched a spiderweb at her shawl, pointed a finger, and the fireball evaporated in a yellow-green cloud.

Gull never even slowed. Hunching his shoulders, fury adding to his strength, he swept the axe in a glittering arc that sheared the undead wizard in two. A snapping like kindling, a surprised squeak like a trapped rat's, and the thing collapsed into a heap of shimmery blue cloth and bones.

But Garth moved, too. Flicking a handful of what seemed to be black marbles before him, he barked a command. Before the woodcutter could assault him, Gull slammed full tilt into an invisible, impenetrable shield. Dazed, nose bleeding, the woodcutter shouted abuse and rapped on the wall to find a way around.

Greensleeves touched a sprig of seaweed at her shoulder, cupped her hand in the air, and tilted it. Garth was deluged by a column of seawater plunging from above. It filled the circular shield he'd conjured, outlining the invisible force like a glass tumbler. Garth merely popped a smooth pebble in his mouth and breathed the water. From his satchel, he drew an object that was chunky and yellow-white: a tooth. Garth blew on it, aiming the puff at a body of cavalry not far away.

Amidst the horses and riders suddenly reared a monster as tall as the trees. Branches broke and leaves fluttered to the ground as the behemoth shrugged its massive flanks, stamped four thick feet, and snapped out a hairy trunk—a war mammoth, twenty feet high at the shoulder, dwarfing even Stiggur's clockwork beast, hung with shaggy hair. Nearsighted, confused by the milling figures near its feet, the mammoth stamped twice, shaking the ground, then raised its trunk and trumpeted loud enough to shatter helmets. Horses, already panicked by the beast's great size and strange smell, reared, backed, spun, banged heads, stepped on soldiers, then galloped away as if an eagle had alighted in a flock of pigeons.

Greensleeves thought for a moment, reckoning how to apply the least force for the greatest result. The mammoth must not overrun the camp and camp followers. Stiggur had sent his clockwork beast careening toward the mammoth. Liko tramped alongside. They might be hurt, the druid decided, so Greensleeves needed to drive it west.

Touching a chunk of twisted burned metal on her shawl, flicking her hand, she shot a fireball that exploded amidst the dead branches of a white oak. The mammoth's tiny black eyes glinted as branches and leaves and old birds' nests crackled into flame not a dozen feet from its head. Sparks spat into the mammoth's oily matted hair, ignited briefly, then went out. But the fire and sting was enough to panic the beast, and it turned and backed, smashing flat a stand of white birches, then blundered west, crashing into the night.

With a rush, Garth dissolved his invisible shield wall, and seawater gushed around their feet. The wizard was dry, the water-breathing spell having protected him.

Rakel half drew her sword, shouted at the men to desist, swore as only an army commander could. Furious and disgusted, she decided to let them fight, get it out of their system. She slammed her sword back in its scabbard and stood, hands on hips, fuming.

Raising his axe as a partial shield, Gull grabbed Garth's collar and shook him like a puppy. Yet Gull wasn't sure what he wanted from this man, only knew he mustn't kill him if he were precious to Rakel. A good bust in the mouth, however—

Jiggling in the air, Garth touched Gull with a finger encased in a dried eelskin.

The spell wracked Gull from head to toe. Electricity shot through him, made his hair stand on end, his eyes bulge, his teeth gleam with sparks, his muscles cramp and spasm. Yet he hung on doggedly, shook so hard Garth's head wobbled and interrupted his concentration. The spell quit. Growling, a frazzled Gull grabbed the wizard's throat and squeezed. Husband to Rakel or not, Gull would break a few bones and teach this wizard a lesson—

A blow knocked him sideways. An animal howl rang in his ears. Looming at his side was a pair of berserkers, a huge man and woman with ratty hair, leather and fur armor, stone clubs held high. Insanity flared in their eyes—they'd passed up a death blow to Gull's exposed side and simply bowled into him with their shields. Gull smelled rancid breath as the man crowded and champed broken teeth at his face—another inch and he'd bite off Gull's nose.

Growling himself, Gull lifted his axe and stopped the slash of a stone club, kicked at the woman to keep her back, saw her club swing overhead to split his skull—

Rakel cried out, sword flashing from her scabbard. Her blade broke off wood from the woman's club, but the man butted her shoulder with his rawhide shield—

Garth saw his wife about to be chopped in half, barked a warning—

And all of them were flattened as an ocean of seawater dropped from the sky.

Greensleeves had conjured a surf's worth this time. The fighters were smashed to their stomachs. Water splashed and gushed everywhere. Even Greensleeves, at the edge, was wet to her knees.

Leaves were swirled away, the forest loam scoured as the water coursed toward the ground. An octopus twitched at Greensleeves's feet, and she stooped, touched and unsummoned it home.

Half-drowned, the sodden crowd flopped like fish stranded by the tide. Greensleeves touched a feather on her shawl and pronounced a sleep spell on the berserker pair.

As Gull and Garth and Rakel pushed to their knees, all instinctively seeking their enemy's whereabouts, Greensleeves called, "No more foolishness, please. It's time to talk."

Shivering, glowering at one another, they nodded.

Wrapped in blankets around a cooking fire, Garth, Rakel, Gull, Lily, and Greensleeves talked while all the army except the pickets listened outside the circle.

Angry accusations and taunts and threats snapped like the branches in the fire, and it was some time before tempers cooled and civil tones were heard. But Rakel, or Norreen, as Garth called her, used to commanding armies, got in her say. Sitting on her lap the whole time, wrapped in a woolen cloak, his hair stubbly, Hammen stared wide-eyed at his spectral father returned from the ether.

"Garth, you neglected your farm *and* your vines *and* me *and* Hammen to pursue magic, and you know it! You fell out of love with *me* and fell *into* love with magic, and you know that! You know it as well as a drunkard knows he loves the grape and will give up everything for one more bottle! You'd toyed with it, wallowed in it, eaten, drunk, and slept it for too long, and you *still* wanted more! And while you've been plumbing the planes for magic like a rat after garbage, Hammen and I have *suffered*! *No thanks to you!* Will you deny this? Can you look me and Hammen in the face and tell us you love us still?"

In the pause that followed this tirade, Gull whispered to Greensleeves, "The same thing I feared for you. That you'd forsake humanity for magic and use us as pawns to further your own dark ends."

"And I told you," chided his sister, "I'd die before I'd give up my friends and family and humanity. Now hush!"

Garth sipped hot tea with his eyes closed, taking the minty fragrance deep into his lungs and body, as if he'd forsaken even eating in pursuit of magic. Finally, calmly, he intoned, "I sought you out, didn't I? I tracked you here—"

"Fat lot of good that did!" snapped his wife. Her anger glowed the hottest of any of them, but she'd suffered the most. "In that time I was tortured, then chased halfway across Benalia, bleeding in the arms of that man and that boy. A good soldier, Ordando, gave her life in my rescue. And Bardo, a paladin, was plucked off a rooftop like a pigeon defending us. We were ripped to shreds in a godsforsaken ashy wilderness by demons! Yet every inch of the way I've been protected and cosseted and comforted by this army, these people—me and my son—because they are good decent folk who stick to their goals and their visions and their promises." She cried now, tears of anger and sorrow, and she felt a fool for it, yet couldn't stop.

"Gull and Greensleeves and Lily and Stiggur and Varrius and Neith and everyone here, from the smallest child gathering fagots, have worked and slaved and trained and fought and damned near died—and many have done just that!—so the Domains might be free of the arrogance and authority and cruelty of wizards flaunting magic! And yet what do they find, after bringing yet another callous witch to heel, but *you* barging in and hurling accusations and spells to assuage your own guilt! Because you have been guilty of arrogance and callousness. And deep inside, the *hero* who returned to Estark to punish even more arrogant bastards for their magic-thieving sins knows it, too.

"So," she concluded hoarsely, "will you admit

you've neglected me and Hammen, and sought only to aggrandize yourself, and apologize to this army—our friends!—for your bullying? Or will you stay aloof amidst the 'higher folk' who disdain humans as pawns and cattle and aspire to be gods?"

There was a long pause, still as the night before daybreak. The entire army seemed to hold its breath.

Rakel's words rang in Garth's ears. He'd almost been a god once, fought for the privilege, then abandoned it to remain human. Where had he gone wrong since?

The black-clad wizard with the star-shaped scar around his left eye thought for a long time.

He put down his redware mug and stood. Gull, disliking the menacing quiet, tightened his grip on his axe, braced his legs to leap.

But Garth faced his wife and infant son. Gravely, he intoned, "You are right, Norreen, and I've been wrong. I have been skating the ether, soaring between worlds. There are wonders out there such as you'd never imagine, things beyond beauty and mystery, things . . . But never mind. Looking at your sweet face, and my son's eager eyes, I realize they are just things and just places, and what really counts in this world and all worlds are people. And I apologize for neglecting you, and you, Hammen. It's been . . . so long . . . since I thought of myself as human, and not a wizard, that I've been sucked into the maw of magic. But I eschew it, once and for all, and ask your forgiveness—"

The rest of his words were cut off because Rakel, juggling Hammen, jumped into his arms and hugged him tight. The boy hugged his father's dark head and cried, "Papa!" Rakel cried with happiness, and both of Garth's eyes, the original and the restored, leaked tears down his narrow nose.

The army laughed and cheered and sniffled and wiped their eyes. Greensleeves smiled. And Lily took Gull's hand, and he squeezed hers back.

* * *

But as always with an army, there were still a thousand tasks to fulfill, a thousand questions to answer.

Having wandered extensively as a one-eyed vagabond years before, Garth filled in many gaps on the cartographers' maps, answered many questions and rumors and stories held by the librarians. One immediate benefit was that Garth knew the lands to the south of Gish and the Honeyed Sea, and could pinpoint the Green Lands of the centaurs Helki and Holleb.

So one afternoon, in a flurry of tears and handshaking and hugs, Garth raised his hands, spun black webbing around the lancer team, and sent them home. He had promised to fetch the centaurs back in a week, to see if they had indeed found their homeland and tribe, but Greensleeves and Gull believed they would never see their four-legged friends again and were sad for it.

Others returned home as the army's knowledge increased. Forced to obedience by the stone helmet, Haakon and Dacian were stood before maps to name areas they'd explored. The king of the Badlands' head wounds and strength had been mended by the healers, but he lacked one eye and always would. In surly growls, he sketched in most of the northern reaches of the continent. The glossy-haired Dacian, from the northeast, bitterly explained the lay of hills and mountains that lay beyond White Ridge. Other islands and continents were laid out, though the two wizards had only jumped across them and knew few details. Dacian revealed the southern peninsula, where she'd hired the red soldiers, Varrius and Neith and the late Tomas, as well as the archipelago where she'd found Liko and reported other giants to live, albeit one-headed ones.

With many farewells, and a wave of black-cobwebbed hands, Garth sent the red soldiers home, then the giant, and handfuls of other soldiers and their families swept up in wizards' wars.

Yet Gull sat before his sister's tent one night,

frowning while he honed his axe. "Don't you see? We've been too successful. Our army had two goals: to stop wizards in their predations, and to map and find the homelands of our friends. We're finding their lands, all right, and they're trotting home like cows to milking. Soon you and I will be all that's left of the army—not much of a force."

Unsure what to do with the captured wizards, Greensleeves finally decided to let them go.

"Are you *mad*?" asked her brother in council one night around the fire. "After all the trouble we went to, after all the lives lost in capturing them? You'd just dust your hands and let them loose? That's like a shepherd freeing wolves!"

Greensleeves shook her tousled head. "There's no point in detaining them. We've got them shackled with leg irons and bound to my will, and I like neither, though it's necessary. And we certainly can't kill them. But since they *are* bound to my will, I can fetch them back at any time and make them state what they've been doing. If it's mischief, we can deal with it. They'll be paroled, after a fashion, with us checking them from time to time. And who knows? They might learn humility, see things from the perspective of those they've enslaved, and decide to help us. So I say let them go."

Gull muttered, "As long as wolves have teeth they'll eat meat. But fine. I hate magic. You deal with it."

Immediately, Dacian the Red and Haakon, self-proclaimed king of the Badlands, were summoned. Like some dotty queen, Greensleeves instructed the wizards to "behave themselves" and released them. Flabbergasted—both had feared they'd be drained of mana and knowledge and then executed—Dacian and Haakon wasted no time in disappearing.

But to demonstrate her resolve, Greensleeves conjured them back the next night. Haakon was grubby and furious, but explained he'd been digging for his armor. Dacian was drunk, set on drowning her sorrows and invisible chains in some midland city. Partly satisfied, Gull grunted, and Greensleeves unsummoned the pair.

"Mad," her brother grumbled. "Someone's mad as an owl, but I'm damned if I know who."

The army received a number of surprises exactly seven days later.

Garth walked to a clearing and waved his hands. Gull, Greensleeves, Lily, and Rakel with Hammen were there to watch, along with many members of the diminished army. All hoped to see Holleb and Helki, if only once more, and learn they were happy.

But the black silky nothingness spun first one, then two, then fifty snorting, stamping, painted and polished centaurs bearing feathered lances. Two of the tribespeople broke away immediately and galloped over to the astonished viewers.

Helki and Holleb looked sharp, their tack and harness new, their spears and armor and flanks freshly painted, their coats polished a glossy red-brown. They halted and saluted formally, but grinned as they removed their helmets.

"Greensleeves, Gull, Lily! Rakel, you most of all! See what we bring! We find our tribe—Windseekers of Green Lands—and make much crying and happiness! See our parents and brothers and sisters, even. We tell our adventures, and quest you follow, how you make sacrifice to stop wizards. And all our people—every one—wish to join army!"

There was a stunned silence. Then Stiggur screamed his war cry and made everyone jump. "*Yahooo!!!* There's *nothing* can stop us now! We can defeat any army in the *Domains*!"

Then everyone, centaurs included, was shouting loud enough to tumble snow from the branches of the winter trees.

Not long after, Garth summoned Varrius and Neith, and they told the same story. Mercenaries by trade, they'd been lied to and manipulated by wizards for too long. For a minimal living wage, the red soldiers would join Greensleeves and Gull's army. How many? How many did they want? Varrius had talked to five centuries—companies of one hundred men—and lost count of the number of volunteers. Gull could only grin, shake his head, and say he'd need to think on it.

Many soldiers returned with similar news. Everywhere they went in the Domains, ordinary folk wanted to join and support an army dedicated to stopping the wizards, for everyone knew someone who'd suffered from magic. Some returnees promised only five or six volunteers—all the able-bodied men and women of their village—while others reported being mobbed by a hundred volunteers waving weapons and itching to fight. Gull clutched his forehead in trying to imagine the numbers that Kwam, as clerk, totted up. "How will we *feed* all those folk?"

Even Liko came back, both heads crying like babies. He was lonely at home and missed his friends—could he stay? Laughing and crying at the same time, Greensleeves patted his one hand and assured him he could.

But then, as if to balance all the good news, the army was saddened by bad.

"We're leaving," Rakel told Gull and Greensleeves in the privacy of the druid's tent.

"Leaving?" barked brother and sister.

Rakel's eyes were misty as she nodded. "Aye. Garth and I and even little Hammen have talked long into the night. I'm weary of soldiering—I've never known but a few years of peace, and I want to settle down. But I won't get fat again, or out of shape. I need to teach my son to be a warrior. And my other children, when we have them."

"I," Garth added, "will eschew magic, as promised.

Well, I might tweak the vines or fetch in rain, and I must set wards around our house in case Benalia comes calling—though I doubt they will after Gull's lesson in woodcutting." He grinned and patted his son's head.

Choking back tears, Rakel took Gull's craggy hands in her own. "Thank you for your help. In everything, for caring for me and—loving me. I don't have any other words than that."

Gull sniffled. He patted her calloused, capable hands. "Thank you for smartening up our army. We'd have no victories but for you. The army will miss you. They love you. Too," he added.

Rakel shrugged, used her sleeve to dry her eyes. "Commanders change like the wind. Anyone can give orders. It's the heart of an army that counts, and this army fights a crusade such as the Domains have never seen. May the gods bless your path."

Garth cleared his throat and hoisted his shaggy-haired son onto his shoulders. The boy giggled. "We must away. There's much to do before the spring rains."

Gull offered his hand, and after a moment, Garth shook it. The woodcutter said, "As long as there are wars, old soldiers can never retire, I've heard."

Garth laughed easily. "Then you've heard amiss, for old soldiers retire all the time, either to a farm or the grave, and yet the wars go on. But if you need us, call. We'll be honored to help. But perhaps you can use this."

Shifting his son, he pulled his magic satchel over his head and gave it to Greensleeves. To her astonished protests, he replied, "Keep it. It's bigger inside than it looks, and contains much you'll find useful in your quest. I don't need it. I have everything I need with me." Still juggling his squirming son, he took Rakel's arm and tugged her gently against his side.

Rakel sniffed. "Good-bye, all."

"Good-bye" said the general of the army and the guardian of magic.

With a flick of a lean hand, black cobwebs encircled them. When the webs dropped away, they were empty.

As Gull passed out of the tent, he found Lily waiting.

"Is she gone?"

Gull nodded. "Back to the farm with her family. I hope they're happy."

"I hope so, too." Lily took his hand and led him away from the tent, out past the perimeter of the camp. "I want her to stay happy so I can enjoy you."

Gull chuckled, but then turned serious. He strove to see her face in the pale moonlight. "Oh? Have you decided you love me? But love yourself first?"

"Yes to both. Now that I can fly, and cut loose of the chains of the earth whenever I want, I feel free. So I'm free to fall in love. With you."

Gull smiled. "I'm just glad you're happy."

"I know. That makes you a special man."

"What does?" He stopped walking, stared at the whiteness of her clothes and her shadowed face.

"Caring about others' feelings. Mine, especially. I might be mixed up, but you've always been patient and waited while I sorted things out."

Gull shrugged, but suddenly Lily was in his arms, holding him tightly, her perfumed hair tickling his nose. "I'm going to hold you, Gull, and never let go. Not ever. But hold me too, please. Sometimes I feel like I'm floating away."

"You won't float away," he crooned. "You're strong and pure and good. But I'll hold you as long as you like."

"And I'll be content to help as I can around here, to be the general's girlfriend."

He chuckled. "How about the general's wife?"

The girl put her head back. "Oh, Gull! What a question!"

"Will you?"

She stared at him. "You'd marry a former dancing girl? And prostitute? Who's now a wizard?"

"No. I'd marry you. Sweet, kind Lily. Or . . . what is your real name, anyway?"

"Thank you for asking," Lily laughed. "It's Tirtha. But I like it when you call me Lily." She tucked her head against his chest and hugged him hard. "No one's ever asked me to marry him before."

"Want me to ask again?" he persisted.

"No! I mean, yes! Yes yes yes yes yes!"

She kissed him, and he kissed her back.

Amma woke Greensleeves in the middle of the night. "Hurry, dear! Chaney is dying!"

Hurriedly, Greensleeves pulled on her slippers and wrapped her cloak and shawl around her shoulders and trotted to the hospital tents. Outside, on a pallet of spruce boughs, lay Chaney. Amma whispered, "She insisted on being carried outside. She didn't want to die indoors."

The words cut Greensleeves to her soul, and she dropped to her knees beside the blanket-laden boughs. By candlelight, the old druid looked more sunken, craggier, paler than ever. But the soft light also showed that Chaney had been a beautiful woman when she was young—perhaps centuries ago.

"Mistress Chaney," said Greensleeves, lapsing into formality. "Don't go! We need you!"

The old druid didn't open her eyes. "We go when we're called, child. No one can stop it, only fend it off, though old age is a wicked price to pay." Her usual rasp was a whisper like the sough of trees in the wind.

"But, Chaney . . . " Greensleeves began to cry.

The archdruid patted the girl's warm hand with her dry scaly claw. "You know much, Greensleeves, and will be a greater archdruid than I. They'll sing legends about you until the Domains cave in on themselves and die in fire. You'll pass beyond druid, and archdruid to—I don't know what. Use your talents wisely, and the power of the stone brain, and put the Domains into balance again. But never forget that the lowliest ant is every bit as important as you . . . no more, no less. . . . "

Greensleeves didn't know what to say, and so remained silent. Tears spilled down her cheeks and splashed their joined hands.

Suddenly, Chaney opened her eyes and stared fixedly. Greensleeves glanced up at a sliver of waning silver. The druid whispered, "I go with the moon. But I'll watch over you and yours. Now kiss me, child, and suck my last breath. You'll need it."

Sobbing, Greensleeves kissed the dry withered lips. And as she did, she heard Chaney wheeze, saw the slack bosom collapse, and she drew in the last essence of the great woman.

And reeled as her head spun.

More potent than any wine, more stunning than any blow, more biting than any pain, Greensleeves felt herself suffused with mana such as she never knew existed. A burning, tingling, howling seared from her lungs throughout her body, to the chakra points behind her forehead, in her breast and loins, in her belly. She hummed with power. Why, she could move mountains with this much—

"She's gone," pronounced Amma. And remembering the dying woman's wishes, did not draw a blanket over her face, only laid a wreath of holly on her breast.

With a flash, Greensleeves felt the strength run out of her body. Exhausted, burned clean. And more alone than she'd ever been before. She put her head on the old druid's breast and cried.

When she'd finished, she heard a rustle behind her. Kwam, waiting, as always.

With a soft cry, the woman rose and ran into his arms.

EPILOGUE

KARLI RECLINED ON HER HAMMOCK, HER SMALL feet propped in the air, her skin as dark as the candlelit night, her soft white hair luminous. Idly, she listened to the desert wind sigh around her tent. Her caravan had stopped for the night in an arroyo protected from flash floods, but even down here the wind howled. She often wished she could harness the power of that wind: it would give her enough mana to take over all the desert country, and beyond. But to grasp the wind . . .

Suddenly she was awake, bolt upright. What was that hissing?

A slithering noise welled through her tent. Dark eyes wide, by the light of a trio of red candles she searched the carpets and chests scattered around the tent. An asp made that hissing noise just before it struck. . . .

No. What was . . . ?

Two small dark shapes grew in the center of the rugs, as if a stump had pushed its way through the tent floor. . . .

Karli bounded out of bed and wrapped a silk

dressing gown around her small frame. The hissing was someone shifting in. With a shriek she summoned her guards, and six sturdy flyers dashed into her tent with scimitars drawn.

By that time, the small shapes had grown, turned solid, mostly brown and silver, to reveal a pair of wizards standing together, both with right hands raised, the universal sign of peace.

A *pair* of wizards? thought Karli. When all wizards were in competition with one another? Seeking a truce? For what?

This bore further study. With a gesture, she steadied her guards from striking.

The woman, with jet-black hair and a brown robe edged with yellow, spoke in a language Karli recognized. "You are the one called Karli?"

"Karli of the Singing Moon is my full title."

"Karli of the Singing Moon, then. I am Dacian the Red. My companion here—" she indicated the huge man in silver- and gold-chased armor and vast horned helmet; yet despite the closed helm, Karli saw he lacked an eye "—is Haakon the First, King of the Badlands. We are all wizards, and we should talk."

"About what?" asked Karli. She yanked the belt of her dressing gown tighter. She was suspicious, but she could be civil, and ordered a servant to fetch buttered tea. She might learn something useful. A wizard needed knowledge more than anything, after all. "But sit. And speak. I'm listening."

Dacian sat primly, crosslegged. Haakon dropped to one knee, propped a spiked gauntlet on it. The woman said, "You have, in the past, fought the army of the ones called Gull the Woodcutter and Greensleeves the Druid, or Archdruid. Haakon and I have also battled them. You came away with nothing, and we lost everything. We propose—"

"How do you know all this?" demanded Karli as she sat swaying on her hammock.

"Because they told us after they captured us," explained Dacian patiently. "We learned of your attack on the camp and how you had to flee. And we know at some point you handled the stone brain—"

"The *what?* I touched no such thing! I was after—well, never mind. But—"

"You sought a pink banded box you thought was a mana vault. It's not. It's a stone helmet that was created by the Sages of Lat-Nam to control the Brothers and end their depradations. The fools were all killed, of course."

Karli held her breath at the ancient names, most sacred to wizards. Bitterly she recalled holding that source of power for only the briefest instant before it slipped away—rejected her. But questions plagued her. "How—"

"I will explain everything *after*—" Dacian held up a hand "—we agree."

"On what?"

"Haakon and I were defeated by the army, but mostly by that stone helmet, the single most powerful artifact ever contrived. Greensleeves has it now, because it responds to her for some reason—no wizard can truly master it—and used it to tag both Haakon and myself. And you have touched it, or else we couldn't contact you."

"Contact me?"

Dacian accepted a cup of tea from a shivering serving girl. Haakon refused. The sorceress went on, "After I was tagged by the stone brain, I could sense it, and Haakon. And you. It's a side effect. *Anyone tagged by it can contact anyone else tagged.* I don't know why, and I doubt Greensleeves knows, but *we* can use it to *our* advantage."

"How? Oh, I see. . . . "

Dacian sipped, nodded. "Exactly. This army of Gull and Greensleeves, this crusade, as they call it, succeeds too well. Everywhere they go they assemble more volunteers, enough to defeat any conjured army, or even a horde of demons. Haakon lost an eye learning that. They will continue to tag wizards as easily as we tag black lotuses. Can you imagine it? With our power under their control, and few to oppose them, they'll become high king and queen of all the Domains, enslave every living thing under the two moons. They'll be like gods on the land, and we less than slaves. We'll be rabbits fit for slaughter."

Karli bit her lower lip, nodding. That's what she'd do with all that power. Only without a "high king." "But what can we do?"

"*We* can unite. Join forces and stop them now, cold and dead. Loot their libraries and artifacts, enslave their followers. Separately, we cannot—that's been demonstrated thrice now. So we must unite or die—a congress of wizards to stop the worst threat the Domains have ever seen. Are you with us?"

Karli sipped tea and demurred, thinking. But Dacian knew she'd agree. She must to survive. The glossy-haired wizard added, "There's more. There are other wizards they've fought and hurt, if not defeated. One is named Towser. And I think I know where we can find him. . . ."

Clayton Emery is the author of *Tales of Robin Hood, Shadow World Book One: The Burning Goddess,* and *Book Three: City of Assassins;* an American Revolution novel, *Marines to the Tops!*; and the "Robin & Marian" stories in *Ellery Queen's Mystery Magazine.* He lives in Rye, New Hampshire. His 1767 house continues to need a *lot* of care, but he works on the gardens when not writing.